A REPLACEMENT LIFE

BORIS FISHMAN

ONE

AN IMPRINT OF PUSHKIN PRESS

ONE

an imprint of Pushkin Press

71–75 Shelton Street, London WC2H 9JQ

Copyright © 2014 Boris Fishman

First published in the United States by HarperCollins in 2014
First published in Great Britain by ONE in 2014

ISBN 978 0 957548 83 1

www.pushkinpress.com/one/

A REPLACEMENT LIFE

FOR MY GRANDPARENTS AND MY PARENTS

All writing is revenge.

—REINALDO ARENAS

SUNDAY, JULY 16, 2006

The telephone rang just after five. Unconscionably, the day was already preparing to begin, a dark blue lengthening across the sky. Hadn't the night only started? Slava's head said so. But in the cobalt square of the window, the sun was looking for a way up, the great towers of the Upper East Side ready for gilding.

Who was misdialing at five o'clock in the morning on Sunday? Slava's landline never rang. Even telemarketers had given up on him, you have to admit an achievement. His family no longer called because he had forbidden it. His studio, miraculously affordable even for a junior employee of a Midtown magazine, rang with echoes, nothing but a futon, a writing desk, a torchiere wrapped in cast-iron vines (forced on him by his grandfather), and a tube television he never turned on. Once in a while, he imagined vanishing into the walls, like a spirit in Poe, and chuckled bitterly.

He thought about getting up, a surprise attack on the day. Sometimes he rose extra-early to smell the air in Carl Schurz Park before the sun turned it into a queasy mixture of garbage, sunscreen, and dog shit. As the refuse trucks tweaked the slow air with their bells, he would stand at the railing, eyes closed, the river still black and menacing from the night, the brine of an old untouchable ocean in his nose. An early start always filled him with the special hope available only before seven or eight, before he got down to the office.

The phone rang again, God bless them. Defeated, he reached over. In truth, he was not ungrateful to be called on. Even if it turned out to be a telemarketer. He would have listened to a question about school bonds, listened gravely.

"Slava," a waterlogged voice—his mother—whispered in Russian. He felt anger, then something less certain. Anger because he had said not to call. The other because generally she obeyed nowadays. "Your grandmother isn't," she said. She burst into tears.

Isn't. Verbiage was missing. In Russian, you didn't need the adjective to complete the sentence, but in English, you did. In English, she could still be alive.

"I don't understand," he said. He hadn't spoken to any of them in weeks, if not a month, but in his mind, his grandmother, quiet sufferer of a cirrhosis that had been winning for years, was fixed to her bed in Midwood, as if the way he remembered her was the way she would be until he came to see her again, until he authorized new developments. Something previously well placed dislodged in his stomach.

"They took her in on Friday," his mother said. "We thought it was only hydration again."

He stared at the blanket around his feet. It was as frayed and fine as an old shirt. Grandmother had scoured it in the wash how many times. The Gelmans had brought it from Minsk, as if blankets were not sold in America. And they weren't, not like this, a full goose inside. The cover opened in the middle, not on the side. A girl had gotten tangled up in there in a key moment once. "I think I need Triple A," she said. They burst out laughing and had to start over.

"Slava?" his mother said. She was quiet and frightened. "She died alone, Slava. No one was with her."

"Don't do that," he said, grateful for her irrationality. "She didn't know."

"I hadn't slept the night before, so I left," she said. "Your grandfather was supposed to go this morning. And then she died." She started to flow again, sobs mixing with snot. "I kissed her and said, 'I'll see you tomorrow.' Slava, mercy, I should have stayed."

"She wouldn't have known you were there," he said in a thick voice. He felt vomit rising in his throat. The blue morning had become gray. The air conditioner chugged from the window, the humidity waiting outside like a thief.

"All by herself, she was taken." His mother blew her nose. The receiver jostled on her end. "So," she said with sudden savagery. "Now will you come, Slava?"

"Of course," he said.

"Now he will come," she said viciously. Slava's mother held the world record for fastest trip from tender to brutal, but this tone had not entered even their arguments about his abandonment of the family. "Now is finally a good enough reason? The woman who would have skinned herself for you. The woman you saw—one time, Slava, in the last year?" She changed her voice to emphasize her indifference to his opinion: "We're doing the funeral today. They say it has to be twenty-four hours."

"Who says?" he said.

"I don't know, Slava. Don't ask me these things."

"We're not religious," he said. "Are you going to bury her in a shroud, too, or whatever they do? Oh, it doesn't matter."

"If you come, maybe you can have a say," she said.

"I'm coming," he said quietly.

"Help your grandfather," she said. "He's got a new home attendant. Berta. From Ukraine."

"Okay," he said, wanting to sound helpful. His lips twitched.

His grandmother wasn't. This possibility he hadn't rehearsed. Why not—she had been ill for years. But he had been certain that she would pull through. She had pulled through far worse, pulled through the unimaginable, what was a bit more?

His grandmother was not a semi-annual hair-tousler. (*Had not been*? The new tense, a hostile ambassador, submitted its credentials.) She had raised him. Had gone into the meadow with him, punting a soccer ball until other children showed up. It was she who found him making out with Lusty Lena in the mulberry bush and she who hauled him home. (Grandfather would have rubbed his hands and given instruction, Lou Duva to Slava's Holyfield, half-nelsoned in Lena's formidable bust, but not for Grandmother loucheness.) When the nuclear reactor blew up, Grandmother cursed Grandfather for bothering with the radio, traded one of her minks (in fairness, acquired by Grandfather on the black market) for a neighbor's Zhiguli, and had Slava's father drive them all for a week to Lithuania, where the mink housed and fed them.

Slava knew her in the body. His mouth knew, from the food she shoveled there. His eyes knew, from the bloated sweep of her fingers. Grandmother had been in the Holocaust—*in* the Holocaust? As in the army, the circus? The grammar seemed wrong. *At* the Holocaust? Of it, with it, from it, until it? The English preposition, stunned by the assignment, came up short—though she said no more than that, and no one disturbed her on the subject. This Slava couldn't fathom, even at ten years old. Already by then he had been visited by the American understanding that to know was better than not to know. She would go one day, and then no one would know. However, he didn't dare ask. He imagined. Barking dogs, coils of barbed wire, an always gray sky.

"Goodbye, Slava," his mother interrupted. She spoke as if she hardly knew him. The line made its noises between them. He had the sensation that only they were speaking while eight million slept. The unreality of it teased him. Heartlessly: Grandmother was gone. Grandmother wasn't.

How long were they silent? Even while talking, they were silent with each other. Finally, in a faraway tone, his mother said: "Our first American death."

Downstairs at the doorman station, Rich was buried in the delivery closet. Slava accelerated to reach the front door first, as he disliked mincing in place while Rich (né Ryszard, Poland), Bart (né Bartos, Hungary), or Irvin (né Ervin, Albania) shuffled toward it. Slava liked to open the door for older men, not vice versa. However, Rich, Bart, and Irvin were eager to take their place in his day, their eyes lit with resentful admiration—a fellow immigrant, risen to heights. Once, Slava had tried to persuade Rich that he had the front door, but the older man only lifted his index finger in warning.

"Slava, how evorytyng?" Rich said now from the depths of the closet. He had buffed the foyer, and Slava, a dozen feet from the door, squeaked with every step. With a dancer's precision, the cumbersome Pole emerged from the thicket of dry cleaning and delivery boxes and slid his hand into the door handle. "Have nice day, pliz, okay?" he said with touching disdain.

Our first American death. Have nice day, pliz. As Slava strode out of the building, the day's what-ifs again presented their tempting alternatives. Rich still got the door first, the 6 train was still inept for the crush of the Upper East Side, and Grandmother was still alive, scratching weakly at her lesions in a bathrobe in Midwood. Sure, her bile ducts were blocked, her bilirubin was high—Billy Rubin, he was a half-Jewish boy, he wouldn't hurt her!— but she was still there, chomping her lips and glowering at Grandfather.

Since the last time Slava had come to South Brooklyn—almost a year prior; his mother could count without pity—a new residential tower had started to grow around the corner from his apartment building, two restaurants on his block had shuttered and reopened as others, and the local councilman had been forced out in a sex scandal. As the train surged above-ground at Ditmas, Slava rode past the same repair shops and convenience stores, the same music bouncing from the tinted windows of spoilered Camaros, the same corrupt councilman on the billboards (only his vice was kickbacks). These people had come to America to be left alone.

Here was a foreign city, if you were coming from Manhattan. The buildings were smaller and the people larger. They drove cars, and for most, Manhattan was a glimmering headache. As the train neared Midwood, the produce improved and the prices shook loose. Here, a date tasted like chocolate, and it was a virtue to persuade the grocer—Chinese not Korean, Mexican not Arab—to have it for less than the cardboard placards wedged into the merchandise said. This was still a world in the making. In some of its neighborhoods, the average time since arrival was under twelve months. These American toddlers were only beginning to crawl. Some, however, had already found the big thumb of American largesse.

Grandfather lived on the first floor of a tawny-bricked building tenanted by old Soviets and the Mexicans who wouldn't let them sleep. His senior-citizen benefits didn't permit him to make an appearance on official payrolls. To the Kegelbaums in 3D, he sold salmon picked off the wholesalers for whose deliveries he waited in front of Russian food stores. Why pay $4.99/lb inside when he could pay $3 on the sidewalk? The boys in the wholesale truck laughed and threw him free flounder and cod.

Next door to the Kegelbaums were the Rakoffs, American Jews. These were aghast by the seafood emerging from the mesh grocery bag in Grandfather's hands. The Aronsons (Soviet, 4A) paid for the nitroglycerine that Grandfather's doctor overprescribed in exchange for a monthly bottle of Courvoisier cognac. To the Mexicans (2A, 2B, illegal basement apartment) Grandfather gave haircuts, because they partook of neither salmon nor nitroglycerine. The churn in which these new arrivals gained body barely had time to spit out cream before it was refilled. Naturally, each batch was thinner than the one that preceded it.

Slava scaled the stairs to the first floor and stood before Grandfather's door. On an ordinary day, you could hear his television from the ground-floor mailboxes—revenge on the basement Mexicans, who smashed tall-boy Budweisers into smithereens until dawn on the weekends. Now it was soundless, on this side of the door the glory of a day just like any other.

It gave without knocking. Usually, Grandfather bolted all three locks—in this part of Brooklyn, eyes still roamed with Soviet heights of desire. But it was a day of mourning. Like Tolstoy's villagers putting on the lights outside after dinner, he was asking for company.

Inside, a sweet glaze hung in the air, dishes clattering in the kitchen. Slava slipped off his shoes and tiptoed the length of the hallway until he could see into the living room. Grandfather was on the beige sofa, the ash-colored down of his hair in his hands. On the street, women noticed Grandfather—Italian cashmere, his hands and forearms needled with sea-colored tattoos—before they noticed the grandson holding his arm. Now the old man was in gym trousers and undershirt, looking like an old man. His toenails were testing the air, as if to make sure the world was still there.

The sofa hissed as Slava lowered himself next to Grandfather. Yevgeny Gelman removed his hands from his face and stared at his grandson as if he were unknown and it was an affront to encounter another person without the woman alongside whom he had spent half a century. Slava was the notice that a million diabolical dislocations awaited.

"Gone, your grandmother," Grandfather whimpered, and rolled his head into the starch of Slava's shirt. He honked out a sob, then sprang back. "It's a nice suit," he said.

"Mom call?" Slava said. The Russian words sounded as if said by another: nasal, arch, ungrammatical. He had spoken Russian last when he had spoken last to his mother, a month before, though he continued to swear in Russian and he continued to marvel in Russian. *Ukh ty. Suka. Booltykh.* These had no improvement in English.

Grandfather searched Slava's face for adequate grasp of his heartache. "Mama's at Grusheff's," he said. "She said to call people and tell them. The

Schneyersons are coming. Benya Zeltzer said he'll try to get free. He owns three food stores."

"Is anyone helping her?" Slava said.

"I don't know. That rabbi, Zilberman?"

"You know Zilberman isn't a rabbi," Slava said.

Grandfather shrugged. Certain questions he did not ask.

Zilberman wasn't a rabbi. As Kuvshitz wasn't a rabbi, nor Gryanik. They loitered in the hospital waiting rooms, Soviet immigrants who had learned a little Hebrew and were conveniently present to ennoble a passing like Grandmother's with Torah-compliant burial guidance for a small fee. And why not? Their brothers and cousins hauled furniture, drove ambulettes starting at sunrise, skim-coated walls until their fingers shredded and bled—so who was smart.

And were these men not delivering exactly what their customers wanted? Were they not, simply, in the American way, addressing a demand of the market? Their compatriots had spent too many years under Soviet atheism to observe Jewish ritual now that they were free to do so, but they wanted a taste, a holy sprinkling, a *forshpeis*. Enter Zilberman et al., temporarily transformed into Moshe, Chaim, Mordechai. These artists of gray zones picked from the religious guidance on Jewish burials selectively. Immediate burial, as per Jewish law—certainly. As for a plain pine coffin, rimmed by no flowers—was that really right? The deceased may not have been a millionaire or an international personage, but he or she had been an anchor of families, a sufferer of world wars, a bearer of plain wisdom. This person deserved greater than #2 pine. Grusheff Funeral Home—Valery Grushev thought the two f's made his name sound as if his ancestors had come with the aristocracy that had fled the Bolsheviks via France in 1917—had coffins from Belarusian birch, California redwood, even Lebanese cedar. Didn't those who'd known the deceased deserve an opportunity to say goodbye one last time at a service? From each milestone of grief, Moshe and Chaim collected percentages.

"I'll help call if you'd like," Slava said to Grandfather.

"I'm almost finished," Grandfather said. "Not that many people to call, Slava."

In the kitchen, a pot crashed into another, interrupting the rush of the sink water. A woman cursed herself for clumsiness. Grandfather lifted his head, his eyes alert once again. "Come," he said, his hand on Slava's forearm. "Things change, you don't come for so long." Rising, he leaned on Slava's arm with more weight than he needed.

They filled the kitchen doorway arm in arm, like a pair of lovers. The blue rims of Grandfather's eyes welled with tears. "Berta," he said hoarsely. "My grandson." Death or no death, Grandfather could ingratiate himself with his new home attendant by formally introducing his grandson.

Like a Soviet high-rise, each floor of Berta was stuffed beyond capacity. Silver polish gleamed from her toes, wedged into platforms that she was using as house slippers; flower-print capri tights encased in a death grip the meat-rack haunch of her legs. Slava felt a treacherous lurch in his groin. She hadn't heard Grandfather.

"Berta!" Grandfather barked. His arm tensed and he rapped the wall with his knuckles. Berta spun around. Underneath its creases and the worried, close set of the eyes, her face had preserved its young, unblemished beauty. A buttery gleam rose from the skin.

"The boy!" she shrieked. Holding up her long yellow dish gloves as if placating a mugger, she waddled toward Slava and enclosed him in the flab of her arms. Berta also had to make a demonstration before Grandfather. One phone call from him to the assignments coordinator at the home-nurse agency, who received from Grandfather a monthly gift of chocolates and perfume, and Berta would be reassigned to a paraplegic who needed his ass wiped and his oatmeal spoon-fed. Slav Berta, whose people had used to terrorize Jews like Grandfather! This—more than the profusion of meat in American supermarkets, the open availability of rare technology, even the cavalierness with which Americans spoke of their president—was the mys-

terious grandeur of the country that had taken in the Gelmans of Minsk.
It had the power to turn tormentors into kitchen help.

Berta held Slava like the flaps of a coat in winter, a hard-on developing
inside his slacks. On the stovetop, a pan sizzled with butter and onions.
That was the sweetness in the air. The after-funeral table would stagger
with food. The guests had to see: This house did not lack for provisions.

As Slava embraced in Grandmother's kitchen a woman he'd never met
with an intimacy neither of them felt, the feeling he had begun to remember for Grandmother receded, like someone gently tiptoeing out of the
wrong room. At the funeral service, he would be accused of indifference
while Mother and Grandfather clutched each other and wailed. The guests
had to see.

It had taken two years of failing to get published by Century *magazine to*
piece together the facts. Our great realizations are slow dishes, but once
they're ready, they announce themselves as suddenly as an oven timer.
Grandfather had helped. Slava was visiting one rainy evening. Dinner had
been finished, the dishes had been cleared by the home nurse, the conversation had dwindled. Grandmother was resting. Grandfather sat sideways
in one of the dining room chairs, his palm on his forehead. Slava watched
him from the folds of a love seat. His mind drifted to the next day's chores,
to the story idea on deck.

Grandfather opened his palm as if making a point to someone else in
the room, and said, "What, is it too late for him to become a businessman?
It's not too late. Not late at all." He flicked his wrist. Not late at all.

To be around Grandfather, Grandfather's neighbors, the whole accursed
neighborhood of Russians, Belarusians, Ukrainians, Moldovans, Georgians,
and Uzbeks—Slava should do it if he wanted to write for a Russian newspaper, of which there were many now in the neighborhood. If he wanted to
live among those who said "we don't go to America," except for the DMV

and *Brodvei*. If he wanted to shop at marts that sold birch-leafed switches
to whip yourself in the steam bath and rare Turkish shampoos that re-
versed baldness, but not *Century*. If he wanted to have his arm gently broken by an ex-paratrooper so he could claim it happened on ice outside Key
Food and get disability. If he wanted to go out with Sveta Beyn, practi-
tioner of high finance, who had just bought a nine-hundred-square-foot
apartment, with balcony. *Bought*. (In truth, it had been bought by her
parents, who took the liberty of decorating as well—lacquer, rococo, pictures of Mama and Papa.)

But if Slava wished to become an American, to strip from his writing
the pollution that refilled it every time he returned to the swamp broth of
Soviet Brooklyn, if Slava Gelman—immigrant, baby barbarian, the fork-
ing road spread-eagled before him—wished to write for *Century*, he would
have to get away. Dialyze himself, like Grandmother's kidneys.

He stopped visiting, stopped calling, left someone else to pass the nights
by Grandmother's gurney as the machines cleaned her liver. It wasn't like
she could tell, most of the time. In his Manhattan exile, which failed to
supply the publication he had expected immediately, Slava would think
about her. With his fork over a plate of kasha; staring at the river that separated Manhattan from Queens; as he drifted to sleep.

This was the price of weathering the divide between *there* and *here*, he
told himself. The facts were old, tiresome, well known: This immigrant
changed his *name* on the way to success in America. This one abandoned
his *religion*. And this one temporarily parted from his family, big crisis.
Slava wasn't leaving to study the human condition from a shack in the
woods. He was going to *Century*—legendary, secretive *Century*, older than
The New Yorker and, despite a recent decline, forever a paragon. No, Slava
wasn't being paid what Igor Kraz was paid for proctology, but he wasn't
palming shit-slathered tubes all day long, either. *Century* had published
the first report from Budapest in 1956. It had been the first to take the
abstract expressionists seriously. It had nailed Ivan Boesky and saved Van

Cortlandt Park. This had meant nothing to any Gelman—all right. (It was the Honda of American magazines, he had tried to explain, the Versace, the Sony.) But educated, discerning people the whole country over—three million of them, the last count had come down from Subscriptions— regarded *Century* as Slava's mother regarded the English queen: with awe, piety, and savage curiosity. Slava wasn't writing there, but the Gelmans didn't need to know that; they never bought the magazine anyway. On the sly, Slava would become a writer for *Century*—success was success, was it not, even if you subbed literature for proctology; he had hardly planned it this way—and then they would see. There was cost, but there would be reward.

Two days before his grandmother died, a stroke of dumb luck—it wasn't dumb luck, it was Arianna Bock in the next cubicle sprinkling her fairy dust—had assigned him an article for *Century* after he had spent three years uselessly trying to achieve same on his own. He had spent Grandmother's last day on earth watching an "urban explorer" climb up the Ulysses S. Grant tomb in Morningside Heights. It was a sodden gimmick—everyone in this impossible city had their thing, and this was this man's—but Slava had teased from the moment a grand essay about politics, continents, love. It was why he had awakened so poorly on Sunday—he had been writing it most of Saturday night while she—knowingly? unknowingly?—marked her last hours. There were no guarantees, but a byline in *Century*? Only a byline in *The New Yorker* meant as much. Entire book contracts were given out on the basis of a byline in *Century*. It was finally happening. Only he hadn't made it in time.

Grusheff Funeral Home occupied half a block of Ocean Parkway, the Grusheff name covering the two outfacing sides of the building. The wide avenue slumbered in the noonday heat, the few passing cars moving without any real desire. The poles of the covered entry were gilded, and the oval windows were frosted with mermaids.

Inside, the hallway to the viewing area, carpeted in a disco mix of abstract zigzags and dashes, was lined with human-height flora, birds of paradise and hot-pink anemones sutured into vertical displays that gave the room the feel of a science fair. Valery Grusheff, cuff links and a pocket square, shuttled among the gathering mourners.

These looked made up for a scene ten years later—dumplings swam under their eyes and tires circled their waists. Grandfather, looking deranged but credibly in grief in an overcoat despite the stifling weather, stood off in the corner cursing them under his breath. In the Soviet Union—where his officially paltry position as a barber at the main train terminal actually left him at the welcome gate of all the commerce that streamed into Minsk on the overnight trains from Moscow, Kishinev, and Yerevan—he had obtained for these people watermelons, cognac, wall units, visas. When the need arose, they had found his phone number easily. But democratic America had empowered them to secure their own watermelons and doctors' appointments. Now he always had to call such-and-such person first, only to be invited for leftovers the day after a party to which he had *not* been invited. He was not counting, but where was their gratitude? They would never see *his* ass in their chairs again.

The individuals in question greeted Slava's mother with the exaggerated intimacy of people who had not seen her in years.

"She is in the skies."—"Be strong for your father."—"It's easier for her now."—"Be strong for your son."

On a metal folding chair in a corner, Slava's father pulled at the collar of his shirt, looking as unclaimed as a child in front of a school at dusk. He was present but unnoticeable, his favorite setting. He hadn't even objected when Slava had been given the last name of Grandfather's line instead of his own.

"Yevgeny Isakovich," a man called out to Grandfather. The summoned looked up and nodded ponderously, grateful to be pulled away from the stream of condolences. His eyes went searching the room. Somehow, Slava knew they were searching for him. When they found him, Grandfather tweaked his eyebrows. As Slava approached, Grandfather extended his arm, and Slava took it.

"My condolences, from the bottom," the man said to Grandfather, covering his heart with his palm. He wore a leather jacket, the lined face of a bricklayer cinched by a short ponytail. A tiny gold hoop roosted in one of the ears. He reached out a grate of hairy knuckles and collected Grandfather's limp palm.

"Thank you, Rudik, thanks," Grandfather said.

"Are you looking?" the man said.

"Yes, yes," Grandfather said. "We need."

"Step into the office?"

"This is my grandson," Grandfather said, turning to Slava.

"Rudolf Kozlovich." The man extended his hand. "What do you—"

"He's studying, still," Grandfather said. "At Harvard."

In the office, Kozlovich unfurled a bluish map of Lincoln Cemetery. It was a small city with avenues and streets named after trees—Walnut, Maple, Ash. A wide thoroughfare ran through the middle, the train thundering above.

"Nothing by the fence," Grandfather said.

"They've got synthetic lawn on it now," Kozlovich said. "Like that stuff they put on the soccer field. You can't see in."

"Nothing by the fence," Grandfather repeated.

Kozlovich's finger traced a line to the other half of the grounds. "The head office is on this side."

"That means what?"

"The grounds crew checks in there. More people around. Downside is—not too far from the train, either."

"Where is the quietest?"

"Quiet's over here." Kozlovich slid his finger across hundreds of graves. "They're building new condominiums on that side, but that's practically over. Tulip Lane."

"She loved tulips," Grandfather said.

Kozlovich opened his hands. "Meant to be."

Rudolf Kozlovich was known. He had come from Odessa in 1977 or 1978. He looked around and settled on a plan. One day he and some hired boys hijacked a truck of Macy's furs. Sable, mink, fox. They returned them one by one at the branch stores, just a lot of husbands coming back with unsuccessful gifts. They were done, over a hundred thousand dollars between them, before the store could piece together what had happened. With his one hundred thousand, Rudolf purchased one hundred choice plots at the cemetery under the el.

There he was at the hospital, at the funeral home. He had an information network—oncologists, nurses, funeral-home directors—that Macy's security could only envy. Kozlovich's business was unofficial, of course, spread among different owners who collected small percentages for the use of their names in the contracts, and the cemetery continued to own some of the plots. But Kozlovich's were the rarest, and as fewer of them remained, the prices went up.

Kozlovich was on a clock, too. His son Vlad had come out of the closet, renounced his father's money, and moved with his homosexual partner to Madrid. There, Vlad had reconsidered and agreed to live off Papa's funds, which Rudolf supplied without objection—when it came to children, his wolfhound instincts went flaccid. But there was no question of Vlad returning to assume any part of his father's burial empire, and Rudolf's ex-wife, the former Tatiana Kozlovich, had absconded to Westchester with a derivatives trader who made her former husband seem like a wage worker. Rudolf was alone.

"I want two," Grandfather said now.

"Yevgeny Isakovich." Kozlovich's eyebrows rose. "A plot in advance? You're tempting fate."

"Well, that's what I want," Grandfather said.

"All right, but I have only four of those left. One family plot and four doubles. The rest is all singles."

"So give me one of the doubles."

"Happily. Twenty thousand."

"Fifteen," Grandfather said. "I'm buying two in one go."

"Yevgeny Isakovich," Kozlovich frowned. "I'm sorry for your loss. But you know I don't bargain."

"Fifteen and—your son is in Europe?"

Kozlovich's face changed expression. "Connection?" he said impatiently.

"Exactly, Rudik," Grandfather said, his index finger rising tutorially into the refrigerated air of the office. "Connection. Why are we here? For them." He poked a nail into Slava's chest. "If this one said, 'I want Europe,' I would build the airplane myself. That's the kind of grandfather I am. But you miss your boy? Exactly. So I am making you an offer. A special kind of telephone. You pick up the receiver and it's already ringing in Paris."

"Madrid."

"Wherever. A special connection just for you and your son. These things, probably the only one who's got one is Bush. And not that money is an issue for a person such as yourself, but: no charge."

"A walkie-talkie," Kozlovich said. "With international range."

"Exactly. The newest thing."

"And where did you get such a thing?"

"Rudik," Grandfather said. Briefly, the sear of grief was gone from his face. His eyes gleamed. "A girl doesn't tell who she's kissed. It's authentic, that's all you need to know. The Japanese navy uses it, or something like that."

When the Gelmans reached the United States, Grandfather had found a "warm" fellow who knew where the trucks from Crazy Eddie's unloaded.

The models of the electronics Grandfather obtained—microwaves, dishwashers, floppy disks—were so new and advanced that no one in the family could understand how to use them. Grandfather screamed into his Pentagon-caliber cordless as if it were a can connected to Slava's wall by a string. But he could obtain a Japanese navy international-range walkie-talkie in the time it took Slava to find a newspaper.

Kozlovich peered at him. "I have one double left on Tulip," he said finally.

Grandfather spread his hands. "Meant to be." From the pocket of his overcoat, which now revealed its purpose, he extracted a Tupperware encasing a snail of hundred-dollar bills. Whispering under their breath, the three mourners counted to 150—once, again, and a third time. Grandfather had not brought a bill more.

When they emerged from the office, Grandfather threaded his arm through Slava's and spat. "*Homos.* If you're going to Europe already, who goes to Madrid?" He looked as if he'd swallowed spoiled milk. "*Paris*, Slava. Don't be a discount aristocrat. Let's walk."

The funeral service was conducted by a Borsalino-hatted, bearded whisperer in Orthodox garb who remarked unspecifically, but in Russian and with key references to sections of the Torah that no one in the audience had read, on the passage of Grandmother's life.

Against the rabbi's gentle reproaches—"We Jews try to remember the person as living," he murmured apologetically into his cuff—the coffin had been left open. In it, Grandmother looked unpersuaded of death. Dressed in a long blue nightshirt, her face diplomatic and cautious, she looked as if snoring politely through an afternoon nap. At the rim of the coffin, Slava stifled back tears, the line of mourners humming behind him. Then Uncle Pasha was at his ear, followed by the sweetish scent of used cognac. "You need to keep it together for the sake of the women," Pasha whispered with sympathetic reproach.

When it was her turn, Slava's mother fainted. Fixed to his seat, Slava watched several men lift her from the ground. A female guest he didn't know—feathered mauve hat, a veil falling from the brim—waved a bottle of salts, and she revived with a gasp.

Afterward, by themselves in the car, his father mute behind the wheel and Grandfather staring wetly at the broad emptiness of Ocean Parkway,

Mother turned from the front passenger seat and, as if sighting Slava for the first time that day, colored. She'd had to handle by herself both these men, one petulant and the other mute, and he thought he could just appear? Her eyes blazed; she looked as if she wanted to strike him. He wished she would. Instead, a gust of something corrective swept her face clean, and again she looked loving. She lunged toward Slava and began to wail into his shoulder from the front seat, two souls bereaved but together.

Mother had taken from Grandmother the condiments without the meal. She clung to Slava but knew not why and did not ask. Grandmother clung because her previous family had been taken without asking. This one she would hold to faster than iron—with this one, she would make sure to die first, in the natural order. ("It is a blessing to die in the natural order."—Sofia Gelman.) The mother clung because the grandmother clung. When Slava stopped showing up, it was only his mother who dialed from New Jersey, badgering and pleading. Grandmother couldn't, Grandfather was too proud, and Slava's father had been made docile by his parents-in-law, though he kicked the television once because why did these people control their lives.

At the cemetery, each of the remaining Gelmans shoveled a spadeful of dirt onto the grave, the rabbi chanting a selection in Hebrew that concluded with Grandfather slipping him a white envelope, whereupon God's messenger vanished into the blurry heat of the evening. The Gelmans stood in front of the pit in a suddenly terrible silence split only by the distant rush of an airplane nosing its way through the atmosphere. Mother and Grandfather grasped each other, two shipwrecks on an island. Slava and his father bracketed them without words.

Berta conveyed her condolences the only way that she could. Two foldout tables in Grandfather's living room heaved with plates rimmed in gold filigree: duck with prunes; pickled watermelon; potato pancakes with dill, garlic, and farmer cheese. A dropped fork or a glass emptied of Berta's trademark cranberry water sent her bulleting into the kitchen with startling litheness. The table droned with the sound of grief mixed with fatigue.

"A woman like her you don't meet nowadays. Fierce as a—"

"Berta, this *soup* . . ."

". . . but mark my words, there wasn't a false bone—"

Slava used to sit at one of these tables once a week, the cooking by a Berta or a Marina or a Tatiana, uniformly ambrosial, as if they all attended the same Soviet Culinary School No. 1. Stout women, preparing to grow outward even if they hadn't reached thirty, in tights decorated with polka dots or rainbow splotches, the breasts falling from their sailor shirts, their shirts studded with rhinestones, their shirts that said Gabbana & Dulce.

Stewed eggplant; chicken steaks in egg batter; marinated peppers with buckwheat honey; herring under potatoes, beets, carrots, and mayonnaise; bow-tie pasta with kasha, caramelized onions, and garlic; *ponchiki* with mixed-fruit preserves; pickled cabbage; pickled eggplant; meat in aspic; beet salad with garlic and mayonnaise; kidney beans with walnuts; *kharcho* and *solyanka*; fried cauliflower; whitefish under stewed carrots; salmon soup; kidney beans with the walnuts swapped out for caramelized onions; sour cabbage with beef; pea soup with corn; vermicelli and fried onions.

On the phone, Grandfather would want to know when Slava would come visit, but when Slava was there at last, the old man would tiptoe off to the television, Grandmother scowling at him. Then she, too, would become tired and, making apologies, shuffle off to bed, her house shoes scraping the parquet. Slava was left with the home attendant. As the day declined and Grandfather made faces at the television, they would compare notes on his grandparents.

"Slava?" Mother said now from the other side of the table. "You're all right?" The skin under her eyes was inflamed.

"Yes," he nodded. "Of course."

"What are you thinking about?"

"Nothing."

"I wonder if someone will say a toast," she said resentfully.

Slava surveyed the table. Grandfather's call-around had netted all the significant relatives. Uncle Pasha and Aunt Viv; the girls from the pharmacy where his mother worked; the Schneyersons; Benya Zeltzer and clan. Even two Rudinskys. The Rudinskys held a special place in Grandfather's catalog of wayward relations. The Gelmans and Rudinskys had come through immigration together, had been assigned to the same guesthaus in Austria, where their documents were processed, and down the block from each other in Italy, where they were processed some more. Vera Rudinsky and Slava Gelman had played supermarket together. They cut cucumbers out of green construction paper, raised a crop of goose bumps on the skin with black marker, and sold them to their parents for prices just below those of the real vegetable market on Via Tessera. Their parents and grandparents laughed, counting out lira, and when the children were gone to restock the shelves of V&S Alimenti, they made jokes about all the money their children would make in America, followed by wordless glances that said: Together? Maybe together.

Money works both ways. After arriving in America, Vera's father had asked Grandfather for a loan to invest in a limo fleet. Grandfather didn't like to part with money unless he could count on interest, and he couldn't bring himself to ask that of the Rudinskys, who had shared with the Gelmans months of stateless dread amid the perverse beauty of Mitteleuropa and the Tyrrhenian seashore. The Rudinskys retreated. No scenes; they just called less and less. Grandfather refused to call until called.

However, the Rudinskys would not disrespect Grandmother's memory. When the men went off to the secondhand market near Rome to pawn what they'd lugged from Minsk, and the women to the firsthand market to spend on provisions what the men made in the secondhand, it was Grandmother who remained with the children, walking them to the pebbly beach, where they splashed around in the bottle-green Mediterranean water. It was she who supervised the children as they distended their bellies with translucent muscat grapes that looked as if filaments of sun had lodged inside. (Grandmother did not touch the grapes. The grapes, expensive, were for the children.) It was Grandmother who tucked the children to sleep, though she didn't read stories. She ran her fingers, the skin flimsy and loose, through their hair until they calmed down and dozed off.

All the same, to indicate displeasure, the Rudinsky high command had sent low-level envoys: Vera had come with her grandfather. The parents (Garik, taxi driver; Lyuba, bookkeeper) had claimed night shifts. It wasn't enough for Grandfather. Slava watched the old man's eyes roll past Vera and her grandfather Lazar, a scowl on his lips.

Slava stared at Lazar. He was stooped as a branch being reclaimed by the ground. In the town near Rome where Soviet immigrants were settled en route to America by some unknown geopolitical contract, Lazar Timofeyevich Rudinsky remained a legend years after the Rudinskys had departed for Brooklyn. The secondhand market was such that people came from Rome itself. Those who had gone through Italy before the Rudinskys and Gelmans sent word about what Italians wanted from their strange interlopers: linen sheets, Lenin pins, cologne, Zenit cameras. Also power drills, cognac, and Red Army caps. Every morning, the Soviet men shrouded themselves in Soviet linens and mongreled into the soft air of Tyrrhenian fall: "Russo producto! Russo producto!"

Lazar Timofeyevich had an idea. He made rounds of the immigrant homes, inviting the men to the little villa assigned to the Rudinskys. His wife, Ada Denisovna, walked around with wafers and tea. Vera and Slava colored in the next room—V&S Alimenti was working on a new shipment of grapefruit. After the men had finished their tea, Lazar Timofeyevich handed out Italian phrase books. Everyone would memorize—he didn't ask, he told—basic Italian numbers. *Diecimila lire, centomila lire.* Whenever anyone looked like he might have a sale at the flea market, an Italian mark ready to spring for a peaked cap or a power drill, one or two of the others would walk over and trot out their new Italian as if they were other customers. Trying to compete with the Italian mark. To drive up the price. *Capisce?*

They stood there in a circle, ten sixty-year-old men, rolling their r's and puckering their fingers like the Italians. *Diecimila lire, centomila lire. Va fangul.* What else was this fucking life going to ask them to do?

They made it happen, however. There were a couple of flops to begin with, Syoma Granovsky losing a nice scarf sale because Misha Schneyerson had become so animated that he outbid all the Italians in the crowd. But then they figured it out and everyone's earnings increased.

Now Lazar was stooped to the waist. Slava didn't have to ask about his wife. The homes of Soviet Brooklyn were filled with men who had been left to themselves by the last people to know how much looking after they needed. The men protected their families in a place liable to go berserk on its Jews without notice, and the women protected the men. They died first, leaving the men the most frightening leftovers: life by themselves. They were terrified of being alone. More terrified than they had been of America, more terrified than they had been of the Soviets, maybe even more terrified than they had been of the Germans.

Next to her grandfather, at the far corner of the other end of the table from Slava, far enough for her words to be lost, though the mascara with which she had burdened her eyelashes would have been visible from across the courtyard, sat Vera Rudinsky. Vera. In Russian, Faith. It was a grown person's name, which explained why Vera had been so irritated by Slava's childish pace cutting out paper eggplant for their supermarket. (Finally, she moved Slava to price tags and took cutting out for herself.) An adult in a child—she had been thin as a steeple, her face blue with pallor, as if life had breathed into her only once—Vera was serious, like Slava's grandmother. Verochka, Verusha—everyone called her by diminutives as if to rub out the age from her name. Ve-ra: the lips shy, then exhaling in wonder. Vera—a wife's name.

But Slava could not find that girl in the person who sat across from him, his first sighting in a decade. Little Vera Rudinsky, studious stork, had been replaced by a bronco with long nails and wild hair, the eyes of a hunter for a husband in the Russian classifieds (as Mama looked over her shoulder), though underneath the thick layer of blush on her face, Slava could still make out the unexpectedly felicitous result of Garik and Lyuba Rudinsky, two penguins, mixing genes on some Crimean beach a quarter century earlier.

Slava closed his eyes. The area behind his chest noised like a beehive. He wanted to go home. He would curl into the blanket and this terrible day would come to an end. And tomorrow, when his story about the explorer came up for judging, maybe there would be good news. He opened his eyes and saw Vera again. Her transformation was so macabre that he could not take his eyes from her.

Grandfather rose, a small glass in his hand. A moment passed before everyone noticed. Berta burned holes in the foreheads of three Slav neighbors from the floor. *The Jews are having a funeral, and you morons are hollering like degenerates.* Probably Grandfather had thought it rude not to invite them.

Finally, the table grew quiet. Televisions from the neighboring apartments howled through the cardboard walls, the wailing heroine of a telenovela mixing with some kind of program about the Russian civil war. "In the name of the Revolution," a wintry voice said, "I am seizing this train."

"Some of you may know," Grandfather said, "twenty-five years ago by now, we were in a car accident. A blue day, blue as . . . I don't know." He pointed weakly at Uncle Pasha's blazer, a bruised blue with white stripes. Grandfather's free hand moved around the tablecloth, looking for invisible crumbs. "This was in Crimea. She lost a lot of blood, so they gave her a transfusion. Bad blood, as it turned out. Everything that came out of there was bad. It was a ticking bomb you don't know it's inside you. Cirrhosis. Well, at least she managed to make it out of there. But, what, it's better that her headstone is in a language she didn't know?"

Berta laid a puffy hand on Grandfather's wrist. "I know," he said. "I know. And look—she spoke English. She did. When we had to study for the citizenship . . ." He turned to Slava. "Slavchik, tell it."

A table of eyes and half-turned bodies regarded Slava with practiced amusement. He had told this story before. He nodded. "To become a citizen," he said. He coughed and straightened. He was going to try. "You have to agree to defend the country. No matter your age. It's called: 'bearing arms.'"

People nodded, smiled cautiously.

"I was thirteen or fourteen," he went on. He sneaked a glance at Vera. She observed him dutifully but gave no sign of seeing anything other than another table loaded with smoked salmon, fried potatoes, and brightly colored bottles, another meaningless feast, though she would attend them to the last of her days without objection. Slava cursed himself. Vera also he had expected to remain as she was when he left her? He ridiculed his naïveté. Then inspected the lurid creation across the table once more, setting up the small laugh at the end of his story with her in mind. "But I had the best English, so I practiced with her for the interview. 'Grandmother, will you bear arms for the United States of America?' She'd make a fist, pump it in the air like Lenin, and shout 'Yes!'"

The table broke into careful laughter. Grandfather nodded, permitting amusement, and some people hooted. These were the stories Slava would tell until his own grave—the "bearing arms" story, the story of Lusty Lena and the mulberry bush. This would be the total of Grandmother, as far as her offspring knew.

"She was better than all of us," Grandfather said, cutting through the noise.

"Hear, hear."

"The new generation continues our work," Benya Zeltzer said, repeating an old Soviet slogan. Eyes turned to Slava, to Benya's hopefully named grandson Jack.

"What we have been through, may they never," Benya's wife said. Arms extended with cognac thimbles, though no one touched rims. Clinking was for celebrations.

"But remember."

"But remember, yes."

"You know the expression," Uncle Pasha said, winking at Slava. "The best way to remember is to start a new generation."

Someone whistled. Eyes returned to the young people, marooned in their obviousness. Jack Zeltzer was, what—seventeen? An apron of fuzz hung over his lip.

Mercifully, the table dissolved in conversation. Uncle Pasha waddled out of his chair and dug his meat-pie hands into Slava's shoulders. Slava felt the enormous globe of Pasha's belly at his back. Pasha had the girth of a bureau, but he wore a silk shirt underneath a nice Italian blazer.

"Slavchik!" He crumpled Slava's jacket like a piece of looseleaf. The scent of cognac encircled Slava again. Pasha ran a limousine for Lame Iosif and drew from a camouflaged flask of Metaxa throughout the day.

"Look at you, Slavchik," Pasha whispered into Slava's ear, sweat from his upper lip touching Slava's earlobe. "Shoulders like a boar. The girls jump for you? I bet they jump for you. We don't need to have the *prezervativ* conversation, correct? Man or not, too young to be a father."

Slava rolled his eyes. "Everything's in order, Uncle Pasha."

Uncle Pasha was Slava's mother's second cousin. Pasha drove a large car, tipped well, and wouldn't let up until he had given attention to every unpartnered woman on a dance floor. Aunt Viv only approved. Smoke machines belching cold mist, strobe lights raiding the dance platform, a heavyset peacock in magenta lipstick belting out *hity* on the stage ("Yellow, yellow roses! You are mine forever! Yellow, yellow roses!"), and Uncle Pasha doing the elliptical: the guarantees of an evening at Odessa or Volga or Krym, the restaurants where they all got together for birthdays, the last reason they got together with the exception of death.

"That's what I like to hear," Pasha said. "Your aunt and I, we could have waited a little bit." He pointed a fat finger at Aunt Viv, bulking in swaths of black crinoline decorated with daisies. Her name was Vika—Victoria—but in America, after seeing *Caesar and Cleopatra* with Vivien Leigh, she had decided that Viv was more glamorous.

"Maybe she's no beauty queen now," Pasha said, "but when she was young? People turned. Not only men. *Women.* That's the highest compliment, by the way, when the women notice. Hair like a fire alarm. Used to be, used to be."

Slava nodded politely.

"What I'm saying is?" Pasha said. "*Tfoo,* you come to say one thing . . ." His jowls jiggled and he scratched at his chin, releasing a belch. "What I'm saying is: Over there you couldn't work like a normal person." He pointed at the black window and, beyond it, their former life. "There was no work. They had five people doing one job. Why work? 'Get yourself noticed, get yourself problems,' as we used to say. But what we have here is normal? I think America's next big invention will be how to live without sleep. I am in the limousine five A.M. to nine P.M., and I am not the biggest earner. Your grandfather is always asking me why I don't come visit. I am in that goddamn car! You think I was this fat back home? I was disc-throwing champion at my high school. Sometimes I ask myself, *nu,* Pasha, how is the trade? That for this? After all, you know?

"But look here. When I come home, I see that woman." A big, hairy thumb pointed to Aunt Viv. She inspected them from the sides of her eyes. Belatedly, Slava realized that it was her lathering that had sent Uncle Pasha into action. "And she sets everything straight. Out there"—now it was America outside the window—"it's someone else's. But with her? I'd go into a foxhole with her. She's one of us. You follow?" The sausage fingers rested inside the black waves of Slava's hair. "You know what I'm talking about, Slava." One of Uncle Pasha's thumbs pivoted inside Slava's shoulder blade until Slava was staring at Vera. "You're off taking care of a man's business, I understand. You think I liked listening to my mother? I went into the Red Army half to get out of that house. Six o'clock in the morning, she'd pull the covers off me. One morning, God bless her, she emptied a vase over my head. But you know what happened when I got into the army? Six in the morning would have been a gift from the skies. How about four-thirty in the morning? And they don't pour water on you if you stay in bed; they break your legs, especially if you're a little Yid with a big nose. They'll take any excuse to give you something to remember them by. I missed my mother a lot in the army. You don't know what you have until you've given it up, like a young idiot. Don't be an idiot, Slava."

Slava didn't say anything. You just had to let the pitch run its course. Uncle Pasha held Slava's shoulders like a rudder. They gazed emptily at the strange horizon before them.

"I have to go to the bathroom," Slava lied.

"Slava, Slava," Pasha sighed. He nodded and kissed his nephew with big blue lips. Then he slapped Slava's shoulders and walked back to Aunt Viv, the army of love in retreat.

Slava rose and ducked into the kitchen. He opened the faucet so it looked like he was doing something and watched the water come down, a solid, unwavering cylinder. With a tick of irritation, he noticed another body enter the room.

"I haven't seen you in forever," Vera said in an English swollen by both Russia and Brooklyn.

Slava looked up at her with a wild, dumb expression. "You remember me," he said.

"How do you mean?" she said, confused. "You look the same."

"You, too," he rushed to lie.

She had a round face with long, lined eyelashes, and her black skirt was tighter than you would find in a funeral etiquette book. Slava could see the unstarved ball of her knee behind black panty hose. He felt a warm liquid slosh in his stomach.

"Your grandmother—" she started to say, then the tips of her nails flew up to cover her mouth, and a second later, she burst into tears. A second after that, she was weeping into Slava's shoulder, a shudder with each sob. Her palms pressed his shoulder blades, her breasts pressed his chest, and her tears dripped into the shoulder seam of his dress shirt. Frantic, he arched out his ass to put some distance between his groin and her groin.

She pulled away. "I got mascara all over your shirt," she said, laughing through the tears. He reached to brush it off, but her fingers closed over his. "No, no," she said. The cubes of her heels clicked past him. She leaned into the fridge, giving him an uncensored view of her rear end, and withdrew a bottle of seltzer, whereupon she began to dab his shoulder with a paper towel soaked in bubbles. His hard-on retreated.

"I must look like hell," she said, and blew her nose into the bubbly paper towel.

"N-no," he mustered.

"She's in heaven now," she said through phlegm.

"Do we have a heaven?" he said. He saw a celestial elevator physically hoisting the deceased.

"It doesn't matter," she said. "Do I have—" She pointed at her eyes.

"No, it's fine," he said. She was an expert dabber.

"Hey, you still speak-a Italiano?" she said.

The words, long unused, floated up like a dog. "*Dove la fermata dell' autobus?*" he said. She started to laugh, but it made her cry again. "I went there last year," she said when she recovered. "On vacation."

"To Ladispoli?" he asked. He had come to think of it as a place that had ceased to exist after the Gelmans departed.

"No. Firenze, Venezia. It was pretty. Personally, though? You could fly to Vegas for, like, half the money and half the time."

"Vegas?" he said.

"The Bellagio?" she said. "The Venetian? I mean, it's like a guy in one of those boats, and he's pushing you, and he can sing if you pay him. Exactly like in Venice. In Italian or English, whichever language you prefer. Why do you need Venice? It stinks there, by the way."

"I see," he said.

"I get a little crazy when I go to Vegas," she said, dabbing again at the corners of her eyes. "Hella fun. You go?"

Recently, Slava had fished out of the *Las Vegas Sun* an item for "The Hoot," the humor column that was his official responsibility at *Century*, but he didn't think he could explain all that to Vera. He shook his head.

"You got to go," she summed up. "I have to go clean up, I can't stand in front of you like this. But listen: You have to come over."

He blinked. "Why?"

"This fight they're having?" She pointed at the living room. "It's crazy. How many years now?"

"So how come you came tonight?" Slava said.

"Because my grandpa said he's going, he don't give a bleep what my mom says. So she said I have to go with him, because it looks bad if he goes alone, like nobody loves him. But she said not to talk to anyone. Be, like, quiet and pissed off. It's nice to see you, though, Slava."

"It's nice to see you, too," he said.

"The children have to fix it, like always. You come over for dinner, and little by little. You know?"

"I don't know," he said carefully. "It's their business." He didn't want to get involved with their argument. But with Vera?

She shrugged. "There's not many of us here. We have to stick together."

She stepped forward and placed her lips, full and soft, on his cheek. He felt the rasp of his cheeks prick whatever she had applied to her own. When she pulled back, the beige powder scattered finely between them. Then she walked out of the kitchen.

When he heard the bathroom door close, he wandered into the hallway separating it from the kitchen and stood there, not eavesdropping. She was humming. Then she flushed and the water slithered down the pipes. He sprang back just before the door opened. Her face had returned to its prior immobility. She winked at him and walked past.

The bathroom swam with the subtle sugar of Vera's perfume. Berta had lined the wall with guest towels, hers and Grandfather's concealed from foreign hands. Slava looked at the mirror. How many times had Grandmother's withered face appeared in the exact spot where he now held his own? Slava knew that mirrors were covered after a Jewish death to prevent vanity. But what kind of mourning was it if you had to trick yourself into it? And was it so wrong to leave the mirror uncovered if it made Slava think of her? Wasn't that the point? He lifted a towel from one of the hooks and slipped it over the mirror, fastening its edges with two containers of Berta's face cream. He waited for this to have some effect, but he didn't feel anything. He flushed the toilet in case someone was waiting. Despite himself, he hoped to find Vera standing outside the bathroom.

Instead, he found Grandfather, looking lost. "Slavchik," Grandfather said drowsily. His hands hung at his sides like a soldier's, only that his shoulders sagged.

"People are leaving?" Slava said.

"No, no," Grandfather said.

"You got lucky with Berta," Slava said.

"She's good," Grandfather said agnostically. "I read in the newspaper about a home nurse from Ukraine who lived with this old couple for five years. Our people, from Riga. They were like family with her—they took her on their vacations. When it was time for her to go back to Ukraine, she said to them: 'I hope you kikes rot in hell.' So you never know."

Slava made himself embrace Grandfather.

"Something I need you to look at," Grandfather said, pointing to the bedroom.

"We're both tired. Let's do it another day," Slava said, wanting to return to the living room.

"Another day with you?" Grandfather said. "Another day with you is a year from now. The deadline is soon. It'll take only a moment."

Grandfather strode toward the bedroom but stopped at the threshold. Slava followed his gaze to the bed, the largest thing in the room. The biggest and softest, Grandfather had insisted to Marat on Avenue Z, and here it was. You could look nowhere else. Now that one had to sleep in it alone, it was grotesque.

"Her slippers are right there, but she's not," Grandfather said. "What sense does that make?"

Slava put his arm around Grandfather's shoulder and brought the silk of the old man's head to his chest.

"This day has no end," Grandfather said. "They're talking out there, but I can't understand a word they're saying."

Slava rubbed his nose in Grandfather's hair, soft and straight as goose down, the hair of someone a third his age. The old man nodded helplessly, a fat, lazy tear at his eye. Finally, he stepped into the bedroom and hooked a papery finger into the handle of a bureau, removing a straw pouch where he stuffed mail until Slava's mother came to translate. *She* came all the time. The item he wanted was out front, backed by circulars and forms. He sat down in the chair next to the bed, eyeing its satin slipcover like an untouchable object. "Look, please," he said, extending the envelope.

Slava pulled out the roughly folded papers and inspected the lettering. He snagged on the Hebrew, blocky but lissome. Then he saw the English and whistled slightly. He had heard people in the office talking about it. " 'Dear you,' " he translated. " 'The Conference on Material Claims Against Germany' . . ."

"I know what it says," Grandfather said. "Mama translated. If you were a Holocaust victim, tell the story and you get funds. They're saying— depending on what you went through—a bigger piece once or a smaller

piece every month for the rest of your life. I did it on the calculator: If you
make it ten months, you come out ahead."

"Who's saying?"

"People at the Jewish Center. On Kings Highway."

"Why do you listen to them?" Slava said. "It's a gossip mill."

"Who else for me to listen to?"

The last page in the packet was blank except for a heading: "NARRA-
TIVE. Please describe, in as much detail as you can, where the Subject was
during the years 1939 to 1945."

"How do they know who to send it to?" Slava asked, looking at Grandmother's name in the address bar.

"Grandmother's registered in that museum in Israel. Vashi Yashi."

"Yad Vashem," Slava said. "Say it correctly."

"Day Vashem."

"Yad Vashem. It's not hard—say it."

He glared and pronounced correctly.

"Sixty years they had," Slava said, "they do it the moment she dies."

"Well." Grandfather hung his head.

They investigated the window, South Brooklyn steaming in the dense
July night. A clothesline strung with large underthings wavered in the
breeze.

"So," Grandfather said, turning to face Slava. "Can you write something?"

Slava nearly laughed. This was Grandfather—the rules were right there,
but he was going to ask anyway.

"She . . ." Slava searched for the word. Gone? *Wasn't*? They hadn't come
to an acceptable word yet.

"Not about Grandmother," Grandfather said.

"About whom, then?"

"About me."

Now Slava laughed. "I don't think they're giving out restitution for
evacuations to Uzbekistan."

Grandfather poked the paper with a square nail. "They are, but it's dicey. Some yes, some no. Either way, it's less money. But ghettos and concentration camps, it's a green path all the way. So, give me one of those. You're a writer, aren't you?"

Slava opened his hands. "Now I'm a writer."

"You write for the newspaper where you work," he said. "That's what you said."

"It's a magazine," Slava said.

"So, this is like an article for your newspaper."

"Articles for my newspaper are not invented."

"This country does not invent things?" Grandfather said, his eyes flashing. "Bush did not invent a reason to cut off Saddam's balls? When the stocks fall down, it's not because someone invented the numbers?"

"This country has nothing to do with it!"

"You don't know how to do it. Is that it?"

"I do know how to do it," Slava said through his teeth.

"Then do it," Grandfather said. "For your grandmother. Do it."

There was a knock on the door. Slava's mother's head—round, defenseless—sneaked in. "Everything okay here, boys?" she said.

"Okay, daughter," Grandfather said with a strange formality.

"There's some dessert on the table," she said. "I think people will start to go soon."

"We will, we will," Grandfather said.

"I ordered the gravestones," she said. "They go up in a week."

"Mine?" Grandfather said.

"Will be blank. There's a plinth connecting them. Says Gelman. Your stone is black, Mama's is lighter."

"The inscription?"

"In Russian. 'Don't speak of them with grief: They are with us no more. But with gratitude: They were.' A poem—Grusheff suggested it."

"Grusheff drank tea with Pushkin, if you believe what he says," Grandfather said. "He probably wrote it himself. We should make sure there are no other stones with those lines. The words are nice, though."

"I'll check, Papa," Slava's mother said and gently closed the door.

Grandfather turned to Slava. "I need to remind you that your great-uncle Aaron—*my* brother—is in a mass grave in Latvia? Unkissed, he died. I wish you could read his letters, they weren't in Yiddish. I went after him with a butcher knife when they called him up. A pinkie would have been enough to disqualify him. In '41, at least. My year? Every boy conscripted in '43"—he sliced his palm through the air—"cut down like grass." He leaned in and whispered, "I wasn't going to volunteer to be cannon fodder. You wouldn't be here. I stayed alive."

"What does Aaron have to do with it?" Slava said. "Look. It says: 'Ghettos, forced labor, concentration camps . . . What did the subject suffer between 1939 to 1945?' The subject. Not you. You didn't suffer."

"I didn't suffer?" Grandfather's eyes sparkled. "I've got a grave already, I didn't suffer. God bless you, you know that?" He snorted, as if he'd been asked to sell a perfectly healthy horse at half value. "All the men were taken right away: Aaron, Father, all the cousins. Father was too old for infantry, so they took him to Heavy Labor. Two years later, there's a knock at the door. I see this skeleton in rags, so I shout to my mother, 'There's a beggar at the door, give him some food!' Not a strange sight in those days. And he starts weeping. It was Father. A week later, they told us about Aaron. Killed by artillery. I wanted to spare my mother losing the last of her men, so yes, I went to Uzbekistan. Not to live in a palace—to pick pockets and piss myself on the street so they'd think I was a retard and not draft me." He looked away. "Look, I came back. I enlisted."

"On a ship in liberated territory," Slava said. "Look, I didn't make up the rules. The paper says: 'Ghettos, forced labor, concentration camps.'"

"What are you, Lenin's grandson?" Grandfather said. "Maybe I didn't suffer in the exact way I need to have suffered"—he flicked a finger at the envelope—"but they made sure to kill all the people who did. We had our whole world taken out from under us. No more dances, no holidays, no meals with your mother at the stove. A meal like this?" He pointed at the living room. "Do you know what it means to have a meal like this? Do you know what we came back to after the war? Tomatoes the size of your head. They'd fertilized them with human ash. You follow?"

"So now you want your revenge," Slava said. "Heist the German government."

"The German government?" he said. "The German government should be grateful to get off this easy."

"This German government didn't kill anyone."

"So, everyone, we should say thank you?" Grandfather slapped his hands, the pop rising to the ceiling.

"What *is* it?" Slava said. "Do you need more money?" He pointed around them: the bureau, the bed, the tricked-out torchieres keeping sentry in the corners.

"Money?" Grandfather said, drawing back. "Money makes the world go round. Money's not the only reason, but I don't know anyone who's been hurt by money."

"Why did you never tell me any of that before? About evacuation?"

"We didn't want those ugly things in your head. We wanted you above us. Enough hands had to go in the dirt so yours wouldn't have to."

"So this is a rose you're asking me to smell?"

"It's family, Slavik."

"Let's skip the big words, if you don't mind. I'm not Kozlovich. It's crime. That's our family? Do you know what the punishment is if we're caught?"

"I would give my right arm for you if that's what it took. That's family."

"If that's what what took?"

"You—safe. You—happy." Grandfather slapped the nightstand between them. "This conversation is over. I don't need your services."

"I don't need your right arm!"

They sat in bitter silence, listening to the muted chatter carrying from the living room. Slava savored his power over Grandfather, like an olive you keep sucking to get every thread of the meat. Now he was a writer. Who was responsible for this deviancy in the first place? In America, unlike back home, the mail came down like a blizzard. The adults hauled it upstairs with dark faces. Was this a letter from James Baker III alerting the Gelmans that a tragic mistake had been made and the family would have to return to the Soviet Union? They couldn't read it.

The letter was given to Slava. His fingers were small enough for the Bible font and onionskin pages of the brick dictionary they had procured from a curbside, somebody who had learned English already. As the adults shifted their feet, leaning against doorjambs and working their lips with their teeth, he carefully sliced open the envelope and unfolded the letter inside, his heart beating madly. He was all that stood between his family and expulsion by James Baker III. America was a country where you could have Roman numerals after your name, like a Caesar.

As the adults watched, Slava checked the unfamiliar words in the bricktionary. "Annual percentage rate." "Layaway." "Installment plan." "One time only." "For special customers like you." The senior Gelmans waiting, Slava was embarrassed to discover himself mindlessly glued to certain words in the dictionary that had nothing to do with the task at hand. On the way to "credit card," he had snagged on "cathedral," its spires—t, h, d, l— like the ones the Gelmans had seen in Vienna. "Rebate" took him to "roly-poly," which rolled around his mouth like a fat marble. "Venture rewards" led him to "zaftig," a Russian *baba*'s breasts covering his eyes as she placed in front of him a bowl of morning farina. Eventually, he managed to verify enough to reassure the adults that, no, it didn't seem like a letter from James Baker III. The senior Gelmans sighed, shook their heads, resumed frying fish.

Slava remained with the bricktionary. Hinky, lunker, wattles. Taro, terrazzo, toodle-oo. "Levity" became a Jewish word because Levy was a

Jewish surname in America. "Had had"—knock-knock—was a door. A "gewgaw" was a "gimcrack," and a "gimcrack" was "folderol." "Sententious" could mean two opposite things, and wasn't to be confused with "senescent," "tendentious," or "sentient." Nor "eschatological" with "scatological." This language placed the end of the world two letters away from the end of a bowel movement.

Russian words were as stretchy as the meat under Grandmother's arm. You could invent new endings and they still made sense. Like peasants fidgeting with their ties at a wedding, the words wanted to unlace into diminutives: Mikhail into Mishen'ka (little Misha), *kartoshka* into *kartoshechka* (little potato). English was colder, clipped, a brain game. But English was brilliant. For some reason, in the bedroom, all this gave him skin against Grandfather.

Grandfather grunted and, avoiding Slava's eyes, rose. Downstairs, a salsa had started up, the dull bass making the same point over and over. Moving toward the door, Grandfather shuddered and lost his stride, reaching out his arms as if he were going to slip. But seeing no help rushing from his grandson, he got his hand on the bureau, righted himself, and walked out.

– 3 –

The east-facing wall of the Spartak Dance Club was not, strictly speaking, any longer a wall. Three quarters of Minsk had been bombed into rubble, which explains why it's so ugly today, rebuilt after the war in the socialist style. But even before victory was declared over the Germans, the Saturday-night dances at the Spartak Dance Club had resumed. The people needed dances as much as bread, Stalin had said. The entire country rushed to reopen its dance halls, those villages without one scrounging to convert something, anything, that could hold a gramophone and a dance platform. Two months after V-E Day, the Spartak Dance Club in Minsk was back in regular operation despite remaining in possession of only three walls, which meant that Sofia Dreitser's older sister Galina wouldn't be attending the Saturday-night dances because, in her view, the other walls could go crumbling at any moment, and then that would be a pretty costly dance, wouldn't it.

But Sofia loved to dance. She had to be more careful nowadays, with no father or brother or mother to look after her, and men back from the war with a hollowed-out look in their eyes and a hunger that even a woman's hand paled beside. So she danced by herself or with a female friend. That was the concession Galina had managed to extract from her wild younger sister; Sofia would go to the dances only if accompanied by Rusya, the Slav girl next door, who joked to Galina with her characteristic coarseness, "You don't mind your sister dead if the walls crumble, so long as she doesn't get raped?" But Rusya went along, and twirl she and Sofia did, casting longing glances at the army captains back from the front in their uniforms, and at the neighborhood boys, who in the span of four years had become men. There was Misha Surokin, the half-moon of a scar running down the right side of his face; and Yevgeny Gelman, the hooligan from Sofia's neighborhood, looking as unserious as she remembered him; and Pavlik Sukhoi, a facial tic he had acquired in the war making him wince twice a sentence. They were the same but not the same.

And so when the waltz started up on this Saturday night, it was Sofia and Rusya, approximating the moves best as they could from the films they had seen before the war, imagining themselves in some grand castle in Austria, switching up the lead every minute or so, Sofia pretending strict indifference toward the men leering from the perimeter of the dance club, Rusya sending them coquettish smiles.

But it was Sofia whom the men were looking at, unblemished skin and two ponytails like cables—Rusya had been blessed with a farmer's fearlessness but also a farmer's face. During a break for boysenberry punch (no alcohol was served, which meant the men had to sneak it in flasks and seltzer bottles, going outside for swigs out of respect for the women), while Rusya was distracted by a bowlegged lieutenant, one of the army captains wandered over to Sofia.

It was as the rule has it: It's the brave ones who get the girl, and bravery has nothing to do with looks; they had the courage to approach. Captain Tereshkin had one such plain face, his chin fading imperceptibly into his neck, halfhearted stubble crowning his jowls. No matter the searing July heat, even starved evacuees sporting healthyish tan glows, Tereshkin was as pale as snow. Who knows what overtook Sofia in that moment; we nurture our defenses, and in a moment of consequence, they simply don't show. Maybe she wanted to feel a man's arms around her; maybe she felt sorry for Tereshkin, because probably he was motherless, sisterless, childless; maybe she simply got tired of saying no. All she knew was that she was dancing the next dance with him, a Rosner jazz tune, Rusya all eyes at her lieutenant, whose own eyes were beginning to wander. Even Sofia, busy with Tereshkin, could see that.

When the curfew bell rang—it was ten o'clock, things still on edge—Captain Tereshkin asked if he could escort Sofia home. It was dark, barely any functioning streetlamps. Maybe that was all he wanted, a gentleman, and Galina would be home in case he tried to push his way in. The way there was long, however, and Sofia wasn't about to take chances. She had danced with him, yes, but because a woman danced with a man, that meant she had to thank him with her body? All the same, she didn't want to insult the captain—because she had danced with him all evening, because maybe he had meant nothing by it, because she was a little bit scared. That was when the idea came to her. She disliked it almost as much as she disliked the idea of having pale-faced Captain Tereshkin accompany her home, and she minced in place, smiling dumbly at Tereshkin while she tried to think of something else. But nothing else would come—her cleverness tended to abandon her these days, as if she had used up her life's allotted supply during the war, staying alive. What a pitiful amount she had been granted, she thought. It hadn't been enough to save anyone but her and her sister. All these thoughts—comically, stupidly—flashed through her mind. Oh, Captain, she thought, if only you knew what you were taking on—an orphan with one dress between her and her sister, because the rest of their clothes, given them by the Red Cross, had been stolen and pawned by the Belarusian collaborator who continued to occupy half their home. Sofia wore it now, not so much a dress as a sarafan, the kind of thing her mother wore before the war to clean the house.

Finally, Sofia excused herself to go to the bathroom, which meant the bushes outside, but the bushes outside would take her past Zhenya Gelman, laughing with his friends in a circle and taking swigs from a bottle with no label, too late in the evening to bother with outside.

Zhenya Gelman was known in the neighborhood. What he was known for was another story. "A child of other people's gardens," people called him before the war. A hooligan, not to say a criminal. He got what needed to be got, whether it was beets from old Ferbershteyn's garden or a set of silver spoons from God knows whom, and you could do yourself a favor by not worrying how.

Sofia was glad to see Zhenya alive, as glad as she would have been for a brother, but she had nothing to do with boys like him before the war, and she would have less to do with them now. Boys like him would be in prison before they turned twenty. Even as she approached him that night, her mind ran with what else she could do, but she had nothing. Her mind was like a still clock. She was impressed with herself for coming up even with this. Besides, Zhenya had a girlfriend. He had ten girlfriends. Maybe he wouldn't want anything from her in return.

She stood behind him for nearly a minute before his friends noticed her and their expressions changed. He spun around. "Sofia Dreitser," he observed, the smile on his face hanging awkwardly.

"Can I talk to you?" she said.

A couple of chuckles followed from the boys behind him, but he half turned and the laughter fell from their faces. Zhenya and Sofia stepped to the side. He placed his hand on her shoulder and leaned in solemnly, but she gave him such a look that his hand returned to his side.

"There's a captain over there," she started.

"Tereshkin," he said.

Her eyes opened wide in surprise.

"The eyes of a reconnaissance man!" Zhenya said with his usual self-regard.

Quite a comment to make, considering Zhenya had been evacuated out east, then had the age on his identity card revised down until the war was nearly over, then, when finally drafted, had finagled his way onto a ship in liberated territory as a radio operator. Zhenya Gelman knew as much about radio operation as she did, but how to get to safe places when the world around him was ending, that he knew how to do better than anyone.

"Let me guess," he said. "The captain wants to take you home."

She blushed and looked down.

"You know, you look like a just-hatched chick in that sarafan of yours," he said.

"Thank you very much, Zhenya," she said angrily.

"And so you came to Zhenya the thug to help you out of your bind," he said. "Not a word for me when things are hopping along, but when trouble comes . . ." The sentence was half out of his mouth when he realized what he was saying, the idiot, her entire family in the ground and she didn't even know where. When it came time to liquidate the Minsk orphanage, the Nazis walked the children into a giant hole in the earth and covered their living bodies with sand. They tossed candies to them as their tiny hands reached out for help. That was what the Nazis did to children. So she hoped her parents and her grandfather had been merely shot. She didn't know how they had died, which was what made her nights endless, but if it was known, it was known only in some army or KGB office, and those places she hoped never to see.

"I'm sorry," he said. "Come with me."

"Zhenya," she said, "I am grateful to you for the help. But I can't thank you. You understand what I mean."

"You've already insulted me once," he said. "Don't insult me twice."

When Captain Tereshkin felt an arm around his waist, he brightened, thinking it was Sofia's; the smile changed to surprise when it turned out to belong to Zhenya Gelman, "a child of other people's gardens," someone who was known to the neighborhood, and known to him, Tereshkin having grown up several blocks away.

"Captain!" Zhenya yelled. He took Tereshkin's hand in his. "I have to pour you a glass."

"W-why?" Tereshkin said.

"Because you've kept my lady company all night long. It was a gentle-manly thing to do—never let a lady stand alone. So I owe you. What do you drink? You know I specialize in Armenian cognac."

Tereshkin turned red as a sugar beet. He had half a dozen years on Gelman, and their bodies were of similar cast, but Gelman had boxed be-fore the war, and in any case, you didn't fight with Zhenya Gelman.

"Zhenya," he said, his face falling. "I'm sorry. I had no idea. Really. You have to believe me."

"But that's what I'm saying!" Zhenya said. "You're a good man, and I want to thank you." Zhenya practically made him drink the cognac. They sucked on the same piece of lemon afterward, Zhenya gallantly giving Tereshkin first taste. They toasted the motherland, then the women around them. There were no women like Russian women. Russian women were made from freshly milked milk, and the rest of the world's women from water. It didn't matter were they Jewish or not—Zhenya couldn't resist forcing the captain to agree with this notion. Russian women were choco-late, like the loam under their feet; they were the butter that went on their bread; the red poppies that swayed in the wind. To Russian women!

"It seems I should walk my girlfriend home, don't you think?" Zhenya said to Sofia after Tereshkin had freed himself from Zhenya's clutches and, pleading curfew, run off. Zhenya winked. Already he had acquired some-where a gold tooth, as was the fashion.

"I don't know if your real girlfriend would appreciate that," Sofia said.

"Who's that?" he said.

"Oh, you can't keep them straight," she said. "Ida. Or whatever her name is."

"Ida?" he said, his eyebrows rising. "I ditched Ida like a sack of potatoes. I asked her to join tonight. She says: 'My teeth hurt.' How do you like that? I was gone like a comet. Sparks coming out from under my feet. You could light a cigarette off my boot heel. Her teeth hurt!"

"Ida." Sofia smirked. "Ida, whose father distributes beer and vodka for the whole city. Millionaire Ida. You ditched her."

"I ditched her," he said proudly.

"Well, even I'm impressed," she said.

"So, what do you say?" he said. "It's insulting that I have to say it, but I got nothing in mind. I just want to see you home safe. We lived fourteen houses from each other before the war. We're practically family."

"How in the world do you know how many houses we lived from each other?"

"Because I counted," he said.

Sofia was right about one thing, though only partly. Zhenya did go to prison, but it wasn't before he turned twenty; he was already twenty-one. Several years after the dance, they were returning from another dance club with friends when they heard from the other side of the street: "Look at those kikes! Would have been nice to have some of that energy at the front, kikes!" She said sternly, "Zhenya, no," but he was already crossing. It wasn't because he was drunk; he would have done the same thing if he had been sober, as he would for the rest of their lives, so while she never knew whether her husband would end his day in her bed or a prison cell, she always knew that it would be without lost pride. Zhenya carried a straight razor for occasions exactly like this one. He cut up the fellow pretty bad. Zhenya's father bribed the judge, so he got only a year instead of three. They were starting to build the soccer stadium around that time, so that was how he repaid his debt to society. Though Zhenya never mentioned it to his grandson Slava, his own hands had poured the concrete for the seats where they sat every week, shouting after Gotsman and Aleinikov.

Sofia Dreitser waited faithfully until Zhenya Gelman was released from prison. Her worst imaginings about him had come true, but once Sofia Dreitser devoted herself to something, she didn't let go. Zhenya Gelman knew how to get to a safe place when the world around him was ending.

And he still had his family, with the exception of his older brother, who had been killed in the war—a large, noisy, argumentative family that took her in the way a wave takes in a body. She wanted these things, and most days that equaled out to she wanted him.

So she ordered her own pride back and waited patiently, faithfully, for his return from prison and welcomed him home with his favorite meal, lamb cutlets and "mashed potatoes in the cloud style," so called by him because they were as airy as clouds, and all without butter. She waited until she became Sofia Gelman; until they produced Tanya Gelman; until Tanya met Edik Shtuts, such a different man from her own husband; until Tanya and Edik produced Vyacheslav Gelman, though she, Sofia, called him Slava for short; until they left the place that was soaked with the blood of her family for a place that meant nothing to her except what it would do for her grandson, for whom she had lived since the moment she had approached Zhenya Gelman at the Spartak Dance Club in 1945 and said can you help.

When Slava abandoned Brooklyn, he bought a small notebook, intending to keep it filled with details about his grandmother's life. That was how he would remain close to her. The problem was that he didn't know a great deal about Grandmother's life. Even when she was well, she regarded her personal history as one regarded a tragic mistake. Some people can't stop working over their tragic mistakes—Slava was this type of person; he turned over in his mind endlessly the mystifying details of his failures at *Century*—but other people prefer to live as if their tragic mistakes never took place. Slava's grandmother was this kind of person. She wanted to know whether Slava had finished his homework; whether he had a girl-friend; whether he had enough to eat: She could make a poached carp that lasted for a week. Slava's life seemed insignificant next to hers, and he felt hot shame in regaling her with what girl had said what to him at school, but Grandmother followed his words with such transport that her lips followed his as he spoke.

With everyone else, Grandmother was prim, unforgiving, impermeable. Even as a young man, Grandfather whined about aches in his chest, aches in his legs, aches in his head; this irritated Slava's grandmother. She glared at her husband as if at a child, embarrassed and angry.

So Slava took advantage of their connection and, in high school, invented a ruse. He pretended that for history class, he had been assigned to extract a family story, for a pastiche on the personal histories of the class. No such thing had been assigned—Slava's teacher, Mr. Jury, was a red-nosed tippler who gave out class-long assignments and napped in his chair—but Grandmother wouldn't dare cost Slava a good grade. "What can I tell you, cucumber?" she said. "Tell me why you call me that," he said. "'Cucumber'?" she said. She smiled shyly; she didn't know; she had never thought about it. "Tell me about the war," he pressed cautiously. She smiled again and began, "Well . . ." The sentence ended there. Her tongue moved but no words emerged. He wanted to say, Tell me because I'd like to tell my grandchildren one day. Tell me because it happened to you, and so I should know. Tell me because it will bring me closer to you, and I want to be close to you. But he was fifteen years old, and he didn't know how to express thoughts like these. He only knew that he wanted to know. He could tell that she would tell him anything but anything, only if he could stand it please don't make her talk about *that*. And though he grasped how important it was for him to know—even if everyone in the family had acquiesced not to trouble Grandmother about it—he couldn't bring himself to make her. So he said to her: "Forget about the war. Tell me about how you and Grandfather fell in love."

He wrote out the Spartak Dance Club story in his little notebook days after he decided not to go to Brooklyn again. His family had yet to understand what was happening, though his mother was already beginning to leave messages on his answering machine, first hectoring, then begging, then feigning poor health, then feigning good news, then claiming to need advice, then loudly giving up. But *Grandmother* understood why he had to disappear, he reassured himself. Even though she never called, somehow she understood, if only because she believed that everything he did was blameless and true.

But the story of how Grandmother and Grandfather fell in love was the only story that Slava had. He traced and retraced its slender collection of details, his pocket notebook as overlarge for the few facts it contained as a widower's bed for its revised list of occupants. He could have expanded its contents, it occurred to him once, by inventing or imagining something—the house Grandmother came from, the way the few working streetlights shone over her and Grandfather's heads on their way back to her house. Hadn't Slava invented a ruse to make her tell the story in the first place? But all that felt shameless now that he no longer saw her. On the pages of his notebook was the truth, and it would be impaired if he invented around it. He wasn't going to lie the way Grandfather did, the way they all had to. His mother had earned the valedictorian slot at Belarus State, but the honor was given to the number two person, a Slav, because how could you have a Jew at the top; Belarus State admitted only two Jews per thousand, and one of them was going to win valedictorian? Invited to say something at the ceremony, a silver medal around her neck, Slava's mother had merely smiled into the microphone and said: "I want to thank the committee . . ."

Stories like these, Slava had too many of. They went around the dinner table with no difficulty. For every story that his grandmother refused to tell, Slava's grandfather told three. He could talk until morning. The usual dinner talk when they all lived together—shopping lists, doctors' appointments, even Slava's doings—bored Grandfather, and he would slink off to make eyes at the television. However, if the conversation touched something from their Soviet life, his eyes would quicken and he would launch into a ceaseless description. These stories were without beginning or end, without the context that would have helped his listeners remember who was who, how things worked. Despite trying his utmost, inevitably, Slava lost the thread, feeling like a failure because he was letting gold slip away in a fast-moving river. But his inadequacy with the details left him free to observe how Grandfather told stories, like a rushing river, indeed. *On zakhlebyvalsya.* He was choking on everything he wanted to say.

4

Everybody's on *shpilkes*," said Arianna Bock, Slava's cubicle neighbor, the dimes of her eyes appearing above the fiberglass divider between them.

"Big day," Slava said, trying to sound casual.

"Big day for Slava Gelman?" she said, flitting the tips of her fingers over an imaginary keyboard.

"Did you see what I wrote?" he said. "It's in the database."

She nodded, a flicker of disagreement passing over her face. He noticed her: pale skin, a slash of red lips, a frizz of charcoal hair. A large birthmark spanned both halves of her right eyelid. It reunited and broke again when she blinked.

"What is it?" he said.

"Nothing, it's great," she said.

The deception cut into him, but he didn't pursue it. "It's time for your walk," he said drily. Every morning at eleven, Arianna vanished for a constitutional, as she called it. Cannons could be firing on the palace, but everything would wait until her return. He admired and resented her skillful oblivion.

She smiled, forgiving the sharpness in his voice.

"And where today?" he said.

"You don't know until you get outside," she said. "That's the point. You should come."

The thought of wandering without editorial purpose filled Slava with anxiety. Unlike Arianna, he had things to do. Slava owed laughs to "The Hoot." Upon ascending to the editorship two years before, Beau Reasons had decided the magazine needed humor, and so Slava was assigned to scour regional newspapers for slipups, flubs, and double entendres, to which *Century* appended a wry commentary (the rejoinder, in *Century* talk). Slava would find in the *Provincetown Banner*:

> *The dog Claude Monet, who was lost last week and whose disappearance has been extensively covered by this newspaper, was found yesterday by the banks of the Pamet River.*

Century would add:

> *He must have thought the light superior there.*

If Slava managed to clear through the pile of *Union-Tribune*s and *Plain Dealer*s on his desk before quitting time, he launched into the stories he himself was trying to write. There was no time for walks to . . . where? They were in Midtown, a cold needle-forest of skyscrapers, striped shirts, pencil skirts, flats, barrettes, crinkling brown sandwich bags of the sort Slava had used to cover his first American schoolbooks, bodies in perpetual sidestep, instructions barked into a cell phone . . . No, Slava didn't want to go outside. His life had a shape, hermetically sealed: on one end the office where he spent the daylight hours, on the other the apartment where he slept, between them the long underground rod of the 6 train. No walks.

He studied the treacherous slingshot of Arianna's clavicle. She knew all about it—in the summer, you could count on one hand the number of times she wore sleeves. Not that Slava counted. Unlike Slava, who remained in the office to work on his writing, Arianna went home at six sharp—"I need to veg" was her announcement, as if she had depleted herself mowing a field. Arianna, a fact-checker, had the eagerness of the red checking pencil anchoring the bun of her hair. He had no time for her, if that's how it was. Besides, Slava stayed clear of anything that could turn into something. He had precious little free time as it was.

However, sometimes curiosity bested even Slava's leonine will, and he listened to the noise she made on the other side of the divider. White, blocky teeth eviscerating the leisure end of an old-fashioned pencil. The hollow thump of a bracelet against the Lucite of which their desktops were made. A back cracking in both directions, then the knuckles. The rabbity progress of teeth down the rims of a sunflower seed. Boots jangly with some kind of spur. Hooting laughter, as if there were no one else in the room.

Sometimes, when she wasn't at her desk, Slava would peek over. Arianna ate almost nothing but salads, occasionally a pair of hard-boiled eggs without mayonnaise. The plastic containers remained on her desk, unfinished and open, until the end of the day, when he heard the day's purchases hitting the walls of the garbage can: coffee cup, salad container, eggshells. Occasionally, these items missed and landed on the floor, or she left them on her desk altogether. Arianna maintained the American attitude toward help: It was their job. Souvenirs from the day's salad decorated her tabletop: a triangle of lettuce, a streaky olive, a full anchovy. After she walked out, Slava tidied up on her side.

It was thanks to Arianna that Slava had found himself assigned to observe a new feat by an urban explorer. Beau had appeared before the Junior Staff pen—it really was a pen; the sixteen Juniors sat behind a railing like zoo rhinos—and thrown out an invitation to contribute to *Century*—*an invitation to contribute to* Century—as if he was merely adjusting ad count for the upcoming issue.

While everyone was busy being stunned—except for Peter Devicki, naturally; Peter, the only Junior to have published anything in the magazine, had his hand up before he knew what Beau was asking for—Arianna stared incandescently at Slava's temple. He looked over. Her eyes were fixed on him like headlights. She would have raised his arm for him if she could.

"Listen," she said now, draping her forearms on the divider. Five copper bracelets rattled against the fiberglass. Her nails were boyishly short and girlishly red. "This is tacky, but sometimes tacky's just the thing. Imagine yourself winning this afternoon. Do something as if you got it."

"Like what?" he said. "Champagne bath in Bean's office?"

"Don't make fun," she said. "I said it was corny. What are you going to do? Get on the phone, call your parents, and tell them to buy next week's issue. Because it's going to have a story by you in it."

"It's bad luck to celebrate beforehand," he said.

"The point is to do it when it's impractical."

"They think I've been writing for this magazine for three years," he said. "That's what I told them when I got hired, so they wouldn't feel bad."

"What would they have you do?"

Slava threw up his hands.

"All right," she said. "I have to go."

He was chagrined to have her give up so quickly. "How did you know I wanted to do it?" he said in a rush. "The way you looked at me when Beau came around."

"You'd have to be deaf and mute not to know," she said.

He watched her walk away. Despite his spying on her, it hadn't occurred to him that she might spy in return. Arianna Bock wasn't really a noticer. This Slava knew with a husband's knowledge—in the last year and a half, he had spent more time within a foot of this hieroglyphic presence than within any other, a melancholy statistic. She marched around the Junior Staff pen heedless of its funereal quiet, forgot what she was told, and cast out of mind things that refused to clarify themselves with efficiency. At the Friday-afternoon Junior Staff assignment meetings, she responded to Mr. Grayson, their voluminous chief, as if they were both senior editors rather than she someone dependent on his goodwill and desire to employ her. Once he had asked her if she was interested in fact-checking a story, and she'd said: Are you really asking? Everyone laughed. Even Mr. Grayson.

He looked down at his desk phone. They were all still there, at Grandfather's. Only Slava had left. The events of the previous day, momentarily sidelined by Arianna, refilled his mind. You had to give her that: She filled the frame of your thinking.

The idea had been Beau's. He had replaced Martin Graves, the Patriarch, deceased after forty-six years at the helm. (Mugging for history, Mr. Graves went not at the breast of some wet nurse but in his office chair, making his faint disapprobations on a sheaf of magazine copy.) Mr. Graves's late phase had some peculiar concerns. There had been a strange piece by a Papuan cannibal (in Dani, the cannibal language), as transcribed by a Canadian linguist, and an even stranger one by Frank Moy, the war reporter, about soap operas. But no one was going to touch Martin Graves until he was retired by the angels.

In any case: An assignment had fallen through; the money had already been spent; what if, in lieu, Beau sent a Junior? These, deranged with dispossession and dreams, thought they could write articles a thousand times better than what those overpaid marquee writers turned in. They'd do it for free, too. *Century* paid writers three dollars a word: You do the math. Beau would send two just in case—two times zero in fees was still zero, and competition bred innovation. He did that sometimes even for the senior writers, which caused no small amount of consternation because book contracts were not given out to someone bylined "Staff." The senior editors would make a clinic of the whole thing: The Monday-afternoon Senior Staff meeting would be open to the full masthead, the choice between Peter and Slava put to a vote.

Berta picked up. In his frailty, Grandfather could not be bothered to answer the telephone. "I'll get him for you," she said.

"Yes," Grandfather said a minute later, as if answering an already posed question. His voice sounded like raked gravel.

"Buy a copy of the magazine next week," Slava said, feeling stupid.

"What?" Grandfather said. "When?"

"Sorry—how are you feeling?"

"What?" he said again.

"Come on. You know what I'm saying."

"Who is this?"

"Just buy the magazine," Slava said.

"Why?"

"It'll have a story I wrote."

"Where am I supposed to find it? What is it called?"

"It's called *Century*. You know this."

"Sancher," he said. "Hold on, let me write it down."

"No—*Century*. You're not trying."

"I am eighty years old, and my wife died yesterday. Do you understand that, or you're already on with your life? S like a Russian S?"

"No. Yes. C. Like a Russian S."

"Then?"

"E. Same in both. Then a backward Ee—N. Then a T—same in both. Then that horseshoe."

"What horseshoe?"

"Just draw a horseshoe."

"Open side down?"

"No, up."

"I had horses. One was called Beetle, and one was called Boy."

"Next is an R. An English R. Like our *ya* but backward."

"*Ya* backward . . ." Grandfather repeated dejectedly. "I need Berta."

"She speaks even less English than you," Slava said. "Come on, you can do it. *Ya* backward. And then—this is the last one—a Y. Same in both."

On the other end of the line, Grandfather studied the paper. "Sancher," he read.

In the preceding years, Slava had tried to propose to his superiors at Century stories of the kind he saw in the magazine every week. He prayed and broke bread with five young evangelical men from Ohio who had come to New York to test their faith in the most depraved place they could think of. He jumped on a trampoline with a runaway to the Big Apple Circus who was a Ph.D. in semiotics and was writing a semiotics of the tightrope. One Saturday, Slava clawed ninety-one dollars from the cold, dead fingers of his bank account and took a Peter Pan bus to the Massachusetts town where the fourth synagogue built in America was going to become the first Staples in town. A town baker who had stayed kosher even though too few Jews remained to notice—he was wise to persist; soon non-Jews would be buying more kosher products than Jews, another story Slava would try to give *Century*—had appeared at the grand opening to protest. ("Destroying a heritage?" his placard said in wandering Sharpie. "Come to Staples! *That Was Easy.*™") The baker gave Slava another lead: an underground international bidding war for Hitler's personal map of Europe by a Belgian industrialist with neo-Nazi proclivities and the British Orthodox Jew (a third cousin of the baker) who wished to procure it first so he could destroy it.

None of it had worked, Slava did not understand why. Had his submissions been received? Slava inquired with the IT department, but his e-mail appeared to be working; Mr. Grayson was managing to get through with brainless new assignments with no difficulty. Archibald Dyson (the senior editor) probably never opened Slava's e-mails in the first place. Slava could write Arch that he had humped his wife outside a liquor mart on Tuesday afternoon and Arch would never know. Arch thought he was spam.

An image of Slava's grandfather spun out of the screen of Slava's desktop one hopeless afternoon: *I have beaten a man eyeless for saying "kike" out loud. I put enough goys in my pocket to get your mother into Belarus State. We left only with what we could carry and now your parents have a Nissan Altima* and *a Ford Taurus. So, lift your ass from your ergonomic work chair and put this Dyson's nose directly into whatever it is that you do, with a little two-finger pinch at the base of the neck if that helps. We have seen your kind, Mr. Archibald, and we have seen worse, so why don't you give this a read.*

Slava did it, minus the pinch of the neck and plus a bout of diarrhea nervosa, but this did not have the result intended by Grandfather-genie.

Slava pressed forward. On a weekend, feeling war-roomish, he bought a wipe board and wrote out on its left side the previous issue's table of contents. To the right of each entry, he assigned the story a category:

- Profile of eccentric personage
- Interview with famous person
- Story of a stunt action
- International report
- Highlight of social issue
- Memoir of picayune childhood experience

Famous people and international reports he could do nothing about—he didn't know any famous people, and he didn't have the money to go to the nearest war. But the rest: They had an eccentric personage, he had an eccentric personage (the baker). They had a stunt action, he had a stunt action (the evangelicals). And while the Jewish evacuation of Rhode Island was perhaps not as pressing an issue as the epidemic of underage mothers, it was along the same spectrum, that could not be denied. Was Slava required to produce a memoir of Little League times or learning to bake with his mother? Slava cursed his mother for never teaching him how to bake, and the full Gelman clan for keeping him busy translating credit-card offers until it was too late to join Little League.

No, it couldn't be the subjects. It had to be the style. Slava returned to the issue and reread every article. Then he went to a bin where he kept old issues and reread the last six issues, this time latitudinally: the opening story across all six; the next story across all six; the closing story. He experienced the Egyptologist's tremor upon stumbling on Nefertiti's lunch bowl: He had decoded the pattern. The wipe board full, Slava started taping note cards on the refrigerator, the fridge burping in acknowledgment of this first garlanding since its purchase.

Article A. Opening part: The Scene. Sentence One: Specific Date. "On January 27, 2005, Avery Coulter went outside to clear his driveway of the heavy snowfall that had blanketed Rochester, New York, the previous night."

The prose made the obvious elegant—you could not very well shovel snow anywhere but outside, could you, but one didn't mind with such a sinuous sentence—and though it stayed well shy of the fences, the tempered, diffident tone was like a mother's hand on the cheek. Absent a mother, a Beau Reasons.

Onward. We watch Avery start to shovel the driveway; his neighbor owns a Range Rover; the township recently cleared a nearby creek's overflow tubes of debris (the randomness of the details only adds to their aristocratic, mysterious elegance); *booltykh*—Avery feels a strain in his lower back. He knows something's wrong. Section break.

Section Two: The Issue. "Tens of thousands of Americans strain their backs shoveling snow every year, leading to millions of lost workdays and tens of millions of dollars in hospital bills. Many Americans have snow-blowers, but quality machines are pricey indulgences, at five hundred dollars and more. It was while Coulter, an entrepreneur, was laid up after his unsuccessful driveway clearing—according to *Forbes*, Coulter has enough money for a million snowblowers, but that morning he wanted some exercise—that he thought: There has got to be a better way."

Section 2A: The Quote. "'I hadn't shoveled a driveway since I was seventeen,' Coulter said on a recent afternoon. 'So I guess it served me right. But it wiped me out for a week. I thought about people who don't have the luxury of that. And that's when I thought: SnowGlow.'

"Coulter, who specializes in domestic use of nuclear energy, imagined a negligibly radioactive field that could melt the snow in your yard [note the smooth intimacy! not *a* yard but *your* yard] at the rate of a square foot a second. Don a protective suit, warn the neighbors, flip a switch, and voilà: snow into snowmelt."

And we're off. A biographical section on Coulter, quotes from a current (ingratiating) and a former (passive-aggressive) associate, a skeptical comment about runoff from someone in Energy, a zoom-out about the state of nuclear, and then the semi-autistic peter-out of the end: "The winter has been especially persistent in Rochester this year. On a recent afternoon, Coulter was in his driveway, pulverizing a snowfall with Snow-Glow. By his count, it was number sixteen of the season. He had been spending more time at home than ever. In his hazmat suit, he looked a little like an extra from *Red Dawn*. It was nearly dark when his wife called him to dinner. 'In a minute!' he yelled. He sounded like a kid reluctant to let go of a toy."

It was too easy. Why had Slava waited to do this till now? He poured himself a celebratory glass of brandy from a bottle that Grandfather, who reacted with dismay to homes without high-quality alcohol, had pressed on him. Slava clinked the bottle with his glass. The peal rang through the room and loosed the Grandfather-genie once more. Again, the genie growled at Slava. How does the clever aspirant seal the certainty of impending success? it asked him. Slava slapped his forehead.

On Monday, he arrived at work bearing four bottles of brandy: one for Paul Shank, the editor of "The Hoot"; one for Mr. Grayson (you had to keep the home front well lubricated); one for Arch Dyson; and one for—what the hell—Beau Reasons himself. Stammering, Slava extended the bottles to their assistants, dropping only one out of nervousness, though unfortunately, this was before Beau's assistant, and he dropped it on her foot. A small gift from his family cellar, he explained, on the occasion of . . . ? He stared at the assistants, who awaited an explanation with puzzled distaste. Slava had failed to invent a plausible reason for the gifts; his grandfather would not have made such a rookie mistake, but the genie had wavered back into the bottle and not spoken again.

"It's a bribe!" Slava said hysterically, but this attempt at humor failed and he didn't dare repeat it, his only solace that he had bombed before Paul Shank's assistant, in the firmament of the magazine not the shiniest star though Shank *was* the editor of "The Hoot," which *was* supposed to be a humor column. Maybe the assistant would feel solidarity and not say anything. Maybe the assistant would keep the bottle for himself! It was not the tsar who failed his people but the ministers, the meddling middlemen! Slava returned to his desk jailed by a mix of anticipation, confusion, resentment, and shame. No immediate word came from the editors' wing. That could be good—he hadn't screwed up too badly. And he remained buoyed by the secret of his editorial discoveries, like a woman who knows she's pregnant but no one else does. Mere days later, *Century* assigned Slava (half assigned, with Devicki, but still) to a story. Coincidence? You make your own conclusions.

The conference room, filled with four times as many persons as usual, tingled with an impending holiday's delirious atmosphere. Bodies crammed the slate floor and the panels over the air-conditioning vents, editorial assistants arrived with extra chairs, toes were boxed with apology, and in general everyone experienced (1) the tipsiness of being closer to one another than was the norm, and (2) the sudden collapse of hierarchy. In his corner, eyeing Arianna several seats down, Slava felt a swell of pride at being in some measure the cause of all the commotion.

At the head of the conference table, his forearms on the back of his chair, stood Beau. On the eve of his ascension to the crown of the masthead, Page Six at the *New York Post* had trotted out the most salacious thing it could wring out of the people he had met on his way to the top: "Beau is 60, looks 40, and acts 20," an anonymous woman had said. This was untrue—wrinkles had settled around his eyes, and two silver wings flanked his butterscotch helmet of hair—but this hardly impugned his haledom. He wore a peach Winchester shirt and rolled a nugget of gum in the pink sea of his mouth with awesome control. The gum was a piece of news he was going to split open and get to the bottom of. (He was an old smoker.) Despite his name—his mother had a fetish for the South—Beau was as northern as the Union. He had started in newspapers: crime on Cape Cod, crime in Boston, crime in New York, over to *Century*. Apparently, they taught in journalism schools the magazine piece that had endeared him to Martin Graves, a complicated twenty-thousand-word two-parter, one of the first pieces about exoneration by DNA analysis, which had set free a man imprisoned eleven years for manslaughter.

Slava had read Beau's famous story many times, but he couldn't build a bridge from it to the Avery Coulter story. The Avery Coulter story gave up its secrets quite readily—it was a grid, Manhattan. The DNA piece was like some kind of Moscow or Paris—everything side streets, dead ends, parabolas, though its conclusion arrived with new force each time he read it, the mystery of which was only more frustrating. Slava studied Beau at the head of the conference table as if this would dislodge from the older man's soul some clue to the information that eluded the younger. But it didn't.

Beau was talking to Kate Tadaka. She clutched a phone in each hand

and laughed into his ear, the plums of her cheekbones bruising into a blush. Kate edited the critics and collected National Magazine Awards in her spare time. Even at twenty feet, it was clear that she was someone who smelled as fine at the end of a long summer day as at the beginning. This filled him with an aimless, futile desire.

He switched to Arch Dyson, in cream linen. Here was a man to make cream linen look fine on a man. Now, Arch could be anywhere between forty and seventy-five. One day the previous year—had so much time passed since Slava's embarrassment?—while Arch was perched in Mr. Grayson's office, Slava took notes on the editor's outfit down to the belt. The next weekend, instead of scrolling and typing, Slava shopped. On the way home, the bags tugged at his hands with the weight of two weeks' salary, and he felt like an ostrich striding into the *Century* office on Monday, but he had purchased for himself an understanding of the American maxim "clothes make the man." Indeed, several Juniors whistled and demanded to know the occasion for his lilac jacket and paisley tie. However, no matter how many times Slava strode past Arch's office, the editor took no note of the sartorial kindred spirit wandering the halls. In the late afternoon, Slava, desperate and defeated, gave up on Arch and, in a final hail mary, redirected himself to Kate Tadaka's many-windowed suite. As Slava neared the consequential doorway, he slowed down, the world shrinking to the airplane roar in his head, and as he came into its field of vision, he hurled in Kate Tadaka's direction the most meaningful look of his life. In the direction of Kate Tadaka's desk, to be exact—she was gone for the day. When, back in their pen, Avi Liss became the one hundredth Junior to ask after Slava's insane costume, Slava barked out that his cousin had died giving birth. The waxy rictus of Avi's face melted, and Slava felt the first satisfaction of the day.

Archibald Dyson, Kate Tadaka, Paul Shank: They shouted at their children for forgetting to compost tea bags, donated old clothes to the homeless with bloodthirsty fervor, and in the pages of the magazine (leaving no room for Slava), broke the nibs of their quills agitating for equitable health care, gay rights, and foods made of whole wheat. What did it mean that Slava couldn't get their attention, may they all get covered up to their heads. Now, in the conference room, he felt the familiar sensation of being in the presence of information obvious to all but himself.

Finally, it was time. Beau took a long sip of his seltzer. An overstimulated sun beat at the office windows, just another aspiring contributor. Across the street, the scaffolding had just vanished from a beaux arts office building, and it stood there not knowing what to do, an old dame amid the sharp-elbowed steel jostling all around it.

The faint rev of a truck rose from the street. Twenty-seven stories below, dots flurried across the pavement with exquisite oblivion. The staff of *Century* was sealed in a chilled container of chrome, glass, and Lucite—for the hundredth anniversary the previous summer, the parent company had gifted a makeover. No more cigarette burns in the carpets. Now the staff walked on radiant concrete.

"I would say we had success with this idea," Beau said, mopping his mouth. "My niece said to me last fall—she's just graduated college, she admires what I do—'Uncle Beau, should I go to journalism school?' And you know what I said? I said, 'Come work at *Century* for a year. Just like journalism school, except you get paid for it.'" Several editors laughed lightly, Arch Dyson baring his fangs like a beached seal.

"All right," Beau said. He squinted at the page in his hands and read out loud: "'Fred Duncan is an urban explorer.'"

Fred Duncan scaled and spelunked municipal constructions. He once hiked the D line, tunnels included, from Coney Island to its terminus in the Bronx. Next up was Ulysses S. Grant in Morningside Heights. The Grant mausoleum—a mere 165 feet—would be far beneath Duncan's highest achievement (the Municipal Building, at 580 feet) but its gray limestone walls were smoother than anything he had summited. "You try to go up the blank face of a wall," Duncan said testily when Slava asked on the phone why the tomb was a target. Slava decided not to point out that it was actually administered by the National Park Service.

Morningside Heights had been leafy and serene, just like the Upper East Side, except here blacks and Dominicans also wandered. Duncan looked about fifty, a clump of seawater-gray hair gathered at the base of his scalp, a bald nest in the middle. He bristled with ropes and carabiners. Peter Devicki was journalistic in a spiffy checked blazer.

"Glad I wore *this*," Peter said, holding up the collar. The ham. Slava considered him hatefully: the indifferently barbered thatch of ginger hair; the bumpy nose; the mouth slightly ajar; faint whiskers sprouting across the unplanted field of his pale, splotchy face.

"Try wearing thirty pounds of equipment," Duncan said, and spat. Brackets of nicotine separated his teeth. He nodded at the mausoleum, two hundred yards away. "Here's what you need to know," he said. "I don't know if one of you wants to write it down and the other's holding his hand?"

"It's an experiment," Peter alerted him brightly.

"Largest mausoleum in North America," Duncan said. "Never been scaled, far as I know. Not—repeat, *not*—illegal. Not clearly, anyway. Not that that fazes me. Half the judges in this town know who I am. Ready?" The young men nodded and withdrew two crisp, slim reporter's notebooks. Duncan, his crotch cinched like an infant's, jangled off toward the mausoleum.

Slava reviewed the notes he had made the previous evening. A history of the mausoleum and its occupant; a *New York Post* story about Duncan's childhood riding subway cars in the Bronx; the equipment Duncan said he was going to use. (Beau liked when you mentioned the brands: It drummed up advertising.) The two of them watched Duncan begin his ascent.

So did many others. They pointed, they shrugged, they kept going. Even an iridescent pigeon at Slava's feet—as a flying creature, arguably prone to curiosity about the gentleman invading its airspace—was more concerned with a triangle of pizza on the ground, approaching it as shyly as a girl at a dance.

Slava marveled, in Russian. There had been a famous mausoleum in the Soviet Union, too. Lenin's Tomb in Red Square. The Gelmans had gone there en famille while they were in Moscow to fix immigration papers. Leaving Russia or not, it seemed heretical to visit the capital without visiting Grandfather Lenin, and only Slava's grandfather resented having to waste time on "that dead dick."

They had waited in a cold, prickly rain. Only a small number of mourners could file through at a time, and no consideration had been given to those who would have to wait outside for their glimpse of the Great Teacher. When the Gelmans finally reached the interior, Slava's chest rattling in dress rehearsal for a cold and Grandmother hissing about the injustice, Slava was impressed to find himself completely unfrightened by the dead dick inside the glass. Lenin was as tiny as an old grandfather, his waxy lips on the precipice of a joke only he understood. It was the *militsionery* guarding him who were frightening. Slava had expected them to be young, crisp, and clean-skinned, but they were heavy men with slow, drunk eyes ringed by ripples of fat.

On the opposite side of the glass encasement, a young boy—Slava's age but with straw-yellow hair and limpid blue eyes—also studied the dead man's face. Slava had slipped his hand free from his mother's to demonstrate his adultness to the man under the glass and noted with pitying sympathy that the other boy still clung to his.

Grandfather had said Slavs were vicious and vulgar, but here was Slava's Slav twin and Slava loved him. They understood each other. So when, drawing nearer to Lenin, the other boy lifted his finger, Slava knew as if the hand were his own that he meant merely to point out Lenin's curious expression to his mother and not to touch the glass, as the nearest policeman assumed, his eyes irradiating with purpose and his nightstick slicing down from his shoulder. Like Slava, the boy had small, easily retractable fingers.

The baton sliced through empty air and came to rest in the policeman's own thigh. He wailed. Slava nearly slapped his hands together. "Scum!" the boy's mother cried at the policeman. It was as if she had spoken out loud the patter of objection that had been coming from Slava's grandmother all morning. "*Tikho tikho tikho tikho,*" Grandfather whispered toward the commotion on the other side of the tomb. Quiet quiet quiet quiet. Grandfather never went at the law directly, but he couldn't resist making himself useful.

Compare Ulysses S. Grant, as considered from the freshly paved squares of Riverside Park: a fall-down failure across the professions—farmer, real estate man, passed over for county engineer—before stumbling onto the battlefield and inducing his country to remain in one piece, like a bull-headed mother. However, those early disasters endeared his late-inning renaissance to his countrymen only more. Meanwhile, Lenin's syphilis was a state secret, his childlessness with his wife, Krupskaya, supposedly the result of his unstraying devotion to the Revolution. You could not touch the man's sarcophagus without corporal punishment. In America, however, love did not require nightsticks.

When Slava remembered Duncan, he was back on the ground, barking impressions as Peter scrawled in his notebook, nodding richly. Slava considered the blankness of his. He moved over and tried to record some of what Duncan was saying, but his mind kept wandering.

It cannot be said that, that evening, Slava obeyed every bit of guidance he had wrung from his exegesis of *Century*'s glimpse into Avery Coulter's entrepreneurial soul. It wasn't hard at all to start with a scene, but by the time Slava remembered the rest of the rules, he was midway done and adrift in a far sea of essayistic remembrance. Slava shrugged: Such is the impulsive tyranny of the artistic heart. Here was the memoir they wanted! Beau hadn't specified the format; why not an essay. With a little patriotism shining from its heart—that couldn't hurt.

Now, in the office, Beau positioned a pair of tortoiseshell glasses on the bridge of his nose. "So, what about these two?" he said.

They didn't talk long. With each comment, Slava slipped lower in his chair. The thirty-four editorial staffers present that day, not counting Peter Devicki and Slava Gelman—fourteen Junior Staffers, eight editors, and the twelve staff writers who were in that day—voted. There were no abstentions. When Beau called out "Piece number one," rereading its opening line, thirty-two hands rose into the air. When Beau followed with "Piece number two"—why was it necessary, for God's sake—the two remaining rose: Arianna Bock, one other fool. As Slava's eyes swept across Peter Devicki, something more terrible than thirty-two hands against began to take place. No, Peter, no, Slava pleaded silently, but in this, too, Peter was going to humiliate him, his hand rising to join two others to vote for Slava.

"I'm taking you out," she said. *"You need to drink and forget."*

"Like I needed to visualize victory?" Slava said. "I got half of Brooklyn going out to buy the issue."

She looked down.

"No, no," Slava said, waving his hands. "I'm sorry."

"What you wrote was lovely," she said. "But what did it have to do with Fred Duncan? They liked it! But that wasn't the assignment."

Instinctively, he looked around to see who could hear. "You saw that as soon as you read it this morning," he said. "Why didn't you say something?"

"I'm not an editor," she said. "The meeting was in an hour."

"You went for a walk instead."

"You would've listened to me?" she said. "I doubt it. You would have looked at me and thought, She has no idea what she's talking about."

He looked away.

"You have two options," she said. "Poetry reading." She counted out on the fingers of one hand: "Bad poems, bad booze, somehow it all works. Personally, I think a little slow for tonight. Number two." The fingers on the other hand: "Band, bar, music, booze. Door prize if you can spot what the two have in common."

"Poetry?" he said.

"Poetry, poetry."

"Do *you* write poetry?"

"I don't know," she said. "Maybe. Let's go to the bar. You need a drink."

"Honestly, Arianna," he said. "No charity required."

"Slava," she said. She came closer, so close he looked away. She waited until his gaze returned to her. "There will be other chances."

"Thanks," he said feebly.

She leaned over Slava's desk, giving him a temporary view of her rear end, and wrote something on his legal pad. "Address," she said, turning back to him, his eyes rising to meet hers a moment too late. "Have a good night." As she walked away, he peered at the scribble. "Bar Kabul. Little Darlings. 361 East Fifth."

Slava surveyed the office. You couldn't give the other Juniors money to look in his direction right now, so he looked freely. How many evenings he had spent staying after all of them had left. There was no printer or fax at his apartment, and here the legal pads were free. As Consuela (Honduras), Piotr (Poland), and Ginger (St. Kitts) vacuumed up the day's traces of editorial life, restoring the office to the errorlessness with which it greeted everyone in the morning, Slava tapped and scrolled, searching out story ideas. He chased them down on the weekends, or mornings when he could invent a doctor's appointment. ("You are the least hale member of Junior Staff, Mr. Gelman," Mr. Grayson, no triathlete himself, apprised him one afternoon.) Slava had lied and lied.

What if, indeed, he went to Bar Kabul? Might Kate Tadaka shudder in disappointment at his lack of diligence? Might Arch Dyson shake his head regretfully as he strode past Slava's empty work chair? Would Beau Reasons howl at his dashed hopes for Slava Gelman, that promising boy on Junior Staff? Slava wanted to dangle each of them off the terrace adjoining Beau's office. Then they would notice.

He sprang from his chair and hurtled after Arianna, colliding with Avi Liss, who was striding contemplatively past the Junior Staff pen, his mouth cheek-deep in a green apple. Avi nearly toppled to the floor, a wounded expression in his eyes. "Sorry," Slava muttered, trying to help him up. Avi's teeth remained sunk in the apple throughout the ordeal. By the time Slava burst into the vestibule, the doors of the elevator were closing with an unperturbed ding.

5

Bar Kabul had imported from Afghanistan nothing more than the name: a dive with brightly painted, uneven walls, and a small stage backed by heavy velour shades. Blissfully, there were no kilim rugs on the floor or kebabs on the menu.

Outside, two whittled young men smoked rolled cigarettes. One wore jean cutoffs, a holey undershirt, and a pair of boots, the other wing tips that didn't match and tight black jeans with a zipper from the shin to the ankle. Slava nodded. They raised their cigarettes.

"Little Darlings?" Slava said expertly.

"Little Darlings." Skinny Jeans nodded, a triangle of hair falling into his eye. "Nice jacket." Risking terminal lateness, Slava had detoured to his apartment and thrown on the outfit he had cribbed from Arch Dyson. It had sat in his closet since the ignominious day, unused and resented.

"Nice jeans," Slava said, to say something.

"Thrift store," Skinny said. "Seventy-Seventh and Third."

"I live nearby," Slava said.

"Stop by," Cutoffs chimed in. He kicked the asphalt with the lip of his boots. "Get you some Clarks. Some of the Earthkeepers they have are pretty badass, too. Practically out of the box."

"People there have nice clothes they get rid of after two wearings," Skinny said. He sang "Score!" and the two exchanged a high five.

"Thirty-four?" Skinny said, eyeing Slava's groin.

"Say what," Slava said, stepping back.

"Your waist."

"Oh," Slava said defensively. "No."

He frowned. "I hate when I'm off."

Slava moved toward the window. It didn't take long to pick Arianna out of the bodies mashed on the dance floor; the place was small, smaller than it had seemed online. She was right by the stage, the bun of her hair loose, her shoulders swaying. The band had a keyboard; a tuba; and a snare drum belted around one of the players. A small circle opened as Arianna and a tall, thin consumptive in a fedora danced with each other. He tried to insert his knees between her legs, but she pushed him away and slimmed back into the crowd, pleasing Slava.

"What's she look like?" Cutoffs said. His hand was on the door handle, Skinny behind him. "We'll keep an eye for you."

Slava smirked. "I don't think she needs any help," he said. "The one with long black hair by the front. In the gray—"

"That's a Balenciaga," Skinny said reverently.

"Don't say you saw me," Slava said.

He watched them go in and stomp the floor. Skinny's dancing style involved a perennial look of surprise, his mouth in an oval. The duo worked its way toward some women and cornered them with acrobatic moves.

Slava stood around, trying to look busy, but this got more taxing than simply going inside. She saw him quickly, the eyes betraying no surprise. She wove her way through the crowd and embraced him, her breasts pushing into his chest. It was more touch than they'd ever racked up. Apparently, they would get to make new rules of engagement here, outside the office. He sniffed at her neck: perfume, shampoo, sweat that was recently vodka.

"What the hell are you wearing?" she said.

He colored: She didn't remember the day he had gotten dressed up. Even then, she had said nothing about it. For a moment, he regretted coming. "You changed, too," he said defensively.

She pulled him toward the dance floor, pausing at the bar to feed him a tall glass of vodka with lemons, generously dispensed because she knew the bartender. Skinny and Cutoffs held up their thumbs.

Little Darlings consisted of four skinny young men in tight jeans and T-shirts, all black save for the pink bows around their necks—they were little darlings—and heads shaved on one side. They performed a kind of rock and roll that was difficult to dance to, though Slava gave it his all, trying to remember the dance moves Grandfather exhibited on the dance platforms of the Russian restaurants where Slava used to accompany him. In the Soviet Navy at the tail end of the war, Grandfather had served with the full panoply of Soviet nationalities, had learned the Ukrainian *kazachok*, the Georgian *lezginka,* the all-Soviet *chechetka*. Sometimes, to emphasize a point, he would break into one, just because. On the paltry square of the Kabul dance floor, Slava twitched in mental approximation. Arianna swayed and pumped with exasperating grace.

"Why is it called Kabul?" he pretended to want to know, the noise level requiring another visit to her neck.

"I don't know!" she shouted back. "Rocking the casbah or whatever? I don't know!"

"Casbah is Moroccan, I think," he said, drawing closer again.

"You should be a fact-checker, Slava," she yelled. "Don't worry about it! Dance, drink. You have things to forget!"

"How can I, with you reminding me," he said.

"Oh, I know I have no influence on that brain." She tapped his head with a fingertip. "I can't feel in that fingertip. Sliced it off with a mandoline once."

He pressed the fingertip like a button. She let him get away with it. "Take nothing on faith," she confirmed.

Onstage, the Little Darlings whined about playgrounds and beer, Arianna's face flashing in and out of view in the hopping red light. Eventually, he persuaded her to sit down. She breathed heavily, like a figure skater just off the ice. There was a spray of freckles around her eyes.

"Show me how you pick up a girl in a bar," she said.

He grunted in objection.

"Are you celibate, Slava?" she said. "Please tell me you never join for anything at work because you're otherwise engaged chasing tail."

"That's it exactly," he said.

"Give me the rundown," she said.

Rundown: Slava walked into his first American classroom with an old man's part in his hair, a striped velour sweater, and the papery smell of the Ivory (cheapest, at seventy-nine cents for four bars) of which the Gelmans availed themselves. Thirty pairs of American eyes assessed this new flotsam and resumed spitballs and notes. Slava could not distract himself from himself as easily. It was not until the following year that he was able to ask for the attention of Diana Gencarelli, whose father owned a bakery in Bay Ridge, which Slava once patronized in the hopes of spotting Diana covered in flour. He would help her dust it off and then they would hold hands as they walked past the Arab groceries. Alas, Diana was not there. Diana was not there even when she was in front of him at PS 247. The rundown ran downhill.

In succeeding years, Slava Gelman was not without attention from the opposite sex. He did not look like most of the people in South Brooklyn. (He imagined that leaving the neighborhood accelerated physical alteration, as if the elements functioned differently in Manhattan.) There was nothing he could do about his height—he was from the stunted plains— but he had finagled from God olivish skin that saved him from being identified as an Eastern European barbarian rather than a sun-dappled Turk or even a Spaniard, black eyes completing the Mediterranean picture. His hand bore a long scar from a bottle shard he had dragged across its pillowy skin at six years old; the stubbled line of his jawbone bore a readiness to greet all interruptions with impatience. All the same, next to Arianna, agitating in her beautiful clothes, he felt like a smudge. He stripped off his jacket. Oh for two. It was too hot, anyway.

Vodka sluiced down the rusty pipe of his throat. The events of the preceding forty-eight hours coursed in the opposite direction. All of it ran together, clotted, settled, drained, ran off. He felt a little deranged. He scratched at his jaw, then leaped up and removed himself to the next table. He relished Arianna's puzzled expression. She listened to him give an imaginary date directions to the bathroom. Then he leaned over. "I have sixty seconds," he said. "She's a lovely girl—*lovely*. But we aren't right for each other. It's an *almost* thing. You've had those—nobody's fault. And then you're sitting at the next table over. Tell me your name. And your number. Thirty seconds."

Arianna stared at him, openmouthed.

"Twenty," he said. "Come on. She pees quick."

Arianna broke into laughter and began clapping. "You can pick me up any time," she said. She curled her tongue in a funny way when she sipped from her drink.

He didn't want to let go of the feeling he'd had a moment before, him advancing on her instead of vice versa. Music clamored from a wheelbarrow-sized speaker directly above them, so it was difficult to think clearly. But he didn't have to think. Everything that had happened at the office was pleasantly falling away—only for the evening, he knew, but good enough.

"Take me to another bar," she said. "I can't hear myself think here."

They took a meandering route through the neighborhood, louche and gentrified all at once. Slava had come here only once or twice, each time in connection with a story he was researching. They kept stopping because she was pointing out landmarks. She volunteered in this garden. Some music club of renown had been located here. Here—she announced overdemonstratively—she'd had a dark-alley liaison. Purposefully, he didn't say anything. "So you're not the only one picking up tail in a bar," she added unnecessarily, and he relished his victory.

He asked about her outfit, in hopes that she would notice his with greater fascination. These were ponte-knit pants, she said. Supposed to be slimming. "'You can hold up a bank with those hips, Arianna,' as my dear mother used to say," she said. They swerved to avoid a phalanx of nearly undressed women eating the sidewalk.

"She's not around anymore?" Slava said cautiously.

"My mother?" Arianna said. "Oh, she's around. Very around." She ran her arm through Slava's, and he tried to fall into step with her. "Brentwood," she said. "Mother Bock had to work out for herself the joy of having a daughter with childbearing hips versus a daughter with wider hips than every girl at the synagogue." She waited. "This is the part where you say it doesn't show."

Slava smiled. "And your father?"

"Spandex factory. Half my yoga class is dressed by the Eagle."

"Why the Eagle?"

"El Aguila," she said in a cute Spanish accent. "That's what the Nicaraguan ladies on the floor call him." She touched her nose with the tip of the dead finger. "He's got an amazing escarpment."

"Not you, though," Slava said.

"Nose job, sweetheart."

"It doesn't show," he said.

"There you go."

"You're close to them," he said.

"My mother called me a dilettante the other day because I'm not kosher out. I'm like, Ma, *that's* a big word! Apparently, the rabbi had a whole *sermon* on dilettantes." She pushed her arm farther into Slava's. "But I like poems, thanks to my dad. Robert Frost was his favorite. 'Frost is like life, Arianna—as deep as you want to look.' Then my mother beat it out of him." They neared a crosswalk and stopped even though the light was theirs. Slava didn't mind. "They moved to a more religious neighborhood. They don't talk about Frost at those tables. The Eagle's an enforcer now."

"We don't have to talk about it," Slava said.

"I don't mind," she said, turning toward him. "I don't mind telling you."

"I want to hear a poem of yours," he said.

"Negative," she said. "I don't write poems."

"That's a lie."

"Don't be silly," she said.

He withdrew his arm and placed it on the cup of her shoulder, turning it toward him. Beneath his fingers, her skin felt taut and giving at once. It was thick, as if the skin descended deep down into her, her center buried somewhere far beneath.

She rolled her eyes. "You have no class. Zero class. You insist on embarrassing me."

"Sorry," he said. "You don't own embarrassment today."

She rolled her eyes again. "No one made you write that. Take as good as you give." She pulled back and looked at him. Her breath was soft, flavored with something human but pleasant. "I loved what you wrote. I knew it was yours when I read the first line."

"Is that why you stood up for me?" he said.

"Of course not," she said. "Most of the Jews in America—that's where we come from. I grew up listening to my grandmother's stories. And you form a certain image. And then you read something like what you wrote, and it's nothing at all like what you thought."

"So that was why."

"No," she groaned. "You're exhausting. Yes, in part, but the number one reason is it was good, really good. You brought it alive. Just that it isn't the kind of piece that runs in *Century*. It wasn't right for Beau—but that means everything?"

He nodded. All of a sudden, he felt very tired. He felt it in his shoulders, a long, draining weight. He imagined himself taking a seat on the pavement and staying there for a long time. "Why didn't we go to the poetry reading?" he said.

"Those things are boring. I go only to see if people are better. If they're bad, I'm the most satisfied person in the room. Satisfied, satisfied, satisfied." She tapped out the words on his chest.

"You say out loud things other people think," he said.

"I am Human 2.0," she said. They laughed, then fell silent.

They watched each other without comment, too long for it to mean anything other than what it meant. He lowered his lips toward hers, his hand on her cheek. They kissed slowly, the human traffic of First Avenue taking them into its indifferent arms, the city's special combination of curiosity and resentment. He tingled with a strange sensation; he was unconcerned with the walkers around him in return, but amiably so.

When he pulled back, he said, "Come on. I want to hear it."

"Jesus!" she said. *"Fine."* She took his arm and pushed him around the corner. The gleam and noise of the avenue receded. Slava felt the building's wall at his back, the bricks still warm from the day. She was shorter only by an inch or two; if she wore heels, she would be taller. She was sideways to him, holding his arm with her palm. "It's a poem about weather," she said in exasperation.

"The weather," he repeated.

"Weather, weather," she said. "The thing people talk about when they have nothing to say."

"The satin skies, that sort of thing."

"Slava!" she said. "In the dictionary, next to asshole—you." She slammed a fist into his chest.

"Sorry," he agreed.

"You've got me wound up, now I'm hot to say the poem."

"Say it," he said.

Her eyes settled at his neck. He tried to lift her chin, but she swatted his arm away. She spoke in such a rushed, low monotone that he had to make her stop and start over. "Just let me finish," she said.

"No," he said, making her look up at him. "Please. Slowly." So she started over. She spoke clearly this time, and he listened intently, but he could hardly focus on the words.

The bar they were heading to, Straight Shooters, arrived too soon. Here, too, Arianna knew the bartender. They really were straight shooters on the alcohol issue, or perhaps it was Arianna's acquaintance that secured them such brimming glasses. The music was mellower, Southern if he had to guess, and there was a more committed row of solitary drinkers at the bar. She made him twirl her before they sat down. His head heavy with drink, he tried, in the noise, to distinguish why he was here—to be with her or merely without himself? Slava was not much of a drinker, but gazing at the solo patrons seated down the length of the bar, locked away from each other and the world by the crisp pints in their hands, he sensed clearly the appeal of their American pastime. His legs helixed with Arianna's at two bar stools.

"You haven't told me a thing," she said. "I told you about my hips, for God's sake."

"My grandmother died yesterday," he blurted out.

"Shit," she said as if she had done something wrong. "Are you serious? Are you all right? Don't answer that. I don't know why people ask that."

"It was a long time coming," he reassured her.

"I'm sorry." She took his hands.

He shook his head to say it was fine.

"Were you close?"

"Yes. No. It's hard to answer." His head weighed two tons. He freed a hand and tried to get the bartender's attention.

She slid off her stool and returned a minute later with two shot glasses.

"You don't clink," he said.

She nodded and drank in one gulp. He sipped his. "Tell me something about her," she said.

Slava gazed past Arianna's shoulder. The bar drinkers were undermining their noble solitude by staring into the blue screens of cell phones.

"You don't have to," she added.

His mouth felt dry. "My grandfather," he said, "you have to give him credit. At eighty, the wheels are still turning." He finished the drink, a brown burn.

She awaited more. "She's a survivor," he said. He tipped his forehead to make his meaning clear—Holocaust survivor—but Arianna did not require the clarification. "Only she and her sister," he went on. "The rest of the family—gone. It takes sixty years for her to get restitution. How do they calculate it? Five thousand for a mother, four for a father, three for a grandparent? What if you were raised by the grandparents? What if the grandparents are the parents? You have to agree: It's tricky."

"Don't say things like that."

He studied her. Did questions like this cease to exist because you didn't bring them up? He took her hand in his. To restrain his irritation? Because it would dispose her toward him? Her fingers felt smooth and dry. She allowed them to be clasped. "The point is," he said, "the restitution letter came just days before she died." He opened his hands. "Isn't."

"I'm sorry," she said.

"My grandfather says, 'Send it in anyway. Write it about me.' But he was evacuated."

"You can't do that," she said.

"Can't I?" he said. "Did you know that they fertilized crops with human ash? After the war, the tomatoes were the size of an infant's head." He gave the words the same inflection that his grandfather did, only in English. They had a new but not unfamiliar sound on his tongue. He knew how to say them. She looked away.

"Can you blame him?" he went on. "You think he had plans to leave Minsk in 1941? No, he ran from the Germans. Then he came back and was a Jew under the Soviets for forty-five years, which is to say a lower life-form. Then America. Here you're not a Jew anymore. Here you're an immigrant. *Go back where you came from, Commie.* You don't think he's due?" The rehearsal of Grandfather's arguments came with wondrous facility to Slava. He rested his hand on his forehead contemplatively, to see how it felt.

"I want to tell you a story," Arianna said carefully. "There was a Soviet family that was settled near us. We'd sponsored them, actually. I had been pen pals with the son before they were released—you know the story. And so Mother Bock says, 'Harry, get them memberships in the synagogue.' And my father, he's not as quick as my mother, but then he will surprise you. And so he says: 'I don't think that's for them, Sandy.' Meaning, they're not religious. And Sandra says, 'How will they ever become religious unless people like us—' and so on and so forth. Harry, as always, in the end, he does what Sandra says, and he gets them synagogue memberships. One hundred fifty a person, times three, and this was fifteen years ago. Also, the synagogue has limited seats, he had to talk to the registrar, get special permission. But we don't see them—the Rubins, they were called. Instead, we see another family, also three—Americans. They get to chatting with my parents, it's Friday-night services, everyone has a couple of shots. And they tell them this Russian family sold them the memberships. Sandra—you should have seen her face. After all the lifts, that face doesn't really telegraph emotion, but at that moment she could have been in the opera. She kept her mouth shut only because she was mortified. Harry just chuckled to himself. She wanted to call the police! And he said, 'Just let them be. Think about what they've been through. Give it thirty years, then they'll ask for it.' "

"Exquisite magnanimity."

"Slava, I'm on your side."

"Why do you call your parents by their first names?"

"I don't know, that's how it's always been. I don't always."

"Your father bent the rules himself—he got a special favor from the registrar."

"Are you really going to compare?" she said. "It was for a good cause."

"Who gets to decide what's a good cause? You said it: a thirty-year dispensation. Let the savages lie a bit to the Germans."

She placed her palm on his forearm. "*You* can't."

"You're full of instructions."

She turned away.

"I'm sorry," he said. "This isn't me. This is—"

"I know."

She knew. There was nothing he could say that she didn't already know. His irritation wouldn't abate, but he forced himself to ignore it. "Are your grandparents still alive?" he said.

"Just my grandmother," she indulged his effort. "Ninety-four young. Swims every morning, e-mails Zen declarations."

"For instance."

She brightened. "'Hi my doll Ari.' That's what she calls me. 'I am finally too old to give a crap what anyone thinks. I wish I'd gotten here fifty years sooner.' And then the next day, 'Ari, doll, do you think a ninety-four-year-old woman can't shake her hips? Yes, she can.' My grandfather's gone, all her friends are gone, and all of a sudden she likes a sip of Maker's and then to the jukebox. Do you know that poem: 'On the way we passed a long row of elms. She looked at them awhile out of the ambulance window and said, What are all those fuzzy-looking things out there? Trees? Well, I'm tired of them and rolled her head away.' My God, I am just rambling."

"Did you cover the mirror when your grandfather died?"

She shrugged. "I was five. I had a dance recital that weekend, so I was doing pirouettes like a loon. I was so sad all the mirrors were covered. I'm named after his father. Ariel. You?"

"I don't know," Slava said. "Slava means 'glory.' Or 'fame.' Depending on what you mean. I covered a mirror. I didn't feel anything."

"It's like weed—you don't feel anything the first couple of times," she laughed, ushering stridency out of the conversation. This time he went along. "A shiva lasts for a week," she went on. "You keep the mirrors covered. Then you see what you feel."

"I see," he said.

"Or not," she said. "You take on too much, so it's too much, and then you want none of it. You'd rather do nothing than have to do *all that*. But you can choose your own amount."

"I would like to teach you something as well," he said.

"Please," she said.

"I meant I also would like to find something to teach you."

"I wouldn't be here if I didn't think you could."

"You're just doing a favor for a colleague."

"If you think so, Slava, you're not as smart as I hoped. But finally, yes, I dragged you out. It was easier to get hired by *Century*."

A slurry smile appeared on his face. "The upside of professional mortification. Why me?"

"You're not like the others."

"That's a foolproof fact."

"What do you want, Slava?" she said. "You want to publish in *Century* so badly?"

"I guess not," he said. "I remember the first time I saw it. I was just killing time in the library. A lot of time killing time in the library at Hunter. I'd gone through half the magazines in the periodical rack. And then *Century*. There was a piece about a rape in South Africa, and Sheila"— Sheila Garbanes (pert, tart, groovy) was a staff writer—"had a piece on these two philosophers at the University of Chicago. Ask me if I knew the first thing about philosophy, but I read the whole thing."

"God, I read the same issue," she said.

"Arch—"

"On the farmers. The father farms organic and the son farms industrial," she said. "Imagine if we were reading it at the same time, fifty blocks apart."

"I want to write something people will read," he said. "And say, There goes the fellow who wrote that."

"So do that," she said. "Wake up tomorrow and write something new. And send it somewhere else. Not *Century*. Some other place. Are you listening? Look at me."

"I will," he said, straightening.

"And another thing," she said. "You don't think about this anymore between now and then. It can't help you."

"Okay," he said.

"And then the third thing."

"Yes." He tried to focus the glaze out of his eyes.

"Take me home."

In the taxi, he ripped the sleeve of the Balenciaga from her shoulder. He sprang back, remembering Skinny Jeans's valuation, but she shrugged it away. Her tongue was cool and thick, her breath smoky and clean despite everything they had been drinking. They bit each other's lips, breathing each other in. He imagined the air spread to every corner of her, down to the dead fingertip, where it stopped.

At the wheel, Hamid Abdul was trying not to watch them. Hamid, his immigrant brother. How Slava was exceeding his immigrant brief with this fine-skinned American specimen. See Slava take the milk of this American skin into his mouth, Hamid. Look at her fingers disappear from your rearview mirror. We are miscegenating with the natives, Hamid, we are assimilating, are we not?

Irvin the doorman did not share Hamid's interest in Slava's quarry. He wanted only Slava's "John Handcocks" for a pair of slacks from dry cleaning.

Slava told him that he was going to buy some skinny jeans and be done with this slacks business. "It is absolute," Irvin nodded obediently.

"What a funny blanket," Arianna said when they got into the apartment, eyeing the rhombus-shaped opening of the duvet cover. Slava stopped in the doorway to the bathroom. "It's old," he said before heading inside.

When he emerged, she was asleep on his clean sheets in her street clothes, the knobs of her knees frowning behind the fabric. He shed the lights, leaving only the desk lamp that had craned above so many drafts. Arianna slept guilelessly, her unnerving alertness finally stilled. He wondered what his grandmother had looked like at the moment she'd drawn her last breath. Had she been aware of it or lost in delirium? Had she been in pain or the opposite of pain? Was she talking now with her dead mother and father and grandfather? *Hello, after all this time. It's you. Where to begin? Let me tell you about everyone who showed up after you left: Zhenya, and the dance hall, and Zhenya, and prison, and Zhenya, and Tanya, and Edik, and tiny Slava, and Crimea, and the car accident, and then America, but first Italy, those fat grapes, the sea—I never learned how to swim!—and then, yes, America . . .* He stopped himself. Her memories were his memories. But what were her memories?

He sat staring at the telephone for a long time. It was late, too late to call, but he lifted the cordless anyway, stepping into the bathroom to avoid waking Arianna. Sure, Arianna, he would write something else.

"What's wrong?" Grandfather said. "What happened?"

"I'm sorry to call so late. You were asleep?"

"What is it?"

"Tell me about Grandmother in the ghetto," Slava said.

Grandfather was silent, trying to understand. "I don't know," he said. "Why are you asking?"

"You wanted me to do something. So I'm asking about her."

"Oh," Grandfather said, startled. "But it would be about me."

"I can't very well write about what Uzbekistan was like. Think."

"Oh," Grandfather said. "I get it. She didn't like to talk about it."

"To either of us," Slava said.

"Well."

"Well."

"I don't know what you want me to say."

Slava was too tired to talk. Drunkenness had left him, as if he were an inhospitable host. Only weariness remained. It was a special kind of weariness that descended rarely, according to internal chemical regimens he did not understand. It made striving difficult, but also falsehood.

"She was in the ghetto," Grandfather said at last. "She escaped. She weighed nothing—the partisans lived on potato peels in the woods. They waded through swamps for so long her skin came off with the boots. They had her run a herd of cows."

"Cows?" Slava said.

"Cows. I don't know."

"What else?"

"What else. She watched a woman in a bunker choke her child to death. There were fascists upstairs. The baby was crying, giving everyone away." He summed up: "It's not pleasant."

Slava cleared his throat. "What about her parents?"

"Her father asked her to come back to the ghetto and get them, but her mother said no. 'Get out, find your sister, don't come back.' Her sister had slipped out already. Imagine leaving your parents and they're killed a month later." He paused. "That's all I know. She didn't want to talk about it."

They were quiet for a minute. "Don't tell a single soul," Slava said.

"Who would I tell?" he said.

"Swear," Slava said.

Grandfather swore.

"Family," Slava said bitterly.

"Ho, listen. I called a couple of stores—nobody has this Sancher. How far do you want me to go?"

"Don't worry about it," Slava said.

"No, I'll get it for you."

"Don't worry," Slava said, and hung up.

Cows. What would partisans, who had to hide and move often, want with cows? Milk, obviously. Did they slaughter them for food? But why would they have put a fifteen-year-old city girl in charge of a herd of cows? Punishment? Even anti-fascist partisans had no special fondness for Jews.

What else did she do during those days and nights, the weather growing cold, the breastplate of the sky turning a bruised black under its necklace of stars? Night watch. (Why not.) Yes, he kept going: During the days, she tended cows, and at night, she kept watch for the camp. "Take pity on a young girl," Slava imagined an older man who knew her from the neighborhood appealing to Zelkin, the commander. Zelkin spat: "You think there are such things as children and adults in a war?" He was respected because he did not take advantage of the young girls the way some commanders did, so the neighborhood man said nothing further.

Slava emerged from the bathroom and was momentarily shocked to rediscover Arianna Bock in his bed. The last two days had brought oddity into his life. "They waded through swamps for so long her skin came off with her boots," he said to Arianna's gently rising and falling form. "She ate potato peels. Her first normal meal, she threw up. She ate so fast, shoveling it into her mouth, she threw up."

Arianna didn't answer. He nodded and moved off toward his desk. He switched on his laptop and shifted the desk light away from Arianna. She released a startled snore and went back to soundless sleep.

Cows, cows, cows. Now his grandmother would talk to him. Now it was no imposition. Now he would follow the movements of *her* mouth. Now he would embrace her and not let go until he could speak as her, until they became the same person.

Sofia Dreitser, fifteen, originally of Karastoyanova Street #45, then, after being penned in the ghetto, of Vitebskaya #111, now of camouflaged *zemlyanka* #6 if you were counting from the bent birch with the bark like split skin. Not that she used the *zemlyanka* overmuch. During the day, she looked after the cows, her thumbs rigid from pulling on teats and her flanks bruised from the anemic knocks of their hooves, and then she sat up on the outskirts of camp in the crisp night, shivering under someone's threadbare greatcoat, by her side a carbine she would not have known how to use. She slept for an hour or two in the morning after she was relieved, her dreams full of her father, who delivered goods by horse cart before the war, galloping in the dream with enormous blocks of ice, faster and faster, because the ice was melting in the hot air of the morning. Her free day was Sunday. She slept all day.

One afternoon, several sleepless nights behind her, she nodded off while the cows were grazing a kilometer from camp . . .

"NARRATIVE. Please describe, in as much detail as you can, where the Subject was during the years 1939 to 1945."

. . . I thought I had been asleep for a minute, but when I awoke, the sun had traveled half the arc of the sky. The animals were gone.

One of the partisans, a Belarusian named Piotrus, said that because I'd lost the cows, I should be killed. One less mouth to feed, what with no cows to supply the grub. Piotrus was a pariah in Khutorka, his village, because he had gone with the partisans. Most of the Belarusians, who had been thrown around by the Russians and Poles for as long as anyone could remember, were only too happy to take up with the Germans. But Piotrus was old enough to have watched Russian limbs split off by German machine guns in the First World War. So he went with the partisans. To the villagers, he became a Jew lover,

because the partisans sometimes took in Jewish fighters. Piotrus couldn't even come back for a meal at his mother's. So he
spent all his time thinking of ways to restore his credentials as
an anti-Semite.

In our unit we had never had to kill one of our own. We had
ambushed a German provisions truck once, the front tires
busted by the tines of a pitchfork Livshitz had spent half the
night burying in the dead earth. And we had executed a Belarusian collaborator. He was slurping his tea, a sugar cube still in
his teeth as he crashed to the floor, his parents observing the
scene with gloomy resignation. But never one of our own.

Zelkin (the commander), Piotrus, and several others were
conferring inside the small tent where Avdosya baked bread. I
had been placed in a makeshift jail. Tsadik, one of the children
we got after the Nazis scattered the Minsk orphanage, was listening in and reporting back to me. Bullets were precious, so
the idea of a shooting was dismissed. To build a gallows in the
middle of the forest when we might have to move at any moment seemed absurd.

As they sat there and pounded moonshine we had taken
from the Belarusian collaborator, there was a distant mooing.
They were coming back on their own! I leaped from my seat;
Piotrus ran out of his tent, squinting. (He fancied himself a big
shooter and was always taking aim at things, even a piece of
bread before tearing into it.) And then, behind the sluggish
mooing of the cows, there was that terrifying sound. It chopped
through the air, then stretched like a string of sap. German.

In that moment, stupidly, I couldn't help thinking how
much like our Yiddish it sounded. I hadn't spoken a word of it
since the night I had slipped out of the ghetto. Suddenly—what
a stupid thought when your life is about to end—I missed it

terribly. *Fargideynk di veg*, my father had said before I left. Remember the way. "Come back for us. We're young yet, we can
work. We can be useful." For the first time in my memory, my
mother interrupted him. "You go and never come back. Find
your sister, stay together. I don't want to see you here again."
She was trying so hard to look stern, and I didn't argue because
I didn't want to embarrass her.

The Minsk ghetto was liquidated one month later.
"Liquidated"—what a strange word. It makes me think of a
deluge, waters rushing in a stream, clear and cleansing. Every
last person was killed. To this day, I can't remember my mother's face clearly. My father's face, I can remember every crease
and warp. My mother's face is a blank.

The Germans sounded as if they were a hundred meters
away. Two of our scouts burst into the clearing where we had
made camp, gesturing wildly in the familiar code. Someone
pulled the levers out of the contraption that maintained the
campfire over a gravelike vault. Several boys got their bodies
behind a mound of earth and pushed it into the fire like horses
leading the plow. Women were frantically tearing down the
wash. In minutes, our entire crew was underground, the *zemlyanka*s innocent under beds of birch leaves. The Germans, following the cows, passed wide of the clearing. That legend about
cows knowing their way home is a bluff. Eventually, there was
gunfire and objections from the animals. The blood was jumping out of my heart. Tsadik was crouched against me, his soaked
pants cold against my arm. From a nearby tent, I heard the
sound of muffled retching.

No one emerged until well after nightfall. Streamlets of
smoke hissed through the earth where the fire had been. They
had never come this close. Some said it was the scouts who

needed reproach, not the cowherd, but most, having lay feet from death for hours, did not much feel like administering it to anyone but the Fritzes. Even Zelkin stood off to the side, smoking queasily. And in this way I was spared. Some irony, saved by the Germans from being killed by your own.

The letter, this new life, had taken all of forty-five minutes. What the Nazis took away, Slava restored. He carried numbers on a pad of paper: Doing this for every person they killed would take 513 years without stopping. Reading over the letter, he felt satisfaction mixed with unease. On the page, it was Grandmother but also not-Grandmother. He couldn't say why, despite rereading the letter several times. Finally, he gave up, double-checked that it included no references to the applicant's gender, and entered his grandfather's name at the top.

He dozed off only when the familiar dark blue started coming into the sky. His head teemed with strange pictures and sounds: a man washing himself from a well, his coarse shirt and suspenders hung over his legs; a gray military truck rumbling over a rutted country road; the high ping of a shot in the woods. And Grandmother. Grandmother wading through a swamp, Grandmother suffocating a child, Grandmother pouring her guts out onto the grass from too many potato peels.

The bed was empty when he awoke. A note was taped to the bathroom mirror. "Did we? We should. XOXO."

−6−

Friday morning at *Century*: Sixteen pairs of feet impatiently tapped the radiant concrete behind the Junior Staff railing in anticipation of the weekend. In his office, Mr. Grayson fidgeted with the classical dial in advance of the weekend's matinees. The writers kept sneaking out of their offices when Beau wasn't looking, the doors schussing open and shut.

Riddle you this: Slava hadn't slept in his bed since sharing it with Arianna, but he had slept with nobody else. They had been together every night since Kabul. She lived across the park, on the Upper West Side, a quick trip by bus. He could return home in under thirty minutes, he reassured himself whenever he thought about how far he had strayed from routine. On Tuesday night, she had stood by his desk until he paid attention. "It's six, time to go," she'd said. "Veg?" he'd said. She laughed.

They meant to take the train, but they walked the fifty blocks. The city was full of neighborhoods Slava knew nothing about, and again Arianna ticked off landmarks as they walked. Her first apartment in New York, where she had sat on the windowsill chain-smoking and listening to Madonna, was here. Her first kiss was on this corner. This was the deli where she had run into Philip Roth. He had asked if she was all right, and she couldn't say anything.

From the high windows of her apartment, you could see the nervy sheet of the river. It was like the river a block from Slava's windows, only browner. "Now what?" he had said, standing uncertainly in the middle of her suddenly vast living room, her cat dashing between their feet. She brought her shoulders into his hands, then stepped out of her skirt. Her thong peeled off like the skin of a fruit, the salty perfume of her hitting his nose, her thighs wet on top of him when they fell into bed. Afterward, they ate leftovers in bed, her cat trying to get at the chicken in her salad. "Don't sleep so far away tonight," she said before shutting the light. It wasn't even nine.

At Grandfather's, the senior Gelmans had read the false testimony the following morning, Slava's mother dipping into the dictionary to translate the difficult words. When they were finished, they called Slava and burst into tears to show their appreciation. Then the waterworks quit and they got off to find a notary public. "You wrote it—because it happened to you, you have to start thinking that way—and you had your grandson translate it," Slava said to Grandfather before hanging up. "Got it?" Got it, he said.

Slava peered dolefully at the wall clock. Eleven-thirty A.M. He owed three submissions to "The Hoot" by the end of the day. After a slow-moving morning, Slava had panned only a single nugget of loot, from the editorial board of the New Orleans *Times-Picayune*:

> *With its cessation of the indigent loophole, the state legislature has stripped the health care law for pants.*

This was Double Trouble: a cliché on top of a flub. He closed his eyes, breathed in and out, counted to three . . . and there it was: "The law for cardigans, however, remains fully intact." It was easy once you'd done one or two.

Slava was not asked to come up with the rejoinder. Paul Shank did that. Once upon a time, Slava had gently flouted this unwritten rule, thinking he would send something brilliant to Paul Shank, impress him, *and* make his life easier, whereupon Paul Shank would sit up and think: This mother is *good*; let him write something longer. But when Paul Shank failed to respond in this way—he did, once, run what Slava had proposed, though without discussing it with the brilliant young man on Junior Staff, leaving Slava to feel like he had been slept with but not called the next day—Slava decided to mount a modest rebellion and quit forwarding rejoinders to Paul Shank altogether. This, too, passed without remark by his superior.

So Slava wrote the rejoinders "for the drawer," as they used to say about the great suppressed writers during the Soviet period. He was Mandelstam, Pasternak, and Bulgakov. He chortled at himself in disgusted amusement. Then noted that he had been communicating with himself at a more frequent rate.

Blearily, he looked back at the papers. A Texas town had renamed itself after a cable network in exchange for free DISH service (*The Paris News*, Northeast Texas). A Vermont man had invented skis for wheelchairs (*Rutland Herald*). But no flubs. The clock ticked. He had the naughty idea to invent a flub. Would the *Rutland Herald* call to complain? Not if he invented the paper as well. He chortled again. For two years, he had spent his weekdays combing through news from Fayetteville, Champaign, Westerly. At first he resented these provincial towns and the news they produced—after a year of strident debate, the Westerly Yacht Club had decided to build dinghy docks—skimming sonorously until he alighted on the haystack needle that would bring him one "Hoot" entry closer to the freedom to work on his own things. At some point, however, he had begun to regard their prominent personages, and the men and women who reported on them, as confederates of a kind. Lubbock, it's you again. He knew many of its streets, if only by name. He wondered what it looked like in real life. He had never been west of New Jersey.

There was a commotion down the hall. Through the knuckles rubbing his eyes, he registered Beau making his way toward the Junior Staff pen. As Beau passed, the heads of writers and editors popped out of the offices that lined the hallway, several deciding to join the boss's procession, as if he were leading a chorus. By the time Beau arrived in front of Junior Staff, he had an entourage.

"Morning," Beau said, surveying the Juniors. With two thumbs, he snapped his suspenders. He held a box cutter. "Mr. Grayson?" he called out. With a great exhalation, Junior Staff's bow-tied captain bounced from his chair. (Mr. Grayson smoked three packs of Merits a day. For his seventieth birthday, the Juniors threw together to get him a carton of Nat Shermans from the Forty-Second Street store, and he still coughed out praise of their fine smoke two years later, though everyone knew they remained untouched in the bottom drawer of his desk.)

Mr. Grayson declined the bald globe of his head. "Mr. Reasons?"

"How many ad pages this issue?"

"Ho, ho, ho," Mr. Grayson said, regarding the floor. "I'll have to count to be sure. Sixty-four, I believe, Mr. Reasons. Sixty-four. Don't quote me on that."

"Sixty-four!" Beau yelled. "What was it two years ago?"

The eyes of Junior Staff swiveled back to Mr. Grayson.

"In the twenty-to-thirty range," Mr. Grayson said obediently. "Is my best recollection."

"Twenty to thirty," Beau said chidingly. "And what was two years ago?"

"I believe when you started, Mr. Reasons," Mr. Grayson confirmed bashfully.

"I raise ad pages twofold—more—and what kind of letters do we get?" Beau said. "'Too many ads.' It takes them an hour to find the first story." He held up his hands. "But that's fine. We're in the business of serving our readers. We're going to change the layout designs. Starting next month, you'll be able to order the magazine in three versions: the regular, the low-ad, and the no-ad. Like milk. But it has to go manual for an issue or two before the layouts are reprogrammed. Who's the Layout liaison among you?"

Heads turned to Avi Liss, who raised his hand fearfully.

"So you'll be the point man," Beau said. He held up the box cutter. "This is top-of-the-line, okay? One slice and it's out, straight down the margin. Watch your fingers—this thing can cut glass."

Avi remained seated, so Beau waved the box cutter impatiently at his employee. "But—" Avi said.

"You don't have to do all three million!" Beau said, laughing. "It's a pilot thing. Twenty thousand. Give or take."

Avi walked up to Beau, closed his fingers around the cutter, and returned to his desk shamefully. Silence took over, ringing phones filling the void. Beau stared at the Juniors. The Juniors stared at their boss.

"That was a joke," Beau said disappointedly. He turned to the editors behind him. "It was funny back there." He turned back to Avi. "Give me that razor."

Avi, his head hung, returned the box cutter, several obliging titters rising from the crowd.

Slava peered at the next newspaper in his pile, wishing Beau would get on with it. On the front page was a photo of earthmovers by a riverbank. A flub invented itself, along with a newspaper to shame:

> *Paiute (Col.)* Star-Bulletin: *"During the night, the concrete pilings meant to hold back the river gave way. 'I'll be damned,' Mac Turpentine, the lead engineer, said on sighting the bedlam at dawn."*

> Century: *"The river won't be."*

"Good issue next week," Slava heard Beau say, nodding at Peter. Slava burned in his seat a little. "I need to know where we are on a couple of things."

Rinkelrinck (Ark.) Gazette: *"Drivers on eastbound U.S. 36 over the weekend reported a naked man on the shoulder by Exit 11, near Fran's Fry-Up. He was brandishing a samurai sword at passing drivers, though he did not cross into traffic. He was taken into custody but almost released due to the absence of penal code for the offense in question. Finally, he was charged with public exposure while displaying a dangerous weapon."*

Century: *"He also had a samurai sword."*

Slava's desk phone rang: 718. Brooklyn. He didn't recognize the number. In the brief pause of Beau's monologue, the ring was shrill and grating. Slava grabbed the receiver and lowered it back into the cradle.

"Mr. Headey," Beau said. "Where are we on food flavoring?"

You just had to give it some specific detail—Fran's Fry-Up—and it sounded real. You might even get away with inventing a town called Rinkelrinck. Let Paul Shank notice. Finally, he would notice.

Charlie Headey answered Beau in too much detail. Beau politely heard him out, feeling bad about the box cutter. Then he turned to Avi Liss and asked about the layout, though he knew perfectly well from the Layout department. Reliably, Ari flubbed the offer of rehabilitation, mumbling for eternity about sources and deadlines.

"Ms. Bock—'Missing Leonardo'?" Beau said.

Arianna delivered a false claim of progress, swiftly and briefly; she had barely started. Beau's eyes thanked her for her quiet efficiency.

Fanning (North Dak.) Advertiser: *"In response to the mayor's claim that the ball was dropped by the developer, Dakota Properties cried foul. 'That's a red herring,' Jim Foulbrush, the CEO, said to reporters. 'They're after me like a hungry pack of wolves because they need a straw man.'"*

Century: *"Hold those horses, McCoy."*

The phone rang again. Slava would really have to change the ringtone. He peered at the display—same number. Watching Beau recede down the hallway, he snatched the receiver.

"Allo?" a hoarse voice said in Russian. *"Allo?"*

"Yes?" Slava answered obediently.

"You are being called by Israel Abramson," the caller announced. *"Allo?* You are very difficult to hear." A throat was cleared on the other end. "Excuse me." Then, with a mix of apology and disappointment: "You are busy?"

"Busy?" Slava said. "No. I'm sorry, who is this?"

"I heard about the letter you wrote for your grandfather," Israel said. "It's very good."

Slava was stunned into silence. It couldn't be. "I didn't write any letters for my grandfather," he said quickly.

"Take it easy, young gun," Israel said. "Your secret's safe with me. By the way, Israel's not my real name. I took it when we came here, to show my support. It was Iosif before, but you know who else had that name."

Slava didn't say anything, his mind scrambling. Did *Century* keep phone records?

"Stalin!" Israel said. "You don't know history? That butcher. In 1952, my cousin was working at the Second Children's Hospital—"

"Wait, wait, wait," Slava said. "Israel . . . I'm sorry—what's your patronymic?"

"Good manners still, that's nice," he said. "Arkadievich. Israel Arkadievich."

"You . . . you . . ." Slava said.

"You want me to get to the point," Israel said. "I understand completely. I want you to write a letter for me also. You wrote a pretty good letter for your grandfather. You need to pinch a couple of things here and there, but otherwise. I do some writing myself, I understand these things."

"Maybe you should write it yourself," Slava said. "Just to make sure you get everything right."

"Oh, don't be a schoolgirl."

"I don't want to talk about this at work," Slava said. "How did you get my phone number?"

"The ghetto inmate himself gave it to me."

"I have to call you back," Slava said, and hung up.

He heard Arianna's fingers rapping the divider. In the past week, they had taken to passing notes around it. Slava would hear a tap, and there would be a folded square of paper between two fingers reaching around the edge of the wall.

> A: *True or False: Leonardo da Vinci had six fingers on his left hand.*
> S: *False.*
> A: *True or False: I am not wearing underwear.*
> S: *True.*
> A: *True or False: I'll stay late if you fuck me in the office.*
> S: *Where?*
> A: *On the couch in Beau's office. Revenge.*

Now her piece of paper said:

> A: *Everything all right?*
> S: *100 percent. Just going to make a call.*
> A: *Mmmmkay.*

Slava began to pound digits. He kept misdialing. If he had Grandfather's calculating acumen, if Arianna had not interfered, probably he wouldn't have dialed from his desk phone. Probably he would have gone into the library and called from his cell phone. Later, he would wonder about this moment.

"Yes," Grandfather said wearily.

"I just had a really incredible phone conversation," Slava barked in Russian into the phone.

"Who is this?" Grandfather slurred.

"Oh, come off it," Slava said. "Do you understand what can happen if someone finds out?"

"Please don't yell at me."

"I'm not yelling, I'm whispering loudly."

"I was proud of my grandson, what can I tell you."

"Don't give me that. Who is he, anyway? You need him for something?"

"I need him for something? He can barely walk."

"You are not acquainted with the law here," Slava said. "But they take this shit seriously."

"You listen to *me*," Grandfather said, his voice stiffening. "Your grandmother died not a week ago. You remember that, or you're already on with your life? Because here, we still remember—"

"That doesn't have anything to do with what I'm saying!"

"Here, we're still mourning," he went on. "And your philosophical questions . . . Your grandmother is in a coffin. There's your philosophy, Einstein. So I don't know what to tell you."

"Who is he?"

"Who?"

"Israel. Iosif. Whatever his name is."

"He's from Minsk, too. We grew up together. We go to Dr. Korolenko together. I've got the gout, and he's got knee stuff or whatever."

"You don't have gout."

"Just don't worry about it. He couldn't come on Sunday, so he called to say his condolences. I thought you were a writer. So here's another story."

"You want to make a family tradition of going to prison?" Slava yelled. Immediately, he regretted it. Grandfather didn't know that he knew.

The old man coughed painfully. He was so fragile, and Slava insisted on committing attacks. Then he said lightly, "I don't know what you're referring to."

"I have to go," Slava said as angrily as he could, and hung up.

His heart smashed in his chest. He made himself inhale and exhale. He was overreacting. *Century* didn't keep phone records—why would it? He would tell Israel no, a misunderstanding, his fabulist grandfather, the usual schemes. Israel would grumble, and then it would be over. He couldn't do it. Could he? Did *Century* keep phone records?

Sweat on his forehead, Slava opened his Web browser. In response to "Holocaust restitution claims," he got a long list of newspaper stories about recent developments in the restitution program. Some group was getting together to advocate for an expansion of eligibility. Not what he needed. "Holocaust restitution claims," he retyped, and then added, "fraud." He had an alibi, if he ended up pinioned in some defendant box. He could have been researching an article, or a comedy item for "The Hoot." Holocaust restitution-claim fraud: yuks.

He got a promising link. Professor Andrew Morton, Stanford Law School, "a leading authority on Holocaust restitution agreements, appeals, and abuses." An alliterationist, to add. It was just after nine A.M. in California. He waited to hear what Arianna was doing. She was busy on a call, so he rose and stole off toward the fact-checkers' library. Out of view in a dim corner, it had been left unrenovated during the makeover. As he was scouring the nooks for *Century* personnel, he remembered that he had left the search screen up on his desktop and, racing back to his desk, nearly toppled Arianna. "What's *with* you?" she said, screwing up her face. "Tell you later," he said.

"Professor Morton's office," a peppy, young voice said when he finally dialed. It had a proprietary air, its owner charged with guarding the oft-stormed gates of Andrew Morton's life.

Slava made himself stop pacing and sit down in a torn armchair. "Professor Morton, please," he said.

"And who may I say is calling?" the sun beamed protectively on the other end of the line.

"Peter Devicki," Slava said. "From *Century* magazine," he added meaningfully.

"Oh," she said. Those magic words always parted the doors. "Just a second. It's *Century* magazine," she announced to the professor, as if she'd gotten Slava to call. He mumbled something and they giggled.

"Hello?" a squeaky voice appeared on the line. "Peter? How can I help?"

"Devicki," Slava emphasized. "We've got a story about the Holocaust restitutions happening now, and an expert of your stature . . ." He waited, then added cautiously: "More about what if there were a fraud of some kind."

"All right," Morton said.

"And the main issue is what kind of liability would there be if, you know, someone were inventing the stories that go in those claims."

"Has something happened?" Morton said.

"To whom?" Slava said.

"You were talking about invented claims."

"Oh," Slava said. "No, no. Strictly hypothetical. We like to cover our bases—you know."

"*Century*," Morton said bashfully.

"*Century*," Slava said.

"I grew up reading it, you know. I'd steal it from my father's shelf because he collected them."

You had to give them a moment to fanboy.

"In any case, the key thing is the money," Morton collected himself.

"Does this person make a profit? Has the bogus claimant been indicted?"

"I'm sorry?" Slava said.

"Indicted. Has the bogus claimant been indicted?"

"Indicted," Slava repeated.

"Well, yes," Morton said. "There's liability in criminal law. I don't have the time to go into it now, but it's money obtained under false pretense. So it's theft—fraud. Criminal law obtains. The question is, is there a federal or state statute that makes this a criminal liability? Where is this happening?"

"New York?" Slava said. "If I had to guess. Is there?"

"I don't know, Mr. Devicki," Morton said, amused. "I'm in California."

"So, we find out if there's liability under New York law," Slava said despondently. Indictment? Criminal liability?

"Then there's German law, of course," Morton went on. "If it's criminal under German law, there may be a request for extradition. I'm sorry this is so hypothetical. This hasn't happened, so there aren't cases to judge from."

"Extradition," Slava repeated. Feebly, he added: "But how can you be beholden to German laws if you're a citizen—"

"It's theft from a foreign government," Morton said. "You don't have to be a German citizen to be liable."

"I see," Slava said. He pumped energy into his voice. "This is very useful."

"My pleasure," Morton said. "Not every day *Century* calls."

"One last thing," Slava said, his finger working a groove in the side of an old wooden bookshelf that held reference books on botany and horticulture. "You Can Lead a Whore to Culture . . ." somebody had handwritten above "Horticulture." "How would they find out?" he said. "That it's false?"

"Every fund has its own verification requirements," Morton said.

"Are there records?" Slava said. "From the war?"

"Very spotty," Morton said. "The Germans destroyed a lot, and the Russians have always kept theirs close. So it sort of comes down to how persuasive the story is. Whether the facts send up red flags."

"I see," Slava said grimly. "Well, I appreciate your time." Morton started asking when the article would run, so Slava hung up. He sat motionlessly, then wished he'd asked what Morton meant by red flags.

"Hey—" Arianna startled him. She was in the doorway to the library, propping the door open with her hip. How long had she stood there? He marveled again at how lovely she was. The fingers as long and slim as pencils, so slender that they were blue by the morning, even though it was a hundred degrees outside. He would rub them between his, twice as thick. "You okay?" she said.

"Come in," he said.

"What are you doing in here?"

"Come here." His cell phone was still flashing Morton's number, ended call. He pulled her neck toward him and kissed her, swiveling her away from the phone.

"Slava, Avi is heating his lentils around the corner *right now.*"

"In the armchair, then." He pointed to a ratty seat around the corner from a bamboo screen, the Austin Miller Home for the Aged. Austin, an editorial assistant, took a powerful south-of-the-border nap there every afternoon.

"Stop," she said. "At home." She pulled away and straightened her skirt. Reassured that she hadn't overheard him, he conceded. "I was going for a walk, if you want," she said.

He was about to refuse when he thought: Arianna would know something about red flags. She was a fact-checker; it was her job.

"I do," he said.

"You're actually going to come with me."

"You only had to sleep with me."

Outside, it was less decisively scorching than the day before. The broom of the seasons was starting to sweep summer under the rug. Emerging into the bright light, they slapped their palms against their eyes. Arianna withdrew large sunglasses from her many-buckled purse. "When I leave this place," she said, "I'm going to write a novel about editorial staffers who work endless hours and then turn into vampires at night."

"Where to?" he said.

"You choose," she said.

"I don't know how to play this game. I don't want to just stand here."

"We *are* the only people on this block standing still." He followed her gaze: The street scrummed around them, itchy and tense. She told him to close his eyes. He was bumped from behind by someone exiting the building, and given a withering look. "Close your eyes," she repeated, oblivious. He threw up his hands and walked away from the revolving doors, to a sad wall where the building's smokers congregated.

"If you just wait for one minute, it'll come," she said, joining him.

"I'm waiting," he said impatiently.

"Sometimes it doesn't," she acknowledged.

He rolled his eyes.

"If I'm with someone who's impatient and annoying, and it just won't come, then I close my eyes," she said. "Then I feel like I am in a van Gogh painting. Everything around is a swirl, and I am a still point in the middle."

He lifted a finger and touched her birthmarked eyelid. She flinched, but her eyes stayed closed. The skin of the eyelid was soft and weary. She never wore makeup.

He saw Mr. Grayson striding out of the elevators, a pack of Merits in his hand like a beacon.

"Okay, let's go," Slava said to her.

"Where to?" she said, opening her eyes.

"The park," he said. "People sit still in the park."

"What do you know," she started to say, but he put his hand over her mouth. She wriggled out and he gave chase. They ran up Sixth Avenue.

In Bryant Park, Midtown was sweating through salads. Having hoped to spend their lunch hour pretending in a corner that humanity was not, in fact, pressing in all around, the park's visitors had no choice but to join strangers at the dollhouse café tables dotting the perimeter. For thirty minutes, they sat next to one another, avoiding eyes.

Slava and Arianna settled onto the grass, still warm in a summer way. Despite being loaded down with a handbag and a wandering skirt, Arianna deposited herself on the ground with a quiet, undemonstrative efficiency. Unspooled against the green, her legs were as pale as plaster.

"How are you holding up," she said. "I mean your grandmother. You haven't really talked about it. Sorry if I'm not supposed to bring it up."

He lowered his head onto her thighs. The air was greasy with summer. "In Uzbekistan," he said, remembering something his grandfather once told him, "when it's hot outside, they drink hot tea instead of the opposite."

"Whenever I ask you about her, you talk about him."

He thought about it. "She was sick for six years. She was in a car accident and the blood transfusion was bad. She got cirrhosis from it. Her liver didn't want to work. All the toxins the liver throws out—they stayed inside. Half the time, she was out of it. Her skin was covered with splotches. They itched her like crazy, she would just about rip the skin off. She had to go to the hospital for hydration all the time. Every other month, then every month, then every week. And through all of this, she didn't complain. You asked her how she was, and she said, 'Very good.' She said it in English, those were the two words she knew, and she said it that way so it could be a joke and you'd laugh and it would take attention away from her. What kind of a person is that?" He looked up at Arianna. "Meanwhile, if my grandfather thinks you've forgotten about him for a minute, he'll remind you. He's the one who talks. So I know him. I don't know her. I would like to. I *would have* liked to."

She didn't say anything, only rested a palm on his chest. He was grateful to her for not saying anything.

"So what do I have to do now?" he said. "After covering the mirror."

"You don't have to do anything," she said.

"But there are rules," he said.

She smiled. "There are rules, yes. You mourn for seven days. Which you would be on the tail end of. You sit on low stools."

"Why?"

"So you aren't comfortable," she said.

"So you remember the person."

"Yes. People bring food so you don't have to cook. Company, to get you through the worst time."

"It's pride to think about it directly?"

"No, I think that would be a Christian problem," she said. "It's just painful. In yeshiva, I had a teacher who said, 'Judaism asks you to be more than yourself and gives you help when you can't be.' That's how I want to live. That's a merciful God."

"I thought he was an angry God," Slava said.

"He's there, too," she laughed. "In the form of my mother. But you really don't have to take all of it. You drown in it and you want to run away completely."

"That happened to you?" he said.

"No, but I can imagine it," she said. She ran her hand inside his shirt.

"This heat is demented," he said.

"August," she said. "You're an erotic hallucination."

"One of yours?"

"I wish."

A lone trumpeter tooted into a microphone on the stage at the western end of the park. There was going to be a concert later in the day.

"Do you try to publish them?" he said.

She shook her head. "It's for me."

"Maybe you're just shy," he said.

"Maybe you're an exhibitionist."

"Do you know what you want to do?"

"Fact-checking not a persuasive career?" she said. "I don't know yet. I'm waiting for a sign. I envy you—you know exactly what you want."

"It's brought great triumph."

"You're not patient."

"Can you tell me about fact-checking?" he said cautiously.

"Sure," she said. "What do you want to know?"

He shrugged. "Anything. I've been sitting next to you a year and a half—I've been sleeping in your bed for a week—and I don't know the first thing about it."

"Will you sleep in it this weekend?" she said.

"Depends how well you answer my questions."

She laughed, the white blocks of her teeth gleaming in the sun. "Fact-checking?" she said, leaning back on her palms. "I don't know. You check the facts in the story." She shrugged.

"The piece you're checking now."

"A missing painting at a museum in Italy. But you can't reach anyone half the time because of their *farkakte* siestas. Also, ask me if I speak Italian. And Sheila, God bless her, doesn't remember the curator's name. But she's embarrassed to hand in incomplete copy, so *she makes it up*. Instead of leaving it blank, she *makes up* the curator's name. Oh, Arianna will find it. Ask me how many hours I spent this morning hunting down Massimo the False Curator."

"But how does it work, you know?" he said. "Like, what sends up . . . a red flag?"

"A red flag," she repeated. "Well, they write the story. Or let's say they *report* a story. For instance, last week: Lehman Brothers. Company of the decade, blah blah. Simons reports the story. I have to go through the entire thing and underline everything that seems like it could be a fact. And then check it."

"But what counts as a fact?"

"A fact? Mr. Grayson would kill me if he heard me saying this out loud, but—a fact is anything that can piss somebody off by being wrong. That's why stories about a murder in the forgotten tribe of Waka-waka on the lost island of Wango-dango are actually the easiest check, in a way. Those people don't read *Century*. They don't care if you counted wrong how many stripes of cow dung they have on their faces."

"But is there anything you don't need to check?"

"Personal impressions. Conjecture. Things that can't be checked can't be wrong, you know? If there's no record, it can't be checked. I'm sorry— *why* are you so interested in this?" He couldn't see her face, but he knew its expression, the way her eyes grew narrow when she was skeptical.

"I'm interested in you," Slava said quickly, and leaned up to kiss her.

-7-

Israel lived in a grotto-like basement apartment on Quentin Road, across from a Russian grocery and near a squat outer-borough edition of the public library. The living room was through a galley kitchen sheeted with the usual gloomy linoleum. Mailbox-sized packs of saltines and tuna-can skyscrapers peered from dusty cupboards—complimentary provisions from the local synagogue. The same dreck piled in Grandfather's cabinets, only his home nurses made Ukrainian magic from it. On Israel's wall was a pharmacy calendar, a bottle of Lipitor reclining suggestively in place of a supermodel. There were four identical calendars from other Russian pharmacies neatly stacked underneath, as if Israel were going to do the year over.

"My small castle," Israel said, spreading his arms and stepping into the living room. It was a line from an old Soviet film about a man who returned home to the wrong apartment because the concrete apartment blocks all looked the same, and fell in love with the woman who lived there. Israel was short and round, a pair of dark blue gym trousers keeping the basketball of his belly in place. His face was as seamed as a topographical map, the curved headland of a nose holding the landscape together. It bucked slightly when Slava introduced himself.

Slava had ignored Israel for a week. His original plan was to ignore him forever. But the week after his call, instead of combing the *Charlotte Observer* and the *East Hampton Patch*, Slava invented three flubs and went to search for his grandmother in the Belarus forest. The night that Arianna had fallen asleep in his bed, his grandmother had come to him. A mercilessly brief visitation, but for forty-five minutes, time had stopped so that he could enter a void and talk with the old woman. As long as he kept writing about Grandmother, Arianna would remain asleep in his bed, the sun would remain banished outside his window, and the city would be kept from reaching the following day. But then the story came to its natural end. That was the mercilessness of a story; you couldn't keep it going beyond where it wanted to end, even to keep your grandmother alive. So, he wanted to travel with his grandmother once more. However, when he tried to write something about her without intending it as a narrative for the restitution fund, without Grandfather providing the spark of a few truthful details, nothing would come. The story had no purpose, no framework. It made Slava feel wretched; what kind of writer was he if he couldn't invent on his own?

On the third day of inaction, he lifted his phone. Israel hadn't called back, and Slava would have sooner knocked on every door in Brooklyn than ask Grandfather, at whose cavalierness he intended to remain furious. Grandfather had told him that both he and Israel had gone to a Dr. Korolenko. "Korolenko gout knee problems Brooklyn nyc," Slava typed, and there was the number: 718.

"Dr. Korolenko's office, you're being greeted by Olga."

"Hi, Olga. My grandfather asked me to call and confirm his appointment?"

"Sure. What day?"

"He doesn't remember, of course. He thinks it's next Wednesday or Friday. Definitely not the first half of the week."

"His name?"

"Israel Abramson. Do you see it?"

"Israel Arkadievich! He's one of our favorites. But no, nothing in the book for Abramson next week."

"No, he definitely said Wednesday or Friday."

"Maybe we made a mistake," Olga said. *"I have a free slot Wednesday morning, if that works for him."*

"Well, when do you have him?"

"I don't have him till September."

"You know what, just leave him there. I'll explain it to him. No, he should remember these things. I bought him a little notebook for his birthday expressly for this purpose, and do you think he's opened it?"

She laughed. *"Go easy on your elders! It's only been two weeks since his birthday!"*

"Yes, of course," Slava said, cursing himself for the unnecessary arabesque. *"I forget he's an old man sometimes. You know how it is—you don't want them to get old. Anyway, Olya, just one last thing. He said last time the ambulette was waiting for him a block up? Can you tell me if you have the right address?"*

"I have 2070 Quentin Road, is that wrong?"

"No, that's right. I don't know why the driver was on the wrong block."

"We've got someone else at 2130, maybe there was a mix-up. I'll check."

"Oh, that's all right. Just a mix-up. You know, he worries for no reason, that man. I'll tell him to cool it."

She laughed again. *"All right. If only all grandsons were this concerned! Come visit us sometime with Grandpa, okay?"*

"I am like the Master here," Israel said with a belch, pointing to the living room window, which cleared the pavement by a dozen inches. A pair of feet clicked past, adding to the thin mist of dust on the glass. *"Master and Margarita.* You've read it?"

Slava nodded. "In class."

"I'm rereading Gogol," Israel said. " 'Whither art thou soaring, Russia?' He knew where they were soaring. Right into the shit bucket." Israel turned back toward the window. "You can tell people's moods by the way they walk," he observed. They watched a lame leg make its dragging passage. "His mood is, 'I want my old leg back,' " Israel said, and broke into hoarse laughter. He coughed brutally into his fist, the bristle of his eyebrows trembling and leaping. "When you have only a little thread," he announced grandly after recovering, "you have to know how to make a whole blanket from it." He placed his hands on his hips, as if about to start calisthenics. "As I said, I do a little writing, too." He coughed again. "My throat is a desert, I'm sorry. Sit, sit, don't stand like an inspector." He motioned to the sofa, its suede haunches cinched by plastic gold bands. "One writer to another, I want to say: I admire the way you work."

"Meaning?" Slava said, falling into the sofa.

"You don't need me to invent the story," he said. "For the claim form, I mean. But here you are. You wanted to sniff around." Israel wiggled his nose. "*Texture*, you wanted."

"Where's your family, Israel Arkadievich?" Slava said.

"You can call me Israel," he said. "We are in America now, you can be informal. Back home, you can save someone from drowning and you won't get a thank-you, but they'll always call you Israel Arkadievich. Here, it's that hai-hava-yoo all the time, but they won't save you if you're drowning. Am I correct?"

"I guess you are," Slava said, thinking about it.

"My wife is dead eighteen months," he said. "May the earth be like down for her. I'm sure you can tell." His gnarly fingers swept the room. " 'The frying pan is not sizzling and the kettle is not whistling,' as we used to say."

"I'm sorry," Slava said. "I didn't know."

"My son . . ." He indicated the window sadly, as if the son were standing outside it. "A couple of years after we came, Yuri got mixed up with those blackhats. They organized the whole world for him over at that synagogue. He stopped eating in our kitchen, put on that hat. My wife was still alive to see it, I regret that she was. And then . . . *poof*—he left. He's in Israel now." Israel stuck out his tongue. "They have these curls down to their shoulders like two swinging pricks, excuse me. How do they get those things to curl like that? Curling iron? Vain bastards." He nearly spat, then remembered it was his living room. "Look." He rummaged in a tin eating bowl on the bookshelf until he held a worn-out square.

Slava unfolded the photograph with his fingertips, the paper as frayed as a dry leaf. On the back, in a smudged violet cursive, it said: "Yuri—too late." From the front smiled a young, round face wispy with a month's beard, the grin toothy and guileless. The teeth had not enjoyed the correction of braces. Already their owner was wearing the costume of the pious. A black suit jacket, specks of dandruff visible despite the mediocre quality of the photo, over a white shirt with a drooping collar, underneath it a white tee with tumbleweeds of chest hair rising above the neckline. Behind him were ponderous burgundy drapes that could have belonged only to a Russian banquet hall in Israel's neighborhood.

"Why did you rename yourself?" Slava said.

"It's not Israel's fault," he said. "There aren't enough of these blackhats over here? Besides, I changed it before any of this started, right when we came. I wanted to show my support. Who's Iosif? Iosif was me in the USSR. That person is finished."

"It's nice to meet someone who knew my grandfather when he was young," Slava said.

"Now there's a story," Israel said.

"He doesn't like to talk about it."

"That's a load. He would tell a horse how to trot."

"Then I don't believe what he says," Slava said.

Israel smirked. "Why would you believe what I say?"

"If you lie, I won't write the application for you."

He laughed. "Very good! You are becoming clever. It runs in your family."

"Meaning what?"

"I meant no offense," Israel said.

"But meaning what."

"Meaning what." Israel leaned forward. "Do you know how your grandfather got that home nurse of his?" He clapped once per name: "Marina. Berta. Olga. They change all the time.

"Your grandmother—may the earth be like down for her—had twelve hours of nurse care a day from the city. That's a lot, by the way. You've got these American grandmothers wandering around, bags of bones, they paid in to the tax base for fifty years, and they don't have any help. It breaks your heart to see these people. I feel like a pole jumper next to them.

"Anyway, your grandfather decides twelve a day's not enough. He wants your grandmother to have someone around the clock. So he gives the twelve-hour nurse some money and tells her to call the agency to ask for an extension on the hours. 'The husband's gone bad from helping take care of the wife,' she says. 'They need someone full-time.'

"So the assessor comes from the city. All this is from your grandfather's lips, by the way, because he's a braggart. The assessor comes and your grandfather is sitting there like a vegetable. Drooling, head keeled over like it's not connected to the rest of him. The assessor starts calling to him— 'Yevgeny, Yevgeny'—so your grandfather starts grunting and gnashing his teeth. He acted out the whole thing in front of me at Korolenko's office. Minus the bowel-loosening. Your grandfather should have moved to Hollywood."

"And they got twenty-four hours," Slava said. "Berta."

"You know who gets twenty-four hours, typically?" Israel said. "Quadriplegics, war veterans, and psychotics. But he wanted it for your grandmother, and he got it. Your grandfather gets things."

"He got me," Slava said. Through the little window, the light was beginning to steal out of the sky.

"You are too smart for that," Israel said.

"Don't be sure," Slava said.

"I've known him sixty years," Israel said. "'A child of other people's gardens,' they called him. He got what needed to be got. The salami, the caviar, the cognac, the minks. Nobody had access to those things but Party people with special privileges. Even I can't tell you how he—a barber—got what he got. Do you know how wealthy your family was at home? In secret, but still. Not everyone had the stomach for it. How many people did he keep in Climat perfume, bananas, free trips to Crimea, so their mouths would stay closed about what he got for himself, your grandmother, your mama, you? I saw him on the street one time. It was hotter than a furnace outside, and he's wearing an overcoat. It looked like he had a piglet in there. I said, 'Zhenya, what's with the coat?'"

"He had something stuffed in there," Slava said.

"Fifteen sticks of salami taped to the insides!" Israel sniggered. "Like rocket launchers! That salami was so fresh it could talk. You understand if you got stopped with fifteen sticks of salami? That's 'intent to sell,' 'private enterprise,' prison.

"One salami went to the woman in ticketing at the Aeroflot office on Karl Marx Street. One went to the director of the kindergarten where your little mama was enrolled. One went to the pediatrician at the local clinic, so your mama wouldn't have to wait three days for a house call if God forbid she got ill. You watched him with awe. My hand never rose to try something similar."

"Why not?"

"Why not. I don't know. Just the way you're made, I guess." Israel coughed into his sleeve. Slava rose and got him a glass of water. The washer was missing from the faucet, and water sprayed all over the countertop. Slava wiped it up with a towel.

"I envied him," Israel said when Slava returned. He lapped greedily at the glass. "Oh, this is good. Thank you. After the war, you'd be at a restaurant with a girl, and these drunk *zhloby* would stumble over: 'Look at these kikes feasting away!' And you have to hang your head because you don't want trouble, because there's a million more where they came from. But you're scalding inside, because until then maybe you were trying to impress the girl.

"But your grandfather, he never just sat there. He got up and he beat that *zhlob* to a pulp, right then and there, while everyone watched, even police. Everybody got stiff when Zhenya Gelman walked into a restaurant."

Israel drained his glass and wiped his mouth with a handkerchief. "During the war, there were seven attempted outbreaks from ghettos by Jews," he said. "Ask me how many times Soviet soldiers tried to break out of German POW camps? Find me enough for one hand. But it was always ' "Fought" in Uzbekistan, did you, kike?' Because the war never came to Uzbekistan. At the end of the war, there were more than a hundred, maybe two hundred, Jews decorated Heroes of the USSR, and you can imagine how many more there would have been if that prick Stalin wasn't an anti-Semite. I mean, you had Jewish war veterans without *legs*. But the way people looked at you, it's as if they thought you amputated them yourself to make it look like you'd fought."

"Were you in Uzbekistan during the war?" Slava said.

"I was getting shrapnel in my leg under Kharkov," Israel said. He gave Slava a little ballet step and hiked up his gym trouser, revealing a veiny, pockmarked calf. "I could use a new leg, too."

"Well, your fearless Yevgeny Gelman was in Uzbekistan," Slava said.

"I'm too old for grudges, Slava," Israel waved. "It kills me more than the other person."

Slava sighed. "I should start heading back soon," he said. "It's a long way."

"I was going to make some dinner for us," Israel said. "Microwave, but not bad."

"Next time," Slava said.

"I've never been to Manhattan," Israel said. "I would like to sometime. All those lights. They show it on television. Can you sleep, with all those lights?"

"You said what I wrote needs an improvement," Slava said.

"Oh, it's good, Slava," he nodded. "It's got that silence of ours. That terrible Russian silence that the Americans don't understand. They are always making noise because they need to forget life is going to end. But we remember, and so we have silence, even when we're shouting and laughing."

"So?" Slava said. "You want silence, I'll give you silence."

"But think about it, Slava," Israel said, clucking his tongue. "You're Fritz Fritzovich reviewing these claims, may all those people get covered up to their heads. And you get this application. Where was the individual between 1939 and 1945. And you get this . . . this . . . Adolf is going to believe that an eighty-year-old man, an immigrant fart, wrote what you wrote?"

"He could have had his grandson translate it for him," Slava said tightly. "That's not unimaginable. The English is the grandson's and the grandson is fluent. Doesn't mean the story has to be false."

"The grandson is fluent, all right," Israel said. "But the story. You're trying to avoid detection or what? It's like a puppet theater, you know? What do they call it? Not puppet theater—with the marionettes."

"I don't know what you mean."

"You've got this movie scene. Beautiful moment, beautifully written, the cows. But no beginning, no middle, no end. Who are we, where did we live? Look at some books. The Minsk ghetto was formed on such-and-such date. We lived at such-and-such address from this date to this date. This is where we were moved when they put up the wire. And then you can do your beautiful sentences. But you need more than that. Nice sentences is like a beautiful woman who doesn't know how to cook. It's not your story. Forget about yourself for a moment."

"And where am I supposed to put all that silence of yours in this encyclopedia version?" Slava said.

"Oh, but that's for you to figure out!" Israel giggled.

"A fact can't be wrong if it isn't a fact," Slava said expertly. "You start feeding numbers and dates in there, they're going to get their record books out. That's how they check facts, Israel. I have it on good authority."

"You'll know what to do."

"Why don't *you* write it," Slava said. "I'll translate. That's the solution."

"No, no," Israel said, waving him away. "Don't get puffy. Listen, you can't teach an old Jew how to make money. I'll tell you a joke, and then you can go to your Manhattan. Two guys are panhandling on a street in Moscow. One has a sign that says: 'I'm Ivanov,' in other words a Slav. 'Please help a poor beggar.' The other's sign says, 'I'm Abramov,' in other words a Jew. 'Please help a poor beggar.' And whoever walks by, they give money only to Ivanov, more and more. It's like they're giving money to Ivanov just to stick it to Abramov. Finally, a Jewish guy comes up to Abramov and says, 'Abramov, what's wrong with you? Change your sign to a Slav name!' At which point Abramov turns to Ivanov and says, 'Look, Moshe, this schmuck is teaching me how to make money.'" Israel quaked with laughter. "What those *shvartzes* pull in the subway? 'I lost my job and I'm trying to get back on my feet'? Pathetic! An old Russian man could run ten circles around them."

"I think you underestimate your black-market skills," Slava said.

"Even a legless man knows how to run when he needs to," Israel said, shrugging. "We're all graduates of that particular academy. But it's too late for some of us. I'm interested in what happens to you, however."

"I am going to be arrested for forging restitution claims for my grandfathers," Slava said.

"No need to say it so loudly like that," Israel said, glancing at the window.

"I'll be going," Slava said.

"For your information," Israel said, peering at him—he was shorter than Slava, but his gaze was strong—"I have no illusions why he mentioned the letter to me. He gives not to give but to show you he gives. Look, it's a kind of compliment to owe something to Yevgeny Gelman, for a man like that to think you can give him something of use—I can barely take three breaths without coughing. But Slava, don't pretend you are doing this to be a good grandson."

"Don't pretend you're a writer," Slava said.

"Opa!" Israel said. "You may be your grandfather's grandson, but you are also your grandmother's grandson. She was the fierce one. That's the nice thing about having children. They take the best of you both. Two for the price of one."

"You get your letter, and I get to be with my grandmother for a thousand words," Slava said.

"Oh," he said. "I see. That's nice."

"Don't worry, it'll be under your name."

"I'm not worried."

"You should be," Slava said. "We're committing fraud. International fraud, apparently. I know that means nothing to any of you."

"We are always behind you, Gogol," Israel said. He clapped Slava's arm. "Have a safe trip."

As Slava walked out, he wondered how Israel had meant it. Behind Slava in defense or behind Slava, hiding.

On his way to the subway, Slava found himself looking around casually—was anyone interested in his progress? The day's last light was leaking away, so it was hard to tell. The street crawled with the usual suspects, grandmothers with mesh bags, a bowlegged Mexican, a cop chewing gum, everyone moving, no one stopping because he stopped. Slava felt resentful relief.

On the train home, Slava went over the details of their conversation—visions of swinging pricks, quadriplegics, Kharkov, and shrapnel sieved through his mind, refusing to snag on some brain branch and bloom—but all of it was either irrelevant or too broad for a claim letter. What had happened to Grandmother after the close call with the Germans? More forest wandering? No, that wasn't the right direction. Overly similar narratives—Slava was sure that was a red flag.

It had been bothering him since that first night. He hadn't gotten Grandmother right in Grandfather's story. Israel was right that improvements could be made, but he was wrong about which. In Grandfather's letter, Slava had described Grandmother's actions, but he hadn't described *her*. What was she like? He couldn't find out through a scene before or after the war, because that wouldn't qualify. And it was hard enough to conjure her as a fifteen-year-old waif without having to disguise her as a boy.

He had three stations before he would go underground. He sighed and dialed Grandfather.

"Hi," Slava said cautiously.

"Hi yourself," Grandfather said.

"News?" Slava said.

"The new bed's here," he said. "It's nice. Smaller but nice. Japanese wood. First they brought a twin, but that's the width of a hospital bed. I'm not sleeping in a hospital bed. Oh, it doesn't matter. I can't live here anymore. How can I live here if I lived here with your grandmother?"

Grandfather had forgotten their argument long ago. He didn't hold grudges. They were impractical.

"How do you feel," Slava said, stalling.

"Like a racehorse. You?"

"Spoken to Mom?"

"More often than you," Grandfather said. "She's been here every night."

"Do you need anything?"

"I need it to be 1975," he said. "Your grandmother and me on the beach in Yevpatoriya. Do you know how difficult it was to get a vacation voucher for husband and wife at the same time? Most people had to take vacations one by one. And the authorities were always wondering why the country had such a problem with adultery. Degenerates. Do you remember when we took you there, you thought it was water in the cup but it was vodka, and you fell asleep under the table on the beach?"

"Can you tell me something else about Grandmother?" Slava said. "Something about the ghetto?"

"I told you everything I know."

"Try to remember something else. I need it."

"What for?"

"I just need it."

Grandfather took a moment to ponder this. "She didn't like to talk about it," he said at last.

"I know, you said that. But surely she said something else. How can you live with someone for fifty years and not know!"

"So now you will educate me on how to live with a woman. Why don't you wipe the snot from your nose first."

"I'm about to go into the tunnel."

"Good for you."

"The phone doesn't work in the tunnel."

"There were pogroms," Grandfather said. "In the ghetto. Thinning the herd, they called it."

"And?"

"That's all there is!"

"All right," Slava said.

"Call more often," he said. "Remember your grandfather."

— 8 —

She slept without any clothes. In the morning, Slava liked to finger the grooves left in her face by the pillow. She twitched so he would leave her alone. He waited and then started again. The cat collaborated by climbing on her head. Its name was Tux, but Arianna always called it the Beast. It didn't look very beastly, just black and white spots that shifted together with its bulk when it moved. Occasionally, Slava and the cat would stare off across Arianna's sleeping body, taking the other's measure.

Finally, she opened her eyes. "You know, if you stopped, he'd stop," she said.

"We can't stop," Slava said. "We're animals about you."

She laughed. "If you're so fond of me, let me sleep."

"You're hot as a furnace inside that blanket. You could power a factory."

"So that's why you sleep so far away," she said. She threw off the blanket and jumped on top of Slava. The cat resentfully gave up its position. The weight of Arianna felt solid and reassuring.

"It's Saturday?" he said.

"I hope you're right, or I'm late for work," she said.

"So you don't—Shabbat?"

"To synagogue? Not every Saturday, no. Some Saturdays. My mother's problem. I pick and choose."

"Why aren't you going today?" he said.

"Because I'm happy right here."

Slava looked up at the ceiling. "Who are you?" he said.

"I know," she laughed.

"Where did you come from?" he said.

"Los Angeles," she said. "City out west."

"What did you think when you got off the plane that first time?"

"Well, I'd been here before."

"You know what I mean."

"I thought: Here is a place where everything will be different tomorrow."

"I think that's why I dislike it," Slava said.

"You don't know anything except your neighborhood," she said.

"That's why I don't," he said.

"Something tells me that's not why."

"Let's talk about you," he said.

"It was lonely," she said. "For some reason, I couldn't talk to anyone in school. Sometimes you feel things very strongly and you need to follow it even if you don't know why you feel that way. And I didn't want to talk to anyone. It's like all this was my secret and I didn't want to share it with anyone."

"You sat on the windowsill and smoked cigarettes."

"Yeah. But then it stopped one day. I got tired of cigarettes. I really wanted to be healthy. The day I had that thought for the first time, I went to a yoga class. When I was finished, I went to another one. And when that one ended—"

"You did a third."

"I went to half of a third. In the middle, I was done. I got up and walked out."

"You're enlightened."

"Hardly. I just stopped wanting to dig around." Her dead fingertip indicated the spot between her eyebrows. "I'll come back to it. There are things I don't have, and that's all right. There are things I want that my mother also wants for me, and that's all right, too. Do you know what I want?"

"Tell me."

"For you to make breakfast."

"I can't," he said.

"*Pourquoi*?" she said, drawing back. "I thought we'd have the day."

"We've had the week? I have an errand."

"What do you have to do at ten A.M. on a Saturday morning?"

"Just something," he said, looking away. "Some of us work on the weekend."

"Don't, Slava," she said, and rolled off. They lay without speaking as she checked her phone. The crown molding near the ceiling was beginning to peel in one corner.

"How did you start fact-checking?" he said cautiously.

She looked over at him. "*Why* is this so important to you?" she said.

"Oh, I just hear you every day," he said. " 'Mr. Maloney, is your bar made of pine or aspen? Can you call the manufacturer?' "

"Yeah, I guess it sounds strange from the side."

"Mr. Maloney's gone his whole life without knowing is it pine or aspen. When has anyone asked him what that bar's made of?"

"What's your point?"

"Does it really matter?" he said.

"I guess," she said, putting down her phone. "But think about it. Maloney's is in New Jersey. Let's say they don't have aspens in New Jersey. I mean, they do—I checked. But let's say. Somebody happens to know that, they see that wrong, they say, What else is wrong? They lose trust. You can't give a reader a reason to lose trust."

"Okay," he said. "But it's not always an either/or situation."

"Meaning?" Her eyebrows gathered.

"Let's say *Century* didn't hire women. You'd raise hell."

"Okay," she said.

"Now, take—I don't know—an Arab woman. An Arab woman might say, 'God willing, they will hire women at some point.' Which strikes you as—"

"Fear-based naïveté."

"Right. She's . . . unenlightened. But she might not see it that way. She may be happier than you."

"Because she doesn't know better."

"But to her it's a fact all the same."

"So you report that American women and Arab women see it differently."

"Would you be a stay-at-home mother?"

"No."

"But you aren't having your direction chosen for you like the Arab woman? If you have a story that says, 'Arab women are unfree,' that may be factually true from an American standpoint. But it's not true from a Moroccan standpoint. Or at least not a yes/no proposition."

"She may be happier than me, but she's still not free, however you look at it. I don't want to be a stay-at-home mom, and let's say it's a mechanical response to how it was with my mother, but I'm free to choose. I won't be harassed for it."

"Not physically," Slava said.

She rolled onto her back. "Slava!"

"During the war," Slava said, "my grandfather ran away. World War II. When he turned conscription age, he had his identity card revised down by a year. Then he got on a train and ran off again, even farther east. If he hadn't, he would probably be dead. And I wouldn't be here. Which would make you less happy." He peered over at her, but his attempt at levity failed. "Is he a hero or a coward? Which is it?"

"I don't know. A bit of both, I guess. A hero to you, a coward to somebody else. A hero to me."

"Pick and choose," Slava said.

"Why not."

"When does 'pick and choose' become 'ignore inconvenient facts'?"

"When you're trying to get at me."

He waved her away. After a moment, he said, "I don't get it. The witness in the box has put his hand on the Bible, so everything that comes out of his mouth is treated as fact unless there's proof that he lied? Talk about naïveté! Because he's put his hand on the Bible? Now lightning has struck and all of a sudden he's unable to lie?"

"You can still check that a woman has two children, not three," she said. "This village was founded in 1673 but that one in 1725. Chickens lay eggs. We landed on the moon. There's video!" She stared at him. "You have to see the limit of your point."

He shrugged and watched the fan spin above them. Arianna did not have air-conditioning. Outside, the sun dimmed under passing clouds.

"Maybe it'll be cooler today," he said.

"You're actually going to talk about the weather."

"It's the stuff of poetry," he said bitterly. The cat cocked its head, sensing an opening.

"This is nice," she said. "It isn't for real until you're fighting. Why is it you can't make me breakfast?"

"I have to run an errand," he said flatly. Then he added: "For my grandmother."

"Oh," she said. "Sure. I'm sorry. You'll come back here after?"

"No, I need to go home."

"Okay, I can come there later."

"Arianna."

"Day apart," she said. "Got it."

"Not that I—"

"It's okay. You're right."

"Tomorrow—"

"Just give me five minutes."

She cantilevered her left leg over his right and lifted herself above him. He could feel on his groin the thin thread of hair between her legs. Even soured by sleep, her breath was fragrant—soap, musk, sunflower seeds. She cradled him in her hand as her lips descended on his. Quickly, he was hard, and she lowered herself on top of him, closing her eyes. She rocked above him steadily, as if he weren't there. As she neared orgasm, she leaned forward until their chests touched, both sweating. The pallor of her breasts was translucent against his chest. Coming close, she placed her palms around his head and began to thrust herself into him. He had never been fucked that way before. He had never been fucked.

She didn't open her eyes until she had come. Then she kissed him on the forehead and said, "Thanks, honey."

He rode home with Arianna drying on his legs. He showered for a long time, just thinking. The violent creak of the stair door as he headed back out roused Irvin from a reverie of Albanian vineyards.

"Hello, Mr. Gellma," he sighed. "Valk?" He walked two fingers through the air. "A little raining." He pointed at the ceiling, frowning.

"I think it's clearing up," Slava said.

Irv, to which the doorman's name had been reduced by some of the tenants, nodded with the enthusiasm of an Albanian spotting a Serb in his garden. *You fockin moron, you could be relax at home on day off, but you go walk in rains.* "Vait, pliz," he said. He opened the delivery closet and rifled through coats. He withdrew a long, sturdy umbrella with a carved handle of a zebra hanging its head. "Mr. Seetrick forget," he said. "But Mr. Seetrick Saturday is dinner come out only—you bring back, okay?"

"Thanks, Erv." In deference to liberal values or immigrant solidarity,

Slava insisted on calling the Albanian by his actual name, and often wondered if the doorman heard the subtle distinction. On this matter, Erv/Irv kept Slava in suspense, which led Slava to try harder in ever more deformed ways, so that he ended up addressing the doorman by some variation of "Aaaairvvv . . ." The latter's mystified distaste in reaction to this *was* clear, though he did not feel entitled to correct a tenant. America had suffered him greater indignities.

"Vait, vait, vait." Irvin held up a hand. "Vait." He disappeared under the podium and emerged with half a loaf of bread in a plastic bag. He banged it against the podium. "For birds," he said. "You give."

Slava hesitated. "Maybe you do it, Erv."

"They hungry now," Irvin said, disappointed. "Afternoon—hungry."

Slava obeyed and took the loaf.

"Small pieces, give small pieces," Irvin said, joining his thumb and index finger. "Bon appétit."

Slava valked. He valked to the river, closed his eyes, and sniffed at the salt in the air. He was an object of indifference to the one thousand pigeons hopping around the pavement, but when he opened Irvin's plastic bag— after ten minutes of trying to unwork the impossible knot, uttering an obscenity, and finally tearing it open—their feelings changed. Following Irvin's instruction, he tore off small pieces and scattered them gently. The pigeons wobbled toward the bread and pecked, bopping one another.

In Arianna's bed an hour before, he only wanted to leave, but now, without her, he longed for her, as if he had a question and she could answer it. Had he just argued with her because he really disagreed or because he resented receiving instructions? If she claimed to find him interesting, why did she forget to ask his opinion? And when she did, she argued against him. In frustration, he chucked the loaf at the railing. It thudded to the ground, scattering the pigeons. They regrouped and stared at him resentfully. He gave them the middle finger and walked off toward the library.

The Yorkville branch of the New York Public Library swam in lazy yellow light. The children's section was full of toddlers crawling on the mats and shrieking occasionally to protest their confinement while their mothers murmured over the baby-size tables. Slava found the reference librarian and asked for good books on the Holocaust in the East. Books with dates, numbers, street names. Books to make an invented claim letter read like a beautiful woman who could cook, too, if Israel Abramson were the judge.

"You sure you don't want Baby Einstein?" the librarian said. He cast a destructive look in the direction of the hollering children. "Research project?"

"Fiction," Slava said.

The librarian nodded. "That's all the fashion now."

Dusk was beginning to settle by the time Slava dialed Israel. Listening to the ring, he watched a man and woman work at a kitchen counter in an apartment across the courtyard, strains of brass in their stereo. Briefly, the music swelled, and she bumped his rear end with hers.

"Hello?" Israel said again.

Slava snapped to. "You're wrong," he said.

"Those were my son's favorite words."

"I'm sitting here with half the library, Israel. Minsk ghetto—formed date such-and-such." Slava peered at his notepad. "July twentieth. A hundred thousand inmates. Largest ghetto in German-occupied territory in the Soviet Union. Et cetera."

"Okay. Very good."

"First of all, someone applying for restitution is not a historian. The people who wrote these books know how many inmates there were. The people in the ghetto didn't get a fact sheet."

"Okay, but they know when it started, they know where they lived."

"You ever apply for anything, Israel, Yuri ever apply for a scholarship? You're the guy reading the claims—*every* claim is going to say it started on July twentieth, we lived at such-and-such an address. But you can't give

him an address. They have records for that. You've got to—I don't know—
distract him. You've got to make him not care that there's no address, that
there's actually no verifiable detail. That's how they check facts, I told you.
I know from someone who knows. Tell a story they'll forget it's a story.
That's our best chance."

"Slavchik, my bird, we're not trying to get into Harvard here. We want
to have a boring little story about poor Jews in the Holocaust." Israel
cleared his nose. "Another old Jew, pity, let's give him a penny. He starts
reading *Anna Karenina*, he's going to have questions. Babel is dead, my
friend. All the best Jews got killed. It's the boring Jews who got left. Let's
give them a penny. You follow?"

"You're wrong," Slava said. "I think."

"You want to hypnotize him. You want to tell him a nice fairy tale."

"Something like that."

There was a pause. "I don't know," Israel said. "We're following you
now, Gogol. Do what you think."

"By the way, Gogol was an anti-Semite," Slava said.

"And you think Jews are a heap of luck?"

Slava hung up with the pyrrhic satisfaction of a child getting his way.
The problem remained. For all the history he read, he couldn't insert his
grandmother into it. Pushing off the endless small-font paragraphs in the
books the librarian had given him, he could smell the rain-soaked canvas
of the trucks that transported prisoners to their workdays breaking concrete outside the ghetto, but he couldn't smell her. What kind of brain was
it that could run so effortlessly with one thing but not with another? He
needed something to start him, but he couldn't figure out what. No matter
what notes Slava made on one of the legal pads he had stolen from the office, the exercise ended in him staring at the wall or at the couple across the
courtyard.

Eventually, they left the kitchen. Probably to the dining room to have
the dinner they'd made. And then to the bedroom in a buzzed glaze, half-

dream, half-reality, the mellowness of body next to body, until they fell asleep, laughably early, the television chattering softly, the bed light carelessly on till the morning.

Around the courtyard, windows were blinking on. Arianna hadn't called. Strange to be together every weeknight but apart on Saturday. Slava dialed her cell phone, but it rang until voice mail. The evening was his, just as he'd asked.

He pictured Arianna in the ghetto instead of Grandmother. Arianna in the midst of a dusty ghetto street flanked by flower beds outside the windows and small gardens in the backyard—homes, somehow, even if inside a ghetto. How effortlessly Arianna objected to having Grandmother's money rerouted to Grandfather. (Did she object? She actually prohibited it—gently, chidingly: You can't.) Not a glimmer of doubt passed over her face. But what if Arianna had eaten potato peels for breakfast and dinner (no lunch) for a year? If she had watched the pale skin come off her beautiful legs from wading in swamps day after day? Would she be of two minds then? Could she go sixty years without mentioning what had been taken, six years without complaining as her body undid itself? And if, in turn, Grandmother had been born in America, would she object in Arianna's fashion? Here his imagination did not dare to go, a sacrilege to imagine so casually the undoing of so many deaths.

He had what Grandfather had said: a factory, a raid, bodies in a basement, a dead child, a bottle of milk. He had what the books in front of him said. He had what he had about Grandmother. The rest would have to find itself as he went. There was an extra layer of confusion in that his protagonist would have to be concealed as Israel Abramson, but that was just a name on top of the page. Was there a reason Israel couldn't have a sister? Was the beauty of invention not that he very much could?

Please describe, in as much detail as you can, where the Subject was during the years 1939 to 1945.

Israel Abramson

It was after the four-day pogrom in July 1942 that I decided I would try to escape from the ghetto, come what may. In truth, it was my sister who decided.

Our job in the ghetto was to sort through the clothes of the murdered. Skirts here, pants here. After a while, the Germans wised up and made people undress first. By the end of '42, the clothes had no holes or blood. You could still smell the people in the fabric, though: sweat and hay and sour milk and something else that must have been fear. It became ordinary to hold a dead person's clothes in your hand, to see a dead body in the street. One time Sonya—that was my sister—saw an infant trying to get milk out of its mother's breast, but the mother was dead, completely dead. And you had to walk by, keep going.

One day we were returning home from the warehouse where I sorted the clothes. It was me, Sonya, two other girls, and a guard in the back of the truck. When we were turning onto Komsomol'skaya, the guard leaned into me and said, "There will be a raid tonight. Don't go home. Hide somewhere." I said I couldn't leave without Sonya, but he made clear the offer was only for me. I didn't know what to do, but Sonya bulged her eyes and mouthed GO. "Now," the guard said. So I jumped. I will always remember him. Herr Karitko. He was old. Thin, wrinkled face. Not tall. Maybe he liked boys. You had different kinds of Germans.

Already, there were bodies in the streets. The Belarusians who worked as policemen for the Germans, they were even more sadistic. Tables had been set out in the streets. They went from street to street, sitting down for a glass of beer and a plate of drumsticks between executions. You know what a drumstick looks like after you haven't seen one in a year? I had scurvy; I'd lost half the teeth in my mouth. I always kept it closed and mumbled because they shot you on sight if you weren't healthy.

My mind was racing because where was Sonya? War makes you make decisions no person should have to make. But also she was the kind of girl who, if she told you to jump from the truck, you jumped. She was steelier than all us boys in the yard. In fact, she was the only girl allowed to play with the boys, not that she asked anyone's permission. One time the boys from the next street were over for a soccer game, and they tripped Khema something awful. He had snot and blood coming out of his nose. Sonya went to the boy who had done it, a real lunk, a meter eighty and not even thirteen, and said, "Watch out for the branch," and pointed up. When he looked up, she kneed him in the groin and kicked him in the shin. While he wailed, she brought him over to Khema by the ear and held him like that until he apologized and wiped up Khema's snot with his own jersey. So she was like that.

I didn't know where to go except our neighbor Isaac because Mother and Father weren't home yet from the factory. (They sewed German uniforms.) Isaac lived with his young wife and a child. They had a double cellar, and said we were welcome there whenever we needed it, may G-d spare us from needing it.

When I got there, Sonya was tapping her foot on the floorboard. "You take your time, brother," she said, and winked. I was about to ask, but there was no time.

We had just closed the door to Isaac's house when the Germans appeared on the street. We were in such a rush to get inside the cellar that Isaac closed the floor latch poorly. By then it was too late to pull it shut; they were entering the house. But what our luck was—one of them jumped in through the window. And he landed on the floor latch, closing it all the way.

We heard them upstairs. "Come out, *Juden*, cheepi-cheepi." I wasn't breathing and clutched Sonya's hand. I could barely see, in the darkness, how many of us were edged into the cellar. A dozen, maybe. Isaac's wife, Shulamit, was next to me, holding their baby. Somebody wept into a fist.

When I heard the sound, my blood stopped. At first it was soft, colicky, like a whine, but then it got louder, pained. Shulamit covered her child's face with hers and began kissing its lips frantically to stop the noise. "Hush, *mein liebe*, hush, *ikh bet dir*, hush." I can hear her saying it now. She would have swallowed that child if she could. But the baby continued to bawl. It became quiet upstairs. For a moment, there was only one sound in the world.

By now, my eyes had adjusted to the dark, and I could see Sonya staring at Shulamit. It frightened me to see that look on her face, to see her capable of that look. I can't say how much of what happened next is because Sonya stared at Shulamit as only Sonya could stare. Would she have torn the child from Shulamit's bosom and done it herself if Shulamit hadn't? Maybe my eyes were merely playing tricks. Maybe I was so afraid that I imagined Sonya had something to do with it. I have never told this story to anyone, and I am telling it now only because Sonya is dead, as my parents—השם יקום—are dead. As all my friends are dead. I am the Last Mohican, as my grandchildren call me.

I didn't see Shulamit do it. She was right next to me, so I couldn't have missed it. I must have shut my eyes, unable to watch. When I opened them, the crying had stopped. Shulamit held a white square pillow over the child. It had stopped moving.

Eventually, the soldiers brought every pot crashing to the

floor and stormed out. When darkness fell, some of us crawled out to the small garden on the other side of the cellar and buried the child, Isaac scooping out the loam with his hands, his eyes blank. Shulamit didn't respond even to Isaac. She lost her mind. She survived the war, but she was never right in her mind again.

We ate from the garden for four days, beets and carrots, one meter away from the dead child. The garden kept us alive.

After four days, we peered outside. It was quiet. Everywhere, bodies. Both of the families who shared the house where my family lived had been killed. The pogrom had started during the workday, so Mother and Father had remained in the factory, hiding in a steel bunker. When they returned to our street and saw the murdered neighbors, my father fell on his knees, thinking his children were among them. Isaac walked to him, barely sentient, and touched his shoulder. "Yours are alive," he said.

They had to pull us out of the cellar by the armpits. I was embarrassed to need so much help. Somebody had given Father a liter of milk. In his hands, it was as white and clean as fresh snow. He gave it to me first as the boy, but I gave it to Sonya, though I couldn't look her in the eyes as I did. She drank from the bottle with the hunger of an animal. I hated her in that moment.

When she was finished, she looked at me and said: "We have to get out. It doesn't matter if we die doing it." The Germans were spreading stories that the Jews escaping from the ghetto were Nazi plants, infected with VD, so the partisans, who didn't exactly need help disliking Jews, were sometimes executing escaped ghetto inmates on sight. But if we were going to die, she said, we were going to die by a Russian hand, not a German. She would persuade Mother and Father as well.

I wanted to disagree, but listening to her also made me want to be more of a man. I had closed my eyes when Shulamit placed the pillow over her child, but I wouldn't close my eyes now. Whatever it took, we would escape.

–*9*–

Slava was at the office early on Monday, his only companion Mr. Grayson dipping his bow tie into a buttered bagel. He waved cheerfully at Slava.

When he heard Arianna arrive, he crawled above the divider. She looked up and smiled.

"We didn't talk yesterday," he said.

"I wasn't really around for yesterday," she said. "I went at it too hard on Saturday night. I got home at four? I slept till noon."

"Oh," he said. In his mind, Arianna had waited at home for him to be ready to see her again. He disparaged his callowness.

"What's the matter?" she said.

"Nothing, nothing," he rushed to say. They shared an awkward silence.

A cough sounded beside them. Avi Liss was standing by Slava's desk clutching a pile of printouts. "I'm sorry, lovebirds," he said. "May I speak? Layout wants to know if Sheila's going to let you cut the Vatican section. Then baseball can run long."

"Sheila's in the desert doing a detox," Arianna said matter-of-factly. "There's an infinity pool."

"I'm sure you know all about it," Avi said.

"They have this massage?" Arianna went on. "Six people work on you at the same time. *Twelve* hands."

"When you figure it out, just let them know directly?" Avi said.

"And Louboutin is opening a boutique there next fall," Arianna said. "Do you know, with the red sole?" She disappeared from view and lifted one of her heels above the divider, the sole demonically red. That was all you could see: the heel with its vanishing tip, the pale knob of the ankle, and the web of the toes pinched by the toe box. She was wearing a dress—anyone passing by Arianna's cubicle could get an eyeful.

Avi and Slava remained rooted in place, bovine. The heel disappeared and Arianna vaulted back into view.

"I have to go," Avi said hoarsely and stalked off.

Slava tried to tamp down the system-wide expansion in his groin. "What was that about?" he said, a little hoarse himself.

"Avi the Jew thinks I'm a JAP. I don't want to disabuse him." Her eyes flashed insolently. He was learning the meaning of her expressions. This one meant: I don't care, but I do. He felt a tweak of satisfaction at this penetration of her invincibility, then instantly felt guilty for it.

"Thanks for defending me," she winked.

Slava stared, dumbfounded. It hadn't occurred to him that she could require defending. She held her expression a moment, then laughed. She was joking.

Slava had spent Sunday translating his letter for Israel into Russian, so Israel could hear what Slava had written. "Well, you certainly don't know how to speak Russian," Israel said, "but it sounds like you might know what you're doing with English. It's beautiful. Who's the girl?"

"Your sister," Slava said. "So to speak."

"I'm saying who is the real-life model."

"No one," Slava said. "My imagination."

"She sounds fierce. Must be one of ours."

"She's not one of ours," Slava said.

"So it is someone!" Israel laughed. "Got you. Oh, you snot-nose. I can barely walk the block, but I can still run circles around you."

"There's an American expression, Israel: 'You get more by honey than vinegar.' Try it sometime."

"My God, you're a stiff berry. I hope you find an American girl, Slava. It's easier for you than it is for us, but it's hopeless for you all the same. But less so for your children, especially if you go with an American girl. And then your grandchildren won't even know where Minsk is, good riddance."

Slava acknowledged the lecture.

"So, did you talk to your grandmother?" Israel said. "It was her: staring at Shulamit, gulping the milk."

"In a way," Slava said.

"Next time you see her, say hello from me. You tell her that before that hooligan Yevgeny Gelman got his claws into her, she had another admirer on Karastoyanova. I wish you to find a woman like her, Slava."

"And what is that like?" Slava said.

"She wasn't an easy person. She held grudges for decades. People she didn't like? She minced no words. And she never did anything she didn't want to. But her heart was big. I've never met a woman who loved that way, and I include in that assessment my dear departed Raisa. There wasn't a false bone in your grandmother's body. For better and worse."

"That is the opposite of my grandfather," Slava said. "What did they see in each other?"

"Marriage is a mystery," Israel said. "In the end, logical explanation is impossible. Tolstoy was wrong: It's the happy families that are happy in all different ways, and the unhappy families that are unhappy in the same depressing, predictable fashion. It's a small miracle, every time, when two people can make one life."

"So it's out of your hands," Slava said.

"No, no," Israel said. "Quite the opposite. You have to work at it."

"Then I don't understand," Slava said.

"I am almost dead," Israel said, "and I still don't understand."

Throughout the day, Arianna a suddenly awkward presence on the other side of the divider, Slava glanced at the telephone, willing it to ring with Grandfather's number. By now he would know that Slava had written a letter for Israel. So, call. When you didn't want to hear from him, he found you, and when you did, he was mum.

Slava lifted the receiver, listened to the dial tone, returned it to the cradle. The phone looked like something Grandfather would appreciate: a spaceship console dressed up as a regular old touch-dial. Slava didn't know what function most of its buttons performed. Conference, transfer, something called ABS. Was that the button for phone records? His limited purview at the magazine was sufficiently served by one through nine. He snapped the phone out of its nest and bashed the buttons.

"How is he?" Slava asked Berta when she picked up.

"He talks at night," she said impassively.

"Saying what?"

"Negotiating, counting. I don't know. It's impolite to listen."

"I'm sorry it keeps you up," he said.

"It's my job," she said. "We honor our old people."

They stalled in an uncomfortable silence. After an eternity, Grandfather picked up the bedroom phone. "So?" he said. "Hello."

"Nothing. How are you?"

"The doctor says it's normal."

"What's normal?"

"Talking to God in your dreams after . . . you know. A passing. I wake up, I don't know what planet I'm on. It's like I have two bodies. Everything falls from my hands. Easy for him to say normal, he's not the one feeling it."

"I'm sure it's temporary," Slava said.

"That's what he said, 'temporary,'" Grandfather said. "As temporary as life or what? *Tfoo*, may these doctors get covered up to their heads. I heard you wrote something for Israel."

Slava smiled to himself. "I did," he said.

"That poor man. His wife—isn't. His son—the roof went on his head. Man has two valor medals, shrapnel in his body, and he lives alone in an underground cubbyhole. You can't compare his apartment with mine."

"Yes, he didn't pretend to be a vegetable," Slava said. "It's cozy, actually. Like *The Master and Margarita*." He mentioned the book as an alliance with Israel. His grandfather didn't read.

"I read the first and last page of that one. His apartment isn't as nice as this one. Look at the size of my kitchen."

"And you've got a woman cooking your meals. He heats soup from a can."

"Exactly."

"You live much better than he does."

"We do what we can, Slava, we do what we can."

"You're really clever and he's dumb," Slava said. He upbraided himself for his orneriness. Not practical if he was calling with a need. He had to think like Grandfather.

"I always tell him at the doctor's office, 'Let me help you think about these things.' But he doesn't have the mind for it, he says."

"You think he's telling the truth?" Slava said.

"Why wouldn't he be telling the truth?"

"Does everyone tell the truth?" Slava said.

"I do. I've got nothing to hide."

"Oh, I see," Slava said.

"Listen, a little birdie flew in here today," Grandfather said.

Slava brightened. Maybe he wouldn't have to ask.

"Said Vera Rudinsky is meeting some friends for dinner."

"Oh," he said, surprised to hear Vera's name. Since the funeral party, Arianna had filled his mind. "And what kind of bird was this?"

"The kind that knows what it needs to know. She wants you to meet them. The friends."

"She's a vulgarian," Slava said unconvincingly.

"She's not Bulgarian, she's one of us. That girl has an ass like a tomato. I saw the way you were looking at her—everyone saw. I'm not saying you have to marry her. Go spend an evening together. Do you know how to do that?"

"You're too depressed to go outside, you're playing matchmaker?"

"I get done what I need. So what, you called to ask how your grandfather is?"

"Why not?"

"Because I'm a couple of days older than you. You want another name."

"And what makes you think that?"

"Because you're my grandson," the old man said with satisfaction.

"And a grandson of yours—"

"Takes opportunity by the balls."

"What is the opportunity here?" Slava said. He didn't hear an answer and asked again.

"Helping people," Grandfather said.

"Your specialty," Slava said.

"Yes, my specialty," he mocked Slava. "Oh, hike up your skirt already. You're flirting a little too long. Do you want a name or not?"

Now Slava made him wait. "Yes," he said finally.

"Then why all the foreplay? Some of us have a limited time on earth. Go out with Vera tonight, I'll give you a name tomorrow. Just let me know if I have to call you at her apartment." He started laughing wickedly. "I was your age, she'd be old news already."

"I don't need you," Slava said without conviction. "I'll ask Israel. He'll give me names. Your neighborhood is full of people who want money for free."

"Do it," Grandfather said. "Just watch you don't say something to the wrong person."

"What's that supposed to mean?"

"I have to go, cucumber," Grandfather said.

"That's what Grandmother called me. Don't call me that."

"I'm sorry," he said, grave all of a sudden. They were quiet while they waited for the ill feeling to dissipate. It was impossible to escape each other. Other people could throw down the phone, move to another part of the country, change their names, but Grandfather and Slava were sealed to each other like a husband and wife. They were married in the old way, without release. They would be vicious toward each other, wait till the burn settled, start in on each other again. They were deathless.

"Your grandmother would have walked under a tank for you," Grandfather said. "And that's the kind of girl Vera is. One of ours. A girl who will think of you first. But no kind of stupid cow, either, painting her nails all day. She's got a salary, an apartment."

"Is it you're too proud to make peace yourself?"

"You don't know *anything*," Grandfather hissed. Slava saw the spittle flying from his gold teeth on the other end of the line. It was the face Grandfather had worn when he cut up that man in Minsk fifty years before, a face Slava had been sheltered from.

"Fine," Slava said. "Give me a name."

"What do you think, I'm a two-year-old?" Grandfather said, pleasant again. "Date first, name tomorrow. Good luck, Don Juan." And with that, he hung up.

Vera called shortly after Slava had hung up with Grandfather, as if Grand-
father had given a signal. The grandfather arranged it:

Slava's grandfather to Vera's grandfather: "He wants to go out with Vera
tonight, but can she call him? He doesn't want to impose."

Vera's grandfather to Vera: "Slava wants to join you, but this one's shy,
apparently. You have to ask him."

Vera to Slava: "What are you doing, Slava? Grandfather gave me your
number. I started telling my friends about our Italian adventures. They
want to meet you."

Vera wore an amber-colored leather jacket over a cowl-necked blouse
and jeans over black heels that narrowed to fine points. They clopped like
hooves down the steps of her apartment building. Her hair, swept up into
a wave captured mid-crash, and her eyelids, fatigued with ultramarine
shadow, sparkled with synonymous gloss, lending a wanton appearance to
a face that seemed still young and unformed.

"Where are we going?" he said. "You look nice."

"Thank you, Slava," she smiled. "Avenue I. By the banya."

"We can take the F," he said.

"No, no, taxi," she said. "Call, please?" She reached into her purse and
handed Slava a card. "Ask for Vova."

Vova was a former cruiserweight, the span of his hands nearly the size
of the steering wheel. A crew cut crowned the square of his head.

"Where tonight, Verochka?" he said when the young people were piled
into the backseat.

"Avenue I. Lara's," she said.

"I'll be taking you back?" Vova said.

"Yes, please."

"Just call when you're ready."

They rode in a festive silence, the streets slick after a brief, indecisive rain. "Your friend, does he speak?" Vova said finally.

"I'm sorry, Vovochka," Vera said. "It was rude not to introduce him. Tell Vova something about yourself, Slava."

"I work at a magazine," Slava croaked.

"One of ours?" Vova inquired. "A fitness magazine?"

"An American one," Vera said proudly.

"An American one!" Vova smacked his lips. "Important people in the car, it turns out. That gives you enough bread, working at a magazine?"

"I'm thinking about driving a taxi," Slava said. He hated these Russian men whose kingdoms were the size of their taxicabs.

Vera elbowed Slava and gave him a cold look. With shame, he remembered that her father drove a taxicab. However, his comment had the intended effect of diminishing the cruiserweight's interest in further conversation.

They pulled up at a building that looked just like Grandfather's—brick, an arched entryway wearing too many layers of paint. Slava hadn't realized young Russian people continued to live in these neighborhoods even though they were old enough to live wherever they wanted. They sat in the car until Slava realized he would be paying. "And how much?" he inquired.

"Ten," Vova sighed.

Slava was about to pass thirteen dollars to the front seat when Vera's eyes sent out an ultramarine blast of distress. Her hand reached into his wallet and removed another five. Speechless, Slava passed eighteen dollars to the front seat.

"He takes care of me," she said vaguely as they walked into the fluorescent embrace of her friend's building.

The guests were in their midtwenties, everyone paired up, and they spoke Russian, normally distressing to Slava, but his had been receiving an unfamiliar workout in recent weeks. Slava stood to the side while Vera exchanged elaborate, lippy greetings with her friend Lara and Lara's boyfriend, Stas.

"Everyone?" Vera said, taking Slava by the arm and walking him into the living room. His discomfort retreated slightly, her hand warm and familiar. "This is Slava. Slava is a writer." The assembled brayed in admiration. "He works at the best American magazine."

"*Playboy*?" said a potbellied young man in a blazer. The other boys laughed. The girl whose arm was entwined with his laid a free fist into his gut.

"That's Leonard and his Galochka," Vera said. "Leonard is our resident literario. You guys will have something to talk about. That's Lyova, that's Oslik. Everyone, introduce yourselves and make Slava feel at home, please. Girls, let's go set the table."

His girlfriend rising, Leonard shook his poetic curls and patted the freshly vacated seat next to him. There were half a dozen boys altogether, drinks in their hands.

"What are you drinking?" Leonard inquired.

"Vodka?" Slava proposed.

"Incorrect!" Leonard announced, and the boys squealed with laughter. He was their ringleader, by the look of things. Each of their glasses held a caramel-colored liquid. "Galina Mikhailovna, my dove!" Leonard called out toward the kitchen, using his girlfriend's patronymic, the way wives and husbands did in the old times.

Galochka, who was setting a plate of herring in oil on a lacy tablecloth, looked up. The girls were working with daunting facility. One was setting the table with gold-rimmed plates, another following with filigreed thimbles, and a third unloading bowls of salad Olivier and boiled potatoes. Slava wished he could be in their circle instead. Vera caught his eyes and mouthed, Everything okay? Embarrassed, Slava nodded.

"Dove, get our guest a glass of cognac, would you?" Leonard bleated.

"I'll take care of it," Vera whispered to Galochka, and moved to open one of the bottles.

"So what kind of writer are you?" Leonard turned back to Slava. "I read a lot. Unlike the rest of these knuckleheads. John Grisham, James Patterson. Suze Orman is very good. Last year, I read *The Count of Monte Cristo.*"

The rest of the boys nodded reverently.

"Why do they call you Oslik?" Slava said tentatively to a skinny boy in jeans and a sweatshirt. "Oslik" meant "donkey."

"Oslik?" Leonard answered for him, grinning. "Oslik!" he said, and brayed. "Why do we call you Oslik?"

"I don't have an elevator in my building," Oslik said, sniggering. "We came back from shopping one day and had to carry it all the way to the fifth floor."

"Like a donkey!" Leonard said.

Oslik laughed with everyone else.

"If Oslik thinks I am going to marry him in these conditions," said a short, bulbous girl who was helping to set the table, "he's severely mistaken." Everyone laughed again.

"Boys!" Vera shouted. "Positions, please! The table's almost ready. Leonard, please pour? Girls, who's drinking what? Vodka for me."

While everyone was trooping toward the table, Slava's cell phone rang. He had opened it by the time he realized he shouldn't have: It would be Grandfather requesting an update. He'd stand over you counting thrusts if you let him.

"Hey," Arianna said. "You're somewhere."

Slava froze. After too long without speaking, he dashed to a corner of the living room. "Funeral," he blurted out.

"What?" she said.

"The shiva?" He worked with what he had given himself. "We're trying it out. Like you said."

"Oh—okay. It's only the seven days after— Oh, it doesn't matter. Good for you. Okay, no problem. I'm sorry to interrupt. Tell everyone my condolences. From your work friend." She laughed quietly.

"But what was it?" Slava said. Looking up, he saw Vera observing him skeptically. He realized he was wedging himself into a corner, his hand covering the phone. He straightened, as if talking to no one other than Grandfather.

"A club, a band," she said. "No big deal."

"That works well for us," Slava said, trying to sound casual.

"Sla-va! Everything's ready," Vera shouted in English. Several people behind her whooped, laughter following. Slava looked at her hatefully.

A long, stinging pause on the other end. Then Arianna said: "I should run."

"Hold on—"

"I'll see you on Monday, okay?" she said, and hung up.

Slava cursed himself. Then Vera. Then himself. Vera called for him again.

When everyone had sat down and the thimbles had been filled by Leonard's pink hand, Vera raised her glass.

"The hosts, Verochka, are supposed to raise the first glass," Leonard said.

"Leonard," Lara hissed. "You know I don't mind. Vera is like a sister."

"Thank you, Larochka," Vera said. "This one's been reading *The Count of Monte Cristo* too much, with his table etiquette." Everyone laughed as Leonard frowned, and Slava understood that Vera was the only person at the table permitted to contradict him. "I would like to welcome Slava to our table," Vera went on in Russian. "And I would like to say a word in honor of Slava's grandmother, who passed away a week ago. A proud woman and a strong woman. I remember her from when I was a little girl. She was so kind, but you never messed with her!"

Again, the table laughed. Oslik slapped the table. "For grandmothers!" he announced.

"Babushka, oh, babushka," Leonard recited with cautious dreaminess. His tone meant that the words were coming from a poem. He was hoping to regain the upper hand of the conversation. Everyone turned to him, but he couldn't recall the remainder of the lines. "Something, something!" he rescued himself, and everyone laughed.

"Slava, what's it like to be at a Russian table?" Vera said as everyone drank. "Different from your American friends?"

"It's very intimate," Slava said, hoping that he was providing the response she wanted.

Everyone burst into hysterical laughter, Leonard's eyes gleaming with his now indisputable restoration to the crown of the male pyramid. Vera laid a hand on Slava's arm. Slava felt her breath on the edge of his earlobe. "*Intimno* is for the bedroom only," she said in Russian. "At a table like this, you say it's very warm, or close."

Slava bulged his eyes for the benefit of the group. The laughter redoubled. Then Slava laid a hand on Leonard's forearm and made flirty eyes. Oslik was so gratified that he had to pull his chair back from the table so he could double over.

"To Slava!" Oslik said. "To Slava!" all of them echoed, even Leonard, slapping Slava's back so hard that Slava nearly spat out a piece of herring.

"So we were promised stories about Italy," Lara said after everyone had settled down.

"Let's eat," Slava tried to encourage everyone.

"Come on!"

"The bourgeois look to the past and the proletariat looks to the future," Slava said, thinking a Soviet slogan might divert them, but he bungled part of it.

"I remember," Vera said in Russian, looking at Slava, "Slava's family had finally been called to the consul. For the interview if you were going to be let into America. And nobody speaks one drop of English. But you can't have a seven-year-old boy answering. So they all stumble how they can, and then the consul asks, 'Why do you want to go to America?'" She said this last part in English. "And nobody understands him. Moments like this—I mean, you know—enough to kill the application. Because they are rejecting people already by this time. Go to Israel, they say.

"And Slava understands, but how can he answer? So he says, 'I want to meet my aunt Frida.' And the consul laughs. And everyone laughs. And meanwhile, his mother or father—who was it, Slava?—understands. Because they practiced this answer, you know. 'Why do you want to emigrate to America?' *Svoboda*. And how do you say *svoboda*?"

"Freedom!" the table shouted.

"How do you remember the word?"

"Aunt Frida!" the table shouted as one.

"And so after Slava said 'Aunt Frida,' one of them remembered and said, 'Freedom.' And they passed. You can say that without him, his family wouldn't be here." She beamed proudly.

The table whooped and rocked with applause. "To Slava!" Oslik whooped. "To Slava!" everyone shouted. Slava gave in and smiled sheepishly. Thimbles knocked his, splashing cognac onto his wrist, palms kneaded his shoulders, and Leonard launched into the "Marseillaise." Next to him, Vera shone with a thousand lights.

Three hours later, a final piece of herring gleaming undesirably in a small lake of oil and a pack's worth of cigarettes crushed into a porcelain ashtray, the group had switched positions. The boys were at the table, finishing the cognac, and the girls were smoking on the couch. Leonard's blazer clung limply to the back of his chair. He had unbuttoned the upper two buttons of his shirt and hung his arm across Slava's shoulder, as if the two of them had served under Kharkov together. Now and then Slava heard his name in the circle of girls and peered over Leonard's Pushkinian curls to make out what was being said. It was difficult because Leonard was breathing heavily into his temple. Slava looked at Vera, who looked at him, as if she came equipped with a device that alerted her every time he wanted her attention. She nodded and smiled.

Leonard's girlfriend, Galochka, wandered over to Leonard and Slava.

"Popochka," she said to Leonard. Little butt. "You're done eating?" She wedged herself into his lap, eliciting a grunt. "I'm going to feed you until your belly is so big no other woman will want you. And then you'll be all mine."

Leonard turned to Slava. "Who said women don't speak directly?" He turned to Galochka: "Dove, please, we're speaking." Galochka pecked Leonard's forehead and removed herself to the couch.

"How long have you been together?" Slava asked, to ask something.

"I don't know," Leonard said, squinting with overfed eyes at the clock. "Our parents have medical offices next to each other."

"I see," Slava said. Leonard downed two fingers of cognac and gazed contemplatively at the wall. "What specialty?" Slava said dutifully.

"Gastro?" Leonard said absentmindedly. "Mine are gastro, hers are feet. You and Vera?"

"We just met again," Slava said.

"She's special," Leonard said.

"That's what everyone says," Slava said. "We haven't really spoken. She clears my plate and runs off."

Leonard tried to focus on Slava through the drink in his eyes. "She doesn't want to interrupt."

"What, this?" Slava said.

"You know what?" Leonard said. "You're okay, Slava. You know why?" He stuck out his fingers—Slava was startled by the gold band on his left hand; he and Galina couldn't be over twenty-five, but they were married—and counted. "One, you don't run your mouth. You observe. It's a gift. People talk too much. They like to hear themselves talk. And two, when Vera said famous Slava was coming, I'll be honest—I'm drunk, so I'm honest—I thought, This guy is going to be a fucking prick. And you are a prick, a little bit. You think you are better than us. But you're all right. I like you."

Despite himself, Slava smiled. Leonard—sloping belly, puffy fingers, the face starting to line—was already a little version of the man he would be in thirty years, to him an achievement. Some questions—America, but a distinctly Russian America; Galina; the medical office he would inherit from his parents—he had answered and would never have to be asked again.

"You're a charming prick, too," Slava said.

"Good." Leonard's face broadened in pleasure. "Let's drink to our women." He reached for the bottle again.

"Galina is driving?" Slava said.

Leonard brought a finger to his lips and winked. Then his teeth closed around the bottle stopper. He extracted it with his mouth and spat it across the table.

"You savage!" Galina shouted from across the room. "I'm not taking you to the dentist when you ruin your teeth."

"Get up, get up," Leonard counseled Slava, a bottle in one hand and a Slava in the other. Everyone looked up from their positions. Leonard made eyes at Oslik, who immediately sprang from his seat and dashed for the stereo. A Russian pop song emerged from the speakers. "Opa!" Leonard shouted, swigged from the bottle, and gave it to Slava, who held it at his side. "Drink, drink," Leonard insisted quietly, pulling Slava, whose right arm now rested around Leonard's haunch, to an unoccupied part of the living room.

"The lilac fog," the crooner sang, "sails above our heads." Slava watched one of Leonard's trousered, loafered feet kick the air, the keys in his pocket producing a businesslike jingle and his center of gravity immigrating position until Slava was nearly embracing him from behind. "I love this song!" Oslik's bulb-girlfriend shrieked. Leonard's leg returned to the floor and he turned to look at Slava: *"Nu?"* Obediently, Slava kicked up his left leg. "Attaboy!" Leonard roared, rubbing Slava's head to indicate admiration for his balance despite his having consumed nearly as much cognac as Leonard.

By now the chorus was up—"Conductor, please don't rush / Can't you understand / I'm saying goodbye / To her forever"—the entire room shouting in unison and swaying in place. Leonard's turn: He kicked up his right leg. Slava kicked up his right leg. Leonard swigged, Slava swigged. They went around the living room, the others singing and yelling. Slava must have revealed an unforeseen aptitude for the primary maneuver, because soon he was alone in the middle of the living room, Leonard seeking respite in Galina's arms and pushing Vera out onto the dance floor. "Ve-ra! Ve-ra!" the crowd chanted, dividing her name into the syllables that Slava had mouthed so many times as a boy. The room swimming, he summoned her with an open hand. Rolling her eyes, she rose to join him, swirling and twirling, demurely coquettish, as he kicked and sprang. They hadn't planned, but somehow they fit together. Grandfather's tutelage, so useless at Bar Kabul, directed his arms and legs, and she—she danced on heels as if on bare feet, though after a while she kicked them off to applause. Finally, the song ended and they collapsed on the carpet. The room thundered, feet stamping the floor.

After they were done, everyone wanted to try it, the dining table pulled back and the carpet rolled up until the living room resembled a dance floor. "Tomorrow the people downstairs are going to have my head." Lara shook her head. "Take this down, apologize, and everything will be okay," Vera said, holding up an unopened bottle of cognac. "See what we started?" Leonard slurred to Slava even though he was buried in Galina's considerable bosom. Slava walked up to Leonard's slumped form and laid a wet kiss on his cheek. "Oh, Galinochka, you frisky, frisky . . ." Leonard mumbled, and everyone burst out laughing. They danced until the clock showed midnight.

Downstairs, waiting with Vera for the cruiserweight's taxi in the stifling air of the street, Slava bristled with a child's excitement. He repeated a maneuver from their pas de deux.

She smiled. "I'm happy you're happy," she said. He toed the curb, recalling the evening, and laughed to himself. "So, listen," she said. "I have an idea for how to get them together." She had switched back to English.

"Who?" he blinked.

"Our parents."

"Ve-ra!" he said, trying to be playful. "Let it be. It's not our business. They're grown-ups."

She shrugged and looked away, disappointed. "I told my mother we talked."

"Was she angry?" Slava said.

"No, she was happy," she said. "She can't do it herself, but if I do it, it's okay. We are too small here to divide from argument. Did I say that right?"

"Sure."

"You speak like an American, like you were born here."

"We came here at the same age," he said.

"But I stayed in Brooklyn. I speak Russian most of the day. Sometimes full days with no English. In Italy, my parents always wanted me to play with you. Slava is a good boy, he studies his translation book. You run away and I stay, and my parents still always say: Why you can't be more like Slava?"

Slava's excitement was emptying into the overheated air. There was a honk, and a second later, Vova skirted the curb with a flourish. Slava, until now no ally of the cruiserweight, felt a tremor of gratitude.

"How was it?" Vova asked cheerfully when the young pair was once again lodged in his rearview mirror.

"Very nice," Vera said quietly.

"And where is my care package from the table?" Vova said flirtatiously. Slava wanted to brain him.

"Oh my God, I am so embarrassed," Vera said, covering her mouth. "And it was a good table. Lara's mom was by earlier and cooked everything. Let me go upstairs."

Vova peeled off before his martyrdom could be compromised. They rode the rest of the way in a merciful silence. Slava thought of Arianna. Despite having been overcome with guilt after she called, he hadn't thought of her again all evening. Only a week had passed since Bar Kabul—he couldn't see friends one night? Then why did he lie about where he was? He moaned in annoyance, raising a look from Vera. "Nothing, nothing," he said.

"That's it, my doll," Vova said when they'd pulled up at the curb of Vera's building. Vova and Slava caught each other's eyes in the rearview mirror and surged into action at the same time. Vera was seated next to Slava in the back, on the other side of the sedan from Vova, so the gentlemen started out even. The driver door (Vova) and the rear left (Slava) opened at the same time, the two of them emerging to circle the vehicle— Vova around the hood, Slava around the trunk—in order to open Vera's door. They arrived at the same time. Vova lowered his head with a taunting smirk, acknowledging defeat.

"Thank you, Slava," Vera said, her lips on his cheek. "Very nice evening. Did you have a good time?" Her drawn face indicated that she didn't expect a reply. She set off down the rain-slicked flagstone leading to her entrance. Slava felt as if he should run after her and apologize, but for what? Vova, next to him, glared like a lunatic brother of the groom. As Vera entered the foyer, she waved. Like a pair in a musical, Vova and Slava waved back. The neighborhood floated in an unearthly quiet.

"Get in," Vova said.

"No, I'll walk," Slava said. "I'll pay, of course."

"Get in, get in, paramour," Vova said. "You need the train for Manhattan, right? At this hour, you need the Q. Let's go." Pathetically, Slava obeyed.

"Quite a performance, Romeo," Vova said when they were inside the car. Perhaps he had insisted on driving him, Slava thought, so he could torment him all the way to the subway station. "Don't feel bad," Vova went on. "With a girl like that, it won't happen the first time. The parents have to meet you, that whole dance. Mama has to give the green light."

"You are speaking from firsthand experience?" Slava said.

Vova studied Slava in the rearview. "I am trying to help you, Casanova," he said. "It helps if there's competition. Wakes them up a little."

"I really appreciate it," Slava said.

"Don't sweat it," he said. "We're just speaking here, like men."

A light rain returned to streak the windows of the taxi. Slava stared at the empty streets of neighborhoods he had not seen in years. He had been wrong about it all looking the same. Here things changed, too, just more imperceptibly. He wondered if Arianna had gone to her club by herself. He saw her hair whipping around her shoulders as she danced to the Little Darlings. He thought briefly about taking Vova's taxi all the way to the Upper West Side, but he couldn't do that now, with Vera's perfume all over him.

Extracting himself from Vova's taxi at the Q station, Slava gave him eight dollars above the owed total. They shook hands through the window, Slava's palm like a peanut in Vova's tonnish maw. "Fear not, *chuvak*!" Vova said, and cleared a pellet of snot onto the pavement. "We're on the same side." And with that, he drove off.

–10–

AUGUST 2006

Even in frailty and mourning, Grandfather performed. After a couple of days, Slava gave up trying to understand, to map and figure the links. Within forty-eight hours, he had calls from a Bukharan Jew named Lev, who had never gone west of Kazakhstan, let alone Nazi-held territory; a young woman who wanted Slava to take down the story of her father, a procurement official in the Soviet Ministry of Forests; a pensioner from Perm who began with a complaint about a willful granddaughter (who, by the way, was single); and a couple from Bashkiria who wanted Slava to know that the Soviet government had created a special home for Soviet Jews in the Far East, where they had visited twice in their capacities as poet laureate of Ufa (he) and the editor of the literary magazine *Kalibr* (she). Slava said yes to almost everyone. He drew the line at one grandmother who wanted a letter to President Bush requesting a larger apartment, and an old man who simply needed a ride to the supermarket. Everyone else, he took.

In their stories, his grandmother went to clear the rubble from bomb damage. She patched up German army uniforms, her fingers avoiding those two hideous thunderbolts. She boiled syringes at the hospital. She revealed herself as a strong-headed young woman. Not very good in school. Obedient. Liked clothes. Lucky that her father was a tailor. Slava watched her savor a piece of dark bread with sunflower oil.

With a hill of unfolded newspapers and magazines on his desk concealing his stack of history books, he watched the office clock crawl with impossible slowness. When the clock hands agreed on six P.M. and Arianna left for uptown, thinking he was staying to work, he ran to the Brooklyn-bound subways. He became a connoisseur of dispatcher accents, the various types of train lurches and grunts, bodega banners, night skies, and Brooklyn's regional humor.

To Lev the Bukharan Jew, he gave Irvin's broken English. ("Camp wall was like giant, bigger than tree. Climb was if you wanted sueycide, and nobody who say nice Polish girl from village give food hush-hush over wall is saying accurate. Wall was impossible. And there was not being nice Polish girls.") The forestry official, ever the Soviet bureaucrat, appended to his claim letter a list of newspaper clippings and maps. He took an academician's pleasure in pointing out that the wild forests of western Belarus and eastern Poland where the partisans hid and that the Germans themselves feared to enter—Perelaz, Zabielowo, Chrapiniewo, Lipiczanska, Jasinowo, Nalibocka, even their names impenetrable—were such inaccessible refuges for those bent on sedition that, after the war, the Soviets turned forestry management into a branch of state security.

On the way to the evening's home from the subway, Slava would stop at a Russian bakery and buy marzipans, chocolates, a round babka, sometimes a bottle. At the store—Net Cost, Smart Cost, Low Cost—he liked when the cashier line was long. The dishes were cooling on the dinner table of the apartment where he was due, but a sin to come empty-handed, and more important, he sneaked a whiff of the old neighborhood in the name of research. He eavesdropped on the conversations in line, Ukrainian if the g's were uttered like h's, Georgian if they emphasized the wrong vowel.

These unlike people had been tossed together like salad by the cupidity of the Soviet government, and now, in America, they were forced to keep speaking Russian, their sole bond, if they wanted to understand each other, and they did, because a Ukrainian's hate of a Russian was still warmer than his love of an American. The brethren who had remained in the old world had moved forward in history—they were now citizens of independent countries, their native languages withdrawn from under the rug, buffed, spit-shined, returned to first place, but here in Brooklyn, they were stuck forever in Soviet times. They had gotten marooned on a new island except for what their children would do. Judging by Vera and her friends, the children would not do very differently.

Sometimes, wandering Bensonhurst, Midwood, Brighton, Slava counted how far she was. She bred confused feelings inside him. At seven, she had been like a sister, but now she was a woman, and though he was ashamed at the feeling—to compare Las Vegas with Italy!—he couldn't think of her without a special recognition filling his chest. So she hung in the back of his thoughts like a pale moon, neither there nor not there. Every time his grandfather was about to give him a new name and address, like a dealer feeding his junkie, Slava held his breath, wondering if the name would be Vera's, also wishing it wouldn't be hers—just as his grandfather could not bring himself to charge a Rudinsky interest, Slava would not dare take a Rudinsky only to bed. The reason why eluded him, and he scratched at it as if at a bump of paint on a wall. Was it something psychological?—she was his lost childhood . . . He would stop himself there: Removed from his elders or not, like them, he had no patience for psychology talk.

Having arrived at that evening's home, Slava would be feted and fed, interrogated about his romantic situation (its inconclusiveness was then mourned over), and bitched to about his grandfather. He would steer the conversation back to the war, the endless war. The assembled—the families before him appeared in full—sat before him as before a judge, the children grasping the mottled hands of the old ones while listening to stories they never had the temerity to prod for themselves. The American dollar would force out the stories that love and consideration had elected not to elicit. Slava, working in concert with the philosophy of the nation that had taken them in—good works as the by-product of self-interest—was able to give the descendants at the table, the children and grandchildren, the gift of knowing, at last, the unknown corners of their forebears, all because the forebears stood to make money. How cheaply they fell—the heart's greatest terrors for a bushel of euros. Slava wasn't a judge: He was a middleman, a loan shark, an alchemist—he turned lies into facts, words into money, silence into knowledge at last.

Arianna had spoken of New York as a secret in her first months here. Now Slava had one of his own. It was a demotic secret. It didn't concern a glorious city. The sharers of his secret were ugly and without taste, uninitiated and crude. Lumpy and bowed, foul-breathed, colored like eggplants, hairy and hairless. But he was writing every night—for a publication no one would see, a readership of no more than a handful, whomever the Claims Conference used to evaluate applications. But the knowledge that someone, *somewhere*, at a time unknown to him (Slava was brushing his teeth, or sitting on the toilet, or absentmindedly heating his lunch), was reading something he had written was erotic to him. Yes, it gave him arousal. He thought of Beau and Arch Dyson with indifference. So what if they didn't know; *he* knew. Every word he put down, every letter he finished, he imagined walking into their offices and dropping them in a pile at their feet. He notched every letter—#7, #11, #20—like a don juan women on his bedpost.

The families didn't want to let him go. They begged him to stay long after the work was finished. Ordinarily martyrs—a rain had soaked only their clothesline, the wafers increased in cost only at the store where they bought—finally they had been authorized (no, required) to speak, which lowered their guard and left them hollering recklessly, as if there were not inquiring neighbors one wall over. It fell to Slava—half listening to what those gathered around him had actually gone through during the war so that he could pillage it later for the oddly specific details he had come to learn made a narrative feel *authentic*—to make sure the windows were closed, and once he even tapped on a wall to test its thickness.

One night, returning to the Manhattan-bound subway from the Dolins in Gravesend (stuffed carp, herring under a fur coat, meat under aspic), Slava sensed that he was being followed. At first he brushed off the suspicion, but no, it was happening. Every turn he took, the leather jacket took with him. Slava took an unnecessary turn; so did the leather jacket. There was no one else on the late street, only televisions flickering behind curtains and the baths at Neck Road sending out steam from the vents. Slava couldn't turn around and get a fair look without making himself obvious. His heart beat unhappily. He'd known this would happen, except it hadn't happened, so maybe it wouldn't. The map of those apartments for which he had written letters—they were dots in a sea of letterless souls, souls who wanted to know what 4C was getting and why. But why would he be followed *to* the subway instead of from? Wouldn't they want to know whose house he was going to?

Finally, turning a needless corner, Slava ventured a peek. It was a boy, all of eighteen. Startled, Slava stopped without planning to, giving himself away. The boy stopped, too. They watched each other from half a block away, Slava's fingers losing circulation from the bags of food with which he was always sent home, which he had to dump in some sufficiently distant garbage can because he couldn't very well bring them to Arianna's, though it broke his heart to throw out food. Not knowing his own plan, Slava spun on his heel and began to march toward the boy.

The boy didn't run. Slava stopped three feet away. In the dim light, he saw a fuzz bristling above the young lips. The boy's hands were stuffed into the jacket—what did he hold there?

"What do you want?" Slava barked in Russian.

The boy leaped back. He didn't expect Russian. He hesitated.

Slava cocked his head, demanding an answer. He felt a heady lack of uncertainty. Let them come at me, he thought. But then his sense returned. His pursuer would be an eighteen-year-old boy?

"What is it?" Slava said warily.

"Do you write the letters?" the boy said.

"Says who," Slava said.

"Down the hallway," he said. "They said you were coming."

Slava cursed the Dolins under his breath. When it came to their own secrets, a crowbar wouldn't do it, but in other situations, they were guileless as schoolchildren.

"What is this, a bribe?" Slava said. "You don't have proof." He tried to manufacture a sneer but didn't believe himself. One didn't need proof to at least call the Claims Conference.

"A bribe?" the boy said, worried. "What for?"

"It doesn't matter," Slava said quickly.

The boy looked around and reached into the back pocket of his jeans. Slava stiffened, which only increased the boy's nervousness. He strode toward Slava and thrust a stapled printout, folded in half, into his free hand.

Oleg Smeshko, the title page said. Slava flipped through the rest—twenty pages or so. The font was large and baroque. Slava saw a sentence he did not like: "His brain thought it would explode." Then something with more promise: "The smoke curled from his cigarette like silver panty hose."

"Can you read it?" Oleg said, studying the pavement.

"You wrote this?" Slava said.

Oleg nodded.

"Why didn't you just knock on the door when I was there?" Slava said.

"They would tell my parents," Oleg said. He rubbed a sleeve under his nose.

Slava looked again at the story. The bags in his other hand were a stone, though they produced a not unpleasant scent: rolls, chicken, pickles. It would all go in the trash. "You're not hungry, are you?" Slava said.

"Hungry?" Oleg said, blinking. "I can eat at home."

"Let's sit down," Slava said.

Oleg looked around. "Where?"

"On the curb." Slava pointed. "Are they going to wonder where you are?"

"No, they think I went to my friend's."

"Have you called the friend and told him to cover for you?"

Oleg frowned and shook his head.

"Here," Slava extended his cell phone.

While Oleg dialed, Slava sat down on the edge of the pavement and looked at the story. "Expensive Trips Nowhere" was the title; that could stay. Slava wrenched a scallion roll from one of his bags, a pickle from a plastic container, then a shred of chicken, stuffed it all together, and handed it to Oleg when he got off the phone.

"You're not eating?" Oleg said.

"Not for several days," Slava said. "They kill your body with this food. I was five pounds less before I started—you know."

"Is it hard?" Oleg said, biting cautiously.

Slava looked over at him. "The letters? It's hard to figure out what to write. But the writing makes up for it."

"Do you get paid?" Oleg said, chewing.

"Paid?" Slava said. "No."

"Then why do you do it?"

Slava laughed and said nothing. They sat watching the street, the occasional car blazing by, leaving the echo of Russian songs in the air. Two elderly men in house slippers shuffled past, arm in arm, evening walk. "They'll freeze off their balls sitting on the pavement like that," one said to the other as they passed.

"What's the story about?" Slava said. He pointed at the bags. Oleg nodded, and Slava started making another roll.

"It's this chip that goes in your head," Oleg said. His large black eyes became larger. "It's a trip you can take wherever you want. Another country, another planet. In your mind, I mean—it's like you're really there, and when you get back, you have the memory of being there. Without your body ever going there, you understand?" Slava nodded. "Do you understand?" Oleg repeated.

"I understand, I understand," Slava said.

"But this guy gets stuck," Oleg went on. "And it's about him trying to get back to earth."

"Like Odysseus," Slava observed. This drew no recognition from Oleg. "And what happens? He gets home?"

Oleg gave Slava a wolfish grin, bit into his new roll, and said, "You have to read it!"

Slava nodded admiringly. He liked sitting there—the day had lost some of its heat; he was not expected anywhere; he was briefly invisible.

Oleg stopped chewing. "Can I read one?" he said. "A letter."

Slava looked over. "Sure. You just have to keep it between us."

"I promise," Oleg said, his eyes full of seriousness, then stuck out his hand, and Slava took it. The skin was moist, a newborn's.

"If you get good grades," Slava said, "your parents won't bother you about your stories."

Oleg nodded gloomily.

"You'll go to college, won't you?" Slava said.

"I'm just going to Brooklyn College."

"Go farther."

"With what money?"

Slava tossed into the roadway a fleck of pavement he had been working loose with his nail. "Write a letter," he said. "That'll be enough for a semester somewhere. You can figure out the rest."

"My grandparents don't qualify," Oleg said. "We're not even Jews."

The Dolins had conveniently neglected to share that they were having theirs made up, at least that.

"In this letter, you can be whatever you want," Slava said cautiously.

Oleg, his face darkened with doubt, nodded. If Slava said to stop eating, return home immediately, and confess to his parents that the practical person they were grooming was cuckolding their plans, Oleg would have done it. So this was what it was like to have a younger brother.

Slava brought the papers to Oleg's eyes. "You see this?" he said. " 'Curled from his cigarette like silver panty hose'? Change 'panty hose' to 'stocking.' Isn't that better?"

Oleg nodded.

"You don't have to agree because I said so," Slava said. "Is it better?"

Oleg nodded again. "Why?"

"I don't know," Slava said. "It just is. Better yet: 'A stocking of smoke curled from his cigarette.' Okay, finish this sentence: 'The heat hangs in the air like a—.' "

"Like a stocking," Oleg said obediently.

"No, no, something new. Cigarette smoke curls like a stocking; heat doesn't look like a stocking. It doesn't look like anything. It's invisible, but it won't go away."

"The heat hangs in the air like a bad thought," Oleg said.

Slava clapped him on the back. "You see?"

The boy smiled diffidently.

*During this period, Slava continued to finish his nights at 322 West Nineti-*eth Street. Arianna didn't volunteer to spend the night at his apartment, and though he occasionally reminded her of the unfairness of this arrangement, in truth he had come to prefer her apartment, only that his refrigerator was full, as Slava had to economize on lunch, and hers was congenitally empty. She ate only takeout, Slava parting with more cash in a night together than on his own in a week, though he didn't bring this up to Arianna, and she never seemed to think of it.

The rest of her apartment, however, was filled with irrefutable evidence of human habitation. None of it was plain—even the wooden lattice that the original builders had installed to give the studio the sense of a one-bedroom; Arianna had painted it white and carved the tops into the crown of a skyline. Then she dotted the panes with black marker all the way down to the floor—windows. "This is what I do when I veg," she explained. "I like to think about what's going on in the windows. What's going on in this window?" Her nail tapped a black dot. "They're arguing," she answered herself.

She loved the city. It made her quiet—her words—an inconceivable idea to Slava because it was so incredibly noisy, though it was this comment by her that made him notice, returning late from Brooklyn one Sunday night, the stone prairie into which the Upper West Side turned at that hour, the bright vitrines gleaming madly for no one. New York gets weary, and New York does sleep. She returned to Brentwood twice a year: Passover and Rosh Hashanah. She couldn't bear it any more frequently—its empty streets made her too lonely, refilled her with the uncomfortable noise of her childhood and youth. Even though she had lived in New York for seven years and knew the parts of it that she wanted to know—she rarely left Manhattan—she continued the introductory walks she had taken as a new arrival.

He envied her love of New York, a feeling he had never experienced for it, or any place, having left Minsk too soon to have any feelings about it save for an unfocused dread of bodily harm due to his being a Jew and the magic scent of the lilac bushes that clotted the yard. Perhaps that was why he didn't mind coming to her, he would reason as he lay in bed next to her, she long asleep. In the small space of her home, the cat darting around like a fiend, the television on to no discernible purpose except to vanquish the silence, he could draw off the sense of home she felt in the city, the way poor people in poor countries got light by siphoning from the municipal wires. He never spoke about this to her. He was resentful to a degree; it wasn't as if she was born there. She was an émigré, too, of sorts. But her relocation was to a place that was meant for her all along—somehow she had sniffed out the right destination all the way from Los Angeles. Slava had neither liked nor disliked the place he was born. He noticed it as a trout notices water. He understood that he was in some *place* only when he was let out at JFK. And this place he hadn't chosen, the way Arianna had chosen New York. Did that mean he had to keep looking? But he couldn't smell what place was right for him. Instead of exhausting him into sleep, this pinballing forced an ever wearier wakefulness, and many mornings he woke blearily tired.

The only thing that Slava preferred back on his side of the island was its river. Sometimes, before heading to work, he would take a detour and head across the park before heading downtown to the office. Across this river, if you kept going past Queens and Long Island, eventually, you would come to Europe and then, a little beyond it, Slava's Minsk. Was it any more his by now than New York? Over there, he would be finished with army ser- vice by now, probably married, probably a child, probably two. Would Grandmother still be alive in this replacement life? he wondered. Maybe the blood from transfusions went bad only if you took it outside of the Soviet Union. Maybe the blood didn't work anywhere else.

Arianna had asked once what he was working on all those evenings at the office. Trying to look her in the eyes, he said he didn't want to say that much about it, would that be all right? It was a family story but unformed, and he didn't want to jinx it. She nodded and ran a hand down his cheek. She never asked the question again. He burned with guilt mixed with sat- isfaction at the mastery of the lie: He had looked her in the eyes, asked her permission not to explain, ostensibly left it in her hands; of course she would do what he asked. He had thought hewing as close to the truth as the lie could afford—a family story—would lessen his burden, but it increased, as if he were teasing her without her knowing.

If ever Slava returned from Brooklyn before she was asleep, their late dinner together often ended with her heading out for a short walk. "To where?" he would say. "I just got here." She never reminded him that she had spent hours waiting for him. "Just a little one," she would say with a smile, and off she would go, her head already in the street. She would return a half hour later, coffee in hand—it didn't keep her up—or a newspaper, or bananas, or nothing. Once she came back with a small painting that a late-night seller had insisted she take because he wanted to know that she had something of his. It depicted, in bright, tropical colors, a pigtailed girl jumping over a puddle.

Slava called for her from the couch one evening, her hands on the shoelaces of her sneakers. "I want to come with you," he said guiltily. "Wherever you're going."

"Just to the park and back."

"I'd like to come with."

"Of course you can," she said. "I didn't know you wanted to."

"Why would you think that?" he said.

"You don't have to do what I do."

"Don't we?"

"Slava, let's not argue. Do you want to come?" She paused, a knee on the floor, a sneaker untied. Her face brightened. "Can I take you somewhere? I think you'd love it."

"To the park?"

"You'll see. We need a flashlight."

"A flashlight?"

"Just come with," she said.

They walked east. He took her hand in his, and she answered: They were going to try. The streets of the Upper West Side were falling quiet with the temporary exception of Broadway. They crossed Amsterdam, then Columbus—they were going to Central Park. But when they reached its edge, she kept going: in, past the perimeter.

"In the dark, Arianna?" he said.

"Don't be a codger."

He tried to erase his discomfort. "Are we uncovering your high school time capsule?"

"You'd have to go to Brentwood School for that. The closest right-end bleacher if you have your back to the school." She marched through the darkness as if it were daylight, twigs snapping under her sneakers.

Slava looked longingly at a vanishing streetlight. "What did you put there?" he said, his shoes crunching through Walden.

"A pack of Marlboro Lights. I can't wait to have one when I dig them out in twenty years." It wasn't entirely dark, due to occasional streetlights, but Arianna was maneuvering away from the lights, looking for tree cover. "Do you know why I love the park?" she said. "It's the only place in Manhattan with no street signs. This could be Eighty-Fifth or Ninety-Fifth. Now they've started putting maps on the lampposts, telling you where you are. I want to rip them down."

Slava looked up at the trunk of a nearby streetlight: There it was, in laminate. Following impulse—he wanted to do something heroic for her—he sprinted toward the light and wedged the map out of the holder.

"Slava!" she yelled. "Put it back." He knew the expression—an awkward surprise—even at a distance, and wedged the map back. They walked in silence the rest of the way. Finally, Arianna paused at the edge of a stand of oaks, the closest light three hundred yards behind them. "This is good as it's going to get," she said. "I haven't done this in a while."

"Could I be allowed in on the plan now?" he said.

She faced him. "Another thing about the park—the homeless have the best view in New York." She pointed at Central Park West, whose peaks glowed dimly beyond the perimeter. "And us," she added.

They walked through the oaks into a clearing, concealed from a bike path by a series of boulders. The grass sloped gently. Slava looked around uneasily.

"No, up," she said.

He followed her eyes. It took him a moment to understand what she wanted him to see, but there they were, as nowhere else in the city: stars. Not many, and the ones you could make out were feeble, occasionally erased by a passing wisp of cloud, but then they emerged once more, charming in their earnest junior performance, like children playing at adulthood. Arianna was beaming—they were her children.

"You come here by yourself at night?" Slava said, incredulous.

"When I was young and stupid enough to walk in Central Park alone at night," she said. "I haven't done this in years. Come on the grass with me."

Slava looked around. They hadn't seen a soul since entering the park. His eyes were adjusting, the darkness turning from black to blue. Nervously, he settled next to her. The grass was careful, the mowers of the Parks Department reaching even this far.

"When I was little," she said, "my father would take me in the backyard, we would lie down just like this, and he would make me find shapes in the clouds. A dinosaur, a briefcase, an apology. Or we would go to the beach and I would tell stories about the waves. The sea is a tongue spitting out seeds. The sea is a head rushing with thoughts. The first time I wrote a poem, it was from one of those days."

"What does an apology look like?"

"Gnarled over. Hunched."

"You miss him," he said.

"He's different now. He would be embarrassed to go look at waves with his daughter."

"Why?"

"I don't know. They don't tell you why they change."

They listened to the city hum somewhere out there, past the line of light that waited beyond the edge of the park. Waited like a bad thought, Slava thought, remembering Oleg, and smiled. In his sci-fi story, Oleg had unconsciously melded the Odysseus story and the failed 1991 anti-Gorbachev putsch, in which the leader of the unfree world learned, upon reaching his vacation site in the Crimea, that power had been seized in the capital. By the time Oleg's hero, sleekly but rustically named John Strong in concert with the technological but agrarian future, had reached his mind destination of Usuria (a bizarre blend of "usury" and Illyria—Slava was getting an analyst's glimpse into the writerly mind), the codes had been rewritten wherever they were written, temporarily suspending all mind travel and stranding in-transit "expeditioners" like John Strong. Slava had sent Oleg edits and, as promised, one of the false letters. Oleg sent back a revision, a second story about the manager of a Japanese café franchise on the moon, and an unshy suggestion on how to improve the Holocaust letter, amusing Slava. Fifteen miles south of Central Park, there labored newfound kin to Slava, a secret operative.

"They say that if you can make out the Seventh Sister, the tiniest one," she said, "you have twenty-twenty vision. Up there." Arianna extended a finger, but his vision was not twenty-twenty. "After Atlas had to carry the world, Zeus turned his seven daughters into stars so they could keep him company."

Slava propped himself on an elbow, as if to get a better look, but really he was studying her. In sneakers, gray tights, and a hoodie, somehow cold even in this heat, she was more beautiful than a woman dressed up. Despite the confusing tenseness between them, this fact presented itself without reservations. He wished to embrace her, but he couldn't bring himself to do it. If he kept his distance, at least he was being true to the fact of his betrayal, not pretending to give while he withheld so much.

He flopped back onto the grass and glared at the stars—where else to look? They would disappear as soon as he and Arianna reentered the light, though they would remain up there, something you had to believe without evidence.

"Saltshaker," he said.

"Hm?" She looked over at him.

"The stars, like somebody shook out a saltshaker." He looked back. "Your turn."

She laughed through her nose, shy and grateful. She took his arm, and he let it be held. "A necklace," she said. "A necklace of stars."

"White cherries."

"Rice grains."

"Rice grains in ink."

"Tonight we are pleased to offer rice grains in squid ink."

"Only the night sky has freckles."

"The biopsy showed a profusion of light."

"A celestial rash—heavenly spores."

"Ew."

"A placenta."

"Who's the father?"

"Only Jerry Springer can say."

"And the children? The Seven Sisters?"

"No, the children are us."

They kissed.

THURSDAY, AUGUST 24, 2006

The Rudinskys' two-story brick slab squatted next to a disheveled pill-box belonging to Orthodox Jews. Half a dozen side-locked children in matching gabardine outfits spun around the singed grass on their side of the lawn. The Rudinskys' half was treacherous with lawn product. To the shrieking children, the young man wending his way through their game was as invisible as a spirit.

Slava's knock was answered with thundering feet, and then Vera swung open the door. He wore a miserable expression in deference to the awkwardness of their last encounter, but she issued a broad, bland smile. She wore a pair of velour shorts stamped with Hello Kitty characters. In the distance, past an ornate Persian-style runner and a lacquered flamingo sprouting a spume of pink tendrils, a large television jumped with Russian pop stars.

"Ver-ka!" boomed from upstairs. "Who is it?"

"Sla-va!" she shouted back.

Slava squeezed out a smile and stepped inside, Vera's bare soles slapping the tile, tiny prints from the television remote on her thigh. Her legs had

yet to slough off their adolescent plumpness. He felt a momentary sting—
she hadn't bothered to dress up. They stood in clumsy silence at the foot of
the stairs. In the living room, chartreuse and puce vases of Bohemian crystal trembled in tune to the permed crooners thrusting on television. Finally, the upstairs voice made its heavy way down: Aunt Lyuba. Slava felt a
second sting at being handed off to the adult. After all, it was Vera who had
called and asked him to come, not that he hadn't thought about picking up
the phone himself many times.

"Slava!" Aunt Lyuba reached the first-floor landing and embraced Slava
with soft, bunching arms. He answered, his arms reaching around the
puckered bun of her. They stood grasping each other as if he'd just come
home from the war. From Aunt Lyuba's grip, Slava watched Vera steal off
to the living room.

"Did you see my God-fearers next door?" Lyuba said, releasing him.
"One year and three months since we bought this house, do you think that
woman—Malka, Schmalka—has come by to say 'Hello, welcome to the
neighborhood'? I made the mistake of going over there once—I needed
flour! Her face turned the color of snow. She just ferries that army of be-
lievers day and night, till Moshe comes home. Then you don't see her. I've
been asking Garik to please go over there; those children trample my lawn
every day. But I have to do everything myself."

Aunt Lyuba took Slava by the hand and strode into the kitchen. "You
saw our Vera?" she said. "Darling?" she called out brutally into the living
room. Vera peeked out. "*There* she is." Lyuba's voice became tender again.
"Not the girl you remember, eh?" Vera blushed.

Lyuba instructed Slava to sit down at the rose-colored banquette around
the kitchen table and went shoulder-deep into the refrigerator, her rump
struck outward. Vacuum-sealed ham emerged, smoked chicken thighs, a
bowl of beet-colored vegetable vinaigrette. "Slava, you are half a meter
taller than I saw you last," she said from inside. "Tell me how things are. I
haven't seen you in years."

"Nothing, Aunt Lyuba," he said. "I work at a magazine—"

"Well, we're making do," she interrupted him. "Garik's driving the cab. He wanted to start a limousine company"—she quit shuffling in the fridge to calibrate how much Slava knew about the argument, though only her rear end could judge—"but it didn't work out. He's a geologist by training, you know. Used to these large open spaces, rocks bigger than a house. Now he's twelve hours a day in that box of a taxi. You should see his eyes when he comes home." She closed the fridge and turned around. "You know what my husband the geologist does now? He sings for his fares. For extra tips. Russian war songs. He was chief geologist, State Institute of Earth Materials, Minsk." She pointed to the cramped square of the backyard, where stones with pretty striations loomed in various sizes like bird droppings. "One day he got a ticket because he was lugging home that chunk of obsidian. God knows where he got it. Isn't that a beautiful name, obsidian? It's like an Armenian name. Vera!"

Vera reappeared in the doorway. "Yes, sweet Mother."

"You have to get dressed," Lyuba said. Then, to Slava: "Go up with her, Slavchik."

"Up with her where?" he said.

"Well, don't go *in* the room, Slava, you seducer," Aunt Lyuba laughed, baring her teeth in satisfaction. "Stand outside the door and talk to her while she's changing. You young people have a lot of catching up to do."

"Leopard-print or the jean skirt with the blouse with the ruffles?" Vera said from the doorway.

"Let Slava decide," Lyuba said.

He followed Vera up the stairs, the skin of her thighs near his nose. "It's nice to see you again," he said, to say something.

"You, too," she said absentmindedly.

"I should let you get dressed," he said. "We'll talk downstairs."

"No, it's okay," she insisted. "Talk to me." She walked into a room decorated with a girl's hearts and pinks. She jumped onto the bed, one leg folded under the other, and shelved her chin on her knee. In front of her was a binder filled with costume-party outfits: sailors, maids, prisoners. She motioned him inside. "Talk to me for two minutes, and then I'll get dressed."

He asked about the binder.

"Work." She swatted the air. "Big event on Monday. So, leopard-print or jean skirt?" She leaped off the bed and rifled through a hundred hangers. A mound of shoes collapsed around her ankles. Kitten heels, stilettos, flats, pumps, platforms, sandals, boots, knee-high and ankle.

"But you don't live with them," he croaked, thinking of the place where Vova the Cruiserweight had dropped her off.

"What? Speak up." The mass of clothes was like an enchanted wood: It killed sound.

"You live here?" he yelled.

"No, I got that place," she said.

"Why did you call?" Slava shouted. The closet was as large as the rest of the room.

Her round face peeked out of the wardrobe. "What do you mean? We needed your help." Slava saw tiny Vera's eyebrows sitting together as she peered at Slava tracing out prices for the paper scallions and plums of their childhood supermarket. How odd that her parents recommended him—in his memory, she was the serious one. His hands were always clammy when she gave him an assignment. But she could be playful as well. One day on their way to the market, she found an opera record, a plump, heavily rouged sufferer weeping on the cover. Vera played it over and over, vocalizing soundlessly into his ear as the singers roared on their thirdhand stereo. Himself, he wasn't enchanted by the music, but he loved watching her.

After coercing an opinion from Slava, Vera settled on the leopard-print dress. She squeezed into it while he stood outside her door. Her heels sank into the furry carpet as she made her way downstairs ahead of Slava, his eyes fixed on the geometrically essential sphere of her ass. Like a gentleman, he had insisted that she take the stairs first.

As they made their way down, two male voices entered the house. Garik, Lyuba's husband, clutched a singing cabdriver's materials: a two-liter Pepsi bottle half filled with water, a seat cushion, and several slovenly sections of *Novoye Russkoe Slovo*. With his free hand, he pushed Lazar, Vera's grandfather. The older man seemed not to recognize Slava even though they had seen each other at Grandmother's funeral dinner only weeks before, but Uncle Garik brightened.

"Slava, you're an oak! Look at him." He came close and hugged. "What's more historic, the Germans giving us money or Slava Gelman showing up in this house? This is an occasion for a glass. Come, let's eat. Lyuba, why isn't the table set? Papa, let's eat. Papa, it's Slava!"

While everyone was trooping to the table, Slava's cell phone rang. He excused himself into the hallway.

"I called the big one, but no one picked up," Grandfather said.

"What big one?" Slava said.

"The earth line. You said I can try you on the little one if no one answers the big one. What are you, sleeping?"

"I'm not at home," Slava said.

"Did I ever tell you about Misha Grandé?"

"Who? No."

"There was a guy in my barbershop back home—Misha Grandé. They'd given him a real shoe box of an apartment, and he had to live there with his wife and his mother. He had begged them for something bigger, he even tried to bribe a guy. Of course, he found the one guy in Minsk who wouldn't take bribes. Then the shah of Iran comes for a visit."

"Is this a joke?" Slava said.

"No, it's a real story, listen to me. The shah of Iran comes to Minsk. And Misha knows the motorcade has to pass by his house, because it's the one road in from the airport. So in the middle of the night, Misha drags his bed into the street. And when the shah rides by in the morning, they all see Misha Grandé snoozing. Naturally, the shah wants to know why there's a man sleeping outside."

"What did they do to him?" Slava said.

"They gave him a bigger apartment."

"Oh. I thought something worse. Look, I'm not at home. I'll call you later."

"With a lady?"

"Yes, with a lady. I need to go."

"Let's talk like men—is she going to pass through your bed?"

"What? I don't know."

"You have to wear a rubber. Because if she's lying down with you, she's lying down with Ivan, and with Sergei, and Isaac."

"It's Vera!" he yelled.

"Aha!" Grandfather said. "Attaboy. Ass like a pear. I guess we'll see each other."

"Not a tomato?" Slava said. "How will we see each other? I have to go home afterward."

"Never mind. I've got bad news."

Slava straightened. "What happened?"

"Volodya Kleynerman. Uncle Pasha's uncle on his mother's side. You don't know him."

"What about him?"

"They got a letter. They sent in their application a long time ago. They got on it early."

"And?"

"And they just got an answer."

"My God, just tell me."

"They got a rejection. 'Ineligible.' What does that mean? They can appeal? If they can send different information? I don't understand it."

"And their story was . . . the truth?"

"And their story was the truth. At the Jewish Center, they told me they're trying to get the deadline extended," Grandfather said. "And the rules expanded for who's eligible? I don't really understand it. You need to come over here and talk to someone. Those goddamn Germans—Volodya Kleynerman was a tank commander. You know what that means? How many Jewish Red Army tank commanders do you think there were?"

"But you know Red Army doesn't qualify," Slava said, feeling relief. "If that's what they said, of course they didn't get it. They told the truth?"

"He's got metal in two hundred places in his body."

"I'm sure it's not two hundred."

"Oh, who can talk to you?"

"Have you thought for one moment what happens if they catch us?" Slava said.

"I'm an old man, Slavik. My wife just passed away, and Section 8 is raising the rent by twelve dollars this year. Did I tell you that? The letter came the other day." He added resentfully: "Mama translated."

"You're an old man, you don't speak English. You're just drooling into your shirt cuff."

"I *am* an elderly man."

"Have you thought about what happens to me?" Slava said. "Do you know what an *indictment* is? *Extradition*?" He had to say the words in English.

"I know extra," he said feebly.

"Yes, you know extra. You're worried about twelve dollars. How about market rates? You don't know what market rates are. They can take away everything you have. Section 8, Berta, everything."

"Okay, let's not wet our underpants right away," Grandfather said. "It's not your name on the thing. I'll tell them I wrote it myself and an agency translated."

"Why did you need this?" Slava said. "Israel lives like a political prisoner. His kitchen looks like there hasn't been food cooked there since his

wife died. He's got these blocks of cheddar, you want to kill yourself looking at them. You have a one-bedroom apartment for a hundred dollars a
month, and you have a woman who cooks all your food. How much more
do you want?"

"I need you to figure out this eligibility business. You could get more
people if they expand it and postpone the deadline."

Slava closed his eyes. "If they expand eligibility," he said weakly, "maybe
you could get in honestly." But that wouldn't change anything. Always
there would have to be some deception for more. More, more, more.

"Berta sent in your letter and the affidavit this week," Grandfather said.
"It's too late." He used the English word—effie-davey. "The Katznelsons
came over the other day. They said you wrote them a good one. I haven't
seen them in two years. They didn't even call after the funeral."

"You saw people who didn't call after the funeral?"

"You lose a little steam in the late years, Slavik. Thirty years ago, they
would've heard from me. They would've heard from your *grandmother*.
But they came, I'm telling you. They brought flowers, they brought your
letter, they wanted to see mine. One of their grandsons translated their
letter, they said he couldn't get his nose out of the dictionary! But I still like
mine the best, with the cows.

"The Kogans came, the Rubinshteins came," he went on. "You remember him, with the cross-eye. Their son just had a boy, they invited me to the
bris next week. And you're telling me you don't want to do this."

"Can't you see, devil take it, this is what I've been trying to explain,"
Slava said.

"I've always been your biggest supporter, Slavik. Who is your number
one supporter?"

Slava dropped his hands. "Forget it."

"How's progress with Vera?" Grandfather said conspiratorially.

"Leave me be," Slava said.

"You're talking to someone who can find out what he needs to know. That girl has a twinkle in her eye."

"That was a kilo of mascara you saw, not a twinkle."

"So she knows how to take care of herself, what's wrong with that? Did you write their letter?"

"Not yet."

"Why not yet?"

"I just got here!" Slava said. "It's not a bread where you add the ingredients together and the dough rises. Look, I have to go."

"Good luck," Grandfather said. "You are my only joy in this world."

In the kitchen, Garik and Lazar sat while Lyuba and Vera busied with dishes and cutlery. Crossing the kitchen, Lyuba paused to admire her daughter. Vera laid her arms around her mother's formidable circumference and smooched her upper arm three times.

"Leave me alone, you rascal," Aunt Lyuba said, beaming. "Slava, how old are you now?" She started setting dishes with faux-Greek fretting in front of the men. "Same as Vera?"

"Twenty-five," Slava said. "My birthday's next month."

"I was already swaddling that one when I was twenty-five," Aunt Lyuba said. "Now look at her." They all investigated Vera. She adjusted her dress, her hoop earrings bouncing.

"You can't compare life over there," Uncle Garik said. "At twenty-five, you had every question answered already."

"Are we eating tomorrow, not today?" Lazar Timofeyevich bawled.

"I'm doing it, I'm doing it," Aunt Lyuba shouted. "I have only two hands. Verochka, my princess, you think you might want to do something?"

Vera pulled down the hem of the dress. "Chicken thighs?" she said.

"Yes, please. Use that knife in the drying rack." Aunt Lyuba turned to Slava. "I expected you a little later, Slava. But there will be a lamb to make you forget your name. Just so you know, Vera can cook something, too, once in a while, if she wasn't so busy with work. Frankfurters and mashed potatoes for now, but we're working on it."

"There's a little place near where I work," Slava said. "The guy makes lamb like it still breathes."

"One of ours?" Uncle Garik said. "Central Asian?"

"No," Slava said. "Lebanese."

"Oh," Garik said. "Ali Baba." He raised his palms and swiveled in imitation of a dervish.

"There is only one solution to that problem," Lazar Timofeyevich said.

"Kill them all!" Vera yelled a little hysterically, obviously repeating something she had heard around the dinner table. Slava watched her fingers work through the chicken thighs, flecks of grease decorating her wrists. With her teeth, she notched up the sleeves of her dress.

"I never said 'kill,'" Lazar Timofeyevich said. "Please don't put words in my mouth. I said 'remove.' Just give them money and please go someplace else. Our people have not suffered enough, they have to deal with this, too? Just leave us alone."

"Where is Lebanon, anyway?" Aunt Lyuba said. "I am always curious now when they are talking about the war on the radio. Is it the same as Libya?"

"It's in the Middle East," Uncle Garik said. "They do make good food, however."

"He has this special layering technique with the pita that he learned from Moroccan Jews," Slava said, trying to steer them to impulses of solidarity.

"I heard on the radio once that Arabs are famous for their hospitality," Garik said. "They invite you into the tent for tea, but once you're inside, they kill you."

"I think that's a legend from long ago," Slava said. "They don't live in tents."

"Don't be naive, Slava," Garik said. "What do you expect, they tell you to put tulips in gun barrels in this country."

Vera deposited a serving plate layered with chicken thighs in the middle of the table. Aunt Lyuba shook her head. "My doll, who serves a plate this way?" She removed the plate and began to garnish its edges with sprigs of parsley. "Voilà!" she said a minute later, returning the dish to the table.

Everyone ate in busy contemplation, the men pushing the food behind their cheeks with their thumbs, Vera wiping her plate with bread. Lyuba was only half seated: more bread, more napkins, more garlic. She'd eat in peace when the men were finished. A flock of shrieks rose outside, the children playing.

"I think it's time for lights," Lyuba said, rising again. "Verochka, tell us about something. How's work?"

"It's daylight outside," Lazar Timofeyevich said. "You're wasteful with electricity."

"Then you should have bought a house with windows," Lyuba said.

"Nothing special," Vera said. "Fashion boutique on Avenue X. Contest for the radio station."

"She works in *piar*," Lyuba said. "She connects Russians customers to American business. Isn't that right, my dove? She earns above fifty thousand dollars a year."

Vera blanched. "I connect Russian customers to *Russian* business," she said. "I have only one account Russian to America. In this country, Mama, salary is a private issue."

"Slava's one of us," Lyuba waved her away.

"Completely senseless," Lazar Timofeyevich said. "If you need toothpaste, you go and buy toothpaste, I don't understand why someone has to advertise toothpaste."

"They have fifty kinds of toothpaste here," Vera said. "You need help deciding."

"I don't need help deciding," he said. "The least expensive one, you buy."

"And then your teeth fall out," Lyuba defended her daughter.

"They've fallen out already," Lazar said.

"As if any of the advertisements tell you something truthful," Garik said. "They just show you a woman throwing her hair around in the shower."

"That I have no problem with," Lazar said. He pointed at the decimated remains of the meal. "Lyuba, please clear. We need to get down to work. We can have tea later. And turn off these goddamn lights."

Lyuba put down her fork and rose to clear the dishes. "Go, go," Lazar dismissed everyone. "Give the men some time to talk." Slava watched Vera, who was still eating, rise and retreat. She didn't turn around to look at him. Lyuba would not walk out until all the dishes were piled in the sink. "I want to leave you a clean table!" she shouted in her defense. At last she left, too.

Lazar was so bent that he couldn't look at Slava directly. His lips were violet, the face like a field darkening under a cloud. "Twenty-five is a grown-up's age," he said agnostically.

"You want us to be both," Slava said. "Adults and children, at the same time."

"Speak into this ear," he said, and swiveled. Slava repeated himself.

"Even as a boy, you wanted, above all, justice," Lazar said. "You wouldn't let your grandfather get on the trolley to the beach in Italy without a ticket. When all of us took the trolley to the market to sell, we bought tickets not for the conductor but for you. You would have made a good Communist. Boy, did they hover over you. When you spoke, the whole table shut up. Four adults got quiet so you could speak. That's a difference between you and Vera. She doesn't expect the world to be something it's not."

"Let's talk about the war," Slava said.

"We'll get to that," he said. "How are things on the personal front?"

"Quiet," Slava said. "Let's talk about the war. I know you weren't in a ghetto or camps, but tell me something anyway. It'll help."

"I was in a labor battalion, digging trenches. Then they conscripted me into infantry. Fought at Stalingrad. Lost half my hearing. End of story."

"Say more. Details help."

"How can they help if you can't put it in?" Lazar slapped the table. "If you were in the ghetto, you get funds. If you had three limbs amputated at the front, you get nothing. I can't tell you what the ghetto was like, I wasn't there."

"Tell me something else, then."

"Into this ear!"

Slava repeated himself, shouting.

"Okay, I'll tell you something else," Lazar said. "I'll tell you a story, though I don't know if you know what to do with it. This was in the fifties. Fifty-two, right before that maniac died. It was getting real bad if you were a Jew. My brother Misha was walking home one night, and these drunks start yelling: 'Kikes, kikes, one grave for all the kikes.' Misha's not one to keep quiet—he and your grandfather would have something to talk about. He took one of their eyeballs clean out. Bam." Lazar Timofeyevich flicked his finger near Slava's eye with a sudden energy. "That sort of thing gets you ten years in the clink," he said. "So what did his older brother do? I had a friend with a military uniform from the Revolution, a collector's item. Borrowed that. Another friend of mine was in a marching band; I told him to get in his uniform. And off we want to Eyeball's house. You follow?"

"No," Slava said.

"Don't be naive, please," Lazar said. "We were pretending to be policemen. So we get to Eyeball's house, and we stick out two little address books like they're IDs. 'Esteemed citizens: We are here on orders of the precinct commander to ask you to drop the charges against Misha Rudinsky and permit the authorities to deal with this hooligan on our own terms. We promise to avenge your son in an appropriate way, if you catch our drift. If you go through the official channels, in prison this kike will have a square meal every day. If you leave him to us, we'll make sure he never walks again. One less pair of Jewish feet trampling the ground.'"

"Did it work?" Slava said.

"No," he said sourly. "They shut the door in our faces."

"Oh."

"You think I stopped there? I got our lawyer to get the case judge to come to our house for dinner. I am twenty-six years old at this point, Slava, basically five minutes older than you. We're toasting to the health of the motherland and all that, and *khop*—I slip him a white envelope. Five large. And my little Misha got three years instead of ten. And I got to pick him up from the prison once a month and take him home for a home-cooked meal and a haircut."

Slava nodded politely. All of a sudden, their twilight upon them, the old men of his old neighborhood were willing to talk about their valorous actions. Initially, they held back so as not to trouble the children with the frightening truth about life. But now, in the last lap, they were frantically unloading, like thieves dumping gold, pursued by the one collector from whom no reprieve. Finally, they had met something more fearful than the prospect of disturbing the sleep of their children.

Lazar Timofeyevich closed his eyes, so slowly and heavily that Slava could imagine the lids never rising again. When he opened them, he said: "You think I am telling you all this to stroke my dick one last time? I am telling you this so you can understand the difference between your own and not your own. Who is your best friend?"

"I'm sorry?"

"You've got a best friend?"

Slava thought about it. The only answer that came was Arianna. "No," he said.

"I had ten best friends back home," Lazar said. "Boys who would slit someone's throat for me. All Jews. Every last one of them Jews. Now, whoever your closest friend is, would he do that for you?"

"I don't know," Slava said. "I don't have—that many friends."

"That girl," Lazar said, pointing at the stairs, "will stand behind you like a tank, Slava. And you need it, with your head in the clouds. She may not know who Sakharov was, but she knows life, loyalty. You get caught doing what you're doing? She would take the fall for you. That's what I mean by your own. You name me one American person who will do that for you, and I will end this conversation. We brought you here, but that means we are Americans all of a sudden? Do you scoop from a box of cherries at the store without looking? No, you pick the good ones. Just because we are here, we have to live a thousand miles apart and call once a week to say hai-hava-yoo? Get a nice job, buy a big house—but you don't have to take any more from this place."

"So we are supposed to be foreigners here?" Slava said. "It wasn't enough for you to have to be a foreigner back there, now you are choosing to be a foreigner here? They have psychopathic classifications for this kind of behavior."

"We will become Americans, Slava, don't worry," Lazar said. "Your children will be almost Americans, and then their children will watch the shampoo commercials without understanding what could be different. It has to happen on its own timetable. You can't rush the facts."

"Life is long," Slava said.

"Life is not long," Lazar said. "At the front, twenty-five was a senior citizen. Lyuba was swaddling at twenty-five, very nice for her, but at twenty-five, I was commanding a Red Army platoon. That's one thing I have to give those crazy medievals next door. They have five kids, six kids, seven kids. We are so small, Slava. We are always in danger of disappearing because of one thing or another."

"Has anyone asked Vera what she wants?" Slava said.

"You have to speak into this ear," Lazar Timofeyevich said impatiently.

"You are willing to give away your one granddaughter to someone who earns half her salary?"

"What?" Lazar whined. Slava wondered if the hearing impairment had been invented for deployment as needed. It had caused notably less interference at dinner.

"It's not important," Slava sighed. "I have to go, Lazar Timofeyevich. Long trip back."

The old man shrugged, too weary to continue. He rose somberly and shuffled off to a corner cabinet. From it he withdrew a sealed white envelope, thick, and dropped it on the table in front of Slava. Then he lowered himself back into his chair. "Make it good," he said.

"What is this?" Slava said.

"Your fee. Two hundred and fifty."

"Thanks," Slava said. "I don't need a fee."

"Your grandfather said not to give it to you, but you're the one who deserves it."

Slava felt warmth in his cheeks.

"Lazar Timofeyevich, you should have waited until they came," Lyuba said reproachfully from the doorway. Garik was next to her, two eavesdropping children.

"Wait till who came," Slava said.

"Who, who," Lazar said, an old owl.

The doorbell rang, a slow tick-tock that banged around the tiled halls for eternity. They stood sealed to their places. On the elders, it dawned that Slava had no idea what was happening. Why had he been kept out of it? Well, he kept his distance now, they had heard. Fucking children, God pardon their speech: You give and you give and they spit in your face. Why *were* they so set on pairing Vera with Slava? That was the only reason they'd said okay when the Gelmans asked to come over. It wasn't the kid's fault that the parents—the grandfather—was a high-nosed prick. But what, the apple falls far from the tree? The kid was a strange one, too—in his own way, but strange all the same. All this flashed through the minds of the elder Rudinskys.

"Must be them," Garik said.

"Who," Slava said, a mild hysteria entering his voice. He knew the answer, but prayed to be wrong.

"Them, them," Lazar said impatiently.

Lyuba disappeared into the hallway. Slava jumped from his chair, Lazar following at lesser speed. When Lyuba opened the door, the three men were bunched in the hallway behind her, wearing pained expressions: Garik because he didn't know what to expect from this encounter—in some ways, he felt responsible for the estrangement, because his need for the limousine seed money had started it, though for the same reason, he also felt the most aggrieved and unprepared to reconcile, though of course he would do it for the children; Lazar because he was halfway to the next world and therefore understood, as only his granddaughter did, the imbecility of such estrangements; and Slava because he was bewildered, one that his grandfather had been charging for the letters, and two that, very likely, there were Gelmans on the other side of that door. Above their heads, Vera's feet pressed the carpeted stairs. She was still wearing her goddamn arousing heels, the stilettos pricking the soft carpet.

The door opened to reveal, indeed, two Gelmans—father, daughter— and one Shtuts. Slava's grandfather wore a white guayabera and an expression of disdain. His daughter was in a multiflowered tunic. Her husband was tidy in a short-sleeved shirt. They held chocolates, cheap champagne, the weight of the world.

"From New Jersey, they have graced us with their presence," Lyuba said. She was aiming for playfulness, but the words came out scornfully.

"What are you keeping them outside for?" Garik said. "You're wasting air-conditioning. Come in, people, come in."

"It's Slava," his mother said, as surprised to see him as the Rudinskys.

"He's on this side of the door already," Lyuba said coquettishly.

The person in question examined his grandfather with blazing eyes.

"I'm so happy you're here," cried Vera, and ran down the remaining stairs into the hallway. She began to relieve the Gelmans of their bags and setting out house shoes from the closet. Massed in the foyer, the Gelmans obediently began to shed their footwear.

"I've cleared the table from dinner already, I just have to set out the china," Lyuba said.

Grandfather's nostrils flared. He was always being invited for coffee and cake after a dinner to which he had *not* been invited.

Dumbfounded, Slava searched out Vera's eyes, but she avoided him. "Why don't we sit in the living room?" she announced, and ran into the kitchen to gather provisions. Slava followed her, though he could only stare.

Her hands were deep in a cabinet. She stopped rummaging and looked over at him. "Are you going to help or not?"

"You're joking, right?" he said. The adults trooped past the kitchen doorway en route to the living room. Lyuba was about to come in, but Vera waved her away. "The good china," Lyuba hissed from the doorway and winked at Slava, an accomplice.

"Why can't you let them settle it themselves," he said to Vera.

"Because they're children, that's why," Vera said.

"I'm leaving," he said.

"You're not leaving," she said. "Help me." Her expression softened. "Please."

"He's charging people," Slava exclaimed. "Behind my back."

"I'm sure it's for you."

"I don't want the money!" Slava yelled.

"What's the matter in there?" they heard from the living room. Vera and Slava stopped to listen. Their bickering had given the adults a subject of conversation. Someone even laughed. "You see?" Vera said to him through her teeth.

The children appeared in the living room carrying two trays of gold-rimmed plates and teacups. Stiff with silence, the adults were wedged into a sofa and love seat, thighs against thighs. The appearance of the children gave them a subject.

"What's for sale today?" someone asked.

"What does the tea cost?" a second added.

"Just like old times," someone announced, because it wasn't like old times at all.

"Today we have a special," Vera said playfully. "Open house at V and S Alimenti. Free snacks and tea."

"Hooray," Slava's mother said tentatively.

Slava wished violence on all of them. After he set his tray down, he reached into his jeans pocket and pulled out the white envelope. Stepping over Garik's feet, he thrust it in his grandfather's face. The conversation stopped. His grandfather looked up at him, fearful and mocking.

"I think this is for you," Slava said. The white envelope hung between them like a poisonous sun. It anchored a galaxy of fat Russians.

"Can we skip business talk this one time, please?" Vera broke in. She snagged the envelope from Slava's hands, folded it in half, and wedged it housewifeishly inside her décolletage. "Looks like I'm getting a shopping trip out of all this." Everyone laughed.

"It's so nice that you wanted to come," Lyuba announced when everyone had settled down.

"*We* wanted to come?" Grandfather said.

"Vera said—" Slava's mother began.

"Oh, what difference does it make!" Vera cried. "You me, me you . . . we're together. We're together for the first time in almost twenty years."

"Well, everyone, you look the same," Garik said, and again they laughed.

"What the fuck did we get ourselves into," Lazar said, not much hilarity in his voice. He meant America.

"Do you know that some people just stayed in Italy," Slava's mother said. She pulled at her tunic.

"If I did it again, I'd stay in Italy," Garik said. "Do you remember these two?" He pointed at Vera and Slava. "They'd be speaking Italiano by now."

"But we're doing well," Lyuba interjected. "We have almost no mortgage on this house."

"They have a Nissan Altima *and* a Ford Taurus," Grandfather announced, pointing to his daughter and her husband.

"I'd stay all Japanese," Garik sniffed. "I understand these things."

"Well, of course, you're in a taxi all day long."

"It takes skill," Garik reminded the older man.

"Wafers?" Vera intruded. "There are cookies and biscuits as well. And what about ice cream?"

While the adults talked, Slava counted. He had written twenty-two letters. Twenty-two times two hundred and fifty was fifty-five hundred. A third of the graves. Or was there a sliding scale? Five hundred for some, two hundred and fifty for others. Did Grandfather say, "Lazar, I charge five hundred. But you let my kid get at your pear-assed progeny, and we'll make it two-fifty. Just do me a favor, don't let him know. He's fragile."

No. It was Vera who'd done the bribing. She had called Grandfather like an equal: Come over, make peace, and we'll buy a letter. Slava in this was a marionette. She knew that Slava wouldn't deny her—was he so obvious, a panting dog?—and with him clearing the way, they would come. She ran circles around him. In public, at Stas and Lara's, she was his shadow. In private, she achieved what needed achieving. She was as tough as Grandfather—tougher. That's why he liked her: He saw a kindred spirit. Slava was writing the letters, sure, but the boy was flighty. Slava imagined Vera wearing Grandfather down on the price, the old man charmed by her enterprise. He didn't want to condescend, however, and made her work for it. They went back and forth: Two hundred. Three hundred. Two-fifty.

Slava inspected Vera with a contemptuous wonder. She felt his eyes and swiveled to face him. Then she pulled out the white envelope and thrust it at him with the eyes of a parent. He took it.

By the time he rejoined the conversation, they were hollering like drunk people. And they were. Vera quickly realized her mistake—what biscuits? They needed cognac. They pulled out the best in the Rudinskys' possession, a bottle of Rémy Martin VSOP someone had gifted a long time before. (Grandfather reminded them that it was he who had gifted it, it was him.) Thimbles were emptied, lemon wedges sucked down, thimbles emptied again. Gallantly, Garik asked to drink for Slava's grandmother. The noise ebbed and they gazed mournfully into the crystal in their hands. "It's nice crystal," Grandfather said. Then they drank. Eventually, Slava excused himself. They became upset. He said he had a letter to write. Then the waters parted as if for a king.

- 12 -

Outside the Rudinskys', Slava was beset by an urgent desire to flee—to Manhattan, to Arianna's. Throughout the preceding month, he had retraced back toward Bensonhurst and Midwood every step that he had taken in the opposite direction two years before. It had happened imperceptibly. You do not notice exactly when day becomes night, but you notice night.

He strode toward the subway. The sun was descending, fluorescent bulbs clicking on and casting a pale blue glow over the pears and lettuces in the bodegas. The heavy-breasted women who supervised the discount-clothing emporia that lined Eighty-Sixth Street wheeled in the enticement racks from the sidewalk, and a grandmother who had been selling *lepeshki* from a foldout table on Bay Twenty-Second Street sang quietly to herself as she stacked the plastic bins into a shopping cart.

Slava had taken the first steps up to the station when he saw him. There was no way to miss Israel Abramson—literary aspirant, anti-clericalist, subject of Slava's second letter—crossing Eighty-Sixth Street. In ninety-degree weather, in his Red Army uniform, faded but crisp, a few medals swinging gently in cadence with his wavering, stiff-jointed lurch.

Israel took the sidewalk the way he had taken Kharkov during the war: left foot, right shoulder, right foot, left shoulder. He walked through the busiest thoroughfare in Bensonhurst, six lanes if you counted the side arteries where cars pulled off to double-park, as if tugging himself through an empty field. A bus blazed by, messing his hair; he didn't even look up. Slava's heart slid from his chest. He set off after Israel, but at a distance. He didn't want him to die, but he didn't want to embarrass him, either.

Crossing Eighty-Sixth, Slava was nearly sideswiped himself, young men staring sunkenly from the windows of an aircraft carrier masquerading as an SUV. "Vot you doo, fahk!" shouted a leery face with smoked-out eyes as the car passed. "I keel you, ha!" As American yearlings, the parents had driven shit-brown Cutlasses and rusty blue Buicks, but now they were able to purchase nice cars for the children.

Israel waddled across Benson Avenue, then Bath, then Cropsey. They were nearly in the ocean before he turned. When he finally stopped, they were in front of a stone building identified by a modest sign out front: Temple Beth-El. Israel regarded unhappily the mountain of steps that led to its heavy wood doors. He leaned on the iron railing that climbed to the doorway, mopped his forehead with a handkerchief, and began his ascent. Left hand clutching the railing, the right foot jerked to the next step, dragging the right shoulder along. Then the left half of him. He paused on every other step, breathing hard.

Five minutes later—maybe longer; Slava was transfixed—Israel's shaking fingers waved at the door, trying to hook the handle. He yanked, nearly toppling, and disappeared inside. Slava emerged from the shelter of a heat-addled spruce and followed, taking two steps at a time. Midway up, he slowed. It felt heartless to fly up after what it had cost the older man.

Shabbat shalom. Inside, Israel was nodding his way down the aisle as he dragged himself toward a small table where memorial candles burned. A man in a skullcap, who stood with the firmness of someone who belonged to the premises, watched Israel with a polite smile, several other worshippers whispering among themselves in a corner. "Shabbat shalom," Israel said. "Shabbat shalom." But it was only Thursday night.

Dust swam in the last light filtering through the stained-glass windows on the balcony level. The panels ran the length of the four walls, like a seating gallery. The ceiling was a soaring cupola. Slava had always thought that this was what churches looked like. He had never been inside a synagogue.

Israel pulled himself to the table with candles and turned to face the rabbi. The rabbi nodded, opened a bureau, and withdrew a tasseled white cloth lined with blue stripes. He walked up to Israel, opened it with the precision of a soldier unfolding a flag, and draped it gently over Israel's head and shoulders. When the rabbi stepped away, Israel addressed the table. "*Dos ist for mayn wife*," he roared in Anglo-Yiddish. The flame of the candle in his hand met the wick of another. Then he muttered something that Slava was too far away to hear. Israel stood for a minute or two, his head bent over the candles, the edges of the tasseled cloth threatening to slide into the flames.

When he was finished, he removed the cloth from his shoulders and began to join the ends neatly. The rabbi stood to the side; it was clear that he had tried to intervene before, without use. Shakily, Israel brought the upper ends in to his chest, as if embracing someone. Pinching two joined corners in his left hand, he ran his right between the edges of the sheet, then pinched the other two corners. His fingers shook. Holding the joined ends in both hands, he turned the cloth ninety degrees and brought it again to his chest. He repeated the folding pattern until the cloth was a simple blue and white square barely larger than his palm, like a flag for the fallen. He placed it gently in the rabbi's hand, kissed him on the cheek, and began the journey toward the door, hauling it open with the whole of himself.

The rabbi had to call out to Slava a second time. Slava had concealed himself in a corner, where he was pretending to make a careful study of the columns and stained glass.

"Yes," Slava answered. "Sorry, yes."

The rabbi smiled. "I said, what brings you by? First time in a synagogue?"

"I saw an interior once from the door," Slava said. "In Vienna."

"The Vienna synagogue?" the rabbi said. He had a light, carefully trimmed beard.

"I don't know," Slava said.

"Big?" He opened his hands.

Slava nodded. The aid society, which would not leave the Gelmans alone, had organized a bus trip to a synagogue.

"Before the war in Vienna," the rabbi said, "only a church could stand freely. So when they built that synagogue, they had to connect it to a residential building. And so they also had to make it look similar, I mean aesthetically. So in 1938, when the Nazis were trashing Jewish property, they skipped it. They thought it was a regular old apartment building. Isn't that a story?"

Slava nodded, trying to think of a way to extricate himself. His mark was vanishing into the evening.

"You know that man?" the rabbi said, indicating the doorway.

Slava shrugged.

"Comes every week. I've tried to show him"—he gestured at the bureau that held the tasseled cloth—"but he likes it his own way. He's seen more than I'll ever see, so I leave him alone. Get him a book once in a while or some matzo. We did have his son's bar mitzvah here. At the ripe old age of thirty-two!"

"Yuri?" Slava said.

"So you know him," the rabbi said.

Shit. "I'm the grandson," Slava blurted out. From one hole into a deeper. Never a dawdling organ, his heart throttled in his chest.

"I don't understand," the rabbi said.

"Two marriages?" Slava said, inventing.

"I had no idea," the rabbi said, raising his eyebrows. "But I can see the resemblance, sure. Why were you hiding?"

"You know," Slava said. "We worry. Crossing the road, things like that. He's proud, though. Don't want to embarrass him."

"I'm Rabbi Bachman," the rabbi said, approaching and extending his hand. "I should have introduced myself at the start. Wonderful to meet someone who knows Israel. I'd love to see you here with your grandfather some time. Maybe even"—he raised his hands to indicate that a man could hope for only so much—"a service?"

"What was he muttering after he was talking about his wife?" Slava said.

"I'm not *sure*," Bachman laughed. "He's got a language all his own. If I were guessing, blessings. For his children and grandchildren. For you!" He laughed again. "For his son." The rabbi shifted his feet. "I know they have a disagreement. Israel didn't even come to the bar mitzvah. But he's welcome here no matter what; I don't see the point of pushing people away. Hey, I bet you speak Russian."

Slava nodded carefully.

"I've had this idea," Bachman said. "A Russian minyan. A service in Russian once a week. With commentary. I do the English, someone like you does the Russian. And brings the crowd, obviously. We'll throw a little Hebrew in, too. Is that something you might be interested in? Talk to some people? Maybe start with your grandfather? The neighborhood's changed a lot in the last decade."

Slava considered the possibility of starting with his grandfather. That day at the Vienna synagogue, he—the real grandfather—had snatched

Slava's hand and slipped away from the group, which had been made to stand waiting for the end of services by their guide, an Israeli in a leather jacket. Slava's insides knitted in worry. His mother and father had not come on the tour, grateful they didn't have to. It was only Grandfather and Slava, and they were breaking the rules.

Holding his hand, Grandfather leaned an ear to the door of the synagogue, on the other side of which a group was praying. "Woo-woo-woo," Grandfather mimicked, and shrugged. Then he slid his hand inside the handle, as large as a torso, and carefully deposited his nose inside the opening. Slava peeked from behind his trousers, which smelled of wool and naphthalene. Inside, in a room as ornate as a Turkish palace, men lurched epileptically, humming like an apiary.

Grandfather looked down at Slava. "Woo-woo-woo," he said again, and turned his finger into his temple. Crazy. "Boy," he said with a formality that made Slava's insides twist again. "Of this, we've seen all we need to. Time for ice cream. The vanilla one they tie up like a sausage."

"But we're not allowed to leave," Slava whispered.

"We, Slavik"—Grandfather leaned down, placing the tip of his finger on his nose—"can do whatever we want."

Slava considered Bachman again. No, Rabbi, I won't be able to provide you with a minyan from the grandfathers, the real or the fake. Their children, perhaps. Their grandchildren, quite possibly. But this—candles, mongreling—was as close as the grandfathers could come. A little foreplay, a *forshpeis*. Slava was overcome by a desire to hear Grandfather's voice, the real grandfather's, as if, like Grandmother, he was going to die and Slava would no longer be able to.

"I'll talk to him about the minyan," Slava said. "I should go now."

"I'd like to see you here again," the rabbi said.

Slava smiled politely and turned to leave. Halfway to the door, he looked back. "Tell me," he said. "When is the mourning over after a death?"

"The shiva?" Bachman said. "There isn't anything else. Judaism's not big on stretching out mourning. You mourn hard, so to speak, but then you let go. You light a candle on the yahrzeit, but otherwise you make your way back to life. Why do you ask?"

"You're supposed to not think of the person?"

"Of course you can think of the person. You can think of the person whenever you want. It's only the rituals that are finished."

Slava considered this. It seemed all right. He thanked the rabbi and started again for the door, his steps echoing on the cold churchy stone.

When Slava thrust open the door, he discovered waiting for him, draped over the stair railing and illuminated from behind by the sun like an arthritic god, Israel Abramson. He looked pink, like a baby.

"Privet, mal'chik," Israel said. Hello, boy. "You took your time in there. What were you discussing, the soul of man? I thought you might want to walk together, help me down these goddamn stairs. They build stairs like they're sitting in heaven."

Slava blinked, adjusting his eyes after the interior's dimness. Maybe Slava was imagining him.

Then Rabbi Bachman opened the door of the synagogue and emerged into the sunlight.

"Hava-yoo, Ravvin!" Israel shouted, raking the air with his paw.

Slava felt sweat on his back.

"Israel," the rabbi acknowledged.

Slava was about to speak when Israel pointed at him and spoke first. Slava closed his eyes as if to shield himself from the blow. But what Israel shouted was: "Grensun!"

You, world, always make new mysteries.

Rabbi Bachman smiled. "I know! We spoke. He's going to help me with a project. Maybe." The rabbi spoke with the extra volume with which Americans speak to those who don't speak English.

Slava turned to Israel. "He says—" he started in Russian.

"Nais, veree nais!" Israel answered with the Soviet immigrant's indifference to comprehension as a primary objective of dialogue. "Bai-bai, Ravvin!" He twirled his crooked fingers.

Rabbi Bachman returned inside, and Israel stuffed his arm into the crook of Slava's. "See these, *mal'chik*?" He pointed to the medals on his uniform. "Reconnaissance, '44 to '45. I had you as far back as Eighty-Sixth Street. Big deal you are—you can barely cross the street. My heart was in my feet, looking at you back there. Let's go."

"Why did you tell him I was your grandson?" Slava said.

"What are you, embarrassed?"

"No," Slava said. "No."

"So why are we talking about this, let's go."

Slava took the steps at Israel's stride. Up close, it was worse. Each step cost him something dear. At home, he had looked sturdy, nearly athletic, in his gym trousers, but the arm that leaned on Slava now was flabby as dough, the left hand trembling in an eternal so-so. Ahead of them, the descending disk of the sun spread a tired lemon glow.

"Let's take a break," Slava said when they had reached the bottom of the stairs. "Let's sit down."

"You can't sit down on concrete, you'll catch cold," Israel said.

"It's a hundred and fifty degrees," Slava said. "Sit down and rest."

"If I sit down here, I'll never get up," he said. "Look how low to the ground."

"Can you lean against the railing? I am going to sit down."

"What are you, a pensioner? Let's go."

"For just a moment," Slava said. He made sure that Israel was attached to the railing and lowered himself. The step was inches from the pavement. Was it simply performing the ritual of sitting on a low place in honor of the deceased that mattered, or were you also supposed to feel something? Slava waited, but he didn't feel anything. The people who covered mirrors, sat on low stools, lit candles, how did they come to feel what they felt? Did you have to be born into it? What was the trick?

There was a terrible rumble next to him. Israel had deposited himself a step above. "If we're resting, we're resting," he said.

"It doesn't bother you to go in there?" Slava said.

Israel blew his nose, a thumb at each nostril. "Where else would I go if I want to sing a song for my wife? The mosque on Eighty-Sixth Street? Masjid Shmashid? No, I am a Jew. I don't go up there, you think that will make him come back? I take what I can."

"Pick and choose," Slava said sourly.

"I guess so," Israel said. "Except I didn't choose for my son to become a fanatic and run off to Israel. All the same, I'd rather he was happy without me than unhappy with. Do you think he might have done that because he was unhappy? Unhappy with me and my wife?"

Slava turned to look at Israel. The old man's face was pinched at the thought. Slava waved him away. "They have studies about this sort of thing," he lied. "I mean atheists who come and convert. It's other factors. It's not family. Weren't you his family in the Soviet Union?"

"Maybe it's something in this place," he said weakly. He looked on the verge of tears.

"Maybe," Slava said.

Israel nodded, the forehead folded. Slava withdrew the white envelope from his jeans pocket. Palmed by many hands, it was acquiring a foxed edge. He extended it to Israel.

"What's this?"

"There was a misunderstanding," Slava said. "I don't know how much it was, but two-fifty to start."

"It was two-fifty."

"Then we're square."

"But who gives you for the work?"

"I've been given." Slava rose and tucked the envelope into the pocket of Israel's uniform. "Let's go. I've got a long night ahead."

"You're still giving us our tales of woe and deceit?"

"Those very same," Slava said.

"And what happens when it's all over?" Israel said. "The deadline's next week. What do you do at that magazine of yours, anyway?"

"If some small newspaper somewhere makes a mistake, we make a joke about it."

"We had that in Russia, too. The capital likes to laugh at the provinces. Makes it feel like the capital."

Slava shrugged. That work seemed so remote. After submitting the fabricated entries for "The Hoot," Slava returned to properly sourced items, though largely because he'd hit a lucky streak and, for a week or two, the flubs were finding him. But he was dry again, and in the past two weeks, he had slipped in a couple of inventions. It didn't matter. Slava's heroic bulwarking of the national decline of small-town newspapers through the invention of the Rinkelrinck (Ark.) *Gazette* had earned notice neither in Arkansas nor *Century*.

"I was going to heat up some soup for us," Israel said. "From a can but excellent."

Slava saw Israel climbing into the cupboard where the synagogue's gifts collected, withdrawing a can of soup too large for one—what he lacked in human variety, Israel made up for soup-wise: carrot ginger, black bean, ten-vegetable—and slurping alone in the falling light outside his ground-level window.

"Next time," Slava promised.

"You said that last time," Israel said, acquiring a pained expression. Slava felt a familiar wave of guilt. Israel cocked his eyebrows. "Ha! Take it easy, I'm kidding. Slow on the uptake, you are." He clapped Slava on the shoulder. "Listen, what is your attitude toward presents?"

"Presents?"

"Presents. Good times, laughter, a long table, a bottle or three. You're a heavy one."

"When I want a good time, I call you to hear a compliment."

"Self-pity flatters no man. I want you to take this money back. And have a good time."

"How many months did it take you to collect that amount?" Slava said.

"This is the use that would make me most satisfied."

For a third time that evening, Slava's hand closed around the accursed envelope.

−13−

Slava dragged the ton of himself home. On the subway, he tried to jot down ideas for Lazar's letter, but he had none. The old man was right— what had happened to him (labor battalion, infantry, Stalingrad, hearing) was useless. Also, Slava was out of ideas. Every single item that Slava had scratched into his notebook from the history books had a line through it.

Eliyahu Mishkin, head of Judenrat—no, Epstein has done.

45 Jews roped together and ordered buried alive by 30 Russian prisoners. The Russians refuse. All 75 killed.

Last handful of surviving Jews when Red Army liberates.

Himmler nauseated by witnessing shooting of 100 Jews. Bach-Zelewski says it was "only a hundred." This has to be done more efficiently—more *humanely*, Himmler says. For the Germans, but also for the Jews. (!) Poison gas arises from this . . . But this won't do, how would an inmate *know* any of this?!

The coarseness of the last entry forced up a nauseating taste in his throat. Was he a monster, the details of death merely the instruments of a story, kindling for a vocation he didn't have the talent to practice another way? However, those details made for good stories—stories that stayed with him days after he'd written them, and would earn money for sufferers. What was coarse, then? When he abandoned his grandmother—that was coarse. When he agreed to stop at undetailed reverence and inquire no further about her—that was coarse. Perhaps one becomes aware of one's coarseness only when it's too late to do anything about it: Isaac Newton's little-known Fourth Law of Motion, Pertaining to the Maneuvers of the Soul.

What was coarser, to revere someone falsely for sainthood, or to know someone's sin but intimately? And if you couldn't know, then invent. Slava had not planned to have his grandmother stare Shulamit into suffocating her baby. (She hadn't, had she? He didn't answer.) Grandmother was fierce, everyone said, and he was trying to make her fierce, but then she wriggled out of his hands and started staring at Shulamit in that basement. (Did that mean Grandmother would have suffocated her own child?) If you wanted to write a good story, the facts *had to* become a story's instruments. You couldn't write without being coarse to the facts.

Slava noticed a cyclist staring at him from several seats away. In fact, he had been staring for quite a while, Slava noted belatedly. As soon as Slava looked back, the cyclist turned back to his phone. When had he gotten on? The same stop as Slava, Slava was suddenly sure. Again, his heart started going. *"Twenty-five-year-old suffers heart attack on the D train. At an age when others are swaddling children and commanding platoons under Stalingrad, he is felled by anxiety at being pursued for a crime. 'He wet his underpants for no reason, that one,' Yevgeny Gelman, a philosopher, said from a low stool."*

They stormed into Fifty-Fifth Street. Slava kept track of the cyclist out of one eye. The train took an eternity to come to a halt. Finally, the doors opened. Slava waited, his heart in his throat. Wait, wait, wait. The conductor began to announce the next stop. Wait. The doors dinged, signaling they were were about to close. Now! Slava barreled from his seat and out onto the platform, the doors sliding closed behind him, no time for the cyclist to pursue him. Slava, a rookie, could not resist turning back to gloat at his pursuer as the train pulled away, but the cyclist was absentmindedly chewing on a fingernail.

Slava sat on the platform, alone, his head in his hands. He took out his cell phone, called his mother, still at the Rudinskys'—now she and Aunt Lyuba were best friends, now they'd go long into the night—and asked for his grandfather.

"You making peace?" Slava said.

"Schnorrers."

"Go into the kitchen, please," Slava said. He waited until his instructions were heeded. "How long have you been charging?"

"It's all for you."

"I don't want it."

"Calm down. They're going to get ten thousand euros, what's five hundred the cost?"

"So you gave Lazar a break? Two-fifty."

"Goodwill."

"I don't want to do this anymore," Slava said.

"It's almost over. The deadline is next week."

"It's not the money."

"Now you don't want to do it? You liked it fine five minutes ago. When you say you're going to do something, you have to do it to the end. That's what a man does. So, what, you're not going to do Lazar's?"

"Give his money back."

"I'm not giving his money back."

"These people *hate* you. Because you do—*this*."

"Who hates me? They envy me. They wish they could do it."

"That's not the truth."

"Who tells the truth."

"That's the truth."

"How did it go with Vera?"

"They dressed her like a doll for me."

"So, she looks after herself. What she does—*piar*, what is that?"

"I don't know how to explain it," Slava said. "It's like advertising. The shampoo commercial with the woman whose hair is like after electroshock? And then she's twirling with the umbrella?"

"Vera sells shampoo?"

"No. I don't know. It's just an example."

"There's a nice girl, Slavik."

"She wants to reunite you—that's all she wants. She's obsessed."

"My heart aches, Lazar is so sick. Your grandfather is a rock compared to these guys."

"You're in pieces every time I call."

"I'm a frail man and my wife's just passed away, what do you want. Do you know how much I've been through?"

"Look, do you know anything about how Grandmother got out of the ghetto? How she made it out, how it all ended?"

"I wish I could say something," Grandfather said. "I've told you everything."

This conversation had become a nightly ritual, a minyan of two, readings from the slender book of Sofia Gelman née Dreitser. Usually, it went the same way—he had told Slava everything—but Slava called anyway. Sometimes a detail floated up through the murk of his brain, and sometimes Slava called just to make sure he was still breathing.

"I wish I'd made her tell me," Slava said.

"It was because you loved her that you didn't," Grandfather said.

Please describe, in as much detail as you can, where the Subject was during the years 1939 to 1945.

Lazar Rudinsky

Soon after the start of the war, an underground network formed in the Minsk ghetto. We organized contacts between the partisans, couriers from outside the ghetto, and ghetto workers who could carry off radios, iodine, cartridge belts. I worked in a tool shop, where I helped in what you could call a negative capacity. We mixed sand into the lubricant they used to clean their guns. We all tried to do something. Cobblers drove nails up their boots. At the auto-repair shop, they ground emery dust into the engine oil; it melted the bearings when they started their Volkswagens.

There was a neighborhood girl named Ada—she is dead now, may the earth be like down for her—whom I would see once in a while as they marched the work columns back to the ghetto. She was on a detail carting firewood for the building that the Germans were using for headquarters. Your heart dropped seeing these girls: our girls, plus some who had been brought from Austria and Germany. (They called these "the Hamburg girls," even though they were from all over.) The Belarusian policemen made them walk on the roadway while city people jeered and threw spoiled fruit from the sidewalks. Not everyone—people cried, too, watching these Jewish girls being led to labor like horses.

Ada signaled to me one time; this was March 1943. We had known each other slightly in the neighborhood, but she didn't circulate with my kind. I was too much a "child of other people's gardens," as we used to say. Maybe that's what made her turn to me for help.

At headquarters, there was a German, a Hauptmann Weidt. He worked in the quartermaster service corps. Weidt had fallen in love with one of the Hamburg girls. Ilse. I had seen her, too. She couldn't have been over eighteen. God had touched this girl—she was radiant. Weidt was almost three times her age. One afternoon, Ada told me, Ilse and Ada had been pushing a wheelbarrow when Weidt pulled them into a doorway and locked them in a closet. Soon, they heard wailing and that *kchyum-kchyum-kchyum* that you never forget. They were shooting the girls right in the courtyard. They had made them take off their clothes and shot them, one after the next.

Weidt had no special feeling for Ada, but Ilse, both of whose parents had been buried alive, was nearly mute, so Ada, who knew a little German, which after all is similar to our Yiddish, became like a go-between. It was the two of them he called when it was time to pick up lunch coupons for the work detail. While Ada choked on a pot of soup with beef chunks that Weidt had called up from the mess hall as if for himself, he and Ilse spoke quietly, their language the only thing they shared. Eventually, Weidt decided he wanted to get Ilse out. His rank was too junior for him to do much. The only way was to smuggle her to the partisans.

"What should I do?" Ada whispered to me. "He's in charge of all the equipment. He can get a work truck for twenty-five people."

"How do you know it isn't a trick?" I said.

"I don't know," she said. "The way he looks at her? The other day he asked me why Jews were being killed. I nearly jumped out of my skin. I should ask him, the blockhead! He said the German officers used to flirt with the Jewish girls during World War I, and now he has to make me cart firewood."

Several days before, the Germans had finished off the ghetto orphanage. Kube, the generalkommissar for Belarus, had made a special visit. He threw candies to the children as they were tossed alive into a pit and covered with sand. It was hard to argue for staying. In the next several days, I made contact with a partly Jewish partisan unit in Rusakovichi. The reaction was mixed, but the commander ordered us to go ahead. Weidt refused to arrange so many, but Ada was tough. She said twenty-five or no one. Eventually, he gave in. He was going to come, too.

I went to speak to my father, but he refused to leave without Zeyde, and the partisans wouldn't take an old, ailing man. Zeyde cursed at my father from the cot, but my father didn't want to discuss it. My father was a ferryman before the war; he delivered safes by horse cart. This was the age before elevators—he carted the safes to the third and fourth floor on his back. The man died without a file at the medical clinic. So you didn't argue much with him. He said I would go and they would follow soon after. After all, they'd made it this far. It was just a matter of time before Minsk was liberated. By then we had heard about Moscow, Stalingrad—it seemed like a reasonable thing to say. You believed him when he spoke.

The cover for the truck detail was an assignment to load cement at the railway station, on the outskirts of town. The partisans had said they would be waiting in one of three villages not far from the station. The driver was an ordinary German soldier. He had no idea about Weidt's plans, but I guess we benefited from the German fanaticism about protocol. As we rolled past the railway station, he didn't say a word.

After hours of driving from village to village, we stumbled onto a forward unit in Rusakovichi, which we had passed twice. The partisans made a mistake; they thought the driver was Weidt and approached off-guard. The soldier had time to fire off several rounds, killing one partisan and wounding another. Weidt had a bullet in the soldier's skull before any of the partisans had time to shoot back.

We slept the sleep of the free for the first time since July 1941, not really believing it—Ada and I, with Ilse squeezed between us like a child, in a tiny *zemlyanka* covered with birch leaves. Weidt they took to the commander's. We woke to shouting, thinking it had all ended so quickly, but it turned out that one of the partisans had lost his temper and was whaling Weidt. It was his brother who had been killed before in the mix-up with the driver. Weidt had his hands bound; the commander waited some time before interfering.

Weidt was gone by the time we awoke. A girl from night watch told us that he had been taken to partisan headquarters for the area; he had begged to say goodbye to Ilse. We never heard from him again. The Minsk ghetto was liquidated a month later. My father had picked such a terrible instance to be wrong for the first time in his life. When the commander made the announcement, I sat down on the grass and could not stand. Then, when no one was looking, I got some rope and walked off until I was out of sight in a clearing with tall trees. I was testing branches for give when Ada appeared. She had followed me. I wept into her shirt until it was soaked. It was a coarse shirt, fashioned from a sack that once held potatoes, and her skin was raw from it. But she managed to stop me.

A month later, I was ordered to join a mobile fighting unit and didn't see Ada again until after the war, back in the neighborhood. She kept her distance, like old times, and never mentioned the day in the clearing. One night about six months after the war ended, there was a dance in a little club on Shornaya. There was a bomb crater in one of the walls; they hadn't had time to fix it. Three quarters of Minsk was on the ground. You could feel the cold air through the wall once in a while. I was with my friends, Ada with hers, but at one point she came over. "Lazar, help," she said. "There's a captain over there who keeps asking me to dance. Says he wants to escort me home. I'm frightened."

"Am I just a thug?" I said. She looked away resentfully. "Fine," I said. "I help you with the captain, you go with me on a date."

She refused, so I returned to my friends, leaving her to stand there alone.

She came over. "So be it," she said. "One date."

The captain and I knew each other from the neighborhood. He lived by Tatar Gardens. You had to take it easy with army captains, but I was something, too. I'm an old camel now, but back then, sparks flew from my feet when I walked—you could light a cigarette if you wanted. I was known in the neighborhood. Anyway, I went over, put my arm around him, and said: "Captain, I just wanted to thank you."

"What for?" he said. He was nervous, you could see.

"For not letting my girl get lonesome." I pointed to Ada.

He turned the color of a sugar beet. "I had no idea. Forgive me, Lazar. You're a lucky fellow."

I walked Ada home that night. On our first date, she sat about a kilometer away from me. But she agreed to a second. I had a while of persuading ahead of me; we weren't married for another two years.

Move forward forty years. We were just about to emigrate to America. I was watching television when I heard Ada scream out my name. In the newspaper, there was an advertisement from an Ilse Shusterman, searching for fellow inmates from the

Minsk ghetto. Ada flew to Krasnodar to meet with her. Except for a lot of wrinkles, Ilse was the same beautiful girl, married to a scientist, a grandmother already, spoke fluent Russian. Before leaving, Ada asked if she had ever heard anything about Weidt. Ilse said that she had been told by the partisans that he had been assigned to a German POW camp. He had died there, for undisclosed reasons.

Did Ilse ever feel anything for Weidt? Ada didn't dare ask, and Ilse didn't volunteer. I doubt it. But it's to them that Ada and I owe the fifty-seven years that we had together.

Eighty thousand Jews lived in the Minsk ghetto, almost all of them killed. After the war, they got a memorial stone by one of the killing pits; it actually said Jews died here, as opposed to "Soviet patriots," which is what it said almost everywhere else—if they put up a plaque in the first place. After the war, the government kept saying they were going to tear down the memorial and fill in the pit.

Generalkommissar Kube also did not live to see the end of the war. His maid, who was part of the resistance, placed a bomb under his bed, timed to go off in the middle of the night. (What did that man dream about?) They had to scrape his brains off the ceiling. I regret it was an instant death.

Lazar wanted Slava to fall in love with his granddaughter, so Slava gave him a love story. The rest he invented, following one detail until it gave him the next. He had started far more carefully with the letters—lists of details, outlines, narrative arcs. He had always known what piece of information would come next. However, the stories came out better if he didn't know everything in advance. In real life, one thing might have happened, but in the letter? It might have, it might not. Was Weidt's plan a trick to root out ghetto inmates who were causing problems for the administration? Would he slip out of his ropes in the middle of the night, club to death the partisan guarding him, and spirit off Ilse? Was he first a devoted Nazi or a Nazi who had fallen in love? You had to write it down to find out.

In their claim letters, the estranged elders of Midwood, né Minsk, spent time together in a way they refused to in real life. Grandmother and Grandfather fell in love in Lazar's story; someone else got Lazar's poor hearing. However, other things were lost, blurred, made false. Mother, Father, and Zeyde killed when the ghetto was liquidated: That is what had happened to Grandmother's family, he was certain of that, even if the fact crowned Lazar's story. But was it her father who was a ferrier? And Grandfather hadn't demanded a date in exchange for helping Grandmother free herself of the leering captain, had he? Why had Slava written it differently, then? That was what the story had asked. The price was, by the end, Slava didn't remember what about it was true and what was invented.

He was startled by the ring of the phone. The last time it had rung this late, it had been to announce Grandmother's last trip to Maimonides. It rang several times before he picked up.

"Mr. Gelmonn?" arrived nasally from the other end. "I hef hea— Vyacheslav Gelman? Slava Gelman? Sam Gelman?"

"Who?" Slava said. No one used his full name. Sam Gelman? He had used that name for a year in junior high school.

"Vee-ya-chess-love Gelman," the nose continued to prod. "Terrific and unusual name. Is the number correct?"

"No, it's me," Slava said. He tried to chase the fatigue from his eyes. "Who's calling?"

"My name is Otto Barber. From the Conference on Material Claims Against Germany."

Slava's blood froze.

"Mr. Gelman?"

"Yes?"

"Your assistance would be most valuable."

"I don't understand," Slava said.

"Mr. Gelman, it has been to us a report," Otto Barber went on conspiratorially. "Regarding some of the letters that have arrived for the restitution. So I am hoping to speak with you."

Slava walked over to his futon and made himself lie down, as if to enforce casualness. "I don't understand," he repeated.

"I will explain all, naturally," Otto Barber said.

"How did you reach me?" Slava said, stalling. He wasn't going to write any more! He was the smoker who quits the day before he finds out he has cancer.

"Ze White Pages? Ze Yellow Pages? It is a listed number, excuse me."

Was it? "You're calling very late," Slava said, then wondered if he was giving himself away, too defensive. He had never thought about the phone. On the street, he turned around every time he was in Brooklyn. Foolishness—what, they were going to swoop down on him with sirens? It's never what you think.

"That is absolutely without manners, I agree," Otto said. "You have to please forgive me. I am like the rodent in the wheel here—meeting number one, meeting number two . . . We have meetings to plan meetings. It is quite unbelievable, actually: It is ten P.M., and have I been eating my dinner? No!" He giggled.

Slava didn't answer.

"Mr. Gelman, the letters are false!" Otto barreled on. "Can you believe this? Do you know anything about it, please?"

"Why would I know anything about it?" Slava insisted.

"Shame!" Otto bellowed, and giggled again. "I had my fingers crossed, I am telling you! Mr. Gelman, I would like to meet with you to discuss this subject. What you can tell us can be very valuable."

"What I can tell you?" Slava said.

"I would not dream of requesting you to come visit us at the Conference here—though it's a nice building and the coffee is free, yes! But maybe you and I drink something stronger together? If so, I'm buying! You are doing me the favor, Mr. Gelman, so I can come to you."

"I don't know what I can tell you," Slava repeated. "I had nothing to do with it."

"To do with it?" Otto shouted. "Oh my goodness, what laughter. You are a joker like me, Mr. Gelman. Together, we will get along. No, Mr. Gelman—*to do with it*? What, *you* wrote the false ones? Ha-ha-ha. No, Mr. Gelman, I want your . . . consulting. You are a complete American. You live on the Upper East Side, you work at *Century* magazine—though I find it quite boring, excuse me, our secret!—and yet you can understand the Russian person's thinking. Why does someone do this, *how* does someone do this. Because I am not trained for this kind of—sleuthing, I learned this word recently. I am, quite frankly—how do you say it—out of my level."

Slava's mind raced. If he turned Otto down, that would only increase suspicion. But why? Slava had every right to wish not to get involved. He had decided to separate from his neighborhood, so this was exactly the kind of entanglement he meant to stay away from. However, Otto knew a frightening number of things about him—how? No, Slava had to agree to a meeting. Under the guise of giving advice, he could ferret out what the German knew. Also, he needed to burn every piece of hard-copy evidence, retrieve the faxes from Grandfather's house, delete the files from his computer . . .

It had finally happened. Even as, all these weeks, he simultaneously dreaded and brushed away the possibility—why did he have to be caught? he didn't—Slava didn't feel surprise at the news on the other end of the line. It was relief of a kind: It had finally happened, the worst was in, and now he could get down to dealing with it. He had to start by meeting Otto. Certainly, he wasn't going to allow Otto to visit him at home; no, he wasn't as easy as that. But it would seem strange if Slava volunteered to go to the

Conference—an overaccommodation. Fine, they would meet in a bar. Slava would nurse a beer and Otto would keep drinking until he started to become careless with his words. That was the way.

"When do you want to meet?" Slava said. "I can meet tomorrow."

"Tomorrow?" Otto said. "Thanks God it's Friday, am I right? No, take the weekend, Mr. Gelman. We are not solving a murder here, ha-ha. This can keep—is that the expression? Is Monday available for you? Monday evening. I am finishing here at six P.M., even if they try to keep me with chains. That's the finishing hour at *Century*, isn't it?"

How did he *know* these things? Slava cursed himself for being too eager. "Seven?" he said weakly. It would be light out still, that felt safer somehow. Slava gave Otto the name of a bar in the neighborhood. If the man wanted advice so much, yes, he could come to Slava. The pub was neither a dive nor fashionable; it was invisible in the way Slava wanted.

"That is so convenient," Otto exclaimed. "I live in the neighborhood! The Yorkville area has a fantastic German history. I am almost like home!" He mentioned a bakery that prepared strudel and a butcher's that had been selling wurst since the 1920s. "I would not say, if we agree to be honest, the Upper East Side is a neighborhood for a thinking person. It is the Florida of New York, no? The recent graduates of the colleges, they are drinking themselves to blindness and everyone else is slowly waiting to die, even if they are forty years old! If the small German connection was not present, I would not live there."

Slava was still processing the news that he and Otto lived in the same neighborhood. Had Otto seen him on the street? Had they eaten at the same restaurant? Had Otto watched him from across a bar? Slava had never thought to look around him in Manhattan, only Brooklyn. *They were neighbors.*

"Akh, Mr. Gelman, you really have to forgive me. It's ten o'clock and I am chewing your ear with this nonsense. We will talk about everything—

about war, and maybe also a little bit about writing—when we meet. I look forward to it! Do you forgive me for calling so late?"

He really wanted an answer. Slava heard himself forgiving the German. The German erupted into a new series of exclamations. Only then did he bid Slava goodbye.

–14–

Slava had spent most of the night excavating the sheets on his side of the bed, grateful for the dead way in which Arianna slept. At last, he rose, the hour too early for light even in summer, and sat at her silver-leafed kitchen table, his hands clasped—a guilty person. He tried to reason through his options, but even though, restless in bed, he could think of nothing but sitting across from Otto, their conversation writing itself in his mind like a false letter, now, at the table, his head filled with a stubborn blankness. He chuckled sullenly. And what would Grandmother say about this turn? Was she an accomplice in Grandfather's subterfuges, and if so, an eager one or ashamed? Slava couldn't imagine Grandmother ashamed, even of sin. And yet, she was an upright person. So upright he couldn't imagine her loving Grandfather more than her own uprightness. But she was upright only toward loved ones. Slava mashed his hands together in agony, his eyes burning with a fatigue that made clear thinking impossible. He had been writing letters about his grandmother for weeks, but in moments like this, he felt as if he knew her barely at all, like a territory that grew larger the more of it you walked. It was the same with Arianna, he noted bitterly.

Worse: Grandmother only became more unknown; Arianna became more unfamiliar.

He checked the kitchen window for light, but you could see little there, as it overlooked one of those poetic brick walls on which so many New York windows gaze. The clock said a quarter after five. Slava stole back into the bedroom and lifted his cell phone from the pocket of his jeans. Arianna remained in oblivion, but the cat opened a knowing gray eye. Slava froze in place, then ridiculed himself—his guilt was such that he was ready to answer to an animal. Advertising his indifference to the bulk of black fur, he strode out of the room.

He swallowed heavily as the telephone rang. She would be up, she had to be at the pharmacy at half past six, but no one dialed for leisure at five A.M., and indeed, when his mother snatched up the phone, her voice was frantic with fear. Now only one old Gelman remained about whom bad news could arrive at this unholy hour—why did old people die only in the night?—and though she had checked in with Grandfather in the evening (he had complained about the springs in his mattress, would these be his last words to her? how hopeless and absurd), her son was now in contact with the old neighborhood more than she was. He might know first.

"Everything's fine, it's fine," he reassured her.

"What is it?" she said, her voice giving up fear but not puzzlement. No one was dead, but her son would not call just to call. She'd had to enter intimate terms with this new understanding in her life, like an illness.

Dear Mother: Was your mother a liar, a cheat? Did she look the other way while Grandfather fenced cars, smuggled gold, sold minks on the black market? Or was she his conspirator, his handler, his Bonnie? Did her uprightness extend only to the people she loved? What would she tell me to do now?

Instead, he said: "Summer's ending."

"Slava?" she said. "What is it?"

"Do you remember Mariela?" he said.

"The Spanish girl?" she said. Slava and Mariela had dated for a year and a half during college and had given it up—unusual wisdom, such young people—when they began to ask more of it than it could give. But for several months, they had been inseparable, the daughter of Colombian Catholics and the son of Soviet Jews making out in an empty room at the Met.

"I told Grandmother about her," he said. "She was sick already."

"Mariela? Have you seen her?"

"Do you know what Grandmother said?" he said. "She listened carefully. Then she said: 'Does she know how to cook?'"

His mother snorted.

"I said no. You remember Mariela—she didn't own a pot for macaroni. Grandmother thought about it, and then she said: 'What a putz.'"

His mother laughed, her voice less cautious. "Have you been going to the grave?" Slava said.

"Every weekend," she said.

"Maybe you should take some time from the pharmacy," he said.

"No, no," she said. "This way, my mind is busy. Working at the pharmacy, you get the impression that there are no healthy people in the world. The normal condition is not health but illness. It makes you feel better in a way—I used to ask God why only she became ill—but then you feel guilty about it. And I still ask God, only a different question: If so many are ill, why did she have to die? And I feel terrible, like a hideous person. But I miss my mother."

"As I miss her," he said.

"You can't sleep," she said.

"I can't sleep," he confirmed. "Would she have gone along? With what I'm doing?"

"She loved you so much," she said.

"But what I'm asking."

"She loved all of us. There was nothing you could do that she wouldn't go along with."

"This is just a nice thought. When she found me with Lusty Lena, she got me by the ears, I can still feel it."

"I don't know what you want me to say, son—we were having a nice conversation."

He apologized and gave in to silence. "It's getting light," he said at last. "Is it getting light by you?"

"Yes," she said. "You know the heat makes me crazy, but I think about fall, and I start crying. It's a crime for a person to die in the spring because everything is just beginning, and it's a crime for a person to die in the fall because everything is ending as it is, and a person can't die in the summer because it's the summer. A person should die in the winter. Only in the winter. I hope I die in the winter."

"Then the ground is icy and you probably have to pay the diggers more," he said, and they laughed at this joke about their frugality, the frugality of all immigrants.

"You have to go," he said. "You'll be late."

"So I'll be late," she said.

"We're performing a service, aren't we?" he said. "You keep them in prescriptions—you keep them alive—and I keep them in funds."

"It feels good to be on the same side as you," she said. "I am envious, however. They get to see you every day. You've skipped over us. I mean your father and me."

"You're too young to qualify," he tried to joke.

She laughed politely. "No, it's true, the grandparents are the ones with the stories. We always thought telling you less was the right way. Maybe your children will come to us."

"Say hello to her when you go to the cemetery," he said.

"You've remembered your Russian so quickly," she said. "No, you speak better than you used to. Shouldn't you visit her, too?"

"I visit her in my own way," he said.

Even though they, each for his own reason, did not wish to end the conversation, they had come to the end of what they could say in peace, and said goodbye.

He returned to the bed, sliding in gently so as not to rouse the cat despite their earlier disagreement. He listened obediently to Arianna's unlabored breathing, intending to be in someone's, something's, good graces. She slept heedlessly, her lips slightly ajar, her face an oval cameo. He discovered an intimate paradox: He had looked at her every day for more than a month but had not registered the color of her eyes. Now that her eyes were closed, however, he was without doubt that they were gray, a shining gray, though they seemed darker because of their thick lashes, which was why if someone had asked Slava what color they were, he would have said black, almost black.

Before they began to see each other regularly, her eyes were filled with a smirking amusement, which irritated him—she was making fun of him, his nose buried in work. Belatedly, he understood that smirk to have been an expression of self-protection, because soon it gave way to tender excitement, even admiration. And periodically to worry, to a futile intent on restraint—the two of them were moving so quickly. It was different now. When Arianna's freckled lids, the left with its divided birthmark, opened from sleep, they would gaze upon Slava with doubt and dread. He wanted her to keep sleeping, as in a fairy tale. Among these thoughts, finally he fell asleep.

The soiree in honor of Century *magazine was taking place in the home of the first girl Slava Gelman had kissed in America. Elizabeth Lechter had just had her braces removed, and her teeth shone in a perfect white row you could make out from across the room. However,*

Elizabeth was nowhere to be seen—it was as if Century *had agreed to have the party at the Lechters', all the way in suburban New Jersey, only if the Lechters made themselves scarce. This was a relief to Slava because his eyes were on Arianna, floating around the room in a red sheath dress, sleeved to her forearms, that ended midway down her thighs, and he didn't want to make Elizabeth feel bad.*

Beau, for some reason, wore a cape, mauve with white polka dots. Avi Liss nursed a gin and tonic by himself. Peter Devicki was chasing Charlie Headey's girlfriend around the Lechters' white leather couch, Headey's girlfriend squealing and their drinks spilling on the leather, to Slava's guilt and dismay. Beau ordered Peter to stop, and Peter wandered over to confer with his boss. Charlie Headey tried to confer with his girlfriend, but she waved him away; there was a kiddie pool in the middle of the Lechters' living room, and that was where she decided to rest. Arianna regarded her with a head-shaking smile from across the room.

A poster board was mounted above the Lechters' fireplace. It displayed the winning article in Beau Reasons's recent competition for a story about the adventures of an urban explorer. Above the article, in the unmistakable Century *font, the byline said: Peter Devicki. Slava strained to make out the story from his perch across the room but couldn't.*

After he finished conferring with Beau, Peter disappeared from the room. When he reentered, he held a black Sharpie in his hands. "That's a big kitchen," he said. "To the Lechters!" Beau shouted. "To the Lechters!" Mr. Grayson seconded. "To the Lechters!" Charlie Headey's girlfriend shrieked. The rest of the room joined in.

While the staff of Century *celebrated the Lechter family of Ridgewood, New Jersey, Peter Devicki went up to the poster board displaying Slava's article, uncapped the Sharpie, and drew a fat line across the byline. Above it, he wrote: Slava Gelman. Again, the room erupted in cheers. "To Peter Devicki!" people shouted. "To the Lechters!" "To the Lechters and Peter Devicki!" Even Avi Liss had risen from his seat, thrusting his glass outward, the Lechters' white couch by now covered with the colors of a half-dozen drinks.*

Slava sat motionlessly. He couldn't rise, though he needed to. He watched Arianna, who was not toasting with the rest of the group, walk up to the poster board and study it like a painting. Then, she turned around and walked toward Peter, who stood by a wall covered with brick faceplates to resemble a wall of exposed brick in the city. She wrapped her hand around his forearm, lowered her eyes, and began whispering into his neck.

A terrible feeling entered Slava's chest. He had to intervene but couldn't move. Was he there? He was there. One person noticed him. His grandfather noticed him. He stood in a corner across the room, like a schoolboy who had been disciplined. Slava felt a needle of irritation—the old man would say something to embarrass him.

His grandfather was wet, head to toe. He wore clothes, his usual clothes, corduroy pants and a wool sweater even though it was summer, but he was soaked and shivering, his teeth chattering, gold knocking on gold. Inside the corduroys, it was as if there were no flesh covering the bone of the knees—the left kneecap rattled against the right. The hands that emerged from the sweater, however, were fully fleshed. One over the other, they covered his balls as he cried out from fright.

Slava awoke with a start, ramming his head into a shelf above Arianna's bed. Whose idea had it been to build a shelf directly above the place that one slept? Was its use, whatever it was, not outweighed by the uselessness of ramming one's head into it immediately upon waking, as Slava had expected to since his first night with Arianna—the expectation haunted his sleep, and when he wasn't dreaming about Peter Devicki, he dreamed that he had rammed his head into the shelf, only to wake up and realize no, not yet. Finally, it had happened, and the dull ache, along with the weary recognition of something one has expected to take place for some time, spread across the back of his head as Arianna shifted in her sleep.

She slept like a tank. War could erupt on West End Avenue. Not that he could say a word about the shelf. She kept her books there, or her night glass of water. "You're not concerned that a glass of water is going to end up on your face in the middle of the night?" he asked one morning. "You're expecting an earthquake?" she answered, and he was made to dissolve in double entendres about earthquakes in bed. When they had sex afterward, he pushed with extra energy because he wanted the cursed glass to fall and *show* her, but it didn't. The second time he mentioned the shelf, it wasn't funny anymore. The third time, she simply pretended she hadn't heard him.

Now she turned toward him and draped her hot leg over his thighs. This one's body temperature rose to dangerous levels in the night, a fever that broke only with dawn, Slava massaging her suddenly blue fingertips until the color returned to them. For this reason, she had no air-conditioning, only ceiling fans attached to peeling, ornately molded ceilings by threadbare chains. Slava spent the night expecting to have his head mashed by the items on the shelf above his head and his legs by the fan dancing above him. That was the reason for his stupid dream! He slept in a state of constant anxiety.

She stirred. "I can *hear* you being angry in my sleep. What is it?"

He looked over. "I just rammed my head into the shelf."

She rolled her eyes. "Slava, for Christ's sake, we'll remove the shelf. You'll be a handy guy and remove the shelf."

"I need coffee," he said to say something.

"Make me a cup?" she said, trying to sound gentle, and turned to face the other side of the room.

He folded his arms across his chest and leaned his head gingerly against the perfidious shelf, a peace offering.

"You had a bad dream?" she said from the other side of the bed, her lips in her pillow.

"You ever think what you would do," he said, "if someone said . . . You have two children, and someone says, 'Choose which one lives.' "

"Jesus, Slava." She sat up and looked back at him. "No," she said flatly. "Can I answer after we have coffee?" She tossed aside the covers and rose. He watched her walk toward the bathroom, the sleeves of her T-shirt rolled up to her shoulders. At some point, she had started to wear underwear and a T-shirt to bed instead of the usual nothing. He wondered now if it was a small gesture of distance. All the same, Arianna Bock in underwear and a T-shirt was better than most girls naked. He swept aside his cover and followed her into the bathroom. Unwilling to miss the action, the cat darted inside after them.

She stood with her hands on the edge of the sink. Whenever she stood in place like this, she rested one foot against the ankle of the other, making a triangle of her legs. Sometimes, as she washed dishes late at night, he would sit at the kitchen table behind her and trace the curve of her ankles as they met each other at the tip of the triangle, an infinite loop.

He came up behind her and slid his arms inside hers, twenty fingers rimming the outer edge of the sink, the tips of hers still frightened and blue, his dark and thick next to hers.

"I don't even know what we're arguing about half the time," she said. She swiveled inside his arms, facing him. "I think about that all day long. That's not what I want to think about all day. I want to be calm." The sleep was gone from her eyes, and she, too, stared at him with the weary recognition of something one has expected to take place for some time. "I'm scared," she said. She exited the rim of his arms and sank down to the floor, running her arms around her legs. She vanished against the white subway tile.

He slid down next to her and took her fingers in his, rubbing out the blue sleep. The cat parked itself on the edge of the sink to listen in from above.

"If you sit on cold tile," he said, trying for levity, "you won't have kids. So the wives say in their tales."

"I like when you tell me about those things," she said. "You never talk about it."

"Gentlemen have much to fear as well, Grandfather says."

"Sexy talk," she sighed. "How is he? With everything."

"He's more fine than he says," Slava said. "He's blessed. He never pays enough attention to anything for it to touch him."

"Don't say that," she said.

"It's the truth," he said resentfully.

The weight of his secret pressed all about him, a stupid, blunt heaviness with no center or edge. He had to hold out only a little bit longer—the application deadline was just days away, and then he would be free, and they would be back to each other the way it was that first night. Slava didn't want to think about the other possibility: that their sudden awkwardness had nothing to do with his secret. That it was, quite simply, them, that the introductory luster of their connection was a fraud now giving way to the pallid fact: They were foreigners to each other. Even in the midst of an argument, they wished to tear off each other's clothes, but the depressing thought struck him that this wasn't enough, necessarily.

He thought of Otto, the day's first recollection out of the hundred to come, an unpleasant dream that wasn't a dream. Slava copped a bit of martyrdom from the victims of fate scattered around South Brooklyn—of course he had to be caught. At *Century*, he could invent entire townships and newspapers without raising flags. Here, no. Someone else gets away with murder. He—he pays.

The list of letters that remained to be written before the deadline burned from the pocket of his jeans across the room, as if it contained the phone numbers of other women and not eighty-year-olds. He had read that a group of survivors was lobbying to press the German parliament to revise the terms of restitution to include a broader cross section of evacuees and, for the first time, Red Army soldiers. He wanted it to end and he didn't want it to end.

"Does your head hurt?" she said. "From the shelf."

"Oh. No. No, it can stay. Really."

"No, we'll get rid of it. It was already here—"

"No, no."

They stopped speaking at the same time.

"Something's strange," she said, a stiff smile on her face.

"Something," he nodded.

He extended his arms. Slowly, warily, she lowered herself into them. The cat leaped off the counter, its paws hitting the tile with a dull thud, and joined them. Slava had never had animals, but he liked the cat. In the moments when he and Arianna didn't know how to be warm to each other, they could be warm to the animal. The animal didn't mind. It nestled between them, a package of simple, dumb, euphoric flesh, and issued a great yawn. The two humans made jokes about how boring their fight was.

"All right," she said. "Let's do something. Unless you're working."

"I'm taking a day off," he announced.

She produced a sound of disbelief.

"Easy, now," he said.

"Let's walk," she said.

"It's a hundred degrees outside," he said.

"Then that's our first clue," she said. "We want air-conditioning."

"It's cool here," he said, eyeing the bed.

She grinned. "Later. Let's get dressed."

He thought about doing what she had done that day several weeks before, when he had to leave for the library. Ask for five minutes, peel off her clothes, and push her down on the bed. She had shown him that you could impose on each other this way; the other would impose another time. Love was not equality but balance. On the bus ride back to his side of the borough, he had felt used but closer to her. However, he couldn't imagine doing the same thing now. The doleful corollary to her rule was that this kind of imbalance was possible only when the rest was steady. It had been in their first week, but less so the more time they spent together, a dismal irony. He rose and got dressed.

The city that had felt mellow and forgiving as they walked from Bar Kabul to Straight Shooters on their first night together now felt hyper and choleric. The thermometer affixed to the doorjamb of Arianna's apartment building said one hundred. However, the heat had emptied the streets, lending them the feel of a holiday weekend, which always created for Slava the illusion that the city was briefly his. "Where to?" he said, swatting at his forehead demonstratively.

They walked in the direction of the Museum of Natural History. When the Bocks of Brentwood began to visit New York with little Arianna, this was always the first stop; the Eagle liked eagles. (Sandra Bock, uncharmed by wildlife, waited in the café.) The museum plaza was empty save for gaggles of pigeons—these would survive the final desolation. Inside, in the sacerdotal dark, the light reserved for antelopes stunned in midleap, camp children mixed with Japanese and German tour groups, individual families gliding between them with the freedom of the unaffiliated. Arianna had dressed in sandals, a low-cut sailor shirt with short sleeves, and black shorts with gold buttons that ended right below the rim of her ass. Men contrived, in the gloom, to inspect this exciting genus, but even more so the women, reminding Slava of Uncle Pasha's insistence that it counted the most when the women looked. Slava thought about Pasha with weary amusement.

Arianna, trained by city sidewalks, cut a lane through the crowds, occasionally reaching back to make sure Slava was there. He followed like a kindergartner. She stopped now and then to say something about the ibex, the lynx, the coyotes that howled in the Los Angeles hills. All the animals looked the same to Slava: horns, hooves, enlarged watchful eyes. He listened with a rancid feeling. To him, she was synonymous with the city, but all this was also known to her. He loved this about her; she brought surprise to his life. But everywhere they went, she narrated. What if he had spent his boyhood trooping through the Museum of Natural History instead of deciphering letters and dictionary-tripping at his wood-paneled desk? Would he know as much as she did? Or was it something about her?

Stopped at a display, he wrapped his arms around her from behind, her collarbone familiar against his forearm. She stopped speaking and leaned into his chest. She had straightened her hair; he inhaled its burnt, smoky dryness. He lifted the tips with his fingers and kissed her neck. "I want to go," he heard himself say.

"You want to go home?" she said.

"I would like to show you a place now." He said it before he was certain of the destination, but the feeling was sure.

She nodded eagerly. "But let's stay like this for one more minute."

Outside, the wet air attacked immediately, and he stuck out a hand for a taxi. She noted the luxury—they always took the subway. He colored, embarrassed. My credit-card statements don't go to the Eagle, he wanted to say, but held his tongue. Did observant Arianna also notice that they had spent every night of the previous month at her apartment? No, this imbalance went unremarked. But he *preferred* her apartment. He was hopelessly tangled. He held the door as she climbed into the cab.

"Where are you taking me?" she said.

"Following the moment," he said, staring at the cabbie's brown neck. He made himself take her hand.

They rode silently. The Upper West Side turned into Midtown, then

Chelsea, the West Village, Battery Park—self-conscious, he splurged for the tunnel—and into Brooklyn.

"Where are we going?" she laughed.

"You don't love being in the dark?" he said as unstiffly as he could, though it came out stiff all the same. Now they had to keep holding hands to pretend they weren't angry at each other. Slava stared out his window. The street slowly revealed itself as familiar—he knew it only relative to the subway, so he recognized it with delay. He had been mugged here. Grandfather and Grandmother lived nearby then, before they found the better subsidized apartment in Midwood. The mugger had been Slav—not a Jew, but still, one of theirs. He had violet splotches of sleeplessness under his eyes and a long knife under his T-shirt—comically long, with a gilt handle, like a circus saber. Graciously, he explained: His family had just spent their savings on bail, and he needed cash for a lawyer.

Slava was with Igor Kraz, the boy who would become the proctologist. He had taught Slava how to karate-kick properly, and how to masturbate into a pillow, so there was use to having him around. He was studded with diamonds. Slava had nothing more than a silver bracelet and necklace, even these like insects he wanted to brush off. The jewelry had nothing to do with them; they were broadcasting their families' progress in America. Grandfather was upset with Slava for agreeing to nothing richer than silver. "But we can do better," he said again and again. "Why does he wear gold and you only silver? What, we don't have?"

When the mugger asked for their jewelry, they handed it over. The young proctologist had forgotten all his karate kicks. And when the thief asked for their addresses, to keep them from squealing, they told him the truth. He must have realized the angelfaces he had collared that day, because then he told the boys to be at the same corner an hour later with a thousand dollars. When they phoned their parents, the first thing they said was they needed a thousand dollars.

They were their parents' and grandparents' children. They did what they were told, parents or muggers, as they had been taught. Compliance with instructions—just say what the rules were—was as molecularly satisfying as a cool plum on a hot day. When he was little, the satisfaction of it reached to the part of Slava that burned when the tea he was drinking was too hot. So how had he turned out a forger? Had his grandfather's fraudulence found its way into him despite the Gelmans' best efforts to raise an obedient person? You can't stop the blood, it goes where it wants? Maybe the Gelmans, older and wiser, understood this and had been trying to keep him close in order to shelter him from it. This part of him—his proper and corrupt soul—appeared only when he squirmed out of their reach. He wished badly to ask Arianna, because he knew she would offer something that he hadn't considered, that would make him think about it differently. But he couldn't. He groaned, and she squeezed his hand.

The taxi stopped on Brighton Sixth. She opened her wallet, but he covered her hand and paid. Whipped by wind from the water, the air was less thick here, the sun exhausted by the punishment it had been meting out all afternoon. They stood looking down Brighton Beach Avenue, Arianna waiting for a signal from Slava. He glared at the doomed souls wandering past them, their legs varicose and bent, the jowls swimming in fat, bellies hung over the legs like overripe fruit. (Had Otto made his way down here, to see firsthand what he was dealing with in his folders, or did he prefer to keep his distance?) Yes, they weren't easy to be near. The mesh bags stuffed with discount tomatoes, the lumbering bodies heedless of traffic lights, the threadbare emporia that had to traffic in furs *and* DVDs *and* manicures to squeeze from the stone of this life the blood of a dollar. And these were the honest ones. After fifty years of Soviet chatteldom, they had come here to get fucked in the ass for a little bit longer before packing off to a spot at Lincoln Cemetery, even this impossible to acquire without money being passed under the table. They never even voted.

"You're always asking," Slava said. "Here it is. Here they are."

"Show it to me," she said.

They walked without plan, happenings from long ago reminding themselves to Slava. In this store, his grandfather had purchased a mink for Slava's mother without paying a dollar. The owner of the store, a man whose existence depended on wringing every penny out of the mink in Grandfather's hands, had ended up pleading with him to take it for free, though Slava didn't recall the exact reason or, more likely, was too young to comprehend the machinations, though he was old enough to understand that minks weren't free and watched his grandfather from below with wonder. That was Grandfather. Arianna reiterated her desire to meet him. People always wanted to meet Grandfather when you told them about him, Slava said. They lit up.

Here were Uzbeks, here Tajiks, here Georgians, here Moldovans. Here you could get a manicure *and* pedicure for ten dollars. (This truly elevated Arianna's eyebrows.) They were staring at the row of identically frost-haired women working the chairs of the beauty salon when Slava froze. Without thinking, he had brought Arianna to a neighborhood where half a dozen homes had enjoyed from him forged letters. What an amateur. His little heart had been wounded—he wanted to show her something that he, not she, knew, and he'd just yielded to the impulse. Grandfather had passed down his fraudulent soul? Slava was a pinkie on Grandfather's hand, no more.

"What is it?" Arianna said.

"So I just wanted to show you," he said quickly. "We can go." He cursed himself a second time; he was retreating as artlessly as he had approached.

"What?" she said. "We just got here. I want to go drink hot tea, Uzbek-style. Take me, please."

As they walked to the boardwalk, he tried to map the homes that required a wide berth and half listened as Arianna babbled on about their surroundings. Where he saw desperation and scraping, she saw another act in New York's great ethnic circus. As they walked past the Key Food, he thought he spotted old Anna Kots waddling out with a grocery cart, but it was a double. At the *chaikhana*, he strongly recommended a table in the back, away from the windows. It was cooler by the windows, Arianna said—they had been flung open, the sea spangling with a heat-crazed blue light past the wide beach. "I thought you wanted to be hot, like the Uzbeks," he said, and she obeyed.

"What *is* it?" she said when they were seated.

"Nothing, nothing," he said.

"Is it strange for you to be here?"

He was saved by the arrival of a waitress in an Uzbek rug cap. An earpiece wire coiled out of her ear. "Are you in the FBI?" he joked to her in Russian. She laughed—this was how the servers communicated with the kitchen. Arianna waited for a translation, but none came. She was asked, however, to choose the tea. Realizing that Slava was accompanied by an American, the waitress became formal. When she returned, she set down the tray and held up each item: "This is green tea, please—*kuk-choi*. This is spoons, please." She held up two rug caps: yes or no? Slava said no, Arianna said yes. The waitress permitted herself a smile and said in English: "I leave, you decide."

"Why does your grandfather know how Uzbeks drink tea?" Arianna said when the waitress departed.

"That was where he was evacuated during the war," Slava said cautiously.

"They're talking about expanding eligibility," she said. "It's in the paper. He might qualify in the end."

"We're hoping," Slava said twice as cautiously.

"I can't imagine what it's like there."

"He was conscription age; he would piss himself in the street so recruiters would think he was retarded."

"You always talk about him."

"You asked about him."

"I meant you never talk about your parents. And I only talk about my parents."

"I even have my grandfather's last name instead of my father's," Slava said. "They made the decisions, I guess. I would like to meet the Eagle."

"Sandra has her charms, too."

"I mean that I like the way you feel about him more."

She looked toward the water. "Do you know that in seven years in New York, I haven't seen the ocean."

"How does it compare to the other one?"

"Whenever I read *The Stranger*, when he kills the Arab on the beach, this is how I imagine it. The water so blue that it's black. And the sun so bright that everything feels bleached."

"You've read it more than once?"

"I reread books all the time. Especially if they made you read it in high school. Then it's like a measuring stick. This is what I thought about it at seventeen, this is what I think about it now. I used to love *One Hundred Years of Solitude*—if you leave out all the chauvinist crap. But I couldn't get through it last year. The woman eats dirt, the colonel's blood flows from the war back to the house where he was born . . . so melodramatic. It's me right now, not the book; I'll try again in a couple of years. I think good books should be translated once per generation. I have a *Stranger* from 1948 and 1982, but from England, and a 1988 American. They're all different." She sipped her tea, holding the *piala* from below with both palms. "García Márquez was brought up by his grandparents. That's the way I think of you."

He laughed. "You're rambling. Are you nervous?"

She smiled. "Maybe."

He extended a hand toward her. She placed a palm inside it. It was warm from the bottom of the tea bowl.

"Was Grandfather telling the truth?" Slava said. "Are you less warm because you are as hot as the weather?"

"I don't know," she said. "Let's go outside and check."

Miraculously, the ocean was stingingly crisp despite having been under assault from the sun for two months. It would stay swimmable until October, this guest welcome to linger. Arianna squealed as the water hit her toes. The rocketing spray climbed up her legs. He had forgotten all about the neighborhood's minefield of betrayal. Momentarily, he felt exempted from responsibility.

"It smells like fish," she said.

"No, fish smells like it," he said. They laughed. She kicked the surf in his direction. He filled his mouth with seawater and wouldn't stop chasing her until he had squirted it down her back.

They fell asleep on the sand, his rolled-up T-shirt for his pillow and his chest for hers. He smelled the brine on her face as he dozed off. His last thought before dozing off was: He was his best with her and his worst.

The sun had slunk off by the time he awoke. Arianna still slept, so he didn't dare move. The departing yolk of the sun streaked a final tantrum of pinks, violets, and golds, a better sunset than the hot, sweaty day deserved. He remembered reading in one of his newspapers that postcard sunsets were actually caused by excess smog. Just as human ash could give you gorgeous five-pound tomatoes. Just as Yevgeny Gelman, Israel Abramson, and Lazar Rudinsky, a hundred years later, would give you Arianna Bock. Everything in between was a loss, a write-off.

When she awoke, they wandered back down to the ocean's edge, the lapping sheets of the Atlantic theirs alone except for a couple petting by the lifeguard stand. The evening was taking on a bruised purple glow. A lone streetlight called them back from the boardwalk. The sand beneath them had cooled quickly, but if you buried your feet, it was still warm below.

"You were born over there," she said, and pointed into the darkness.

"The ocean in the dark freaks me out," he said.

"Me, too," she said.

She took his hand and they tiptoed into the cold black water. Slava had been staring at the river from the edge of his neighborhood for years, but this was his first step inside the water that bordered New York on all sides. When you thought about it, it was as waterbound as a Venice, or an Amsterdam, but here, this natural boundary had been reduced to a sideshow. You did not think of New York as a water city. What if the water rose, as the scientists kept saying now and then. What would go first? What would be carried away, and what would rise in its place? The thought of a different city, a city he could have a hand in, made him excited and gave him the boldness to wade deeper into the impenetrable ocean.

-15-

On Monday, the *Times* carried a story about a lawsuit against the German government by a group calling itself Advocates for Historical Justice. The plaintiffs, represented by an Australian attorney with the surely invented name of Howard Settledecker, had "made an appeal to the German Holocaust restitution funds to revise eligibility requirements to include those on the Eastern Front who had never been incarcerated in a ghetto or a concentration camp but had suffered nevertheless as a result of the German invasion."

Beau wore suspenders over a pink shirt. The sleeve creases could cut. His eyes gleamed with a weekend of rest, sport, and other diversions. He greeted everyone and slid his thumbs under his suspenders. "The fall issue this Friday," he said. "We might have late-breaking up front. Gruber is still filing. But it has to be shuttered on Friday. Acceptable to everyone?" Everyone nodded.

"There's a story in the *Times* today about Holocaust reparations," Beau went on. "Anyone read it? You know how I feel about the *Times* beating us, so we might ignore it. But just in case, there's a press conference this afternoon at the Museum of Jewish Heritage. Howard Settledecker! You're in for a treat. Mr. Grayson, when did my profile run?"

"I'll look it up, Mr. Reasons," Mr. Grayson said. "Nineteen ninety-seven, I believe."

"Who wants it?" Beau said. "I want two."

A familiar hand rose, the cuff of the blazer riding down to the elbow.

"Peter," Beau said. "Excellent. Who else?"

The cubicles produced no response. Slava's mind was floating with Otto, trying to imagine the angles.

"How about a rematch?" Beau said. "Mr. Gelman, can we have the honor? Let's see what our little clinic accomplished."

Slava looked up, startled. He felt Arianna at his temple again. He couldn't understand what she was trying to telegraph. Do it? Don't do it?

"Mr. Gelman?" Beau said. "Should I plead for you to take an assignment from *Century*?" The group tittered nervously.

Slava didn't speak.

"I'll take that as a yes," Beau said.

"Want to just go downtown together?" Peter said. "Split a cab?"

They whooshed downstairs in the glass elevator. Outside, Peter surged toward the curb and stuck out his hand. "There's a system," he explained once they'd climbed into the taxi. "You have to find the biggest building on the street and get ahead of it. Most people don't think of that. They just stand in front of their buildings and wait."

"Doesn't the building with the most people also have the most cabs emptying out?" Slava said.

Peter scratched the wisps sprouting from his chin and admitted that Slava had a point.

They continued in silence. They hadn't spoken since the competition. They hadn't spoken much before, either, but now their distance had an ill-feeling cast. At Thirty-Fourth, Peter turned to Slava. "Can we clear the air?" He extended a hand.

Slava nodded and took it. Despite his near translucence, Peter had a firm, dry clasp. "Thanks," Peter said. "I'm glad."

"Tell me what it takes," Slava said.

Peter looked at him quizzically.

"They publish everything you give them."

Peter threw his head back, flattered and exasperated. "About one out of ten things I give them."

"What does it take?"

"What difference does it make?" Peter said. "You don't like what I write, anyway."

Slava, confronted with the truth, said nothing.

"There's a style," Peter said. "It's not your style."

"I want it to be my style," Slava said.

"You don't," Peter said. "Otherwise, it would be."

Despite the choking weather, the press conference was taking place outside. Slava didn't understand why Settledecker was passing up the opportunity to be photographed inside, next to the cattle cars and shoe piles advertised by the banners lining the drive to the museum. Slava had skimmed the *Times* story before walking out with Peter: Australian Settledecker (he owned a quarter of some sparsely settled territory in the country's hinterland), "the unapologetic mastermind of controversial publicity campaigns that have succeeded in compelling United Nations resolutions, the return of looted art, and university firings." In resentment, Slava had declined to peruse Beau's article.

On a broad gray dais, Settledecker swung his long arms and scratched his beard. He wore an ill-fitting three-piece suit. You could see his ankles when he gestured with special intensity.

"What's with the suit?" Peter said. "He looks like a tailor from the shtetl." He pronounced "shtetl" carefully, as if he had learned the word that morning in the *Encyclopedia of Jewish History* in the fact-checkers' library.

Peter had instincts; he was right without knowing it. The vest, the striped shirt underneath it, the usually fastidious beard allowed to go unkempt: Settledecker was subtly channeling a poor Jew.

There were three rows of black folding chairs to the side of the dais, filled with pensioners holding on to reedy bouffants in the suffocating wind off the Hudson. By the cheap jackets shielding them from the clandestine ravages of the breeze, by the gold teeth sparkling in the strong sun, by the dazed faces—you knew. *Nashi.* Russians all.

Slava made the next observation in his notepad with astonishment: Underneath the jackets, they wore prison uniforms. Striped prison uniforms. They could have been from a Halloween store. Numbers had been embroidered on the chests, yellow stars taped beneath them. Some of the seniors, worried about the lost impact of stars concealed by outerwear, had un-Velcroed the six-pointed stars and were trying to affix them to their overcoats.

They snacked: cylinders of cookies, bread-and-cheese sandwiches, yogurt. Behind the seating, a long table covered in white tablecloths held bowls of sandwiches and bottles of water for the postcoital repast. The seated periodically turned to make sure no one was making unauthorized advances on the food. On the rim of the meadow, penny-colored seniors visiting from Florida paused to take in their less well-preserved contemporaries on camcorder.

"Why would they put all these old people in the heat?" Slava said to Peter.

"You think they could fit this arrangement inside?" Peter said, his pen moving fluidly down his notepad. "I'm going to walk around." He nodded toward the chairs.

Two young women were trying to attach a large banner that said "Remembrance" to a fence behind the dais. It kept kicking up in the wind.

Settledecker yelled at them from the platform, the coils of his hair leaping and crouching. Eventually, he gave up and began to choreograph a camera crew unfolding its mantises. He shouted for an assistant to weigh down the napkin towers on the serving tables.

Peter was bent above a turtle-faced pensioner. "Look at that *kikele*," the older man was shouting, pointing his sailing cap at Settledecker. "Ai-ai-ai. You have to admire how far a Jew can go in this country."

Peter looked at Slava and smiled dumbly, pointing his pen at Turtle-Face. The Devickis, nobles of Poland, had partaken of Russian boar and timber but hadn't bothered with the language. Peter was straining for the dim corners of long-unvisited brain rooms where a grandmother or grandfather once used words that shared more than they didn't with Russian. From where in Poland had Peter's ancestors come? Slava would have to ask him. Minsk had been the western edge of the Soviet Union until 1939, the villages west of it Polish territory. If it wasn't for transliteration and history, he and Peter could have been countrymen. Peter could have been Slava's Slav twin.

Slava was about to start across to help when one of Settledecker's assistants appeared before them. She knelt in front of the old man, her black top hot just to look at. Settledecker seemed to surround himself only with women. Peter said something to the girl, then looked back at Slava, thumbs up.

At last everything was ready—the seniors seated, the assistants lined up behind Settledecker, the cameramen staring into their viewfinders. Settledecker scratched at his beard and approached the microphone, his modest potbelly jiggling. Cautiously, he tapped the head, as if it were the first microphone of his life.

"Ladies and gentlemen," he said. He swiveled to face the rows of folding chairs. "Survivors," he nodded. He returned his gaze to the cameras and looked ahead without speaking. All at once there was too much silence. Settledecker coughed. Then he turned back to the folding chairs. The pensioners were motionless. Settledecker rolled his eyes and, half turning,

hissed to someone behind him. One of the assistants ran down the steps of
the dais and whispered into the ear of the woman in the corner chair of the
first row. *Oi-oi-oi.* The woman slapped her forehead and pulled at the
nylon jacket of the woman next to her. "*Poshli*, Roza, *my idyom!*" *Let's go,
Roza, we're moving.*

The first row followed with discipline. Then the second, waiting patiently until the first had filed out. Settledecker nodded from the stage.
The lead woman, the assistant's hand gently steering her back, began to
mount the platform. Roza and the rest followed. Ghosts, they were going
to file past Settledecker as he spoke.

"Ladies and gen—" Settledecker started again, but a tugboat blared
from the Hudson. He opened his hands to the sky. "We will begin, of
course, only when God wills it." Light laughter from the grass. "Ladies and
gentlemen," he said. He half turned again: "Survivors." He pointed at the
cameras. "And I do call them survivors. Because they are. I am going to
pose a question to you. Any of you. You, sir." He selected a cameraman.
"Imagine your country—our country—is invaded. Imagine our
conquerors—and make no mistake, we've been conquered—our conquerors have no special feeling for Americans, but it's New Yorkers they really
dislike. Oh, they *really* hate them. Difficult to imagine, isn't it?" Another
round of laughter. "The rest of America is more or less autonomous, but
New Yorkers they herd into concentration camps." Settledecker lifted his
hand and began to count on his fingers. "Starvation. Disease. Extermina-
tion. Gas chambers. You see what I'm getting at. Sir, where are you from?"

The cameraman whom Settledecker was pointing to uncoupled his face
from his viewfinder. "The Bronx," he shouted up to the stage.

"The Bronx!" Settledecker repeated. The prisoners filed behind him,
professional grief in their faces, their bodies tired and slumped. They didn't
know what was being said. Someone had told them that doing this might
get them money. In their heads, calculations were being made about what
those euros could buy. A new car for the son-in-law. And a limousine me-

dallion. Enough to help the children get a down payment together, because everyone else's children already owned a home. They would crawl across the dais if that's what it took.

"The Bronx is an internment camp, my friend," Settledecker went on. "Your family—you got a family, sir?"

"Two kids," the cameraman shouted. There was a bored practice to his tone.

"Two kids," Settledecker said. "And a wife who brought them into the world, I presume?" He paused again for mild laughter. "Well, they are in Camp Bronx. But—last question, sir, I promise—your name?"

"Joseph Rumana," the cameraman said. "Junior. You want to know what we're having for dinner?"

The other cameramen laughed. Settledecker smiled tolerantly into the microphone. "*Thank you*, sir."

The cameraman cocked a finger at Settledecker and pulled the trigger. He was a plant.

"The Rumanas are rounded up. But Mr. Rumana—loving husband and father—finds a way for his family to slip out, leaving him alone in the camp. His wife and children spend the next four years wandering the country, living off scraps, fending off attack, suffering the worst kind of humiliation—because by now there are people in Utah and Texas who say, 'Let them have New York. Then they'll leave us alone.' The war is so long, Mr. Rumana's boys become old enough to join the U.S. Army. In trenches they fight. Mrs. Rumana works twenty-hour shifts in a factory, making munitions.

"It's like this for years, ladies and gentlemen," Settledecker went on. "*Years*. When it's over, there used to be eight million in New York. Now there are two. Imagine this city with two million people. I know, I know—room to walk. But I'm serious. Miraculously, Mr. Rumana has survived. He weighs a third of what he used to, he's sick with things medicine has yet to describe, he's seen things that none of us can imagine. But he's alive. For decades, Mr. Rumana must agitate against the German government to have a value put on his suffering. Can it be measured in numbers? That's not for us to answer." Settledecker pointed an index finger at the sky. He was warmed up now, swaying.

"But something that we *do* have to ponder: German restitution covers only Mr. Rumana. That's right—everything that his wife and his boys went through, all because New York was invaded by Germans, and they won't see a cent. Sixty years later! Mrs. Rumana is eighty-seven years old! These are her last days on earth. She has gout, arthritis, glaucoma. From day after day working in the dark, casting artillery shells. But no! The generous German government doesn't cover anyone who wasn't—I quote to you from the official documents—'incarcerated in concentration camps, ghettos, or forced labor battalions.' Shame, ladies and gentlemen!" Settledecker was thundering, his cheeks quivering. "Shame!" he bellowed, and for a moment it was easy to imagine that there was no act in his speech. He blinked several times, his words echoing. The survivors had finished filing past him. They milled on the other side of the dais, unsure what to do.

"But why resort to fiction?" Settledecker said quietly, now in the transport of tormented appeal. "Why don't we hear the facts from the survivors themselves? And then you decide for yourselves. You won't hear from me again. Decide for yourselves. Decide if you want to petition your congressman, your senator. The choice is in your hands. No one else can help these people, only your word. But who will speak up when they come for me? Yes, please."

Settledecker, eyes afire, turned to the pack of seniors and gestured to the woman who had been in the first seat in the corner row. The woman was a cake, concentric tiers of flab from her face to her waistline. But her nails were tidy semicircles, and thick amber earrings hung from her ears. She lolled her head weakly.

"Yes, yes," Settledecker confirmed, dribbling his head. "Now, please." He lowered the microphone. The cake shrugged and separated herself from the crowd. Panting, she climbed the stairs, Settledecker lifting her by the elbow. The wind had stolen several strands from the golden fog of her hair. They fluttered around her face like streamers, so light in the sun that it was easy to imagine what she looked like as a young woman. In 1941, to this woman, as to Grandmother, the world must have felt like the final version of itself. Nothing could make the lives they were living seem obsolete. After the war, Grandmother would pretend to agree with the neighborhood: Grandfather was unsuitable, a hooligan. But she no longer had parents or grandparents, and in her mind, Grandfather was like a rock against whom even the worst things might break.

Had Grandfather told Slava this, or had Slava made it up?

Slava's father, when he came to court his mother, was also unsuitable, only for the opposite reason. He was shy and hid behind his wife. Mother pretended to agree with her parents that he was unsuitable, but in her mind, he was a rest from rock-Grandfather's dictations.

What was Slava's place in this sequence? Would the woman he wanted to marry have to lie to her parents about the kind of person he was? In the historical pattern, he was supposed to repeat Grandfather, a rock.

On the dais, the woman, unlike Settledecker a genuine technological novice, leaned in so closely that her lips touched the microphone. "I'm sori, pliz," she said. "I no spik English." She looked over at Settledecker. His face was a rictus of exasperation and rage. He wheeled around and blinked at the crowd. Finally, he found whom he needed. He began to snap his fingers.

The young woman who had saved Devicki with Turtle-Face began pardoning her way through the crowd. Slava could see her in profile, her makeup glittering in the sun. From the side she looked like a painted doll, the pear of her ass swaying in a tight skirt. She mounted the stairs and turned to face the crowd. Now Slava could see her face in full.

"Hello, everyone," she said. "My name is Vera. I will translate." Then she turned to the older woman and whispered in Russian: "Speak."

*The seniors piled their mesh satchels with diagonally sliced halves of south-*western turkey wraps. They worked with a martial exactness, words rarely passing between them. *Sima, syuda. Dai sumku. Net, te bez myasa.* (Sima, over here. Give me the bag. No, don't bother, those don't have meat.) The husband removed the stones keeping the napkins in place, the wife plucked open two napkins, the husband nested the sandwich between them. Those without spouses worked with friends, neighbors, new partners.

"So this is the Russian-to-American account," Slava said when Vera had finished a row of interviews at Settledecker's side.

"The one," she said, nodding. "I thought maybe you'd come to this."

"Why didn't you say anything?" Slava said.

"It's no big deal," she said. "It's not like what you're doing."

He spun around and counted the television crews. She shrugged.

"It's so hot," he said. "Why is everything outside?"

"We tried. The museum didn't like the prisoner trick. They wanted an association, yes, but they said outside only. Doing it on the lawn was the bargain. Off the record, okay?"

"You have to say that first," Slava tried to joke.

"You're the professional," she shrugged.

"This was your idea, not his, wasn't it?" Slava said.

She nodded.

"You're good," Slava said.

"Are you surprised?" she said. She pulled uncomfortably at her blouse. It was too coarse for the weather, but it outlined her chest handsomely; probably Settledecker had made her wear it. For ten minutes after the ceremony, the cameras interviewed Vera while Settledecker steamed beside the dais. Though he wanted the attention, he knew that he was getting what he wanted with her in front of the cameras.

"Slava, why are you doing what you are doing?" she said.

Slava looked away. "I don't know anymore. Truthfully."

"So maybe you don't know everything," she said. "Your head can be a watermelon sometimes. A lot of juice but a lot of water. You know, you could have asked me at the house what were the scrapbooks with the Halloween costumes. But you were not interested. You like to put us down. I don't care, Slava, for your information. But them? They are old, Slava. They are in a place they don't understand."

"And what do you want?" he said.

"I want them to have comfort."

"You, you," he said irritably. "Not them."

"I don't know what you want me to say."

Slava looked away. The woman who had been calling for Sima earlier shouted to find out if Sima had found the cake. Sima replied that she had, Fanechka, thank you.

The wind had won a temporary reprieve from the heat and, added to the shade they had found, was actually pleasant. You could imagine the world cooling down.

"I earn half as much as you do," he said. "And I want away from all this. Why would your parents want us to be together?"

"For someone who wants to go away, you spend a lot of time in the neighborhood."

"It's temporary."

"You sure?" she said. She watched the camera crews folding up. "You used to be different. They think it's a phase."

"And you agree with them."

"You're still one of us, Slava. A strange you is still better than an American. They can understand you."

"Do you know what I think?" he said. "You don't want this. They want this."

She lifted a palm to his cheek. "You talk and talk," she said. "You make everything so complicated. I'll see you tomorrow."

"What's tomorrow?" he said.

"At your grandfather's?" she said. "Everyone's getting together. The applications are due the next day."

"I know when the applications are due. No one told me."

"They came up with it at our place last week. Your grandfather didn't tell you? I think he's a little afraid of calling you. But it's not like you're not invited. You are the author."

"My grandfather invited people to his house?" Slava said. She had to have mixed something up.

"It's a nice idea," she said. "Really an excuse to spend time together. Our old people are lonely."

His grandfather was going to have over the Katznelsons, the Kogans, the Rubinshteins? Whose grave inconsiderations he had borne with an unspeaking pride all these years? But six weeks ago, an evening hello from an investigator for the Claims Conference also would have seemed far-fetched.

Slava peered past Vera at Peter, skulking around the seniors, strands of Yiddo-English rising into the air. Slava wouldn't bother trying to file a piece for *Century*. Peter would get only the cream of the story, but he would write about what had actually happened: the survivors' agenda, their quotes. It was far better for these old people to have Peter Devicki file a piece. His was far likelier to see print.

He turned back to Vera. Of course he would be there.

−16−

Otto Barber had a professor's wild, unkempt hair, its loose gray strands billowing mildly in the line of a fan thrumming from above the bar. All around Otto, young people were working through liter-size pitchers of lager, but the German had ordered in the European manner, .3 liters. Lifting the glass, he barely wet his lips. Watching from the doorway, Slava was reminded of a walk he had taken with his father in Italy. After many aimless turns, they stopped, Slava not sure why, at the window of a café like a hundred others. This one had only a single customer, sidled up to the copper-top bar. It was the lunch hour; he was in his postman's uniform. He ordered a juice—Slava's father, of lesser eyesight and lesser Italian, asked Slava what kind it was, and Slava proudly said, reading the label, pera, grusha, pear. The barman retrieved the potbellied bottle from a fridge, followed by a lowball from a rack. He deposited a small square napkin on the bar, on it the empty glass. Then he tipped the bottle of juice over the glass. The two men continued to talk while the barman poured. He poured for a minute. The final drops slid from the neck of the bottle with torturous slowness. Finally, the bottle was empty, the glass filled to its neck. The two men spoke for another minute before the postman reached for the glass, as if his thirst were not pressing. Once he had taken a sip, the juice barely touching his lips, the barman vanished, the bar the postman's alone. He unfolded a newspaper, and both Slava and his father thought they could hear the snap of its crease before it landed next to the juice. Slava's father looked down at his son and smiled in a resigned, fatal way.

"Mr. Gelman!" Slava heard through the noise of the bar. Otto was barreling toward him like a castaway. "Well, it is you," he said proudly on reaching Slava.

"You can call me Slava," Slava said.

"My assistant says it's a name with great meaning," Otto said. He pumped Slava's hand and even bowed slightly. "She's also a Soviet émigré," he hastened to explain. "Lyudmila. Please, Mr. Gelman—Slava, excuse me—let us not stand here like guests." He extended his arm toward the back of the bar, where the bartender had placed a coaster over Otto's glass.

"What is your poison?" Otto said as he lowered himself in his chair. "Did I say it correctly? As promised, I am buying."

Slava looked up at the bartender, but he was experimenting with the foam on a Boddington and had no interest in their conversation. Not to prolong matters, Slava asked for the Boddington, but in his nervousness, he elbowed it onto the bar. When he looked up apologetically, the bartender only shrugged. "I'll practice the perfect Boddie till kingdom come," he said. "You'll have to pay me again, though."

"*I* will pay," Otto shouted. The bartender, mopping up the spill with a dirty towel, looked up at the odd pair before him. Otto waved him away. "Mr. Gelman, I will tell you a story," he said. "One time my father and I met for tea. I had just finished university—I was struggling to find a direction for my life. It is a problem for all men at twenty-two, but in our country, with a father like mine—you understand. He was a serious man, a strict man, but in the most positive sense, and he believed that the value of going around without a goal, well, it was nil. Better to file the same bolt over and over at the motor factory, not that he was a great ad-mirer of such things, than wander the streets and drink coffee and think about—what?

"Anyway, we met for tea. I was wearing yellow running shoes! Oh, it was the 1970s, and I imagined myself an adventurous person, but how foolish to meet your father for a discussion about the direction of your life in yellow running shoes!" Otto slapped the bar, delighted at his callow-ness.

"Anyway, I was so nervous. The waitress brought over the tea in these two very attractive small pots, and what did I do? I spilled the whole pot in my lap. All over my yellow shoes, all over my jeans, so it looked like—excuse me—like I went to the bathroom." Otto hiccuped from the beer and apologized.

"I think it is taking all of my father's power not to shake his head. I excused myself and went to the bathroom to wash up. And in that time the waitress had brought a new pot of tea—for free, I would like to add, Mr. Bartender, ha-ha! No, I am joking, it is okay. And what happened then, Mr. Gelman? Can you guess?" Otto's eyes sparkled with anticipation.

"You spilled the tea all over again," Slava said grimly.

"That is correct!" Otto shouted. "That is so very sadly correct. You see? You are a storyteller. You know how it ends. But also it doesn't end that way!" He wagged his finger. "My father rose from the table, and I thought, He is going to walk away in disgust. I could see the waitress laughing be-hind the bar. But he took me by the shoulders. And he said: *Ich bin fertig aber dir gehört die Welt. Sei dir selbst treu.*" Otto gleamed at Slava as if they spoke the same language. Finally, he relented and translated: "'I am a fin-ished man, but you have the world. Be true to your own strange kind.' It was lines from literature. Did I think my father read a single page of literature in his life? No!" Otto looked off and recited: "'I am a finished man . . . But you are quite a different matter: God has prepared a life for you . . . Become a sun and everyone will see you. The sun must be the sun first of all.'"

He turned back to Slava. With bewilderment, Slava realized Otto was waiting for an assessment of his performance. Slava mumbled a compliment. Otto nodded demurely.

"Mr. Gelman, my position is, how do you say"—Otto made the motion of cuffed wrists—"but at sixty-five, you are free. With a nice state pension. I will not say this even to my wife, but I will say it to you: There is a book inside me. Maybe there is some advice, even, you can give me. Isn't this the biggest task of them all? To organize these thoughts running around inside us, to stop the river of time just one second?" He shook his head tragically.

"I can hardly help you if I have no idea what's going on," Slava said, trying to sound casual as he delivered the line he had practiced so many times. What he really wanted to know was why he was sitting there if he wasn't the accused, and how Otto knew so much about him, but that he couldn't ask. He counseled himself patience.

"Pathetic," Otto said, shaking his head. "I would much rather speak with you about life and the books we can write than . . . Maybe it's because I am nervous? I'm telling you, this is not exactly what I do every day." He held up his hands. "This"—he moved his finger between them—"was not in my job description. Do you want to see the job description? It says: 'Boring, boring, boring. Paper, paper, paper.'" He laughed. "So, when this arrived on my desk, I confess to you, I was quite excited. I hope you understand I am not playing light with the subject, it's just exciting sometimes to step outside your skin and play Sherlock Holmes."

"And what do you do?" Slava said. From another table, a chorus of cheers marked the downing of a whole liter in one go.

"Me?" Otto's expression became serious and sad. "I try to make it so the money comes more quickly for the old people. Sometimes this one paper becomes lost in the channels, or this office is on vacation, and for no very good reason, the old Russian Jewish person here in America is waiting for money and thinking the worst things about the Germans—again. So in this small way . . ." Otto trailed off. He had a broad, kind face, almost square, the jaws pressing out of the skin, academic in the thin owlish glasses perched atop a broad ex-boxer's nose. In surface area, it bested a Jewish nose, but the shape was non-Semitic. Jewish noses amplified vertically, while Aryan noses metastasized sideways.

"Here is the complication, Mr. Gelman," Otto said almost apologetically. "Germany is a democratic country. Sometimes too much so. But it is all a reaction to—to what was. Regardless, it is a democratic country, with some parliament members positioned against this law. Not because they are anti-Semitic, Mr. Gelman, don't rush to conclusions. Simply, they say that because of all the documents destroyed by the Nazi soldiers, and all the documents that the Russian authorities will never share, proof is impossible. So, the restitution program, it is almost asking for fraud. There is a way to give reparations, but this is not it."

"And what is?" Slava said.

Otto spread his hands. "I don't know, Mr. Gelman. I am not in the law-making mechanism. But I would like to do my part to prevent Herr Schuler from Niedersachsen from saying, 'I told you so.'"

"And this—" Slava said.

"This equals 'I told you so,' yes," Otto nodded. "Because I have this report. My professional obligation is to investigate the report. If I come to zero, I have no choice but to make a declaration to Herr Schuler, who runs the committee in parliament. And then Herr Schuler has a press conference in front of the Reichstag, and then there is no telling what will be the result. You can probably say kaput to this new proposal for expanded eligibility, that's what. Not to mention some legal consequences for the guilty person. But if I can find the results by *myself*"—Otto poked himself in the chest—"well, it couldn't be more simple. We take them out. 'Internally handled' is the phrase. It never happened. If the person who is doing this gives up the fake ones, he can save the ones who are real. Or she, or she," he hastened to add. "In this time, we must be politically correct about identities of criminals also, ha-ha." He leaned forward with coppery breath.

"But you know what, Mr. Gelman? I don't care who's doing this. Herr Schuler is a rigid donkey. And what Herr Schuler doesn't know isn't going to murder Herr Schuler in his sleep."

Slava laughed. "So you are going to commit your own fraud to prevent the original fraud?"

"Fraud?" Otto sprang back. "Who said the original issue is fraud?"

Slava's face fell. "I thought you said . . ." He felt his face color.

"Ha!" Otto broke into laughter and slapped the bar with his hand. "I got you! I am pulling your leg, ha-ha!" He buried his face in the crook of his arm. "I'm sorry, Mr. Gelman," he said, emerging. "I am truly unprofessional. This investigation business is overexciting sometimes. No, you are right—it is a smaller sin for the sake of a big justice, that's right."

"Why can't you just pay them?" Slava said. "Just pay them all. So what if they're false? What if a thousand of them are false? What if you pay every—all the people who want expanded eligibility now, the soldiers, the evacuees. What if you pay every one of them? It wouldn't break Germany, and it still wouldn't be enough. It will never be enough."

Otto looked at him chidingly, as if at a petulant child. "Mr. Gelman, do you know who my father was? He was a soldier in the Wehrmacht. And my mother was a nurse for the wounded soldiers. But that is not why I am sitting here. I do not believe in the sin of collection. The war was over six years when I was born. I will not deny anything about my father—not what he did during the war but also not that he was a wonderful father. But those Red Army soldiers did not rape woman after woman in Berlin?" He held up his hand. "Mr. Gelman, we can go on and on like this. This is why there is a law. If I was born six years after the war, you were not even a shine in the eyes of your parents. Even your parents did not exist yet. The suffering of your grandparents belongs to you not any more than I belong to the crimes of my father." He held up both hands. "I know what you say next in this dictation: 'My parents almost did not exist because of people like your father.' I know. The dictation is well practiced. Let us go beyond the dictation.

Let's take this down from the sky. I understand there cannot be justice. So all there can be, then, is the law. This is about people who deserve help. Let's help them."

"But what is it that you want from me?" Slava said.

"I want to understand what makes someone do this, Mr. Gelman. You have just argued to me on the moral ground. They all deserve it and then in addition. All right. Is this the deciding factor, or are there others?"

"Why not?" Slava said.

"Well," Otto held up his hands. "I don't know. It is somehow too handsome. Too easy. The moral defender."

"You are not a moral defender?" Slava said.

"Akh," Otto waved his hand. "What kind of a defender am I? Paper-pushing. I am making sure there are no interruptions, that all papers go where they need to. Yes, it is my small contribution, but morality is a big word. A word from a capital letter. I am not a moral defender."

"The letters—it's the same thing," Slava said. "A smaller sin for a big justice."

"I don't know," Otto said. "Perhaps. You know, the motive doesn't matter, only finding the false ones. The motive I am simply curious about. I began to look into this, and— Well, it is more interesting than 'put this paper here, put this paper there.' I started to think."

"How did you find out?" Slava said, tiptoeing.

"Someone called the Conference."

"Who?" Slava said indifferently.

"You know I cannot say. They said: 'Letters are being forged.' Which letters they did not say. 'Who is forging?' This part they did not say also. 'Why are you calling?' 'Because to do justice.' This part I do not believe. More like they are getting back at someone for something. But does that mean what they are saying is a lie? I don't know. What do you think?"

Slava shrugged. "I don't know," he said cautiously. "I need to know more." He straightened and went for it: "Besides, why me? I'm sure there are people who study this."

"And you can reach them in one minute!" Otto exclaimed. "In Germany, to speak to such an individual, I would have to file a request with the academic dean, wait one week, then another form. Here? The gentleman's direct number was on his Web page. 'Andrew Morton, speaking.' Can you imagine?"

Slava's heart stopped. Otto eyed him like a wolf, the cheekbones ravenous.

"And what did he—he explained—" Slava stumbled, his skin burning.

"So it is my lucky day, I guess," Otto said. "Because this gentleman says he has just received a phone call on the very same subject from a writer for *Century* magazine, named—named—one second"—Otto rummaged frantically in his pockets, pulling out a crumpled Post-it—"Peter Devitsky."

"Devicki," Slava corrected, his face a wreck.

"Your colleague at *Century*," Otto affirmed.

"He's not a writer," Slava said.

"But he is a writer, Mr. Gelman," Otto said. "I searched for him on the Internet, and I found several articles. Short articles, but with him as the author."

"You think he had something to do with it?" Slava said, trying to hold his voice steady.

"No," Otto said, shaking his head resolutely.

Slava wasn't ready to have Devicki indicted for fraud, but he was disappointed by how quickly Otto gave up the possibility.

"Let's think about this together," Otto said. "Devicki is a Polish name. Why would he be forging letters for Russians? They can't even speak to each other."

"The languages are similar," Slava said feebly.

"Something tells me you are not Mr. Devicki's first friend," Otto giggled, surveying Slava's collapsed expression. "No, Mr. Gelman, it is also something else. One look at Mr. Devicki's articles online, and it is immediately obvious—it's not him. He is not that kind of storyteller."

"Why not?" Slava whined.

"Why not." Otto looked at Slava with rebuke. "I'll show you why not." He unclasped the gold buckle of his briefcase and withdrew a manila folder. From it, he began to extract letters that Slava had written. Otto had marked certain words and sentences with fat red circles and asterisks. He called out the names as he slapped the applications on the warped wood of the bar: "Shlomberg! Feinberg! Shpungin! Abramson!" Raising his eyes at Slava: "Gelman.

"Sometimes there is this maneuver," Otto said. "Really, I take my hat off to the author. My hat is practically on the floor about this. The sentence begins with a formal expression, and then, boom! Suddenly, it is something very— I don't know the word. *Umgangssprachlich.* I love this maneuver. It makes the sentence sound so . . . It makes you forget you are reading a story."

Slava was speechless, stooped in his chair.

"Colloquial, I think," Otto said. "*Umgangssprachlich* is 'colloquial.' In any case, it is not Mr. Devicki's style."

"Then whose style is it?" Slava said, his mouth dry.

Otto's eyes shone with amusement. "Whose style is it?" he repeated. "Ha! You are a joker, Mr. Gelman. Why, it is your style!"

Slava collected every last bit of deceit inside him and managed to laugh in Otto Barber's face. "They couldn't pay me to do this," he said.

"It was very clever, Mr. Gelman, to say Peter Devicki," Otto went on. "It took me some time to understand it was not Peter, that was a distraction. And then to get the flowchart for the departments at *Century*, and then who is on Junior Staff, and study the profiles. That young man Avi Liss—I think he is not the most suspicious person in the world." Otto's eyes lit up. "Do you know how I did it, Mr. Gelman? I called the magazine and I said, 'I am from the Media Blue Book Directory.' I learned this from the letters, Mr. Gelman; you must include one specific detail, like the color. Would you have believed my story about the tea if I had not said *yellow* shoes? Anyway, I said I needed the flowchart for our annual issue. I don't know why they sent me to this Layout person—what *is* layout?—but could he please just save my day and fax me the flowchart? I mean, it was really too easy." Otto shook his head again, as if remembering a great wartime exploit. He turned to Slava, knocking him with a knee in excitement. "You know what, Mr. Gelman? It was addictive! It was a high. You put down the phone and you say, 'I want more!' I want to look someone in the eye and state a complete lie and have that person nod with great feeling because he thinks I have just told him the truth. What a power! It is God's power, Mr. Gelman. It is sublime. It is dangerous! The author of these letters, Mr. Gelman? I *became* him for the length of one phone call!" He leaned toward Slava in conspiracy. "Also, I believe Andrew Morton is sleeping with his assistant."

"You have it wrong," Slava whispered at his glass. He was sick to his stomach.

"Your poor lip is twitching," Otto observed.

Slava raised his finger to his lips, but they were still. "You're wrong," he repeated. "Otherwise, why haven't you called the police?"

"The police?" Otto laughed. "Are we on an episode of television? The police. Perhaps I should call the lawyers as well. No, Mr. Gelman, I don't want to talk about the legal side. The lawyers can talk about the legal side. The newspapers can talk about the legal side. We will talk about the human side."

"Why can't you just let them all in?" Slava said.

"Because I have the conscience of my position, Mr. Gelman. And also some pride as a starting investigator! Now I need to know. I need the satisfaction of holding my prey in my mouth. You have poisoned me with this hunger. I am your creation!"

"So then just take them all out," Slava said. "Every single one with your—your—your *umgang* . . ."

"It is an insane language, I agree. No, Mr. Gelman. Though I have been drinking from the cup of God's power, I have not crossed into lawlessness. I can't take them *all* out; what if some are real? All I have is my conclusions. This is not a dictatorship. I need proof. Either proof or a confession."

"And you don't have proof."

"Depends on what you mean by proof," Otto said. "I don't have the gun still smoking, but I have enough to call Herr Schuler."

"Unless you get a confession."

"Unless I get a confession. Then I can take care of the matter on my own." Otto took a sip from his glass. It remained over half full. He observed the baseball game on the television above the bar. "I only want to understand what is a shortstop," he said. "The bases I understand. The hitters I understand. Bunting, designated, pinch—okay. But a shortstop?"

"Why this charade?" Slava said. "Why not just call and say, 'It's you'?"

"Do you think it didn't work?" Otto said, a little hurt. "Remember, I am a novice. But if I said on the phone, 'Aha, it's you!,' or we must meet right away, I steal from myself an opportunity. Oh, I am giving away all my amateur secrets.

"No, Mr. Gelman. If I had real evidence against you, of course I would attack. I had no evidence except an anonymous verbal report and my sleuthing, so it must be a matter of conscience. Better to permit a guilty conscience to keep walking around, to increase the weight of its guilt! Unless you are a monster, a *psychopath*, in which case it doesn't make a difference." He considered Slava coquettishly. "You are not a psychopath, are you, Mr. Gelman?

"Also, I will ask you to remember that I was quite vague on the subject of evidence, quite vague. If I say, yes, there is evidence, there's no room this way or that"—with his big hands, Otto enacted a fish trying to maneuver from a trap—"why, you would stop worrying, for better or worse. Because it is done. They say that at Sevastopol, the people were in a terrible fright that the enemy would attack openly and take Sevastopol immediately. But when they saw that the enemy preferred a regular siege, they were delighted! The thing would drag on for two months at least, and they could relax!"

Otto sipped from his beer philosophically. "You don't know this, but I am, in general, a student of military campaigns, Mr. Gelman—it is my great petting interest. To visit the neighborhood of Brooklyn Heights: You are standing where George Washington stood! There is history underneath your feet! New York City is a war, a constant war! In Berlin, truth and justice is with the lower classes, but here in New York, it is with money and power. And all the young people, instead of making doodles and eating drugs and scratching the cars of rich people, are pursuing this power and this money, ha-ha! They want to defeat the people with power and money, but only to take their positions! They want to eat their lamb chops! It is war by other methods. There is no rebellion. Which is a rebellion in itself, wouldn't you say?"

Slava didn't speak.

Otto leaned back on his stool. "It is poor manners to give compliments to oneself, Mr. Gelman, but by the way your lip is continuing to twitch, I think I had all the effect that I wanted."

This time Slava kept from raising his hand to his mouth.

Otto sighed. "How terrible for someone of talent and promise to labor in darkness. Well, the subjects of the letters know, but we both know that isn't the same. You *wanted* to get caught, Mr. Gelman. Tell the truth. The similar maneuvers, the details?" He rummaged in the manila folder. "Look: Everyone is from Minsk! Night watch here, night watch here. A ferrier here, a ferrier here. The war took place only in the Minsk ghetto?"

Slava ignored him.

Otto shrugged and faced the bar again. "I understand the attraction of telling me to go to high hell, Mr. Gelman. I release your letters to Herr

Schuler, he holds a press conference, there is a leak, an excerpt in *Die Zeit*, then the *International Herald Tribune*, the *New York Times* . . . An audience of millions. Only no one knows who is the author. And what am I offering you in exchange? An audience of one? It's not the readership of *Die Zeit*, but it isn't an audience of zero. One person has meaning. And unlike Herr Schuler, I will know who the author is. I will know it is you. And with me, I take your word, the false ones go out, but the real ones stay in. With Herr Schuler, everything is under suspicion, *everything*. I am sure you understand the full weight of this, Mr. Gelman. Tell me which you forged, and you save the ones who are real. Don't tell me, and you send them all under the guillotine."

Slava kept staring blankly. He could not account for what would come out of his mouth if he spoke. He had to wait him out. Walk out, think, *think*.

"Mr. Gelman?" Otto said.

"I understand," Slava croaked.

Otto slid the folder back into his briefcase and slid from his bar stool. "They have less time than you, Mr. Gelman," he said. "You must choose them." He laid a soft palm on Slava's shoulder. "I'll be waiting for you."

–*17*–

The earth is the color of chocolate, so damp and moist it looks like you can spread it on bread. It runs into everything—coffee, underwear, letters. Slava is writing a letter. In Yiddish. His hands make out the sinewy bends and blocks, the letters bowing and scraping. The battalion commander is down in the trench, too, smoking a Belomor, the filter crushed between his fingers, and laughing at the letter.

"You owe the fascists, Yid. We weren't distracted, you'd get your ass strung up for writing letters like that." He kicks some dirt toward Slava, but halfheartedly, with a friendly contempt. "So it's like they say, then," he says. "The Yids and fascists are in cahoots." He laughs again, mirthlessly this time, loses his smile, spits.

Several yards from the trench stands a simple wooden table with two high-backed chairs lodged unevenly into a mound of black earth-chocolate. The table has been hacked together from the Belarusian birch that rises synonymously all around. The chairs—wicker chairs, with seat cushions tied by neat bows at the backs—are the first chairs the Gelmans had in America, lifted on a lucky evening from some curbside.

Every minute or so, the table and chairs tremble from a distant eruption. Uncle Aaron—Grandfather's brother, the unkissed virgin whose fingers Grandfather hunted with a butcher knife to disqualify him from the draft—sits in one of the chairs, his arms folded, looking at a heap of mackerel dripping oil onto a jaundiced copy of Komsomol'skaia Pravda, *the words running together. His field jacket is unbuttoned. A tuft of chest hair pokes out of the open collar.*

Grandfather is seated on the other side of the table, pointing angrily with his right hand. He's trying to explain something. His left hand is closed around his neck, as if he is wounded or trying to protect himself.

Aaron becomes angry. His arms go wide, as if to say, Well, what do you want from me? How can I change that? Grandfather slaps the table. Another muffled boom. Aaron folds his arms and looks down at the table. "Vi gob ikh ikent visn funderuf?" *he says in Yiddish.* "How was I supposed to know?"

There is another boom, closer this time; it kicks clods of earth onto the table. Slava waves his hands from the trench, trying to get their attention, but they are busy arguing. He tries to climb out, but the earth is too wet and crumbles in his hands. The chocolate smears his fingers. The battalion commander is laughing again and banging his fist on the ground. The booms are one after the next now. The mackerel has slipped to the ground, swimming in a chocolate sea. Slava is shouting so hard that his throat is tight, his hand rising to shield it.

Finally, the table is knocked to the side. Aaron still has his arms across his chest, but both he and Grandfather are staring regretfully at the earth floating beneath them. Then Aaron looks over at Slava.

He is clownish, almost: a squat face with a broad forehead, the nose like a young potato under broadly lit silver eyes. The hair rises in a wave above his forehead, the face smudged with grease from his Degtyaryov. It's a worn face, but still young underneath, the unkissed boy, and it lightens when he sees Slava.

They stare at each other, preparing for something. Then Aaron's face lifts, as if he has found the thing he's been looking to say, and he's starting to lean forward when the next boom hits. A hailstorm of damp earth. Like sediment in a stream, it carries a soldier's peaked cap, Yiddish letters, gold teeth.

Slava awoke in Grandfather's new bed, already darkness outside, only a tube of light at the foot of the door: the Katznelsons, the Aronsons, all those who had accepted Grandfather's invitation to come and kibitz while their applications received finishing touches from their adjutants, the children and grandchildren. The applications had to be postmarked to the Claims Conference by the following morning. The applicants were not going to wait to find out if the German government would expand eligibility so they could apply legally.

Walking from the train to Grandfather's, Slava had kept to the shadows, turning around periodically as if Otto Barber were panting somewhere behind. Then he moved to the center of the sidewalk. He could be walking to his grandfather's for perfectly innocent reasons. Besides, he had already been caught. He was free.

Little by little, the bedroom revealed its shape in the darkness: Grandfather's new bed; the armoire where some of Grandmother's things still hung; the stockpile of paper towels, footbaths, and mouthwash that Grandfather acquired under some unknown arrangement with the pharmacy.

Slava rose heavily and pushed open the bedroom door, the voices rising. How long had he slept? He came straight from work. He crossed the threshold, and all of a sudden pudgy, jeweled hands were at his forehead, remarking on its pallor. *"On prosto ustavshi, skol'ko zhe on pishet, predstav'te! Otpustite ego, zhenshchiny!"* He's simply tired, imagine how much he's been writing; let him go, women! Grandfather watched uneasily, his left hand covering his collarbone, just as in the dream. He had taken to keeping it there lately.

It was Grandfather's idea: everyone who hadn't mailed the application, in one place, the evening before the deadline. Everyone was surprised that Grandfather would propose it. Berta undertook an epic shopping excursion while Slava's mother called everyone on a list he had made of the letters he'd written. No one wanted to be disqualified because he forgot to photocopy his birth certificate. For this, feuds and misunderstandings could be laid aside for a night, insults temporarily forgotten, dead friendships briefly revived.

Someone's enterprising daughter drew up a checklist, taped to the refrigerator (she had taped it to the wall, but fearing marks to Slava's father's paint job, Berta moved it discreetly):

Did you fill out Form 88-J? _____

Did you photocopy your green card/citizenship certificate/ permanent alien card/passport? _____

Did you include two witnesses? _____

From the guest list Slava's mother had prepared, the young woman copied the last names of everyone of these permanent aliens, forming a table. Before anyone left, they had to check all the boxes. Next to the list was a stool: paper clips, a stapler, folders, pens. It was a war room.

Slava watched, unnoticed, from the threshold of the living room, forks scraping against plates and wafers being dunked into tea: Anna Shpungin (Kishinev/Bay Ridge), Feyga Shlomberg (Riga/Sheepshead Bay); Borukh Feinberg (Gomel/Borough Park). Slava had written letters for them all: the insulted and the injured, monsters from a place their blood would never know again.

They had been there since the afternoon, the stapling and filing staffs gradually joining, the younger generation's professions determining the order of appearance: the physical therapists, then the pharmacists, followed by the publicists and accountants, and finally, the lawyers and doctors. It was already past nine. They were still waiting for the investment bankers.

Who had called Otto Barber? Was it Lyuba Rudinsky, unable to let go of her grudge before one final comeuppance for the high heads of the Gelmans? Was it someone Slava turned down, angry at having to do without what everyone else was getting? They had struck a moral bargain with themselves; they would say someone was forging, but they wouldn't say who. Or perhaps Otto had lied about the *Century* goose chase, and Slava really was named by the caller. But why? Slava stopped himself. Once you started making things up, everything was up for doubt.

Slava crossed into the living room, and the conversation stilled. A male voice said: *"A vot nash pisatel'!"* And here is our writer. They began to clap, everyone, the old and the young, the sound loud enough to reach the Mexicans downstairs, and someone—it was Garik, Vera's father, the full complement of Rudinskys had come—even stuck two fingers in his mouth and whistled, which made everyone laugh. Vera laughed, too. She caught Slava's gaze and smiled. He smiled back. The sight of her after the evening with Otto was consoling to an erotic degree, a surprise.

Soon others arrived, and with their appearance, the moment vanished. Slava kept checking the door for Israel—if he could hobble over to the synagogue, he could hobble over here—but there was no sign. Someone arrived with a whinnying infant. The little head wobbled and lifted, wobbled and lifted, like a drunk person's. What customs would this small person follow? Would his little tongue curl away from *kvass*, the tiny nose indifferent to the smell of butter and onions in a linoleum kitchen? In some yard sticky with summer, the now grown fingers wrapped around a can of warming beer, would his head whir to calculate, for the benefit of some pale-skinned American girl, what portion of itself it owed to the chocolate loam of that other place? When, some years on, his great-grandmother, for whom his uncle Slava had once forged a letter, passed away, the Holocaust-funds-renewal certificate trailing her death by a month, would he trace the uncertain curlicues of her name in English as if her hand were his own? Or would he follow the law?

When no one was looking, Slava took into the bathroom a matchbox and the lined piece of notebook paper with the names of everyone for whom he had written letters. There was no point: Otto knew what he wanted to know, and yet. The paper burned quickly, the edges curling into his hand, so that Slava had to drop it in the sink and start again. This would be more difficult with the list affixed to the refrigerator; Slava's mother wanted to frame it. She was out there now, she and Lyuba Rudinsky clutching each other like lost sisters.

Slava stepped out of the bathroom. On the edge of the beige leather sofa, an older man whom he didn't know was lecturing a wild-eyed boy in a FUBU T-shirt. The boy didn't seem to know Russian too well, but he listened, nodding politely. Next to them, one of the granddaughters was leading her grandmother through the letters on the boy's T-shirt, an impromptu English lesson. "Foo-boo," the grandmother telescoped her tongue. She really wanted to learn.

"And he says, 'I am going to be a writer!'" Slava heard Grandfather say to the woman next to him on the love seat. She was nodding wearily; she knew the routine. "How do you like that? He was getting offers from— Hey, Slavchik!" Grandfather yelled. He waved Slava over. When Slava approached, Grandfather wrapped his free palm around Slava's forearm like a glass of water.

"What is this new affectation?" Slava said, nodding at Grandfather's other hand, wrapped around his collarbone.

"Nothing, nothing," Grandfather said, dropping it to his side. He turned back to the woman. "This university, that university, some bank, a senator," he continued to lie. "They all wanted him. Six figures. But Slavik said, 'Not for me. Anyone can become one of those financiers. I want to be a writer. I want to help you, Grandfather.' And so we said, 'We will do everything'—Regina Alekseevna, I don't have to explain, do I?—'whatever you need, we are going to help.'"

Regina Alekseevna nodded obediently.

Grandfather looked up at Slava. "Who wanted you to work for him, Slavik? Who was that senator?"

"Schumer," Slava invented. "The senator from New York."

"Not Kennedy?" Grandfather said disappointedly.

"Not Kennedy," Slava said, spreading his arms in apology.

"Well, anyway," Grandfather said. "This Shuma wanted them to write a book together, you see."

As Grandfather talked on, Slava ran his free palm through Grandfather's hair. It felt different than Slava expected, rough and dry instead of silky and ageless. That memory of it, Slava realized, was a decade old.

Slava knew why Grandfather kept a hand at his neck: a talisman. Against undefined rasps in the throat, against illness, against death. Slava wanted to pry it away, return it to the lap of Grandfather's natty corduroys, to Grandfather's forehead, so it could keep the mental abacus warm as Grandfather made his calculations: No, it's not too late for him to become a businessman, not late at all . . .

One morning after Grandmother's death, Berta had found Grandfather in bed surrounded by a moat of chairs, the backs facing him. "No, no, no," Berta exclaimed, rushing the bed. "You can't, you can't." He didn't know how they'd gotten there.

Maybe Grandfather had begun covering his neck long before Grandmother died, only Slava hadn't been around to notice. Maybe, while Slava was gone, Grandfather got old, his lying mind his only health. If you can invent, you must be alive still. Grandfather *is*. What would Grandfather tell Otto Barber?

Slava knew. Grandfather would shrug. He would express the deepest desire to help. Unfortunately, he had no information to offer but would as soon as he heard anything, naturally. Grandfather would let the letters go to Herr Schuler, may they all get covered up to their heads. And Grand-mother would look on approvingly from the side. How else could it be? If she had wanted Grandfather to stop, she would have made him. Slava didn't know many things about her, but he knew her power. And she didn't stop Grandfather. Why would she have? To a friend she would not lie, but to the law she would not tell the truth. (What law? Where was the law when the Minsk ghetto was being "liquidated" along with her mother, fa-ther, and grandfather?) For a person like Grandmother, there was no law but what we find in each other. And Grandfather was the man she had found. Slava lived in a different country. A lie meant something different here, even if it was easier to pull off thanks to the American insistence on imagining the best about the next person. It wasn't difficult at all to lie here, Slava had discovered with some regret, as it devalued his duplicities compared to Grandfather's. Slava's new country asked less of his ingenuity than the Soviet Union had asked of his grandfather. It would take nothing for Slava to deceive Otto Barber.

Slava patted Grandfather on his no longer silky hair and kissed his forehead, the kind gesture allowing Grandfather, in the calculus of affec-tion demonstrated to Regina Alekseevna, to release Slava's arm. What if Slava, naive Slava—his grandfather would run circles around him until his last day—had it backward about Grandfather's friends? What if Grand-father *wanted* to have them in his life but couldn't because he had lied about his age during the war to delay the draft? He told big stories about needing to mind the official records in Moscow or Minsk, but it was the Katznelsons, Kogans, and Rubinshteins that he had to continue to fool, to persuade that simply he had been too young for the draft in 1943, the year that was "cut down" in full: the year Dodik Katznelson lost a brother, Grisha Kogan three brothers, and Nina Rubinshtein enough cousins to fill a village, as they had before the war. The Katznelsons, Kogans, and Rubin-shteins were Grandfather's undisappearing accounting, long after he had disappeared from the Soviet Union. He hated them for it. This was why no one appeared in his home. He didn't want anyone there, stumbling accidentally on the truth.

He couldn't explain it this way to Slava, so he invented their insults, their distance. He kept inventing and inventing, unable to stop, until he had ended up alone, without friends, without his grandson. He had survived the war at the price of punishing himself for the rest of his life with the lie that had made it possible. Vera had saved Grandfather with the Rudinskys. Had tricked him when no one else could, granted him reconciliation without requiring a reckoning. Slava had saved him with the rest.

It was close to midnight by the time the guests started to leave. There were long kisses, embraces inside humid necklines, unmeant promises to call regularly now.

Slava watched Vera help her grandfather Lazar into his jacket. Lazar's eyes were empty. He trembled as Vera walked him down the hallway, a branch quaking in the wind. When he pulled even with Slava in the line of farewell-wishers—Mother, Father, Berta subbing for Grandmother, Grandfather, Slava—Lazar lifted a trembling hand and clasped Slava's, pulling it gently. He was phlox-colored, the skin stale and soft, the mouth in decay. Closer, closer, he gestured. Slava placed his ear next to Lazar's spittle-covered mouth, thinking he wished to say something, but Lazar only turned his face until it was even with Slava's cheek and kissed him there, his lips flat and dry. They left no trace except what Slava imagined.

"Here," Lazar said. "Here." He lifted his right hand, gnarled and shivering, and wedged a piece of material into Slava's hand. In Slava's hand was a rectangle of white cloth with an address, the kind Jews in the Minsk ghetto were required to wear underneath their yellow stars. It said: "54 Krymskaya." And underneath: "Rudinsky."

"My great-grandmother," Vera said, leaning into be heard. "Grandfather's mother." Slava could smell her perfume, jasmine and honey. She spoke to him in Russian, so Lazar could understand. Her English was plain, colorless, sometimes even incorrect, but her Russian—at least to

Slava's ears, because she owned it far better than he—was as elegant as a palace. He felt overseen by it; for a passing moment, the two of them felt unnoticeable in the most crowded place in the apartment.

"This is a hallway, not a dance club!" someone farther back in line said half jokingly.

"Why don't you let the youth speak, cow!" Lazar said with startling vigor. And then, under his breath, "If you lost some weight, you wouldn't have trouble squeezing past."

Vera and Slava laughed. "He wants you to have it, that's all," she said.

"Do you have to go?" Slava blurted out.

She thought about the answer but not long. "There's a bar close to where I live," she said. She gave him the name. "I'll wait for you there."

*The bar had bordello-red velvet couches and multiple television screens show-*ing sports. They were the only ones there; the bartender, a young woman wearing an olive-green tank top and leather bands on both wrists, was flipping through a magazine.

"What are you thinking about?" Vera said. She sat in a high-backed banquette, her back arched, the edge of her skirt lapping her knees.

"Someone I wrote a letter for," Slava said. "He wasn't there tonight."

"You spend a lot of time with old people now," she said.

"You said they are lonely," he said.

"Let's bring you back to young-people time," she said. "Let's dance."

"Here?" he said. There was a sneering song coming out of the speakers.

"Wait," she said. She rose and walked over to the bartender. A moment later, the music changed.

"I think she wanted to close," Slava said when Vera returned.

"You just need the charm," Vera said.

"You have an effect on men and women both."

"Stop talking, Slava. Let's go."

The song was slow. In a blue something. Slava's arms slid neatly into a crevice in the small of Vera's back. The bartender lifted her eyes, winked at Slava, and returned to her magazine. It wasn't the kind of bar where people danced.

"Do you remember," Vera said, "when you smacked your face in the window in Vienna?"

Slava tried to remember, but all he could recall about Vienna was the synagogue, cobblestones, Grandfather. All the other slots in the slide projector showed empty.

"We were just walking around," she said. "You stopped because you saw these kitchen pots in a store window. They were very beautiful, with designs on the side in bright color. You started walking toward them because I think you wanted to touch them. And then—bam!" Vera's palm met Slava's forehead softly. "The window was so clean, you didn't understand there was a window there."

They both laughed. Slava wanted to remember. He liked being the person who gave her such satisfaction.

She leaned into Slava's chest. "You are so serious now," she said, so quietly that perhaps she didn't wish him to hear.

"That's not true," he said.

"Prove it you are not," she said, looking up at him.

He pulled away, lifted her, and twirled her in his arms, her skirt making an accordion in the air. She yelped. The bartender looked up and smiled again.

They walked to Vera's apartment. The streetlights ticked and buzzed, playing with one another in the cool night. It was practically September. In this neighborhood, Slava had never walked to a home at such a late hour, only from. In the last month, he had spent more nights around here than in the preceding two years, but always he left well before now.

Slava remembered only one thing clearly about Vienna, from the afternoon he had peeked inside the Vienna synagogue from behind Grandfather's pants leg, Austrians streaming past them. How could they walk by so indifferently, Slava had thought, if they once wished to exterminate all the people inside? Slava felt shame for the worshippers. He didn't want to look at them because it would have connected him with their destruction. That was when Grandfather made them disappear with a release of the door, a finger in his temple to say they were crazy. All the knots in Slava's stomach gave way.

The Gelmans managed to leave the Soviet Union only because all sides had agreed to pretend that they were going to Israel. The Soviet government wouldn't release Soviet citizens directly to the United States. But it would release its Jews to Israel, "family reunification" being less humiliating to the USSR as the refugees' reason for emigration than discontent with socialism. If there was no family in Israel, as there usually wasn't, it was manufactured. Scribes popped up to supply people like the Gelmans with an Aunt Chaya in Haifa and a Cousin Mumik in Ashdod. These invented Chayas and Mumiks filled out affidavits in the scribe's hand requesting the Soviet government to release their relatives. The Soviet visa office quietly acquiesced.

Intermediary countries—Austria, Italy—facilitated the deception; after all the invention, the refugees couldn't very well fly from Sheremetyevo to JFK. So the Gelmans took the long, slow train to Vienna, a month later another to Italy, several months later the airplane to New York. At every step, everyone had lied about everything so the one truth at the heart of it all—that abused people might flee the place of abuse—could be told.

Grandfather was already a liar—this kind of liar—when he twirled his finger in his temple that afternoon in Vienna, and Slava was young enough to understand such lies as a better kind of truth. It wasn't until they'd come to America that the truth started to mean exactly what was said and not something else. The calculus had changed in America. Here you could afford a thirty-two-inch television on a doorman's salary, as Bart at the front desk kept finding ways to mention. Here you could afford to be decent.

If you find yourself on one of the lower-alphabet avenues in South Brooklyn— Avenue U, Avenue Z—you are sure to come across a furniture emporium. Russian-owned, Europe-minded. Collezione Eleganza, La Moda, and, to reassure those concerned that Europe-minded means Europe-priced, Discount European Furniture Warehouse. Inside, you will find leather couches with armrests wide enough to serve as ottomans, in elusive shades of tan and ocher. You will find lacquered tables with tapered legs and faux-sapphire inlays; paintings in every color but primary; and curves, everywhere curves.

Vera's bookshelves curved. Her lampshades curved. Her fridge would have curved if only the maker obliged. The balcony, where Vera's tour of the apartment ended, was covered with synthetic grass and additional leather furniture.

"It doesn't get ruined when it rains?" Slava asked as they surveyed the neighboring homes, the occasional clothesline breaking the baked tar of the roofs. The ground floors were for dirt, exhaust, and cheap living. It was soundless and cool up here in the clouds.

"I cover it with plastic every morning before I go to work," she said.

"But if you go away somewhere?"

"I don't go anywhere."

Out of her intimidating freezer, Vera withdrew an ice-encrusted bottle of vodka. The ice on the bottle sparkled like diamonds, and the clear liquid poured from it thickly, a clear honey.

They clinked, downed in one gulp, and gnawed on frozen strawberries while listening to the quiet. Slava stood at the dark window. On the other side, Brooklyn made the sounds of sleep. The early morning and the night, those were his favorite times, before everything began and after it ended.

"I can't tell," he said, "if this is real or it's because you and I cut vegetables out of construction paper together in Italy. Because you remember things about me that even I don't remember. Because when I say 'Grandfather,' you think the same thing I think."

"That is what means it is real," she said from the sectional.

"We cut vegetables out of construction paper and made our parents pay in real money. Your grandfather with the secondhand market in Italy. My letters, your press conference. All we do is lie. Germans make Volvos, at least. We lie."

"Volvos are from Sweden," she said, and asked him to join her on the couch.

He continued to look out the window. "They know about the letters," he said at last. "Where the applications go."

"What does that mean?" she said, her voice stern. "Look at me, please."

"Someone ratted," Slava said, turning around.

She was squinting against the light, trying to get this new lay of the land. Her shoulders fell. "One of ours did it?" she said. Her worry was convincing. Was it expert? Was she acting, covering up for her mother? He hated himself for the thought, but was it unreasonable? He had seen her in action.

Slava sat down next to her. He smelled the vodka on her tongue, mixed with strawberries. Every part of her had a different scent, like departments in a department store.

"I don't know," Slava said.

"Anybody else knows?" she said.

Slava shook his head.

"So . . ." Her head hung forward as she tried to understand.

"If I tell them which ones I faked, they will quietly take those out. As if they never came in. That they can do."

"And if you don't tell them?"

"They have no choice but to make a public statement. Make it an official investigation."

Vera exhaled slowly and fell back.

"If I deny everything," Slava said, "that's kaput for Settledecker's plan, too. If they have to go public, there's no way anyone's approving an *expansion* of eligibility requirements."

She sat up. "Slava." Her hand clasped his arm. She was sober, conspiratorial, in control. Lazar Timofeyevich was right about his granddaughter. "You need to say you have no idea what they are talking about. I know how this works. They're not going to do press conference. No way. They will just make private investigation inside by themselves. They're saying it to do the guilt to you. It's— What do you call it? With cards."

"Bluffing."

"Exactly. If they can't make you confess, they will not risk press conference. Think about it. If no Claims Conference, no job for them, no salary. They're never gonna go for that. They will bury it. You start saying yes to anything, and you're guilty of— It's not going to end. Don't be a *pioner*. Boy Scout."

She studied Slava's face to see what he thought, her attention resting on him like a mother's. A vein came through her temple, steady and unruffled, a blue valley. Slava knew every bend here.

"It's going to be okay," she said. "I promise you. I will make." Her hand rose to his cheek and playfully scratched the stubble. His hands answered her—her face, her neck, her shoulders. She wore a V-neck silk blouse, dark blue except for black bands at the hems of the sleeves. The knobs of Vera's shoulders were as round as her face, thick and solid. As she shimmied out of her skirt, a Soviet woman's coarse panty hose remained, and then nothing. In three years at *Century*, Slava marveled viciously, he had made no advance, but this bounty was his just weeks after meeting Vera again. She was like the language they shared: He had done nothing to earn it, but it was his. He resented her for accepting him so easily. But these were the perks he could expect. If Slava gave up his mysterious objections, this was what awaited, the dark collapse between Vera's legs said.

His hands stopped.

"What is it?" she said.

"I can't," he said. "I'm sorry." He made himself look at her.

Her eyes became frightened and uncomprehending. Then came a look of loathing and disgust, as if he had failed a manly duty. He gave her an ugly, meaningless smile.

"You are a sad example, Slava," she said finally. "A puddle. I hope you find what you're looking for."

"Vera"—he tried to hold her arms, but she recoiled—"you don't want this."

"So you are doing me a favor," she expelled.

He started to speak, but she raised her hand. Go now, please.

He tried to gather his things, though nothing would move quickly, their clotheslessness grotesque. He felt her eyes on him. Eventually, she busied herself with her phone, the awkwardness like a third person.

Outside was warm and stuffy after the chillbox of Vera's air-conditioning. Slava considered dialing Vova the cruiserweight, the admiring nod Vova would give upon pulling up at the address he knew so well, but Vera would correct the record the next time she saw Vova anyway. No, Slava wanted away from all that.

He flagged down an ordinary livery cab. Ninetieth and West End in Manhattan? The driver was incredulous at this kind of fare at this time of the night. As they bumped through the taciturn streets, Slava thought about Israel—the scratchy voice, the desert throat sending up coughs, the eyebrows leaping and waving. About his own grandfather. Where were you, old men, when your instructions were needed? But it was three A.M., the streets were empty, and there was no answer.

By now, Arianna's night doorman knew Slava's face, and even though he hadn't seen Slava in several days, his hailing from Bratislava inclined him to give Slava the benefit of the doubt, the inauspicious fate of the Czechoslovaks under the Soviet yoke notwithstanding. Which left him with a predicament now because it was three o'clock in the fucking morning, and Slavic brotherhood encountered its limits at the shoals of Western decorum.

"Ring her, ring her," Slava said, reading his face.

The Bratislavan pressed pause on a personal video with great fanfare. "It's late time," he observed.

"She's expecting me," Slava lied.

The Slovak eyed Slava distastefully. Slava lied again, despising it: a late flight, delayed arrival, an exchange of phone calls with Arianna around midnight, she'd go to bed but leave dinner under saran wrap. It was the saran wrap, the specific detail, that got him. Otto was right about you have to mention the shoes had been yellow. If you say there are elephants flying outside your window, no one will believe you. But if you say there are six elephants flying outside your window, it's a different story.

Bratislava made his calculations. Of course, he would rather have let Slava go up than be responsible for having woken the tenant. Slava needed to push a little bit more, he saw. "What's your name?" he said.

"Bujnak," the Slovak said. "Vladimir Bujnak. Vlado, you can call."

Slava extended his hand and said his name. "I'm sorry," he said, looking at the stairs he was about to mount. "Sorry."

Slava stood before Arianna's door a long time. Then he stood another long stretch after he had rung the bell. He had to ring it several times.

Finally, she called out in a worried voice. Slava told her who it was, putting a note of apology into it. He knew the Bratislavan was listening up the staircase. She opened the door wearing a T-shirt that Slava had left.

"Where have you been?" she said, her voice full of sleep. Slava only smiled dumbly. Suspicion and fear streaked her face. He tried to meet her eyes and not give way to tears. The cat, stirred from its slumber, minced curiously at her feet, skeptical and alert.

"Come to bed," she said. She left the door open and retreated down the hallway, holding her head. Slava heard the opening of cabinets, the clinking of glasses, the glugging of alcohol into a tumbler.

Slava walked in after her, the cat watching the arc of his legs. Before Slava could close the door, it hurtled out into the hallway, and Slava had to turn around and retrieve it, the animal's hind paws dangling helplessly in the air, disdain on its snout.

"Vodka?" she said.

"Everybody's drinking vodka tonight," he said.

"Oh, yeah?" she said. "Who's everybody." The cat rubbed its scalp against Slava's ankle.

"Before the war," he said, "there was a boy named Pavlik Morozov. He really took Communism to heart. His father was forging some kind of documents. So Pavlik turned in his father. Can you imagine? Guess what happened next."

She shook her head wearily. "I have no idea, Slava."

"They murdered the kid. The family murdered him."

"Why are you telling me this?" She poured herself another glass, shorter this time.

"Because I can imagine myself as the person who's forging. But I can also imagine myself as the person who turns in the forger. How can that be?"

"I don't know, Slava," she said. "I don't know what you're talking about, and I'm not interested in finding out right now. Can we go to bed?"

"Her name was Vera," he said. "The one drinking vodka tonight."

Arianna considered him helplessly. She sank into one of the kitchen chairs, too tired to wedge her legs under the table. She covered her face with her hands and moaned. Then she opened slits between her fingers. "I wondered was it something like that," she said. She laughed nastily. "And then I thought, no. What a cliché."

"Nothing happened," he said. "That's the truth."

"Oh, yeah?" she said, still wearing a foul expression.

"It's not where I was all those nights."

"Oh, yeah?" she said again. "So where were you?"

He answered her truthfully. He told her everything. From his mother's call, and the funeral, and the funeral dinner, and what Grandfather asked, and Beau, and Vera, and Otto, and the rest, the words tumbling out without any through line. At this late moment, he couldn't tell a good story.

She lost herself in his narrative all the same because, frankly, it was unbelievable. She forgot to remove her fingers from her face, and she sat listening this way, latticed against him. When he finished, she said, "I am actually wishing it was only that you were fucking somebody else." Her fingers finally moved away from her face and she dislodged a hysterical laugh. "He works on the sly, this one!" She went to drink again, but her glass was empty. "I'm too tired for this," she said, and covered her face again.

When she opened her eyes, he was on the kitchen floor, next to her legs. "I'm sorry," he said.

"What are you apologizing to me for," she said in a desultory way.

"To you, to you," he said. He tried to slide into her embrace.

"Don't," she said, lifting her elbows away from him. He withdrew but remained sitting on the floor like a drunk. They sat without speaking, the clock ticking at them from the wall. "I am counting how many times you had to lie in the last month," she said at last. "You might be better than anyone I've met. And I've met some talented liars."

"I didn't lie about this." He gestured from her to himself.

"Somehow, I know that's true. Remarkable. They do studies about people who won't face the facts."

He pulled himself up and rested his palms against the table. He waited until she was looking at him. "You are unlike anyone I've met," he said. "I know you feel the same way. But often we are not happy with each other. And not because of what I just told you." As he said it, he knew it was persuasive because it wasn't servile. It was also the truth.

She didn't respond.

"I would like to try," he said. "I would like to be the kind of person who loves someone like you."

"Just be the person who loves me," she said. In retrospect, it would occur to him, she was merely correcting him. At the moment, however, her words sounded like reluctant forgiveness.

He lowered himself to the floor again. This time she let him rest his head on her thigh.

"What am I going to do with you," she said, her fingers in his hair.

"I have to tell the truth," he said, looking up at her.

She took his face in her hands. "You have to tell the truth," she said.

18

WEDNESDAY, AUGUST 30, 2006

Two days before the closing of the inaugural fall issue, Junior Staff crackled with pre-holiday anticipation, much as the Gelmans had washed windows and waxed floors on New Year's Eve in Minsk. The issue would include the Italian story that Arianna was checking; a roundup of back-to-school items; a piece on fall styles; Peter's piece about the press conference; a baseball piece by the dignified, sweatered man who had been doing *Century*'s baseball pieces for most of the century; and comments by Beau on the arrival of autumn.

A specially commissioned painting would appear on the cover: a pointy-nosed, ponytailed lady defying metaphysics by holding in hand the issue in question, the leaves changing outside her auto, the road ahead stretching unsubtly. The work was by Serge, one of several monomial artists used by the magazine. Serge was unable to paint unless entirely in the nude, an awkward discovery made by the magazine the previous year during a reader-appreciation watch-the-artists-paint-reproductions-of-famous-covers event.

Having dropped off the week's "The Hoot" (66.67 percent factual) on Paul Shank's desk, Slava felt a twitchy, unfamiliar lightness. The final claim letters had been sealed and sent off that morning from different post offices by special emissaries (Berta, who regarded the matter with more gravity than all the Jews added together, coordinated the couriers). Slava felt as if he were sending soldiers into slaughter; he had told only Arianna about Otto—though who knew whom Vera had told by now, whether out of revenge or concern. He lifted himself above the divider and watched Arianna until she noticed him.

"Get out before they find you new work," she said.

He nodded.

"You'll go soon, won't you?" She meant Otto.

He promised. He reached far over the divider and ran his knuckle down her temple. She stiffened, but then eased into his hand.

*Manhattan is the imperial seat from which the various subway lines sail to-*ward Brooklyn like an armada. The Soviet armada is the color of yolk: The D, N, R, F, B, Q, heading to Bensonhurst, Bath Beach, Midwood, Gerritsen Beach, Mill Basin. The rest—the red 2, the green 5, the blues flirting with Queens, the browns making their excretive way across Williamsburg and Bushwick—are the trains of other countries.

The last days of August: the Sunday of summer. The Labor Day weekend was the only thing dividing the people from the full enfilade of fall sales, styles, and shopping. For the last handful of days, the mouth of American commerce—subway platforms, the flanks of buses, bus shelters, the radio—still whispered sweetly about barbecues, swimming pools, weekend getaways, and last chances.

Israel's door was locked. No one answered the doorbell or Slava's knocking. He thought about leaving a note, but then the gate creaked open at street level to reveal an old woman in a housedress. Slava called up to her in Russian and asked about her downstairs neighbor. Her ice-blue eyes radiated blank amusement.

"Abramson?" Slava tried. "Lives in the basement apartment. Short. Big eyebrows." He wiggled his.

"When I moved into this neighborhood fifty years ago," the woman said in blocky English, "there were a lot of immigrants here. Poles, like me. Germans, Irish, Italian, Hungarian, Croat, you name it. It never occurred to us that we should just speak our own language to the next person in the street."

Slava blanched. He was about to repeat himself in English when she waved her hand.

"Mr. Abramowitz is in the hospital," she said. "They picked him up over the weekend. I don't know how serious it is, but I had to call the family."

"In the hospital? Why?" Slava said, as if one chose to go to such places.

"I don't know," she said. "He called the ambulance himself. They found him on the floor. The medics gave me the note."

Rooted in place, Slava appropriated this new information. The thought that swept through his mind was: I am about to lose another one.

"He was a heavy smoker when he was young, you know," the woman said. "I caught him smoking on the steps here once. I said he shouldn't. I was afraid he thought I was telling him simply not to smoke on the steps. But he understood. He came back with a piece of graph paper. I think he had somebody write it out for him. It said, 'Life is death if you don't have a cigarette now and then.' We had a nice laugh about it."

"You had to call the family?" Slava said. "In Israel?"

"Oh, yes. I had a time figuring out the codes."

A gust of wind crept through the spruce above them. Amid the remaining heat, you could occasionally make out autumn loitering at the door.

"Do you know what hospital?" Slava said.

"Maimonides," she said. "The whole street was lit up with sirens."

"Does he owe you anything for the call?" he said hopefully.

"Oh, no," she said. "The son took it collect."

Slava was in a part of Brooklyn where yellow cabs did not roam, but he had Vova's card foxed in his wallet. He kept misdialing. He made himself stop and take a long breath. The stillness he was pleased to discover inside himself that morning, a quiet readiness for his meeting with Otto—Arianna's gift—was gone. At last it rang. "I have to get to the hospital, Vova," Slava yelled into the phone when the cruiserweight picked up.

Vova spoke with a solemnity that soothed Slava. As a taxi driver in the southern reaches of Brooklyn, where they died every moment of every day, Vova was no stranger to calls such as this one. "I will be there in ten minutes," he said. And he was.

The aging sedan squeaking and grunting over the potholed roads, Slava's mind was stuck on the onion of Israel's frame, horizontal on a hospital gurney. *He* hadn't been called, Slava thought with a sting. But why should he have been? Who was he to Israel? They had met twice, once by accident. He was the letter writer; he wasn't a family member. He wasn't needed. But he was going to go anyway.

"Ho, listen," Vova said. "I'm sorry to bring this up now, but I've got you in the car."

"Sure," Slava said listlessly.

"It's like this," Vova said. "You ever heard of New Orleans? Where the fuck is that?"

"Down south somewhere," Slava said.

"Right—well, they had this dustup with the atmosphere last year. You hear about that?"

"I'm amazed you've heard about it."

Vova checked him out in the rearview. "You underestimate your blood, *chuvak*."

"So?" Slava said.

"So there's a situation down there. A warm situation, if you know what I'm saying." Vova waited to hear whether he should go on. He did anyway.

"All these homes beat to the ground after the storm. And if one of them's yours, you can get money. A lot."

"Okay?" Slava said.

"So there's sixty thousand homes. And some of them are getting filed on, to get dough from the government, and some of them are not. Because the owners died, ran away, whatever. And so there's this *claim* you can fill out— there's some kind of process—I don't know the details, this isn't my territory, this is why I'm talking to you. But the word is it's not hard, for those abandoned homes, to move the title to yourself. And qualify for that money."

"And what is your territory?" Slava said.

"My territory is setting it up," Vova said. "Not the paperwork."

"What if you apply this energy to a legal business?" Slava said.

Vova consulted the rearview. "Should I regret I told you about this? Don't make me regret it. You didn't even give me a chance to spell out the details. You get a cut, obviously. They said five percent, but I am going to push for ten percent for you, because without you, it can't happen, and I understand that. Some people undervalue the desk part, not me. And you can go there if you want, flight paid. Scope it out, get the flavor. They got African ladies down there to make your underpants wet. You ever make it with a black girl?"

"No," Slava said.

"It's a different ball game than—" He pointed outside the car to indicate Vera.

"Why are you talking to me about this?" Slava said.

"You write the letters, don't you? You're the paperwork guy."

"Does anyone keep a fucking secret?" Slava said.

Vova started laughing. "You know how we are."

"How are we, Vova?"

"We live in the real world. You'll think about it, won't you?"

"I won't do it," Slava said. "I'm sorry, it's not personal. Though your secret is safe. If mine is safe with you."

Vova considered this. "I see. Well, I admire a direct conversation." He turned back to the wheel. They rode in silence, each chewing on Slava's answer. Then Vova said, an olive branch: "I know a good flower store right by the hospital. We'll be there in five minutes." And they were.

From the curb, Vova extended his hand through the driver's-side window. "No hard feelings," he said. "The offer, it was a sign of respect. I wish you health for the person inside."

Slava shook to match the force in Vova's grip, as if the power would transfer to that person.

In the vestibule of Maimonides hospital, Slava was the one with the bouquet of carnations: white, pink, and red. Grandmother had liked carnations, and when Slava thought of illness, he thought of her. Now they looked paltry, the ruffed heads bobbing on the weak stems, too feminine for the sack of leather in Room 317. On the day Grandmother died, the sun blazed with an infernal fury, as if it had overheated. Now, however, the weather looked like one of those ads in *Century* that Avi Liss almost had to slice out: the soft sun; a long, narrow, white-clothed wooden table; towheaded children at play in the breeze; a pharaonic repast on the endless table itself. The sainted sun outside the hospital shone on an endless row of florists, bakeries, and kosher butchers, encased in ancient, artisanal concrete. The Brooklyn where the Soviet Jews lived was as ugly as the rows of apartment blocks they had left behind in the Soviet Union. Perhaps that was why they lived here.

On a monitor in Room 317, a spiky green comet shot across the beeping surface of a dark night. Spiky was good. Israel was asleep, the giant raisin of his face loosening and closing with each breath, a happy brook of saliva dribbling down his chin. Only a Gogol splayed on his chest, and he would have looked like he was napping at home. Slava pictured him licking his finger, turning the pages, and slumping over from a heart attack. But it didn't happen that way. Israel had written out a note with instructions. That part didn't make sense.

Slava stepped into the hallway. Maimonides looked as empty as if it belonged to them alone, as if all the illness in the world was theirs. It was pleasantly ramshackle: Paint peeled in a corner of the ceiling, and the counter behind which the nurses worked was scuffed and dented.

"Can you tell me what happened?" Slava rushed after a nurse. "Abramson. Room 317." He pointed.

"Abramson?" she said. Her voice had a thousand cigarettes in it, though her teeth gleamed whitely. She ran her finger down a chart. "Oh, honey, he'll be fine. His blood is normal, everything's fine. Heartbreak hotel."

Slava stared quizzically.

"Lonely," the nurse smiled. "Old and lonely. We see it all the time. Seventy, seventy-five, family far away. The insurance company should come up with a code. Let me go, honey, I actually need to give him a new IV."

Slava returned to the room. The sun shone luminously through the wide window. It seemed especially outlandish to be ill during such weather. One of Israel's eyes popped open, like a diver emerging from the deep.

"Oh, shit," he said, and snapped it closed. He opened it again. "Where did you come from?" He coughed.

"Are you sick, or are you not really sick?" Slava said.

"Me? I'm fucking tired," Israel said, and closed his eyes again. Then he opened them.

"Hollywood's crying after *my* grandfather?" Slava said.

"Did they say anything about—" Israel started.

"Yuri? He's coming," Slava said. He had no knowledge of this, but Israel didn't need to know that.

"Might as well be the Messiah himself," Israel sighed.

"Nice play," Slava said.

Israel looked up at Slava. "I am at your mercy," he said.

"Don't worry, your secret's safe."

"I'm sorry, Slava," Israel said. A tear rolled out of his eye, then stopped in place, as if, like its owner, it was too tired to go on. "Yes, I envy your grandfather, but not because he has a twenty-four-hour home nurse. Because you're one borough away."

"So you will go with Yuri to Israel," Slava said.

"If he takes me," Israel said. "I'll die in the Jewish homeland. That's not so bad."

"Where would you prefer to die?" Slava said.

"In Minsk. I don't want English on my headstone and I don't want Hebrew on my headstone. In Russian: 'Iosif Abramson. Date of birth, date of death. The tea was bitter and he blamed existence.'" He broke into hoarse laughter.

"You're tempting fate, Israel."

"I've had enough," Israel said. "Just let me look at my son one more time. He's coming, isn't he?"

"I'm sure he is." Slava took the old man's hand, dry and crabby. "You don't have to go, you know. I'll come for soup."

"You already have a grandfather," Israel said.

Slava took the old hand with both of his. They looked through the windows at the lunatic sunshine. "Will you do what I say?" he said to the old man.

Israel cocked an eyebrow. "Like how?"

"Just do what I say right now. Get up and get dressed."

"I don't understand."

"'We're following you now, Gogol'—who said that? That's the problem with all of you: You don't mean what you say. You use the big words, but they're worth a turd. Come on."

"But my son is supposed to come."

"You think Israel is two hours away? We'll be back well before."

"Where are you taking me?"

"You're trusting me."

"What if the nurse finds out?"

"So when it's your own hide, you cry. Show me you have balls, Israel. Show me you don't hide behind the young ones with your big words."

While Israel pissed, Slava made a phone call. "Come back?" Vova said on the other end. "I can be there in ten minutes." Vova was always ten minutes away. But Slava needed him to switch cars. "Are you serious?" Vova said. That was going to be extra. "I know, just do it," Slava said impatiently. "You didn't reconsider our arrangement, did you?" Vova said. "It could be fifteen percent if you want."

After Israel was done, Slava heaved him back onto the bed. The old man was faking his unraveling, but he was no colt. In Slava's hands, Israel surrendered, shy when Slava removed his blue gown. These old men had fucked their way through Minsk, two million people, but they remained modest as children.

Israel was left in a pair of checked boxers, the white belly that had seemed so estimable while hidden settling meagerly over the band of the underwear. The belly skin was as soft as a newborn's. While Slava retrieved Israel's clothes from the locker, the old man crossed his feet like a boy and peered with perplexity at the squares of his toenails.

First Slava pulled on the trousers, leg by leg, Israel playing inept. Then an undershirt, Israel's arms like slabs of pale, old salmon struggling to come through the openings. A short-sleeved summer shirt followed, then a pair of white socks and white sneakers.

"There you are," Slava said, surveying his work. "Ready for the first day of school. Come on."

They peered out of the doorway like two burglars. Only one nurse at the nurse station. "Wait for me," Slava said. He walked up to the nurse and started asking about the prayer room, located on the side of the hallway facing away from the path Israel needed for the elevator. When the nurse, Slava giving her his best smile, looked that way, Slava waved his hand behind his back and Israel waddled toward the elevators around the corner from the nurses' station. When Slava joined him there a moment later, Israel stuck out his thumbs. "Not bad," he said. "Where are you taking me?"

You had to give Vova credit. Ten minutes, like he said, plus five to switch his sedan to a limo. He even found a livery cap somewhere, the actor. "What the fuck is this?" Israel stopped in his place, sighting the vehicle— black, sleek, pouncing, beautiful.

"You said you wanted to see Manhattan," Slava said. "If you're moving to Israel, this is your chance."

While Slava wedged Israel into the backseat, Vova ran down the block to the liquor store (flowers, bakeries, liquor—these establishments filled out the block where Maimonides was located, proving that certain claims about the efficiencies of the American market were not overstated), coming back with an Asti Spumante that a true Soviet citizen preferred to better champagne.

They saw it all, Slava seeing most of it for the first time himself, though thanks to Arianna, now he could imagine how one led to the other. The Statue of Liberty, the Chrysler Building, the Empire State Building, Times Square, Rockefeller Center, St. Patrick's Cathedral, Central Park. At stoplights, Slava made Israel raise his head through the sunroof. Around them, Fifth Avenue anthilled in oblivion, sublime and grotesque. "The women!" the old man shouted. "Look at the women!" Slava raised the bottle of Asti Spumante, and he and Israel drank to the women of Fifth Avenue, the tourists stopping to snap pictures of them peering out the sunroof, though the natives continued to march on, officially untouched.

They went as far north as Riverside Park, Slava asking Vova to swing by the statue of the American president Ulysses S. Grant. Slava told the old man all about the American president. Israel listened like a schoolboy. "I want to get out," he said. "I want to feel it under my feet."

While Vova idled, they strode arm in arm onto the grass of Riverside Park, the bottle of champagne in Slava's hands. They sat down on a bench and swigged from it like two homeless men.

"So, this is it," Israel said.

"This is it," Slava said.

"It's leafy."

"Like spinach."

They hollered like children.

"This is what you spent the two-fifty on, isn't it?" Israel said.

"Russian limos cost less than American limos. There's plenty left over."

Their shouting and vagrancy attracted the squint of a patrolman from the pavement on the other side of the grass. Open consumption of alcohol invited more law-enforcement attention than freelance climbers of municipal property. Slava tossed the empty bottle of Spumante into the bushes and they made legs back to the car.

The desk nurse rose in flames when she sighted the pair, still laughing, emerging from the elevators on the third floor of Maimonides. She began to shout, wresting Israel from Slava's hold. Israel patted the arm emerging from her uniform. "Nice," he said in English. "Beautiful lady." He and the false grandson laughed again, though Slava let go. The nurse walked Israel back to 317, Slava following. "I should have you barred," she hissed at the young man as she settled Israel in the bed. "I just need another minute," Slava said. "If something happens to him, we're no longer responsible," she said angrily, walking out. "It's happened already," Slava said after her.

He stood by Israel's hospital bed. "Do you need a book?"

"I came prepared," Israel said, and nodded toward the locker. "Come closer."

Slava leaned toward Israel's face. It smelled of cellars, mushrooms, earth. Israel's hand enclosed Slava's, and lifting his head, the old man laid a pair of blue lips on Slava's forehead.

"You didn't send it out in time, did you?" Slava said.

"I've had a little attack here," Israel said, "but I'm not brain-dead."

Slava smiled.

"Go forth, my son," Israel said.

19

THURSDAY, AUGUST 31, 2006

The New York headquarters of the Conference on Material Claims Against Germany was neighbored by the offices of German economic initiatives and foundations, as though these could not rightly proceed with their business without a reminder of what their forebears had wrought. Where had this gray-haired man, a lanyard swinging over his bow tie, been? What had he done? Or not done.

The woman at the front desk, her cheekbones as sanded as a promontory and a bundle of black hair bridled by a zirconia-studded barrette, was whispering to someone in Russian on the telephone. Lyudmila, a nameplate made clear. She smelled of clothes freshly removed from the closet. On sighting Slava, she extended a manicured finger toward a red leather chair without interrupting her conversation. Slava tried to gather his thoughts, but they refused to stay put, and he simply gazed at the oatmeal-colored carpet.

Ten minutes later, he still hadn't been called. Apparently, as far as Otto was concerned, Slava could have risen and gone four ways at once. When he inquired with Lyudmila, she reminded him that "he will see you very soon, please" and indicated once more the red leather chair, into which Slava hopelessly sank.

When Slava was finally led into Otto's office, the big man rushed over to pump Slava's hand and apologize for the wait. "Everything is upside down because of the renovation," he said, mashing Slava's palm.

Slava looked around aimlessly. He hadn't noticed anything amiss in the hallway.

"No, it's not important, it's not important." Otto waved him in. He beamed at the receptionist, as if it were an achievement to have a personage such as Slava in his office. "Thank you, Lyudmila." He turned back to Slava. "Coffee, would you like, tea?"

"Coffee," Slava said weakly, and Lyudmila nodded with elaborate competence.

The vaguely classical motifs inscribed on the wood paneling in Otto Barber's office lent it a conservative authority that was undercut by the same oatmeal carpet and rec-room love seats. It looked as if the receptionist had made her own trip to the furniture emporia in lower Brooklyn. A triumvirate of miniature flags—Germany, Israel, and the United States—decorated Otto's desk.

If they had Russians, why had Slava been given the German? he wondered. Had the Conference done research and determined that one of his own was less likely to make an impact? Had the "suspect's past rejection of his community" been highlighted in the report? "Mr. Gelman maintains an adversarial attitude toward people from his community. It may be more productive to present him with someone from a neutral or unfamiliar background." He could have written it for them.

Having deposited Slava in a leather chair on the other side of his desk, Otto sank into his own and pointed at the air-conditioning panel behind him. "Is it too cold for you? I am an arctic person at heart."

Slava shook his head weakly.

"Mr. Gelman, I can't hide my excitement to see you. But you, it seems, could be more excited to see me!" Otto sniggered.

"You weren't concerned I'd run off?" Slava said, trying for defiance.

"That's very funny!" Otto said. "It's very funny that you are thinking this way. No, I knew you would not run away."

"Why is it funny?" Slava said. "Were you so sure?"

"Well, perhaps it is because you are innocent!" he laughed. "You seem to be not considering that possibility yourself!"

Slava hung his head. "You have your evidence," he said derisively.

"Incorrect! You have the evidence. You hold all the power. And so if I say, 'You must come to me tomorrow,' pathetic! *I* don't have the power to make you do this. You must come when *you* want to come."

Slava's forehead was clammy with sweat, but he didn't dare acknowledge it by swiping at it.

"Then again, I have read that a good investigator begins from far away. *Misdirection* is the word. And then he jumps like a jaguar!" Otto tore out of his chair. "So perhaps I am catching you! With the fish. How do you say."

"Baiting you," Slava said morosely.

"Yes," Otto said, settling back in his chair.

Lyudmila walked in with a tray bearing implements for coffee for one. The tiny spoon clinked against the porcelain cup in her hands. She disappeared as quietly as she had arrived. Otto rubbed the space between his eyebrows.

"Did you bring the china with you?" Slava said, sitting up. He coughed self-pityingly and tried to focus.

Otto looked up. "I'm sorry?"

Slava pointed at the coffee cup. "Is it German?"

"No. I do not know, to be honest. I can find out," Otto said, leaning toward the intercom.

"We had a set of German china when we lived in the Soviet Union," Slava said. "My grandfather collected china. This one set from Germany was his prize possession. Cobalt with gold trim. He had to leave most of it behind because there was a limit on how much we were allowed to take with us, but there was no question this set was coming. My grandmother wrapped it up in newspaper. That bundle was half as big as a person. We trundled it all over Europe."

"Mm-hmm," Otto nodded.

"When we finally got to JFK, we relaxed," Slava said. "My uncle was meeting us at the airport. Everybody was crying and hugging. He wanted to show us he was a big man already, he could take care of things. So he picked up the suitcase and threw it into the porter's cart. We all froze. We all thought the same thing."

"No," Otto said. "They were broken."

"Only one. When we got to my uncle's house, my mother and grand-mother went into the bedroom to check. Only one cup had broken. The rest were okay."

"Well, that is good luck," Otto said. "But you see, the manufacturing in Germany is superb. If my father could hear me now. It was his wish that I pursue a position in the private sector instead of the government."

Slava didn't respond. It was unpleasant to think of Otto's father as also a father.

"So, Mr. Gelman, you have rushed in almost the very next day," Otto said. "Two days later. Why is it so? Was the guilt tickling your nose hairs?"

It must have been an expression in German. "I wanted to help," Slava said feebly.

"Yes, we are talking about something very important," Otto said. He rose from the chair and strode toward the window. The sky had become overcast again: the unreliability of late summer. "Tell me now, Mr. Gelman," Otto said gravely. "Tell me everything."

Slava listened to the muted honks rising from the street. "What do you think I should do after this, Mr. Barber?"

Otto turned around. "Are you leaving the magazine, Mr. Gelman? I think you can do anything. This is beneath you. Maybe you should go to a different place. New York City does not feel like your natural condition."

"I would like to see Lubbock, Texas."

"This would certainly classify. It is different from New York, you can say that."

"You know it?" Slava said.

"I am sure you have not been to the Statue of Liberty as well. Visitors take a different interest in your country than people who live here. I spent two weeks in Texas visiting the sites of the Mexican War. Don't mess with Texas, ha-ha. But Lubbock, Texas—it is not quite Shangri-la, Mr. Gelman, if that is what you are expecting."

"They are installing a bike share," Slava said desolately. He stared at the coffee, regret forming at the sudden upswell of camaraderie between them. He had to return the conversation to its original subject. "I will tell you everything, Mr. Barber," he said. "But first I want to give you one last chance to do the right thing."

Otto smiled combatively. "And what would that be, Mr. Gelman?"

"Pay them all," Slava said. "Because you are responsible. Or because you can. Fate has put you in this lucky position to do the just thing."

"Would you call this position lucky?" Otto said. "I do not call this position lucky. I do not wish this position on anyone. Mr. Gelman, please tell me you are noticing that I am handling all of this differently from the way my superiors probably wish." He shook his head. "Can I ask you something? What is it like, to sit there writing the letter and think: No, this detail is not gruesome enough. I have to find something more gruesome. Is 'gruesome' the right word?"

"It's not hard to find gruesome details," Slava said.

"But you must choose. This is gruesome in the right way, this is not. Does it give you a chill?"

"No," Slava lied. "A chill is what was done to them."

"You are a curator of suffering."

"And you are the purveyor. Which is better? You have given me too much to work with. You think of that time as a museum, an aberration of history, but someone goes through it all the time. Your Turks go through it. The blacks here go through it. Jews go through it everywhere except Israel and America, more or less. Things get better, there's no more lynching, and they don't break your knees for being a kike in the Red Army. But it goes on all the time, somewhere."

"Don't use that word, please."

"Are you sensitive, Otto? It's quite a business you've chosen if you're sensitive. My grandfather says 'kike' all the time. 'Die among kikes, but live among Russians,' he says. You ever hear that one? He likes to show his home nurse he's not clannish. It makes her uncomfortable, just like you. No, Otto. This man lost his family, lost a limb, lost his hearing, lost his sanity, but he is not eligible because he was a soldier. This one was in the ghetto and slipped out—that person *is* eligible. Who is the curator?"

"But is it not strange to take that memory and use it for profit?"

Slava laughed. "A man of means acquires them God knows how and then lectures the man without means about honor. Is it not strange to kill diligently and then commemorate diligently? That profit is for old, pathetic people who can't understand anything other than dollars."

"I am disappointed not to have changed your mind."

"My mind is changed. By you or not, it is changed."

"I meant it when I said something better awaits you."

"You don't have to tell me who called, Otto. Just tell me if it was one of us."

Otto considered this new bargain. "And then you will tell me?" he said.

"Then I will tell you everything."

"Yes," Otto said.

"Young, old?" Slava said.

"Mr. Gelman."

"I will guess old."

"Fine," Otto said.

They worked over this new information without comment. Then Slava said: "Do you want me to tell you how it works?"

"Very much," Otto said. "I want to put this behind as much as you, Mr. Gelman."

"I don't want to put it behind," Slava lied. "I had only just started when I heard from you."

"Are you implying you're going to continue?"

"That's for your sleuthing, isn't it?"

Folding his brows, Otto withdrew a note card from a desk drawer and scrawled something. The pen wouldn't collaborate, and he threw it into the garbage with irritation, the stem thunking the side of the basket.

"You were in such spirits when I saw you last," Slava said. "You were laughing, as if we really were just two friends talking in a bar."

"Do you have many friends, Mr. Gelman?"

Slava pressed his lips together. In his mind, he counted Arianna, Israel, Grandfather. "Yes," he said. "Average age a hundred."

"I would like to remind you, Mr. Gelman," Otto said. "This could have happened very differently. I am trying to be sensitive. I am trying to help."

"I know." Slava hung his head. "That's why I will tell you everything." He straightened in his chair, defeat on his face. "I don't know what you were told," he said, so softly that Otto had to move closer to hear. The German's eyes shone wetly with anticipation of Slava's disclosure. Slava aimed for a look of perseverance despite complete conquest. "But I'm going to guess." He tried to look at Otto, purposefully failing. "Has Lyudmila explained to you about these old people? They live on envy. You had it right—your caller was getting even for something. There wasn't enough of the most basic things where they lived. If you were a Jew, you got even less. But there was always a guy who had more. Because he knew the right people to bribe. So he could get his ham from the back of the store, the good cut before the rest was laid out, half of it spoiled. Do you understand what I'm getting at?"

"I am listening with great interest," Otto said.

"Well, that was my grandfather," Slava said. "The guy with more. The guy with china from Germany. Do you know what it meant to have china from Germany? West Germany, not East Germany. East German china would have broken before we finished packing. But he didn't know how to keep quiet. He was the world's biggest braggart. He still is. He couldn't help it. It made everyone angry."

"So, what are you saying?" Otto said, his forehead creased.

"I like it more when we can talk seriously," Slava said. "It looks like a joke to you, jumping around, playing investigator, but we are talking about people I love. We are talking about people who have suffered, Mr. Barber. People who eat soup from a tiny can six times a week, and then one day they get something from the synagogue. Even if they are liars, they deserve respect."

Otto's face fell. "Mr. Gelman, it is crushing my heart to know that it was received in this spirit. You must forgive—"

"I did forge," Slava interrupted him. "You have that correct. It's a relief to say it. But your details are wrong." He nodded at the stack of applications on the desk. He had forged every one. He could recite sections of many by heart. "I faked only one. I faked my grandfather's. He was in Uzbekistan, not in the forest. The next morning, he called everyone. Real victims, people who had been in the ghetto, the forest, the camps. Told them I did his and ten others, so they were already behind. You can imagine what a job I had trying to persuade these people, who don't believe anything, that he was lying. Phone call after phone call, all morning long. Between us, I had a woman in my bed, and not a bad one, and I didn't even notice her leaving, I was so busy dealing with this. They would not leave me alone. So I made a deal. Even if their stories were real, I would not do it. But I would teach them how to write. That's why you have the similar phrases, the maneuvers. Do you know what they say about the Russians, Mr. Barber? They don't make anything, but they copy better than anyone else. The sushi you will have in Moscow is better than the sushi in Tokyo. They followed every rule. They followed the rule to the letter."

Otto stared, stone-faced.

"I refused all these people because the law, like you said, is the law," Slava said. "But if you want to know the truth, I wish I hadn't. Your law is a puddle of rain next to what they went through. Because of your country. Because of you, Otto—because *you* are all that is left of *them*. I didn't, in the end. Still, I couldn't say no to my grandfather. *Family.* I hope you can make sense of that."

Otto leaned against his desk and regarded Slava with an amused, admiring expression. They listened to the noise from the street a dozen stories below. The coffee gleamed blackly from its porcelain cup, an oily penumbra gathering on the surface. Finally, Otto exhaled a long column of air. "I can make sense of it very well, Mr. Gelman," he said. "It doesn't change what I have to do. Your grandfather's application will be denied."

Slava nodded.

Otto crossed his arms. A strange expression, disdain coupled with merriment, played in his eyes. "Thank you for your honesty," he said.

"It didn't come simply," Slava said.

Otto smiled mournfully. "I have learned a lot from you, Mr. Gelman. You are free."

At his dining room table, returned to its habitually abridged position, the wings retracted and folded, Grandfather was counting pills: powder-blue ramipril, white meclizine, pink clopidogrel. Each set corresponded to an envelope stuffed with prescriptions. Grandfather slid several pills from one pile to another, noted it on a torn piece of paper, licked his finger.

Slava had come directly from Otto's office. It was easier to be here, in front of Grandfather, than far away. A brief rain had fallen, then settled into a cool evening, the air carrying the impending decay of leaves. In the kitchen, Berta was slicing and dicing, preserving and pickling for the long winter ahead.

"What is all this?" Slava asked Grandfather.

Grandfather finished writing down a figure. "You have to know how to make money," he said without looking up.

"How?" Slava said. If you taunted him—if you said, No, it's impossible, no one could do this—you could get out of him any answer you wanted.

"How," he snorted. Then, in his *forshpeis* English, he said, "I no steal, okay?"

"So you knew English the whole time," Slava said. "You could have written your own letter."

Grandfather picked up a box of prostate tea and began to demonstrate his English. "No shoogar. No gloo-ten." He squinted. "No pre-zer-va-tiv. What is that?"

"No chemicals."

"Hm." He put the box down skeptically.

Berta appeared in the doorway of the kitchen, one plate heaped with fruit, the other with pastries. "Time for snacks, young men," she said. "Fortify yourselves."

"You are an angel, Bertochka," Grandfather said. To Slava: "She's an angel."

"Food is the way to a man's heart," Berta affirmed, laughing.

"We did notice, Slavchik, you've been coming around more often." Grandfather winked, and he and Berta laughed. Slava joined in, reaching for a triangle of pastry.

"Excuse the interruption, men, I'm back to the kitchen," she said.

"Somebody had a date with Vera Rudinsky," Grandfather said matter-of-factly. He winked again.

Slava laughed because there was nothing else to do.

"Nice place?" Grandfather said.

If Slava said yes, Grandfather would be envious. If he said no, Grandfather would put her down. Slava said nothing.

"So, how was it?" Grandfather winked.

"None of your business," Slava said kindly. "Nothing happened."

"You went to her apartment and nothing happened?"

"Yes. Nothing happened. We talked and I left."

Grandfather's face fell. "Slavik," he whispered, gold teeth glittering through his scowl. "Tell me that's not true."

"It's true," Slava said.

Grandfather's face turned dark. "Slava, for God's sake. You went to a girl's house and nothing happened?"

Slava said nothing, only waited. Let it come.

"I won't believe it," Grandfather said. "Tell me the truth. You—" He smacked his fist into his palm. "You did, right? Like a man?"

Slava watched the pain in his grandfather's face for a long moment. "I did," he lied. "Like a man."

"Attaboy!" Grandfather shouted. He yelled out to Berta in the kitchen, "Watch out for this one, girls! He's no kind of homo!" He turned to look at Slava in triumph, but Slava couldn't bear to look at him and looked away coldly. Grandfather's triumphant expression faded into remorse. He would never understand his grandson. With a thick finger, he began pushing around invisible crumbs on the oilcloth.

Finally, Slava rose, the feet of the chair making a loud noise on the parquet. Grandfather looked like a boy regretful for having made another mistake. He had seen Slava three times in a month, three times more than in the year before, and now his mouth would send Slava away once more. Send him away for reasons he would never grasp, but send him away all the same, that much he understood.

But it wouldn't. Slava walked over to Grandfather's side of the table and laid his arm around the old man's head. Grandfather reached up and squeezed Slava's hand. "Love you," Grandfather burbled in English through the tears in his throat.

Love you. I no steal.

The Bratislavan in Arianna's foyer was relieved to see Slava so early in the evening this time. He beamed, a crooked molar showing. "Nice!" he roared, pointing outside. "Cool down!" Slava pushed out a smile and hauled himself up the stairs. Someone was baking: The staircase was thick with butter and sugar and heat. Again he stood mincing in front of her door. Again he listened for noise on the other side like an intruder. Did he come here only for absolution? That wasn't what he wanted. He wanted to tell the truth, if only to one person.

He could hear music rising electronically from her laptop, her voice joining occasionally. Now and again, she addressed the cat. At last, he knocked. She opened the door and lowered and raised her eyes quickly—she did this when she was nervous. Often she didn't announce what she was feeling, so he had to decode on his own. He got it wrong many times, but many times right, not meaningless considering they had known each other so briefly. Six weeks before, she was a voluptuous shadow on the other side of the wall.

"It's from here," he said, sniffing.

"I bake when I'm anxious," she said. "Come in?"

He stepped inside and embraced her. He tasted all the ingredients on her tongue: lemon cake. Again her eyes fell and rose. When this happened, her face acquired an unkind crease around the lips, as if she resented him for having to become uncomfortable: If he understood what she wanted to know, he should just tell her.

"I didn't," he said.

She drew back. "What do you mean?"

"Or I did, but not exactly." He worked the dome of his head into the crook of her arm. She pushed him away and lifted his face to hers. She called out his name. It was a question.

The cat offered its diversionary services, parking the front paws on the side of Slava's right knee and staring up expectantly, what for only the cat knew. Slava forfeited the out and motioned to the couch. There, he told her what he had said to Otto Barber.

He had expected her sympathy, but none appeared on her face. "That wasn't what we talked about," she said coldly.

He rubbed his eyes.

"Slava, you promised. You swore. You said it yourself. We agreed."

"It had nothing to do with you," he objected.

"But then you forced me into it. You could have left me out of it, but you came here, you pulled me into it. Did you know? Did you already know what you were going to do when you promised me?"

"If I had kept lying, you would have felt even more betrayed. But because I told you, I forced you into it?"

"You're right, Slava, this situation is so unfair to you. You try to do the right thing, but the world won't notice."

He groaned.

"Did you know what you were going to do when you promised me you would tell the truth?" she said. "Just tell me that. Did you come here simply to share the burden?"

"No," he said. "I don't think so. I'm—" He felt a great unhappiness rising within him. "I'm trying to be honest."

"It doesn't matter, does it," she said despondently. "Whenever you did know, you didn't come to me. You didn't tell me."

"Probably I didn't know until I walked into his office," he said. "I'm telling you now. Arianna, please."

"Oh, I know," she yelped, and covered her face.

She crossed her legs and looked outside while her teeth worked the edge of her nails. He had never seen her do that. In the window, an old tree swayed tentatively in a light wind. A finger-sized bird, iridescent with emerald plumage, skidded onto a branch, unshamed by its meagerness from setting the bulb of its head at a magnificent angle. The branch swayed a little in answer. Unlike Slava's windows, which looked into a courtyard, Arianna's faced into the city. He felt quieter but lonelier at his place.

"Please go," she said. "I'm not strong enough to insist on it."

"Arianna," he whispered. "No."

"I love when you call out my name," she said. "You do it rarely. You called it out during sex once . . . I knew it was because you were so gone, you'd forgotten I was there. I loved that."

He was on the floor beside her again. "Arianna, it's over. Don't you see?"

Her face twitched and she drew a finger under one eye. "Don't *you* see? You didn't take me with you into that room. We agreed you would tell the truth. But you didn't. At the last moment, you changed your mind. You left me at the door, you looked only after yourself. But how else could it be? You've been answering to someone for so long. Oh, why are these things impossible to see in advance. You're not up to this now, Slava. And I don't want you like this. Please go."

His insides drained. He wobbled, trying to stand up. He had become so accustomed to her understanding that he didn't know what to do when she withheld it. He scratched out her name, all he could say.

"I can't do this with you now," she said. "Tomorrow we'll talk—next week. Please go. Be kind to me and go."

"You're not a Boy Scout, Arianna," he mumbled. "Pick and choose? You don't care about the rules."

"Don't I?" she said. "I do care about the rules, Slava. The rules that we have with each other, I do."

He felt bewilderment. How could he know that *this* rule, for her, was the unbreakable one? There were so many others that didn't matter. He could follow instructions—he would now, he would—but not without receiving them in the first place! Once again, he felt himself in the presence of information only he didn't understand. Everyone was slightly embarrassed that he didn't.

"You know, Slava," she said without looking at him, "when it started and we disagreed all the time, I liked it. I'd rather disagree with someone who's interesting. Also because those disagreements felt like the frosting; underneath we were the same. But I was wrong, Slava. We are different— all the way through."

"But I want to be like you."

"But I'm not looking for a student. And you are not looking for a teacher." She sighed heavily and walked to her bureau. When she returned, she held an old issue of *Century*. "Happy freedom," she said.

It was the issue from all those years ago, the first issue of *Century* he had come across, in the Hunter library.

"I stole it," she said. "From the archive." She laughed barbarously.

He didn't want to—if he took it, he was agreeing to something. But he didn't dare disobey. His heart curdled at the foxed feel of the old, tawny pages.

" 'Now she snaps her wings open, and floats away,' " she said bitterly.

He called out her name again, but she looked at him with such a helpless, crazed expression that he understood the loving thing would be to go. Holding the magazine, he did.

-20-

What do the holy books say about the paying of respects to the deceased on the Sabbath? Is it a form of work, prohibited on the sacred day, or a kind of rest? There is no Arianna to ask. Slava might not be long for the answers, but he will look them up anyway. He has to get ready to teach those who come after him.

From the train platform, the rows of headstones look like children gathered for an assembly. Up close, the graves of the American Jews are as unlike the Russian as two siblings whose parents scratch their heads, wondering how the children turned out so differently. The American graves are enormous slabs, saying only: "Fisher b. 1877 d. 1956." The Russian are smaller but make up with ornament: scalloped shoulders, roses climbing the panels, multipeaked crowns, and on the stones themselves, beneath suns setting on menorahs that the family of the deceased never lit while he was alive, inscriptions:

"We miss you, dear one, like the earth misses the rain."

"Words have little room, but thoughts fly free."

"An evil whirlwind has passed above this earth and taken you into that other world."

"Little son, why did you leave us so soon?"

The mortuary Seurat who has etched the face of this last unlucky addressee in a pointillist style rendered even his incipient mustache. Eighteen years old. Auto accident. He is the cup and saucer who broke on arrival, the rest of the set having to carry on incomplete. It is a blessing to die in the natural order.

You can tell the anniversaries by the heaps of flowers. The cemetery has set out notices about stagnant water and West Nile virus, so the flowers are mostly plastic, a rare act of civic obedience. These last longer and require less maintenance anyway.

You can tell the new graves by the eight-by-elevens, encased in cellophane to defend from rain, wedged into humps of freshly turned earth. A Soviet-Jewish family tends not to wait a year before unveiling a tombstone, as Jewish custom dictates, but neither does it erect one immediately, as it would have in the Soviet Union. It strikes a murky compromise between worlds whose logic is clear only to its members: one month or two.

Slava's secret descendant, he of the beer can and the accentless tongue, how long will he wait? There is a Hasidic belief that three generations of deceased ancestors keep watch over the newlyweds under a chuppah. Slava wants an inversion of this teaching—three generations of unborn descendants keeping watch over a grave. As he strides down Tulip Row A, approaching Grandmother's plot, flowerless but with a notebook in hand, they wait for him by her stone.

How will I explain to you how we lived, there and here? There, our evenings spent in some living room—for there was really nowhere to go—fearful but safe, insecure but joyful, guarded but open? And here, the re-used paper towels, the boxes of instruction manuals saved for some future loss of direction, the receipts organized in an accounting of every indulgence?

But you must know these things, for you will replace me as I am replacing them.

In the distance, a mower whines in the hands of a groundskeeper. Behind the noise, you can hear—after all—the train running its fingers across the ribs of the tracks. It comes through the pavement and into your feet.

The pair of tombstones in front of Slava grows apart only at the hips. Gelman, the common plinth says. Grandfather's is blank; Grandmother's has the poem. Her face is etched in the same pointillist style; the local Seurat must have a monopoly. Grandfather's stone is black, Grandmother's the stippled chestnut of a bay horse. The crown of his stone rises slightly above hers, a shoulder.

The turf is even on both sides of the plot, flecks of freshly cut grass clinging to the knees of the common stone. The custodians must have mowed since Grandfather and Berta last visited; Grandfather wouldn't permit the flecks to remain, Berta nicking them away with her mother-of-pearl nails.

Slava sits down on the paved path that runs alongside the plots and gives his greeting to Grandmother. He decides that she does not need small talk. They will talk in a different way. He would like to meet her all over again, their recent encounters untrue. How? He opens his notebook. A blank page looks at him with doubt. Doubt enough of his own he's got. He touches a pen to the paper, moves it off, brings it back. His untrustworthy imagination whispers to him, the sound of new treason. He listens, waits, listens, brings pen to paper again.

> Q: *Did I betray you by inventing all those things?*
> A: *How? You're being foolish.*
> Q: *I would like you to be truthful with me.*
> A: *No, you did not.*
> Q: *I am here only to talk with you. There is no other reason.*

A: Then why do you have the notebook?

Q: It's how I understand things. You will live in it.

A: I live in your heart.

Q: The heart is unreliable, a notebook is forever.

A: That isn't why. But it doesn't matter. Write, write.

Q: When you slipped out of the ghetto, did you know you would never see your parents again?

A: No. The mind doesn't prepare for death.

Q: Were you afraid, going to the woods? You were only fifteen. I think of myself at fifteen.

A: I was a city girl, of course I was frightened. But I don't remember being frightened. You are in such terror that you don't feel . . . anything. You move because there is something working inside you, you don't know what. And then another day, for minutes, whole minutes at a time, it seems as if everything is normal, absolutely normal—it's the old you, and things are just as they were . . .

Q: What should I say from you? To Grandfather or Mother.

A: He can't live without your admiration. And she—call her again, for no reason.

Q: Can I bring you something?

A: This is how we used to talk when we were calling from a trip: "Can we bring something?" No—you're here, what else do I need.

It isn't her, because she never spoke like this. But she is no longer around to answer for herself. And so she will have to live on in the adulterated form in which he must imagine her. He cannot strip himself out of the imagining. If she is to live, she will live as Slava+Grandmother, one person at last.

"Boy! Boy!" a woman shouts as she rushes down the path, the plea of a fist in the air. She is already clothed for winter—a heavy coat, a beret on her head. "Boy," she repeats as she draws near, out of breath. "How could you sit on the pavement like that? You will catch cold, and then what? How would your"—she squints at the grave, considers the years of birth and death—"how would your grandmother like that? Answer me."

Slava smiles and rises. "Thank you," he says.

"The weather's changing," she says. "That's always the vulnerable time. Look after yourself. God bless you for looking in on your grandmother."

After she disappears down an alleyway, Slava returns to the ground, though not to the pavement; after all, he has promised. He comes down to the grass, to Grandfather's unused side of the plot, next to Grandmother. The pavement already holds the chill of autumn, but the grass is still heedless and warm, as if summer is never going to end. He thinks of Arianna, the singed grass of Bryant Park underneath them, his head on her thigh, the saxophone going off at the other end of the park, the ordinariness that hides the miraculous.

The world above is endless and blue. Slava runs his fingers through Grandmother's side of the plot, the short, prickly grass like Grandfather's face after a day without shaving. Her pliant, puckered flesh was so inadequate to protect the fragile body beneath it that the last time she had enough strength to go out, the sons of another family—each the size of a bureau, each overjoyed to see her well enough to come for a party— embraced her so fervidly that they broke two of her ribs.

The plastic carnations that fill Grandmother's vase are too firm to sway in the light wind, but behind them, a thin greenish stem with a space helmet of white puff bobs in the earth. It was the costume of every meadow outside Minsk; you pinched the stem and blew the puff out like a candle. Slava can summon the name of the flower only in Russian, and in the moment before he scatters the down across what remains of his grandmother, he knows—a fact, he made it—that he will never look up the English translation. The white wisps settle like summertime snow. *Oduvanchik.*

Acknowledgments

$\mathbf{M}$y first thanks are to my grandmother. She really was better than all of us.

Then to my grandfather. A friend of mine once said, "You're smarter than him, you're more enlightened than him. But both of us can fit inside his left nut." Hard to argue.

To my parents, for loving so well and for not giving up.

To Polina Shostak, a woman of singular fortitude, and the Shostak/ Gold family—the only ones who remain.

To Alana Newhouse, for inspiring so much. To Annabelle, for the oxytocin. To the Liguoris of Rhode Island, my second family, and especially to the memory of Antoinette Parise, who loved Robert Frost.

To the friends who read drafts, talked shop, and held me up, especially Rob Liguori, Nicole DiBella, Vance Serchuk, Amy Bonnaffons, Chad Benson, Luke Mogelson, Kseniya Melnik, Julian Rubinstein, Ellen Sussman, Meredith Maran, Jacob Soll, Joshua Cohen, Tom Bissell, Ben Holmes, Dan Kaufman, Jilan Kamal and Justin Vogt, Joshua Yaffa and Kate Greenberg, Will Clift, Andrew Meredith, Rebecca Howell, Louis Venosta, Vica Miller, Joseph DiGiacomo, Michelle Ishay and Michael Cohen, LuLing Osofsky, Jules Lewis, Anne Gordon and Andrew Garland, Teddy Wayne, Arthur Phillips. Special thanks to Susan Wise Bauer, who spans categories and is one of the most brilliant, generous, interesting people I know.

To the teachers: Lawrence Weschler, Brian Morton, David Lipsky, and, especially, Darin Strauss and Jonathan Lethem, two of the greatest teachers (and mensches) I've encountered. They are not only teachers but mentors, too rare a mantle these days. I met these people because of the NYU MFA program, run by the incomparable Deborah Landau, who redefines patron. To this list, add Joyce Carol Oates, who taught me first and has remembered me always; Star Lawrence, who was the first to give me a chance; William Zinsser, who gives more without eyesight than most with it; Vera Fried, the Pink Dynamo; and the great Jim Harrison, who made me want to write.

To the residencies and organizations that so very generously gave time, and space, and sustenance by many definitions: Norton Island Residency Program in Maine; the Fine Arts Work Center in Provincetown (with special thanks to Salvatore Scibona for his insight and encouragement); La Napoule Art Foundation in France; Mesa Refuge in Point Reyes Station; the New York Foundation for the Arts; the Albee Foundation in Montauk; Wildacres Retreat in North Carolina; Blue Mountain Center in the Adirondacks; Brush Creek Art Foundation in Wyoming; Djerassi Resident Artists Program in Northern California. It's hard to put value to what these people and institutions give to artists.

To Henry Dunow. They say the right agent is like the right relationship—elusive until it finally happens, and then it feels destined. Thank you, Henry. You are so good at what you do, and you are such a class act while doing it. You have my gratitude and admiration. Thanks as well to Betsy Lerner and Yishai Seidman.

To Terry Karten for a rare kind of patronage; for having faith, wisdom, vision, and a flawless touch. You gave an incredible blessing, and the way you steer is a model and inspiration.

Thanks as well to Elena Lappin, who has been an exceedingly generous and incisive champion of this book.

Finally, to the walking wounded who survived the degradations of a life in the Soviet Union. For all their warts, they, too, are survivors.

Author's Note

The line between fact and fiction, invention and theft, is as loose as the line between truth and justice. My adopted culture knows this in practice but forgets it in theory—we are transgressives in private and puritans when caught, itself a savory self-deception. This affects literature as much as politics or mortgage lending. Sometimes we struggle to remember that fiction is often nonfiction warped by artifice, and nonfiction unavoidably a reinvention of what actually happened. (I am stealing these words from myself, from a book review I once wrote.) There are lines, of course, but they're further out than we think. Life is sin and art is theft. Let mine in this novel register as a reminder of this, as well as a tribute to authors who have said something of meaning to me.

22 The line "Every morning, the Soviet men shrouded themselves in Soviet linens and mongreled into the soft air of Tyrrhenian fall: 'Russo producto! Russo producto!'" appeared previously in a piece I wrote, "Paid in Persimmons," in *Departures* magazine (October 2007).

52 "He studied the treacherous slingshot of Arianna's clavicle" is gratefully stolen from Kseniya Melnik. A different version of the expression appears in the story "Kruchina," in *Snow in May: Stories* (Henry Holt, 2014):

"Masha looked at Katya's thin neck sticking out of the collar of her night-gown, the slingshot fork of her clavicle and ropy shoulder, the pollen sprinkling of freckles, just like her mother's."

106 "August, / you're [just] an erotic hallucination" is from Denis Johnson's poem "Heat," in *The Incognito Lounge and Other Poems* (Carnegie Mellon University Press, 1994).

152 "The lilac fog / sails above our heads" is from "Don't Rush, Conductor," a Russian pop song by Vladimir Markin.

163 "Expensive Trips Nowhere" is the title of a story by Tom Bissell, in *God Lives in St. Petersburg and Other Stories* (Pantheon, 2005).

165 The phrase "stocking of smoke" comes from the story "Islands" in Aleksandar Hemon's collection *The Question of Bruno* (Nan A. Talese/Doubleday, 2000).

208 The third false Holocaust narrative is a version of a story that became widely known after the war. I learned of it, in addition to other valuable details, from David Guy's book (*Innocence in Hell: The Life, Struggle, and Death of the Minsk Ghetto*, trans. Nina Genn, self-published, New York, 2004).

224 "[Her eyes] were gray, a shining gray, though they seemed darker because of their thick lashes" is a variation on *Anna Karenina* (Leo Tolstoy, *Anna Karenina*, trans. Richard Pevear and Larissa Volokhonsky, Penguin Classics, 2004). The original sentence reads, "Her shining grey eyes, which seemed dark because of their thick lashes, rested amiably and attentively on his face . . ."

254 "I am a finished man . . . The sun must be the sun first of all" is from Fyodor Dostoyevsky's *Crime and Punishment*, translated by Larissa Volokhonsky and Richard Pevear (Vintage, 2012).

254 "Be true to your own strange kind" is a variation on Louis Simpson's poem "The Cradle Trap" in *At the End of the Open Road: Poems* (Wesleyan University Press, 1963). The original reads, "Be true, be true / To your own strange kind."

262 "Better to permit a guilty conscience to keep walking around, to increase the weight of its guilt!": Dostoyevsky, *Crime and Punishment*.

263 "They say that at Sevastopol, the people were in a terrible fright that the enemy would attack openly and take Sevastopol immediately. But when they saw that the enemy preferred a regular siege, they were delighted! The thing would drag on for two months at least, and they could relax!": Ibid.

280 The italicized words in "This was what awaited, the *dark collapse* between Vera's legs said" is from Chang-Rae Lee's *Native Speaker* (Riverhead, 1996).

281 "If you say there are elephants flying outside your window, no one will believe you. But if you say there are six elephants flying outside your window, it's a different story" is a variation on Gabriel García Márquez, "The Art of Fiction, No. 69, Gabriel García Márquez," interview by Peter H. Stone, in *The Paris Review*, no. 82 (Winter 1981). There is no indication who translated the interview. The original reads, "For example, if you say that there are elephants flying in the sky, people are not going to believe you. But if you say that there are four hundred and twenty-five elephants flying in the sky, people will probably believe you."

292 "The tea was bitter and he blamed existence" is a variation on Bernard Malamud, *The Fixer* (Farrar, Straus and Giroux, 2004). In the original phrasing— "It tasted bitter and he blamed existence"—the "it" does refer to tea.

297 "Slava could have risen and gone four ways at once": Dostoyevsky, *Crime and Punishment*.

299 "I have read that a good investigator begins from far away . . . And then he jumps like a jaguar!": Ibid.

311 "Now she snaps her wings open, and floats away" is from Mary Oliver's poem "The Summer Day" in *New and Selected Poems* (Beacon Press, 1992).

About the Author

Boris Fishman was born in Belarus and immigrated to the United States at the age of nine. His journalism, essays, and criticism have appeared in the *New Yorker*, the *New York Times Magazine*, the *New Republic*, the *Wall Street Journal*, the *London Review of Books*, and other publications. He is the editor of *Wild East: Stories from the Last Frontier*, an anthology about Eastern Europe after the fall of Communism, and the recipient of fellowships from the New York Foundation for the Arts and the Fine Arts Work Center, among others. He lives in New York City. *A Replacement Life* is his first novel.

AN IMPRINT OF PUSHKIN PRESS

ONE, an imprint of Pushkin Press, publishes one exceptional fiction or non-fiction debut a season. Its list is commissioned and edited by the writer and editor Elena Lappin, who selects the best writing by authors whose extraordinary voices, talent and vision deserve a wide readership and media focus.

THREE GRAVES FULL
Jamie Mason
"A ripping good novel" *The New York Times*

A SENSE OF DIRECTION
PILGRIMAGE FOR THE RESTLESS AND THE HOPEFUL
Gideon Lewis-Kraus
"Here is one of the best and most brilliant
young writers in America" *GQ*

A REPLACEMENT LIFE
Boris Fishman
"Mordantly funny and moving" *The New York Times*

Forthcoming in 2015

THE FISHERMEN
Chigozie Obioma
"Obioma's remarkable fiction is at once urgently,
vividly immediate, yet simultaneously charged with
the elemental power of myth" Peter Ho Davies

www.pushkinpress.com/one